Reality in Chaos

Monique Kelley

Black Rose Writing | Texas

The author grants the final approval for this literary material.

First printing

This is a work of fiction. Names, characters, businesses, places, events, and incidents are either the products of the author's imagination or used in a fictitious manner. Any resemblance to actual persons, living or dead, or actual events is purely coincidental.

ISBN: 978-1-68433-619-7
PUBLISHED BY BLACK ROSE WRITING
www.blackrosewriting.com

Printed in the United States of America
Suggested Retail Price (SRP) $20.95

Reality in Chaos is printed in Georgia

*As a planet-friendly publisher, Black Rose Writing does its best to eliminate unnecessary waste to reduce paper usage and energy costs, while never compromising the reading experience. As a result, the final word count vs. page count may not meet common expectations.

To the women who somewhere along the way lost themselves, forgot the beauty of who they are, and feel like their dreams will never be realized. May you realize the light within you still shines and the world is ready to see it....

To my mother Rosalyn McPherson... love you to the moon and back!

Reality in Chaos

Even in chaos, you may find a life-changing reality
that ultimately brings you inner peace...

Prologue

Hampton University, May 8, 1999

The air of celebration was thick. Outkast's album "Aquemini" was being played in the background on full blast. Hundreds of students milled outside the Big Café, doing the unthinkable ... doing what was the rite of passage once you were officially on the list of approved graduates – they were dancing in the middle of Ogden Circle. Right in the center of campus, in front of Ogden Hall and the Big Café.

People who visited Hampton University's beautiful waterfront campus nestled along the banks of the Virginia Peninsula on Chesapeake Bay could never understand how the grass on Ogden Circle stayed so green and pristine. You would never see students on that grass. It stayed untouched, never walked on.

The legend went that if you walked on Ogden Circle, or had any contact with it prior to being placed on the official graduates' list, you would never get a degree from Hampton University. And that was a legend that every freshman who entered Hampton did not have the guts to challenge. The only time students actually walked on Ogden Circle was the night before graduation, and then it was for a big party.

"Where the hell is Jacqueline?" Simone asked with her usual impatience. You knew she was annoyed when she used her full name instead of just Jackie.

"She knows what time we're supposed to meet. And you know she's always late." As usual, Taylor tried to calm Simone down.

"I have waited four fucking years to walk across Ogden Circle and now this heifer has me waiting longer? And all because she almost didn't pass an elective sign language class and is just now finishing up her extra credit assignment?" Simone had her perfectly manicured nails stuffed in her jeans pockets like a five-year-old who was about to have a temper tantrum. Taylor couldn't help but laugh. She looked like she was about to blow a gasket. But just as Simone was about to lose her mind, they heard Jacqueline running up behind them.

"Girls! Girls! Girls! I signed my way to a degree!" Jackie was out of breath as she dropped her shopping bag on the ground to hug Simone and Taylor.

"Well, it's about fucking time!" Simone said. "I still can't believe you waited to the last minute to take an elective course and almost had to stay here an extra year over some bullshit! Really? And when in the hell will you ever use sign language anyway?"

Jackie rolled her eyes and stuck up her two middle fingers. "Well, now would be the perfect time for me to start using sign language!" The three of them started cracking up. Even Simone had to laugh. "I mean loosen the fuck up! I'm here now. And now I can add sign language to my résumé as a skill. You never know when Hollywood will be looking for an actress who knows sign language! Duh!"

"Hell, I was worried that $5 I owed the library for late fees was going to have my ass not on the list," Taylor complained. "I heard they have the folks from the accounting office at the doors at graduation to collect any money owed before they even let your ass in the Convocation Center."

"You know President Harvey is all about getting those coins," Simone said. "Well, I'm glad we're all good. Because if you had us waiting here for nothing, Jackie, I was going to kick your ass!"

"You weren't going to do shit! *You'd* risk breaking a nail for Jackie's ass? Yeah, right!" Taylor scoffed.

"Now that you're finished grilling me, can we get to the business at hand?" Jackie said as she pulled out a bottle of Dom Perignon champagne and three red Solo® cups.

"Are you crazy? You know we're not supposed to have alcohol on campus and right in the middle of Ogden Circle. I'm not going to mess around with your ass and have to be out by five the day of graduation!" Taylor was justified in her concern. Hampton was famous for their strict rules regarding student behavior. If any student dared to violate the code of conduct, they were escorted off the campus by 5 p.m. that same day. If that student were found on campus any time after 5:01 p.m. the day of their expulsion, police were called and they would be arrested for trespassing. Some would think the rules were too stringent, but these were all things President Harvey (the university President for decades) implemented decades ago, which made Hampton University home to the best of the best and most elite Black college students in the world. It was a reputation current students and graduates were proud of and wore like a badge of honor. It also set Hampton apart from all other HBCUs (Historically Black Colleges and Universities) and was what made acceptance to the university so hard. That's why it was referred to as the "Black Harvard."

"Relax... Even Bullet ain't tripping," Jackie said, referring to the infamous security guard who stood at the front entrance of Hampton University's campus. He monitored who came on and off the campus. If he suspected you weren't a student, just some local riffraff, you would not gain entrance. Or if you were a student who didn't have clearance to have a car on campus and did not have the proper decals, he wasn't letting you on campus. Although he could be a complete pain in the ass, by the end of freshman year there was a respect factor that he earned from the students in his brassiness. "Don't you realize we are about to be alumni in a few hours? This is when the tables turn and the university will start kissing our asses for that good ole' alumni money! And that's why I have the red Solo® cups for discretion – uh, but wait, looking around, half the people here have red Solo® cups and I know they ain't drinking milk! Well ... maybe they do if it has Bailey's in it..." Jackie began pouring the cups to capacity to finish off the bottle.

Simone laughed and held out her cup and wiggled her knees, dancing. "This will be the only time you will ever see me drinking champagne out of a plastic cup, girls! You know this is tacky as hell! But top me off a little more!" Jackie emptied the rest of the bottle into her cup.

"Ladies...are you ready?" Taylor took a deep breath and the three girls slowly made their way to Ogden Circle. Right before they stepped onto the green grass with the other partying students, the three girls looked at each other, smiled, and touched their feet on the grass. It was the most exhilarating feeling. Four years in the making. A huge accomplishment – this is when it all became real. Tomorrow they were going to walk across the stage and get their bachelor's degrees.

At the moment they were in the very middle of Ogden Circle, Simone lifted her cup. "Toast time!"

"Oh, Lord..." Taylor and Jackie said in unison. Simone loved her toasts.

"Please, keep this one under 10 minutes, if possible. I would like to drink this expensive champagne while it's still chilled," Jackie said.

"Ha... ha... ha... very funny!" Simone rolled her eyes in good humor. "Anyway, before I was so ruuuuuudely interrupted... Ladies, we did it! I know I couldn't have made it through these four years without you ladies. Now we are embarking on our real adult life and I know we are going to do big things. And I am so excited we are all moving to L.A.! This is just icing on the cake! Jacqueline, you are going to become the first Black actress to get the Best Actress Oscar®. You are so damn talented. You are going to take Hollywood by storm. And please just make sure I am on the guest list for the *Vanity Fair* Oscar party. Taylor, you are the next John Biggers and Romare Bearden of this century. I admire your creativity. Your masterpieces will be hanging right next to the John Biggers murals in the university library one day! I know you will be HUGE and I want one of your pieces to be in the living room of me and my future husband's estate. Don't worry... I'll put it up high enough so our kids don't fuck them up! This is just the beginning! You girls aren't just my friends, you are my sisters for life."

"Cheers!" They said in unison and started to praise dance in the middle of Ogden Circle.

"I can't believe you two convinced me to move to L.A.!" Taylor yelled above the music that was blasting.

Simone laughed. "We wouldn't have it any other way! This is fate. I got the job at Deutsch and Jackie is going balls to the wall with her acting career. The three amigas aren't about to split up because of geographical challenges!"

"Besides, being in warm weather, close to a beach, and looking at palm trees seems like a no brainer for artistic inspiration," Jackie chimed in. "You can't create masterpieces in the snow! Haven't you heard of brain freeze?"

"I can't argue with those points. Let me stop fronting, I'm actually excited too!" Taylor put her shoulders around Jackie and Simone and gave them both kisses on their cheeks.

"To new beginnings and the three amigas!" Simone said as she again raised her cup. They then started chanting their class name with the rest of the students on the circle celebrating, "The O-the-N-the-Y-the-X, it's Onyx! It's Onyx!!!"

They kept hugging each other as they danced their way around Ogden Circle in a full-on party that would go on into the wee hours of the morning.

This was just the beginning. They knew their lives were going to turn out just like they had planned...

Meet Simone Monroe Lee

18 Years Later

When I woke up this morning, I knew it was going to be one of those days. I just felt it. Not one of those life-changing good days, but one of those days where the shit was going to hit the fucking fan. I didn't know if it was going to be from someone at work or if it was going to be my husband. After all, I did what he wanted me to do. Not only did I go to church, but I went to Sunday school and I even endured going to his mother's house. This woman made it her life's mission to make my life miserable and make sure to point out any inadequacies she felt I had as her son's wife. I even sat at the table with his brother and his wife, a woman who at that very moment was pregnant by another man. The parents had no idea. How could they? That couple managed to put on the façade of the century. She was at church every Sunday in the front row sitting next to his mother, praising the Lord.

I was learning to do what my husband and the rest of his family did. Sit there, smile, and pretend like everything was perfect and fine, and eventually the problem would magically go away.

I managed to get in a great round of sweaty, raunchy sex with my husband just two days ago. You know, the kind of sex you have before you got married. The kind of sex that knocks you both out afterward, and you wake up in the middle of the night still naked from the session. That was an area we never had problem in. Shit, that's how he got me in the first place. But lately even that department was lacking and occurring less often. And lately, that's all it was, just sex. It wasn't making love, it was just pure fucking. That's great every once in a while, but not all the damn time. There was a disconnection.

Just six months ago, we had the wedding of the century. Over 300 guests at The Montage in Laguna Beach. I waited until I was I was 40 years old to get married. It wasn't by choice. I thought I would have been years into a marriage by now, with two kids and a glass balcony overlooking the ocean. But living in L.A. for so long and not accepting bullshit, I waited for the right man and I did it the right way.

Travis and I met on a blind date. When I initially met him, it wasn't major fireworks. My panties did not get wet when I first laid eyes on him. After the date I called my friends and laughed at the fact he had no swagger and didn't know how to dress. He was a little more on the corny side than what I normally dated. But I was trying to do things differently. Unlike my relationships in the past, I didn't want to allow my puss to do the thinking. I was trying to make better choices.

After my ex-boyfriend, who had swagger for days but was one of the biggest man whores in L.A., I said to myself, "Simone, be practical. You're hitting your late thirties and you want to get married. Here you have a handsome, church-going, successful real estate developer, who is family-oriented, and it will be easier. A lot of the boxes on your long list of requirements are checked off with this man."

I wasn't getting any younger and my biological clock wasn't just ticking, it was sounding like a hammer banging a nail into a concrete wall. I had dated so many assholes to this point, and now I wanted to sift through the superficial bullshit and get to know the character of a man – not just the size of his dick and bank account ... well, at least not initially.

With Travis, I took my time and got to know who he was. He was such a refreshing change from the guys I typically dated. He was consistent, loving, reliable, and he wasn't easily annoyed by my self-admitted battiness. Not to mention, on that first date he asked me questions about myself. He really seemed to care about my wants, needs, and desires. He looked me in the eye when we talked. He made me feel cared for and loved. He was ready for marriage and children. We were both approaching our forties and we were both ready for that life.

I eventually fell in love with him, and I fell hard. The first time we made love it was magical. He didn't just fuck me for a bang ... he made love to my heart, my soul, and my every fiber. When we were entangled in the aftermath I could feel his heart beating. I was experiencing love. And it felt so right. I felt like all the bad romantic decisions I had made in the past were worth the very moment that we fell in love. We enjoyed dating each other and we had fun together. To the outside world, Travis was shy and introverted. But in our own world he was fun, goofy, freaky, and passionate. I knew the Travis that the outside world didn't know.

What drew him to me was that I was unlike anyone he had ever dated. I was feisty, driven, fun, exciting and made him break out of his shell. In time, I helped him get that swag that I needed. I took him shopping for his non-work attire. My husband could rock a suit any day of the week, but I helped him step up his weekend game. I got tired of seeing him in baggy jeans, white T-shirts, white sneakers, Sean John sweats, or hideous short-sleeved checkered shirts. I introduced him to Seven7 Jeans for men... fitted T-shirts that showed off his muscular shape, Kenneth Cole leather sandals, and nice button-down shirts.

Although he was an educated brother, he still had a lot of 'hood in him and could be downright country at times (his family was from Mississippi). He didn't even have a passport when I met him. His travel consisted of visiting Mississippi in the summer to see his grandmother and going to his church convocation. His most exotic trip was a field trip to Hawaii when he was a freshman in high school.

Here I was, a well-traveled woman who had even studied abroad, in Paris, dating a man who didn't even have a passport. His lack of travel wasn't due to lack of finances; it was lack of exposure. That was an easy fix and he was willing to make the adjustment. I was determined to make this work and at the time he was open to change. The definition of insanity is doing the same thing over and over again and expecting different results. I had dated the well-traveled Harvard man and that shit just wasn't clicking. I was switching shit up!

Need I mention again that sex with Travis was next-level freaky, nasty, and off the hook? We shared a passion that was unparalleled to anyone else I had ever been with. And not to sound like a total skank ... I had many men to compare him to. Travis was super-duper successful and I felt like we could build a great life together. So, we got him a passport and he surprised me a few months later with a trip to Cabo San Lucas where he proposed to me during the sunset and presented me with a five-carat cushion-cut diamond with diamonds that surrounded the band. It was beautiful.

We dated for a year before getting engaged. But then, things seemed to change. The fun-loving, goofy Travis I fell in love with started to succumb to the demands of his very religious, dogmatic family. He started to morph into the Pentecostal, straight-laced, boring folks his family were. The very thing that made us attracted to each other and fall in love seemed to be what was beginning to pull us apart.

I could not change how enmeshed he was with his family. His brother lived two blocks away from us. How he could afford a house in our neighborhood I could never understand. He owned a failing tech-support business, which is why I think he decided to get into the ministry at his father's church – so he could have an extra paycheck. His wife, Lindsey, worked as a secretary. His mother, Karen, had a key to our home and ruled everything her sons did, from the decoration of their homes to their weekly schedules. She would show up to the house unannounced. When I started adding my touches to the house, she flipped. She wasn't about to let anyone come in and change that up.

Karen initially liked me, or at least that's how she acted. But as I got closer to her son and exposed him to a life outside of their small church world, instead of appreciating me for broadening his view on life, her resentment toward me grew. She was the matriarch, used to running the show when it came to her two sons and her husband. The threat of me coming in and destroying that dynamic, which she had carefully orchestrated and perfected for decades, made her disgusted with this Jezebel who was taking away her favorite son! She used every single moment before the wedding to put doubt in his head about marrying me. I wasn't like her other son's wife, who came from a small family, and didn't have much – for her, this family was her come up.

I came from money. I grew up in a huge house on a lake in Princeton, New Jersey; I spent summers on Martha's Vineyard, traveled the world with my family. My first car was a Nissan 300ZX, and I was a debutante. I was not easily impressed by his family's religious following or their new-money house in Baldwin Hills because I was from the East Coast and had family money that ran long.

The Lee family's weekly schedules consisted of Sunday school, church, and Sunday dinners at Karen's house as well as Thursday evening Bible study. We had to go to his uncle's for Fourth of July weekend, his mother's for Christmas, and church on Christmas morning. Since my family was on the East Coast, his family got the majority of our holiday time. I almost broke up with Travis when we were dating because he didn't come home with me for Thanksgiving. He made up some bullshit excuse. I was beyond pissed. But he apologized and promised we would alternate holidays moving forward.

Every summer we were expected to go to Mississippi for a full week to attend the church convocation; we had to be in church every day for revival. To say this life was exhausting was an understatement. Now don't get me wrong. I love God. I grew up in the church but my family members were not "Bible Beaters" or "Holy Rollers." I didn't like his father's church; I only joined because it was his dad's church, and my husband was not willing to come with me to my church. An old school Pentecostal church, it preached the Bible as if we were still living in the eighteenth century. His father once preached a sermon on how gay marriage was wrong. Ironically, that happened to be the Sunday I invited my gay best friend of twenty years to the church. It was awful.

Before we got married, Travis's father informed us that in order for him to perform our ceremony, he would have to be the one to do our marriage counseling. How asinine is that? I had to go to marriage counseling with my husband's father? I fought it; I begged my husband not to make us do it. I told him how uncomfortable it made me. Although I genuinely liked his father, and he seemed to like me, I didn't feel like discussing our issues with him.

But Travis wasn't budging, so to make him happy, I acquiesced.

We didn't move in together until a week before the wedding. We even stopped having sex three months before the wedding. It was Travis's idea, after his father preached an hour-long sermon about how premarital sex was a sin. The whole time he preached the sermon I could feel his mother's evil eye glaring at me.

What started as the fairy-tale courtship was beginning to crumble. I found myself fighting to make him stay in love with me and see things my way. Despite these potholes during our engagement, a year-and-a-half later, I found myself walking down the aisle, looking at the man of my dreams standing at the altar. I felt like we'd ironed out all of our kinks prior to the wedding and all would be just fine once we were married.

I had been scared that I was going to end up one of those successful women who had no man, no family, and lived in a big house by herself. Thank God I was smart enough to freeze my eggs in my thirties, which took the pressure off. But I was not about to try to pull a Janet Jackson and have a baby in my fifties! I would look at my friends from high school and college on their social media pages and see the smiling faces of happy families. During the holidays I would be bombarded with Christmas cards from them, showing off their beautiful children and perfect families.

I was ready to post pictures of me and my boo on Facebook and Instagram. I was ready to send out family-photo Christmas cards instead of a newsletter that highlighted all my travels and attempted to make the single life I was beginning to loathe seem glamorous and fun. I was about to be 40, I was lonely, and longing for a mate. And I had no question that I loved this man and he loved me. My pre-wedding jitters would vanish. I believed all would work itself out after the wedding madness was over...

•   •   •

And so today, six months later, here I was... married. I turned over to hug my husband but he was not in bed. This was beginning to happen more often. I would wake up in the middle of the night to find him gone. I would find him asleep on the couch. I'd wake him to come upstairs and go to bed with me. I thought if we made love we would fall asleep in each other's arms. But lately that wasn't the case.

Although I was now married, I never felt so alone and lonely. How was this possible? How can you live in the same house with someone and yet feel so alone? I thought I'd made all the right jokes at dinner last night with his family. Did I not smile enough? Did I not do enough to help his mother clean up after dinner as his sister-in-law and brother sat there and did nothing? I had no idea what I was doing wrong. But the distance was growing and the more the distance grew, the more my anxiety grew. I didn't know how to fix this.

I forced myself to get up and get ready for work. I splashed water on my face and extra water on my eyes. I looked at myself in the mirror. I rocked the stylish short pixie cut that Halle Berry made famous and had gone with blondish brown highlights. In this town where most sistahs' hair is weaved down their backs, my short haircut allowed me to stand out in a crowd.

I stood 5'8" without heels, but I always made it a point to wear killer heels that push me to stand over 6 feet tall. My wardrobe staples were pairs of designer jeans that accentuated my figure, along with a variety of stylish tops. But when I wanted to switch it up and be corporate I could also rock a DVF dress to meetings and some Manolo Blahnik shoes.

I have been told my best assets are my long, muscular legs and my smile. Despite sucking my thumb until the age of 17, my teeth are completely straight, I never had to wear braces and, to top it off, God blessed me with caramel-bronze, smooth skin; the only time I got a blemish was around the time my period was due. Thank God for creating wax – I was able to keep my eyebrows perfectly arched. I am definitely blessed in the looks department, if I say so myself. I still had my weekly hair appointments so that my hair was always shiny and perfectly in place, and kept bi-weekly manicure and pedicure appointments.

I've always had a lot of confidence in myself. To the outside world I was the most confident person on the planet. Often described as a diva or high-maintenance, the image I presented to the outside world was a good one. Simone Monroe, now Simone Monroe-Lee: successful ad executive, beautiful, smart, in all the right social circles, member of Alpha Kappa Alpha Sorority, graduate of Hampton University, funny, gave great parties, loyal friend, former party girl, now doting wife of Travis Lee, a successful real estate developer and son of Bishop Lee.

The image was a good one – one I worked my whole life to perfect. I knew when I walked into a room I could light it up. I knew I had the power to get people to open up to me within minutes of meeting me. I was a people person. And I loved living life to the fullest.

But today I didn't know the woman who was staring back at me in the mirror. I was staring at someone who, despite a full eight hours of sleep, was exhausted. Now that I was 40, I found myself looking at my eyes to see if the crow's feet were beginning to appear. As I undressed to get into the shower I noticed my once full, perky, double-D breasts were beginning to lose their fight with gravity. Despite hitting the gym four or five times a week, my gut was damn stubborn and not going anywhere. I grabbed at the gut and shook it. "Go away!"

Just last week, I noticed a few gray pubic hairs! I couldn't believe it. I was a few days late for my regularly scheduled bikini wax and "grandma pubes" decided to appear. I told the lady who does my bikini wax to take it all off and no longer leave a landing strip. I was terrified to grow out my blonde highlights, which I spent hundreds of dollars every few weeks to maintain. If I was getting gray pubes, I could only imagine what my natural dark brown-colored hair had in store for me! Was this 40?

Oh, how I envied the young girls in their twenties. Sometimes I felt like I took those years for granted and didn't enjoy being able to eat whatever the fuck I wanted and maintain my washboard abs. I missed living life without consequence and having time to correct my mistakes – which had worked.

Life had proven to be financially and professionally successful for me. I had been promoted to V.P. of the North American sales team at my advertising agency. I had a team of 25 that reported into me. I got to travel throughout the U.S. and Canada to meet with my clients and wine and dine them.

I bought my West Hollywood condo in my early thirties and when I sold it prior to my wedding, I made a huge profit. So I was sitting pretty financially, and even though my boss was a total lunatic, I enjoyed the perks and the visibility of my role with the agency. I was at the pinnacle of my career, and now I was married.

As I was giving my daily pep talk to myself about making this marriage work, my husband walked into the bathroom. He was a handsome man. He towered over me with his 6'3" football build. His chocolate skin was smooth and rich. He worked out on a regular basis. His eyes had a slight slant to them. He had full lips, a low fade and rocked a super-neat and well-groomed five-o'clock shadow beard. Like me, his teeth were perfectly straight and bright white. He had a deep voice of sophistication with a slight street edge to it that showed he was from the hood and hadn't lost his cred despite his education.

"Good morning, baby." He kissed me on the lips, handing me a hot cup of Starbucks coffee. "Skinny vanilla latte with almond milk and a double shot of espresso."

"Well, good morning to you, sunshine. Thank you. I didn't know what happened to you when I woke up and you weren't in bed. You fell asleep on the couch again?"

"I was watching the sports highlights and fell asleep."

"You seem to want to fall asleep on the couch more than cuddle with me these days." I tried not to have the sound of irritation in my voice, but I had a feeling I wasn't being too successful at it.

"Are you really starting in on me first thing in the morning about that? Did you not get enough sleep?"

"I got enough sleep, but I probably would have gotten more sleep if my husband was holding me in his arms instead of the damn remote control."

I rolled my eyes and proceeded to the shower. Although I didn't have time to really luxuriate in our 4-person, walk-in shower, I still put on all the various shower heads at different angles. Instead of addressing my being pissed off, Travis did what he always did: went about his business without acknowledging that I was pissed off. Asshole!

I was going out of town the following day for work so the last thing I wanted was for us to be arguing. I was tripping. Really, what's so bad about him falling asleep on the couch? I was probably being a little too needy. Maybe my ego was a little bruised. Shit, I was used to men that begged to hold me and I wanted to sleep in the same bed as my husband, like in our premarital heyday. Perhaps I needed to try a different approach.

I walked into his home office, where he was on the computer. "So... I was thinking, since I'm going out of town tomorrow morning, let's have a date night."

"What do you have in mind?"

"Let's go to Beauty and Essex. I took some clients there last month and you'll love it."

"That's cool. Make the reservations and it's a date."

"I will do that." As I said that the phone rang. I went to pick it up and saw it was the same 800 number that kept calling the house. "It's that same robo call."

"Well, just ignore it, it's probably a telemarketer."

"They called at 8 o'clock at night the other day. It's getting ridiculous. I thought we were on the 'do not call' list."

"Me too, but you know how those things go. You put your name on the list and end up getting more calls. Just ignore it."

I put on my zebra print 6-inch heels that sassed up my black fitted pencil skirt and crisp white button-down blouse and got ready to leave for work. I yelled as I was leaving, "See you tonight. I'll make our reservation for 8. I love you."

"I love you more," he yelled back.

Okay, so things weren't that bad. I was just tripping. I was probably about to get my period and I was extra-sensitive. See? A little bit of compromise goes a long way.

Meet Jacqueline McKinley

After all these years in L.A., I knew this was going to be my big break. I had spent hours the day before with my acting coach, and even he was moved to tears of laughter from my read. I was ready! The first two auditions went great. Now I was getting to read for the producers. There was no way that I wasn't going to get this part! All the stars were in alignment; I even found a parking spot right in front of the building. Lord knows I was so tired of struggling and being broke.

But you would never know I was living paycheck to paycheck, working part-time at publishing company. You would never know that at this very moment I had three payday loans to cover my hair, makeup, and a coaching session for this audition. I would pay those folks back with my first big check and never have to use them again. It was so demoralizing having to walk into those loan places, the same spots that destitute folks go when they're desperate for money.

But my credit was shot and I didn't want to go to my mother for any more money because I knew I would hear her mouth: "You need to get a real job." And I just wasn't in the mood to hear it. I had an image to maintain and I wasn't going to let anyone or anything stop me from achieving my dreams.

I had lived in L.A. for the last eighteen years and I wasn't about to give up. I studied theater arts and lived in London for a year so I wasn't one of these starlet, non-talented bitches that just moved to L.A. because they thought they were cute. I studied my craft; I lived and breathed my craft. With each guest-starring appearance and day-player parts I landed, I knew I was getting closer and closer to becoming the star I was born to be. When my agent called me about this part I felt within my every fiber that this was going to be it.

I knew I looked the part. I pulled down the car visor so I could look at myself in the mirror. Yep, I was looking good. My skin looked like it should be wrapped in a silver wrapper and labeled Hershey's Kiss®, my hair hung to the middle of my back, and my eyes had a little bit of a slant to them.

Many times, people would ask me if I had Asian in my family. I can't tell you how many times some ignorant membas (my terminology – I use it instead of saying the N-word) would say to me, "You look good for a dark-skinned girl."

And I would roll my eyes and reply, "You look good for an asshole."

In L.A., your game had to be tight, especially as a dark-skinned girl. You had to bring it ten times more than the next bitch. Seriously, I was overlooked time and time again for different parts because the producers thought I looked "too ethnic." They wanted to go with someone who had more of a "universal" look. I was waiting on the Morris Chestnut/Idris Elba Effect to happen for Black actresses, in the same way it happened for Black actors. We were getting close.

Tika Sumpter was making it a little easier for us. But the bitch was booking parts that I should have gotten. I could act circles around her. But the studios always picked the same Black actors and actresses for each movie because they were afraid to take a chance on a new breakout star. Especially a dark-skinned sistah.

But I felt like times were changing. They needed to change. Shit, I was 40 years old; I could only pretend to be twenty-five for so long before the jig was up. I'd walked into different auditions and seen that actress who represents my biggest fear. The 40-plus woman trying to go out for the part of a twenty-something with caked-on makeup, bad skin, and ill-fitting, out-of-date clothes. That couldn't happen to me. There was no way it would happen. Perhaps if I could meet a rich man, that would help my chances. That way I wouldn't be so stressed out about money and I could really concentrate on my craft and quit working at that boring publishing company. I figured if I could get on TV, some NBA or NFL star would see me and fall in love, we would get married and everything would be okay.

It happened for Gabrielle Union and LaLa Anthony. Those groupies weren't fooling anybody. I knew the deal. They'd scope out clueless athletes, ask entertainers to be in their music videos, or just happen to be in a club they frequented. Most athletes are from country bumpkin towns in the south or the projects of inner cities, so they grow up idolizing these women they see on TV, or whose music they hear. Being totally enamored by their celebrity status, they fail to realize they are being worked by these famous women in the same way a regular groupie would. These women know their music careers are dying and their acting roles are drying up. They are just as desperate as the no name groupies for a come up but, because they are famous they are able to disguise their desperation. The next thing you know, either the girl is pregnant or engaged. I knew that game like the back of my hand. Shit, I tried that card and hadn't been successful yet. One thing I refused to do was get pregnant before I was married. That's just not a good look. People will always think that you trapped the guy, even if you get married and live happily ever after.

Where in the world was my happily ever after? The idea that I was 40 and still going to auditions was a sobering reality for me. URGH!

Okay, let me get out of my head. *Stay focused, Jackie, stay focused.* I got out of my Range Rover. As cute as the car looked, it had become a major pain in my ass. My car note was almost two months behind, my registration was expired, and I definitely didn't have the money to pay it since it went to my new headshots last month. To top that shit off, when I went to start the car, the engine stalled, so I knew there was another $2,500-plus repair around the corner waiting to knock me down. But there was no way in hell I was going to drive around L.A. in a putt-putt car at my age. That was cute in my twenties, but I had to step up my game. As I walked into the building in my brand-new Louboutin red bottoms, my black leather skinny jeans that felt like butter, and burnt-orange wrap shirt I looked every bit the part of the diva fashion executive I would be portraying in this new TV series.

I walked in as my character. I scanned the room and saw the other three girls who were my competition. It took everything in me not to laugh out loud. This was my competition? They should have just left the room right. They all looked a hot-ass mess. One of them had a *tired* weave. You could see the tracks, not to mention her hair didn't even pretend to blend in with the weave hair. The other girl had on open-toed shoes that exposed her bunions and she literally had a corn on each toe. One toe had two corns on it. She wore a cheap Forever 21-looking top and her nail polish was chipped. I gave the third girl props. She looked decent to say the least. She pretty much looked like a lighter-complected version of me. Actually, all of them were light-skinned. I began to wonder why I was there… was I the honorary dark-skinned girl? Did I even have a chance?

However, all these girls lacked the confidence and flavor that I brought to the room. My flair was ingrained in me. It was impossible not to grow up a diva when your mother was part of the Who's Who of the East Coast. My mother owned and ran a top non-profit firm. She was what most would consider an overachiever: graduated from high school two years early, then went on to Hampton University, and from there went to Harvard for her M.B.A. – all by the age of 22. She went straight through; she didn't take any summer breaks.

From there she worked her way up the corporate ladder and when she was at the peak of her career, she decided to branch out on her own and open her own non-profit firm to take advantage of her golden Rolodex and her love of giving back to the community – and having people stroke her overinflated ego. She anticipated I would ultimately run the firm once I graduated from college.

And for a while, I did keep with her script, following in her footsteps to Hampton University. Not because she pressured me to go, but because the first time I visited the campus, I had never seen so many fine ass Black men in my life! That's all it took for me to decide to go there, although I let my mother believe that it was her influence that made me decide.

As much as there were benefits to being the daughter of the unstoppable Angelique McKinley; I was burdened with the expectation of perfection, along with the expectation to become a top executive. But that wasn't who I was. I was never that person. I always knew from the time I was a child that I wanted to be an actress.

Perhaps it was all of those Jackie Collins novels I read, or maybe it was the time I watched *Carmen Jones* and fell in love with Dorothy Dandridge's on-screen presence. When I was onstage and in character I felt like I had all the control and power in the world. For that period of time I controlled people's emotions and perceptions. I was able to live the life of another person. So it was not hard to imagine my mother's dismay when I told her I was majoring in Theater Arts.

"You're what? I'm not spending hundreds of thousands of dollars for you to play make-believe for four years. What are you going to do with that degree once you graduate? Become a waitress?"

"No, Mother, I am going to move to L.A. and pursue my acting dreams."

"L.A.? Do you know how many wannabe starlets land in L.A. every day and think they are going to be the next Halle Berry, only to find themselves years later, broke, destitute, and without a real job? Why are you setting yourself up for failure?"

The concern in my mother's voice was real. It wasn't an attack; it was a genuine concern for my well-being. She sacrificed a lot to make sure my sister and I lived a good life. When she and my father divorced I was only four years old, and she became the mother and father. My dad was still active in my life, but even he knew better than to contradict or question Angelique's parenting skills or decisions. She made sure we never wanted for anything. We went to the best private schools in Princeton, we spent summers in the Hamptons, we traveled abroad as a family, and we lived in the most elite neighborhoods in the D.C. Metro area. Basically, we were raised to be *Our Kind of People* women, and graduating from Hampton University to become an actress-waitress was not part of the master plan she had in mind for her daughters.

I was thirteen years older than my sister Julia. She was technically my half-sister; she was my mother's daughter from her second marriage that also ended in divorce. Julia and I were like oil and water and had nothing in common outside of the fact that we both issued from the same womb. But I had to give my Millennial sister her props. She was smart with how she pimped my mother for money.

She was what I would call a "professional student." She finished her bachelor's in Political Science at Hampton University... yes, she managed to attend the legacy university as well. And I suspect she did it for the same reasons I did... All those fine-ass Black men! From there she went to Princeton to get her master's in psychology, and now she was working on getting another master's in business. I already could see through her bullshit. But my mother loved the idea of telling her friends all about her younger daughter's ambitions, which typically resulted in me throwing up in my mouth.

My younger sister didn't have to work because my mother wanted her "focused" on her studies. So when I would go home for the holidays and see this 20-something rocking Gucci fur slides and an Hermès belt, I would mentally slap the shit out of her and want to shake my mother and say, "Can't you tell this heifer is pimping you?" Outside of my career, most of the major arguments my mother and I had were over her indulgence and spoiling of my entitled baby sister. Anyway, I digress. I said all that to say, appearances were everything to my mother. And just like my baby sister knew how to work her, so did I.

"That's not going to be me. I am going to study my craft and learn it. You've got to trust me," I pleaded.

"Well, if you're going to study theater you should explore moving to New York after you graduate. At least the people there have more culture. L.A. is a bunch of wannabes. You'll like New York better."

Instead of arguing the point with her, I knew I had to agree. At the end of the day, my mother held the purse strings and there was no way I was going to risk pissing her off and cutting my monthly allowance and tuition. "You're right, Mother. I will definitely look into that."

"Jackie, you know I support you and I love you and I want you to be happy. But you also have to be practical. Make sure you have a backup plan."

How I hated that phrase, "backup plan." Whoever came up with it must have been an underachiever. To think of a backup plan was like admitting to myself that I wasn't going to make it before I even started. I didn't need a backup plan. I had talent.

So as I sat in the audition room, scanning the competition, after living this "dream" for the last eighteen years, I knew this audition was the make-it-or-break-it audition. I needed this part for more reasons than financial concerns.

You see, I was beginning to lose faith that I was good enough. I was beginning to lose hope that the years I spent in L.A., the year I spent in London studying Shakespearean Theatre, the semester I spent in Paris perfecting my French, and the four years I spent studying acting at

Hampton were going to lead me to the life I always dreamed and believed I could have. I was terrified of failure. I was tired of living a lie.

I felt like a Monet painting. From a distance I was beautiful and well put together, but close up and inside, I was falling apart. I didn't have a backup plan and the last thing I wanted was to admit to my mother that she was right. More than anything, I didn't want to admit to myself that perhaps it was the end of the road. Perhaps it was time for me to come up with a Plan B... because my Plan A wasn't working

"Jacqueline McKinley." The casting director came out with her clipboard and my headshot in her hand. "We're ready to see you now."

Meet Taylor Ross

I closed my eyes, took a deep breath, and let Pat Metheny's guitar lead me to my next masterpiece. I envisioned the bright colors I was about to cover the canvas with. Lately, I had been reflecting on the end of the chapter of my thirties and was getting used to the idea that in exactly five days I would officially be 40 years old. I still can't believe how fast the time went, but how slow it seemed on some days. This canvas was a huge one. Taller than me.

I used a ladder to help me cover all areas of it. Height never got in the way of my creations. I knew from the time I was ten that I was going to be an artist.

I'll never forget my first visit to the Museum of Modern Art. I was in the fifth grade and our class took a field trip. Unlike most of the other kids, I found myself mesmerized by the work of Edgar Degas. When I looked at the ballerinas in his paintings and drawings, I could feel their stories and their struggles. Not bad for a ten-year-old, huh?

I've always been deeper than most. I look at life from a perspective that most people don't. Perhaps it was from growing up with a brother who is bipolar. I never knew from day to day what the mood in my household was going to be.

My brother was diagnosed when he was 15 and I was 12. This was back in the early '90s. People didn't understand what bipolar disorder was back then, and it certainly was not understood in the Black community. People just assumed if he went to church, the "demonic" spirit could be prayed out of him. I never really understood, either. I just knew one day me and my brother would be having a great time playing Donkey Kong on our Atari system and then the next day, he would be sitting in his room in the dark staring at the walls.

My mother and father didn't know how to handle it. Before he was diagnosed he would get in trouble and they would spank him. My mother figured the harder she spanked him, the more he would get it. My father was the complete opposite; he invented passive-aggressive communication. His tactic was to ignore my brother and make him feel like shit, like he didn't exist, like he had the plague.

When my father and mother divorced, my dad became what you would call a weekend dad. He had this amazing ability to just check out completely. Shortly after their divorce, my father met and married some random white woman after knowing her for only six weeks. Not only did her marry her, but he also adopted her young mixed daughter, and it was as though his first family didn't exist. And little by little, we literally became the "ghosts of family past" to him.

First, the phone calls lessened, then he went from a weekend dad to a nonexistent dad. I remember sitting for hours looking out the window on the weekends he was supposed to pick us up. He never came. Even worse, he stopped supporting us financially. The brunt of raising us was left to my mother, which caused her to drink more and work longer hours.

My mother was college-educated, but she made the mistake many women made when they got married. She became a full-time mother and was completely dependent on my father's income. Men can wake up one day and change their minds, leaving the woman with nothing. Since my mother had no real work experience she took jobs that were blue collar, for people with GEDs, not bachelor's degrees. I'd hear my mother's sobs outside the door of her bedroom many nights. The devastation and hurt that my father not only left us, but also started a new life with another woman, sent her over the edge. The bills were piling up and she had to handle everything on her own.

Initially, she was able to hide her alcoholism fairly well. She was at first a functioning alcoholic. But as the years went by, her ability to hide that addiction spiraled out of control. There were times when my brother and I had to do a team effort to get her out of bed to get her to work. She would cry in our arms, "I'm so sorry children... I let you down... Mommy will fix this... Mommy will fix this."

My brother Michael and I were each other's confidants. When the doctors would attempt to level out his medications and he had the severe shakes, he would come to me to ask if it was as bad as it seemed. And me being the honest sister, I would be like, "You're just a little stiff. Try to loosen up."

My mother would wake up in the morning and fix herself a rum and pineapple juice, with a splash of cranberry juice, on the rocks. On those many days when she was too hung over to get out of bed, I knew the exact amount of rum to mix with the pineapple juice and splash of cranberry juice. I would make her some toast and brew up the coffee, and my 11-year-old self would take her hangover cure down the hall to her room, place it on the bed, open the blinds, and wake my mother up. This was normal in my household. I never knew which way the wind was going to blow with my mother.

It was a day-by-day thing. If she woke up in a good mood, then everything was good. But my God, on those days when she wasn't in a good mood, everyone suffered. The more grown-up I became, the more anger she had toward me. If she was in a bad mood, the mere sight of me wearing lip gloss would send her into a fit. She would look at me and the violence would strike. She would grab me by the neck and smear the lip gloss off and start pounding me in the face or choking me, or she'd grab scissors and try to cut off my hair. That's when Michael would save me. He would pull her off me until she calmed down. I would run and hide and wait for the episode to pass. Museums became my safe haven.

So when I bought my first ready-made canvas and started painting, it brought me freedom – from the madness of my life as a child. It was so damn hard growing up. But I didn't realize that it wasn't normal until after high school, when I went off to Hampton University, where I studied art history. Hampton had one of the largest African American art collections in the country. And the university granted me a full ride academic scholarship for maintaining straight A's in high school.

While most students spent long hours in the library studying, I would spend long hours studying the two John Biggers murals that hung in the lobby of the library and attempting to imitate some of the intricacies of his art. While most students spent Saturday morning sleeping in after partying it up on Friday night, I would go to the art museum and study the various artists' work. Don't get me wrong, I still got my party on – but my passion was art.

After I graduated from Hampton, I moved to L.A. and began working at one of the most exclusive art galleries in Beverly Hills, which gave me the opportunity to learn the business side of being an artist. After working at the gallery for a year, I decided to show the owner my paintings, and she was amazed at my talent. Keep in mind, this was work from the time I was in high school through college. In no time, she held a show of my work at the gallery and all 30 of my pieces sold out.

From that point on, I focused on cultivating my talent and selling my paintings. In time, I became one of the most sought-after artists in L.A. Who says you can't have it all at 39? I most certainly do. This birthday, I have such an overwhelming feeling of gratitude.

I dipped my brush into the paint. It was a butter pecan color that reflected the color of my skin. I let the strokes guide me. One stroke at a time, carefully selecting each color. Within an hour, I could see the foundation of this painting was me. The big curly wash-and-go hair that was my signature statement when I walked into a room gave it away. Most folks thought I was much taller than 5'2", and it was probably because my hair added a good four inches to my height. The bigger the hair, the closer to God.

I was now in my groove. Each color represented a different decade in my life. My childhood, dealing with an absentee father and a mother who used alcohol as a crutch. My brother, in the early 90s, when doctors had no idea how to treat a young Black man with bipolar disease and used medications that did more harm than good. Those were the quick strokes that had fire red, blood orange, and dark gray under tones on the canvas.

The next color strokes of eggplant and black reflected my teens. Days when I had to put my mother to bed after she passed out. Days when lied to my friends at school and told them Michael was in boarding school so I didn't have to deal with the shame of having a brother who was "crazy."

Then came the softer period of my life. Late teens and early twenties and Hampton University, where I met my true sisters for life. The time when my dream of becoming an artist came to fruition and I was encouraged to hone my talent. The strokes of pink, lavender, and teal helped add to the softness of the painting. And then came the strokes of yellow, gold, green, and silver that represented my thirties. My passion and love of art had become my career, and I was one of the few people who could make money doing what she loved. I had made peace with my mother shortly before her death. And there was a certain tranquility that came with her leaving this earth. The strokes were free and long and airy.

I hadn't realized I'd been painting for damn near six hours until my phone rang. My girls knew Sunday was my painting day and not to disturb me. I walked over to the phone, wiping the paint off my hands, annoyed and ready to go off until the caller ID told me it was my brother. I was relieved; I hadn't spoken to him in a few days and I was beginning to get worried.

"What's up, bro?"

"Hey, T-Squito." This was the nickname he gave me in my pre-pubescent years when I had a completely flat chest. He used to call my boobs mosquito bites. "How's the birthday plans coming?"

"You know Simone is treating this like it's her wedding, so it's going to be off the chain. When are you getting into town?" I walked to my fridge to get a bottle of aloe vera water.

"I'll get there Saturday afternoon. I know you'll be busy so I'll Uber it over. I was calling to let you know I talked to Dad earlier today – "

Before he could even finish, I knew exactly where Michael was going. I hadn't spoken to my dad in years, and he wanted to reach out now that I'm damn near 40? *I don't think so.* "Michael, I already told you I don't have any plans on talking to him. And you better not even think about telling him about my party."

"Calm down, T-Squito. I didn't tell him about the party. But how much longer are you going to stay mad at him? You got to let it go."

"Well, maybe you're fine with him, but I'm not. And you better NOT give him my information." I hated when my brother got all "big brotherly" on me.

"I told you I wasn't going to."

"Was that the only reason you were calling?"

"I just wanted to check in on you and make sure the party planning is going well." He sounded slightly defeated. "Why do you always think

I call you because I want something? I'm your big bro. You know I worry about you."

"I'm sorry. It's just that talking about Dad really gets my blood boiling. I hate that he left our family and then went and started his new family and forgot about us, the originals."

"I hear you, T, but you have to learn how to move past that shit. He can't unscramble eggs."

"And do you see how he brags about that bitch of a wife and her daughter on Facebook, like we don't even exist?!"

"Who pissed in your Cheerios this morning? Damn T, you're on one today. Maybe I need to give you one of my pills to calm your ass down."

"You're right. But I'm not like you. You've always been so damn forgiving. I just haven't gotten to that point yet. Anyway, enough about that, how are you doing?"

"That's what I was calling about. I started writing my book and I'm almost done. I wrote 200 pages in the last two days. I want you to do the artwork for the cover."

"Wow! I'm impressed. Are you getting any sleep in between your writing, Shakespeare?" My brother was always an amazing writer. And he was now writing for *IT* magazine, New York's new "it" publication.

"I'm on a roll, T! I don't want to lose the stuff before I get it out. I just keep writing so I don't forget anything."

"I can't wait to read it. Two hundred pages in two days is A LOT. Are you getting sleep?" I again broached the subject.

"I bet you've been up the last eight hours painting, now you're worried about my sleep patterns?"

Fuck it... he knew me so damn well. But I was tired of beating around the bush. "Michael, are you taking your meds?"

"Damn, way to shoot a brotha down! Yeah, I'm taking my meds. They're just adjusting my levels, and you know how that goes."

"But you are taking the meds you have in the meantime while they are making the adjustments, right?" I tried not to sound like I was beginning to panic, but I knew the signs. One of them was when my brother wasn't sleeping.

"Yesssssss, T!" he said, sounding like an annoyed teenage boy.

"Okay, okay," I said, feeling like a totally pain in the ass nag. "Of course, I will do the book cover. I would be honored. After all, we need to keep the coins in the family."

"Now you're talking. I'll see you on Saturday, T-squito!"

"Bye, Soul Brother Number One!"

I hung up, knowing in my spirit that something wasn't right. I knew that sound in my brother's voice. I knew this was about to start the roller coaster ride that I was all too familiar with... I went over to my painting and grabbed my brushes to clean them.

Chapter One
Jacqueline

How could I have ever doubted myself? I rocked that audition! I had the producers and director eating out of my hand. The casting director, who typically has a poker face, could barely contain her laughter. I have never felt more confident that I was going to get a part. I couldn't wait to call my mother and tell her the good news...

But where in the world did I park my car? I thought I had parked it right in front of the building. I had so much on my mind, I'd probably parked another block down the street. I walked a block and didn't see it.

"Okay," I thought. "Let me walk in the other direction." A black Range Rover isn't hard to miss. I began to walk the other direction and still didn't see my car. That's when panic struck. *Where the fuck is my car?* At this point my feet were beginning to hurt. And the last thing I needed was to begin to sweat because I did plan on returning this $200 shirt to Neiman's. I was only "renting" it for the audition. "Just *think,* Jackie," I said out loud to myself.

I took a breath and walked a little farther down the street. *I know I parked my car right here.* Just when my panic was about to get to the next level, a guy came out from one of the shops. "Do you drive a black Range Rover?" he asked.

"Yes, I do. I thought I had parked it here..." I said.

"Sorry, ma'am. They towed your car 15 minutes ago."

"What?!" I yelled, as if he'd said he towed my car personally.

"It was a black Range Rover, right?" He had a thick Persian accent but I could understand every word he was saying.

"Right, yes."

"Yep, they towed it," he said, confirming my biggest fear. I knew why. My registration had been expired for well over eight months. Every time I got in the car I was always scared I would get pulled over. I mastered the art of driving on side streets where I knew police wouldn't be around. I also valet-parked my car whenever I went out so I wasn't parked on the street. My audition lasted 30 minutes. Who would have thought they'd tow my car so soon?

"Shit... Shit... Shit... Fuck." I took my phone out of my purse to call Taylor. I was hoping and praying she would answer.

"You can wait in here if you'd like," the guy said in a sleazy, disgusting tone as he smiled revealing his missing tooth. His tone matched his shop: one of those cheap and trashy lingerie places on Hollywood Blvd.

"I'm okay," I said, quickly walking away down the street to a café. Taylor's phone rang and rang. She wasn't going to pick up? I knew she didn't like to get calls while she was painting...

"Hey there, future NBC series regular. How did it go?" Taylor! She sounded so excited for me. In a matter of minutes, the high I had from a slam-dunk audition was overshadowed by the reality of my life.

"The audition went great and I'll tell you all about it, but first I need a favor."

"What's up?" Taylor always sounded so relaxed. I guess that yoga "namaste" shit worked.

"Can you pick me up? My car got towed."

"Damn! Of course I can get you. Where are you?"

"I'm on Hollywood and Vine." As I was trying to maintain my calm, my competition from the audition walked past me and got into a beat-up Honda Civic. Go figure! Her car might have been beat up but her tags were current and her car was where she left it.

"All right, I'm on my way. I'll be there in 15 minutes."

I could always count on Taylor. She, Simone, and I were closer than I was to my own sister. I was never embarrassed to tell her the real deal. But she had no idea about my financial situation. That was the one aspect of my life that I kept a secret from my friends. Sometimes I felt like I was living a lie. My friends had no idea how broke I was.

Welcome to the madness called Jackie's life! I was so fucking broke! I didn't pay the registration because I had to pay my rent and my cell phone bill. How in the world had I gotten myself into this mess? I looked down at my brand-new Louboutin shoes and wanted to smack myself for making such a shitty decision. After all, Steve Madden made a knock-off and it was only $125 versus the $1,025 I spent on these. I needed a break. I needed to finally have a career... a real career.

I felt like such a failure. Just as a tear was about to makes its escape down my cheek, my phone rang. I assumed it was Taylor trying to figure out where I was.

"Hi," I answered as I stood up to see if Taylor was outside.

"Hello, dear," said the powerful voice of my mother.

FUCK! Angelique was the last person I felt like speaking to right now. How is it that she always managed to call me at the worst times? "Mother, now isn't a good time," I said, not hiding my annoyance.

"What's going on there? I can tell something is wrong." She sounded genuinely concerned.

"Everything is fine, Mommy..." I dabbed the tear off my check and straightened my shoulders, going into full actress mode. "As a matter of fact, things couldn't be better. I booked the NBC series regular part." What the fuck? The lie came out before I had a chance to stop it. "You did?" She sounded shocked... which really pissed me off.

"You sound like you can't believe it." I said, as I looked up and down the street for
Taylor's car.

"Well... it's about time. I was wondering how long you were going to be living out there in fantasy-land. You're 40 years old."

"I am? I didn't even realize that." My sarcasm was evident.

"Jacqueline, I'm just saying at a certain point you have to grow up and get a real career."

"This *is* a real career, Mommy!" Luckily, Taylor pulled up in a brand-new black Porsche Cayenne S. "Mommy, I have to go."

"But – " I hung-up before she could finish.

"This is gorgeous, Taylor! When did you get this?" I exclaimed as I got into her car. It had a red leather interior and she looked damn good in it.

Why do some people have it so damn easy?

"It's a little early fortieth birthday present for me. I got it yesterday. I was planning on showing it off this weekend."

"Well, I love it. It's about damn time you upgraded from that Explorer! How are you going to fit your paintings in this?"

"Girl, I still have the truck. This is my fun weekend car."

"Wow."

"They finally towed you for the late registration, huh?" Taylor said, looking at me over her sunglasses.

"I got caught. You would think the city of Hollywood had something better to do with their time, like clean up the sidewalks or fix the potholes in the streets. But, noooooo, they just had to tow my damn car."

I was about to start a long monologue, but what was the use? So I did what I am gifted at doing: turning the conversation around and making people talk about themselves. "Anyway, enough about me. How's the party planning going? I hope you're planning on having some men there."

"Well, of course I am. But you're not going to like any of them. They're not ballers; they're more of the creative type."

"You're right about that," I said as I reapplied my lip gloss. "Unless they're some creative types with a bank account."

"Girl, you are crazy! You know Simone is planning this like it's her second wedding. Let's focus on getting your car out of the impound lot first." She shifted gears, the engine revved, and we drove off.

When we got to the lot, panic set in. It was probably going to be $500 to get my car out of the lot.

I could handle that. My cell phone and cable bills would just be paid late.

"Thanks for the ride, girl."

"Do you want me to wait for you? We can grab a cocktail afterwards. I'll call Simone and see if she can meet us as well."

"Sure, I shouldn't be long." I walked into the office and of course there was your stereotype stank, full-of-attitude Black woman behind the counter with her long, square acrylic nails and bad hair weave.

"Can I help you?" she said.

"Um, yes. My car was impounded earlier today."

"May I get your license please?" I handed my license to her and she started pounding keys on her keyboard. It seemed like it was taking forever. And the more time it took, the more I started to panic. I could seriously forget about returning this shirt because the amount of sweat I got on it would make it obvious I had worn it. Good-bye, $200.

"Okay, that's going to be $1,183.22," she said nonchalantly.

"I'm sorry, I thought you said $1,100...?" I chuckled. My ears must have been deceiving me.

"No, ma'am. I said $1,183.22," she repeated in her dry, monotone, ghetto voice.

"There must be some kind of mistake. My registration is only $549." This had to be a mistake. "Are you sure you're looking up the right car?"

"You are Jacqueline McKinley, and you own a black 2010 Range Rover, correct?"

"Yes." I was really getting fucking annoyed. And why did she have to be such a bitch about it?

"Then it's the right car. You have a late fee, parking tickets, returned check fees, towing and the impoundment fees. That will be $1,183.22."

Holy shit! That would wipe out my entire checking account! I began to take out my checkbook. I figured I could write a check and by the time it got to my bank I would have enough time to figure out a way to cover it. I still needed to pay my rent and car note.

"We don't take checks. Only credit or debit cards."

This can't be happening. Why the hell didn't I just pay the damn registration when it first came and was only $549? I had nothing else left to do but pay up. I handed the bitchy clerk my debit card. I had just gotten paid from the publishing company, so I had money in the bank. After I paid this, I'd be left with a total of $26.87 in my debit card account. I had no idea how I was going to pay my rent or the car note.

Twenty minutes later, I was driving my car out of the impoundment lot and following Taylor to Katana for a drink. I felt lower than low and didn't have a clue how I was going to pull a rabbit out of a hat this time to pay my bills. Once again, I was beginning to feel like it was the beginning of the end.

Chapter Two
Taylor

Katana is one of my favorite spots in L.A. It is an outdoor rooftop restaurant with Asian-themed décor, a fabulous Asian fusion menu, and a live DJ after 5 p.m. It was hip, trendy, and no matter what time of day, always packed.

The artist in me loved going to places where there were beautiful people. It inspired my artwork. Looking around the outside patio, everyone had a story – whether it was the overly cosmetic, surgically enhanced woman clinging onto her youth, not realizing the surgery made her look even older; the young twenty-something starlet with bleached blonde hair sitting next to an overly tanned, balding, fat man with obvious wealth; or even the beautiful, young, Black Hollywood starlet with a bad weave and cheap clothes, carrying a fake Louis Vuitton purse, trying to appear relevant. This place hosted the gamut of folks, and it was also a place where me and my girls would often meet. It was our version of "Cheers."

Jackie and I spotted Simone at our usual table. Sometimes, it still amazes me that we are 40. that it's been that long since my first day at Hampton University:

Hampton University, August 1995
One thing about a Black university that is unlike most predominantly white schools is that it is also a fashion show. When I got to my room in the Twitchell Hall dorm and saw some of the things that the girls were unpacking, I began to feel like a "Bama." Although my clothes were nice, they didn't have the flair the other girls' clothes had. I dressed for

comfort. I was wearing a pair of sweatpants and flip-flops. Who would have thought girls would be wearing heels with sundresses or jeans to unpack a dorm room? I was beginning to realize I might be out of my league.

Las Vegas, where I come from, isn't exactly the fashion capital of the world. Most people don't realize that outside of the famous strip, Las Vegas is a hillbilly town.

Most of the folks there look like they work on ranches. Here I was at the most prestigious HBCU in the world and "Yeah, I'm from Vegas!" wasn't going to work. I was beginning to feel insignificant. Everyone had their parents to help them. I just had myself. I was on a full academic scholarship to Hampton; all I had to do was maintain a 3.0 GPA. I was grateful for the scholarship that the Vegas chapter of Alpha Kappa Alpha Sorority, Inc. gave me to cover my books and day-to-day living expenses.

I had worked so hard to attend this university, but now I stood in my dorm room and all I could think was, "Now what?" *Seventeen* magazine hadn't covered this. No one told me that once you unpack your room, there was such an empty feeling, especially when you didn't know anyone. I was sitting on my bed, trying to figure out my next move, when in walked another new student. She was wearing a pair of Express jeans, heels, and a cute white tank top. She had diamond studs in her ears. They were at least three carats but had such an understated elegance. Her nails were perfectly manicured. She had her hair in a choppy bob and she didn't have on a lot of makeup – just a little bit of blush, mascara, and lip gloss. Her smile lit up the room. She was so confident and friendly. She embodied the typical Hampton University girl.

At first, I thought she was looking for my roommate, Keisha. She was not at all friendly and had made it a point to get to the room first, leaving me with the shitty bed, and she seemed to know everyone. Keisha was a member of Jack and Jill. I had no idea there was an entire Black organization named Jack and Jill. I thought it was a nursery rhyme. Her friends that came by the room were girls whom she grew up with in Jack and Jill. She never did bother to introduce me to any of them. It was obvious she figured I didn't fit into her clique. And I was never one to kiss anyone's ass. So, I automatically assumed this bougie-ass girl was one of my unfriendly roommate's friends and would ignore me once she realized I was a nobody.

"Hi, I'm Simone Monroe." She sounded like Hilary Banks from "The Fresh Prince of Bel Air." As a matter of fact, if I was talking to her over the phone, I would have assumed she was a white girl with blonde hair and blue eyes.

"Hi, Simone, I'm Taylor. Are you looking for Keisha? She just left."

A lot of new students had come to Hampton during the summer for the bridge program. Some of them were required to pass "bridge program" classes in order to secure their enrollment into the university. Other students came just to get a jump-start on their college life. I felt like I was the *only* girl who hadn't attended the program. Everyone seemed to have formed their cliques already because they had a chance to hang out during the summer. I didn't see the point. I was determined to graduate from college in four years. Not to mention, my scholarship only covered four years. I was going to have to work part-time, too. Besides, not only could I not afford the summer program, but that summer my brother had just started an outpatient program, so I wanted to spend as much time hanging out with him before I left home.

"I don't know who Keisha is." Simone said after I asked her if she'd done the summer program. She was standing just five inches away from the painting of ballerinas I did when I was a sophomore in high school. "Wow, this is a terrific painting. I don't mean to sound like a know-it-all, but I wouldn't hang up valuable pieces of art in a dorm room. You should save that for your house once you graduate."

I laughed. "That's not a valuable piece of artwork – it's just a piece I did a few years ago."

"You painted this?" she exclaimed. She was so damn animated, I was slightly embarrassed. I wasn't one who just talked to strangers. In fact, I was surprised I hadn't kicked her out yet. But there was something so intriguing about this bourgeois girl. Besides, I was so relieved to finally have someone in the dorm pay me the time of day.

"You are so talented, Taylor. Wish I could paint. This painting might not be valuable now, but it will be. And when it is, I will make sure me and my husband buy it from you and hang it over our couch in our 10,000-square foot mansion."

"Thanks." I was stunned. I had never had anyone say something like that to me. "But are you engaged?"

"Oh, God no! Not yet. But I know I will meet my future husband here. We'll date for the next few years, he'll go off to medical school, and then once he's finished his residency we'll be married."

"Wow! You have it all figured out, huh?" She seemed so focused.

"But then why don't you just get married before the residency and be a stay-at-home mom?"

"Are you kidding me? I could never be a stay-at-home mom and spend someone else's money! No way! I am going to be an executive and make my own money. My husband and I will be a power couple. We'll be featured in *Essence* magazine, throw the best parties, and live a fabulous life!" She spun around and fell on my bed, her hand clutching her heart. "A woman should never ever give up control to a man. Instead, you must look at your future husband as a partnership prospect."

"That sounds like a business deal." My parents split up when I was young. They met in high school and were married by the time they were twenty-three.

"Well, at the end of the day, that's what marriage, is. At least that's what my mom always told me. Listen, I'm sorry I digressed."

"That's okay." I could sit here and listen to this girl talk all day; she was something straight out of a movie.

"So, here's the deal, Taylor. I don't know anyone here and I think you're cute. And my mother always told me it is important to surround yourself with cute friends. I never understood girls who insist on having ugly-ass friends. That won't get us any play at the Kappa, Que, or Alpha parties. And I'm not hanging around with any skanks!"

"Well, I don't know anyone here either because I didn't go to the summer program."

"Neither did I! Some of them are acting like assholes, like they run the fucking campus. But us not going was the smartest thing we could have done. You see they have already made their way through campus. So we are the true and official undiscovered meat."

"I don't know what you mean."

"Oh, boy, where are you from?" Simone asked as she cocked her head to the side like she was staring at a child.

"Las Vegas."

"That explains it. Well, let me break it down for you. None of the upper freshmen guys have seen us yet, so there's going to be a certain amount of curiosity. Whereas, the girls that were at the summer program already have their big brothers, and I can guarantee you some of them have already fucked a few upper classmen... That reminds me. If we're going to hang, you can't be a ho. That's not a good look for either of us. Oh, and before we leave this room, we are going to have to do a mini-makeover."

Simone was going on and on. And I was listening to her intently, even though I was shocked that someone who had so much class had such a vulgar mouth.

But I liked her. And I didn't know anyone else. I also didn't have the guts to tell her I was a virgin.

"What did you plan on wearing, Taylor? This is going to be our first impression on campus. We will never be able to unscramble the egg once it's cooked. You should go for an edgy artsy look, since you're an artist."

Hearing her say it made me think that maybe I really was an artist. It had such a flair to it. "Artist." It did something to my spirit. It's amazing how Simone could say something so nonchalantly and not realize she was changing the course of your life.

"How about this?" I pulled out a pair of light baggy jeans, a blue vest and a t-shirt.

Simone stared at it. I could see the dialogue playing out in her head, trying to figure out how to tell me that the outfit was hideous.

"Okay, we can work with this." She sighed. "First, I'm going to need you to burn this vest. It should never leave this room ever again, as long as you are a student here at Hampton University or living a human existence on this earth."

She rolled up my jeans, and tied the t-shirt back so it was fitted. She at first insisted I show some midriff, but at Hampton University there was a dress code and showing midriff was forbidden. She had me put on a bunch of bangles and espadrilles. She took some makeup out of her purse and by the time she turned me around to look at myself in the mirror, I was no longer a girl from Vegas in a cheap Charlotte Russe outfit, but a funky-looking girl with flair. I couldn't believe it.

"Oh, my goodness. I love it," I exclaimed as I began hugging Simone, jumping up and down.

"You stick with me and I'll show you some things. Now we can go over to the Student Union and make our debut as two of the fiercest, flyest freshmen on campus." She turned around and stopped dead in her tracks. "Taylor, who is this fine-ass guy? Is this your boyfriend?"

She had seen the picture on my desk. I was used to girls reacting this way to him. "That's my brother."

"He is fine. Know that any guy you meet has to at least look as fine as your brother! You can't mix just any blood with those good genes."

•　　•　　•

Simone and I walked out of my dorm and set off across campus. Here I was, an actual student! The campus was like a painting. It was surrounded by water. The buildings were brick and stately. The university president's white house was right in the middle of the dorms, like a king looking over his kingdom. The university Chapel stood majestically on the campus, reminding students of a higher power. Hampton was now officially *my home by the sea.*

And though I didn't know anyone that morning, now I was walking around with one of the funniest, engaging girls I had ever met. She was entertaining as hell.

Simone talked nonstop!

"I knew that I was going to make sure I built a circle of friends that were the baddest, classiest bitches on campus," she said again. There she went with that bad mouth – she really was a Jersey girl at heart. "I hope that doesn't offend you. I use the word 'bitch' as a term of endearment. You know... Being-In-Total-Control-Herself."

"I'm not offended at all." I knew she wasn't calling me a bitch in a derogatory fashion.

She went on to break down the various Hampton University cliques for me. There were an awful lot of groups: The Jocks, The Frat Boys, The Sorority Girls, The New York Fly Girls, The Fraternity Groupies, The Jock Groupies, The Bamas (aka Country Folks), The Geeks, The Weed

Heads, The New York Crew, The Cali Crew, Ebony Fire Dance Team, The Cheerleaders, The Student Leaders, and The Universals.

She explained that we could consider ourselves a part of the Universal classy chic clique. As a Universal we could navigate in and out of each clique and get along with everyone. People wouldn't have anything bad to say about you. You were a student leader, or a sorority girl, but you could also enjoy a good party. In general, you were well-liked by all the various cliques. I had no idea how she came to have all this information. But she was confident in everything she was saying, and I bought it.

The campus had so much energy! The freshmen were busy moving into their dorms, hugging their parents and pushing them off. The Student Leaders wore identifying T-shirts and were extra bubbly. The football players were wearing their jerseys and flirting with the "freshmeat."

"Oh my gosh, T. She already had a nickname for me.

"Did you see how short that girl's shorts were? She is bound to get a yeast infection! Oh, my goodness," Simone whispered to me as we passed by one of the "hos."

"I thought they had a dress code here," I laughed.

"She obviously missed the memo! At the rate she's going, she will not only need Monistat 7 but probably need penicillin too. You know she is going to be getting it in!"

I was laughing so hard I was almost crying We passed some Alphas, from the intellectual fraternity, all cutie-pies wearing their frat jackets. Each fraternity and sorority had an area near the Big Café where they congregated. The Ques gathered by a big oak tree and the Alphas' turf was the stairs on the side of Ogden Circle.

Simone started to laugh a little harder and tilted her head back. Just so they could see she was having a good time and also so they could get a good look at her perfectly straight white teeth, one of her best assets outside of her long, lean, toned legs. But then Simone was suddenly in the air. I tried to grab her hand and save her but I was too late. She hit the ground with a loud smack. She'd missed a dip in the sidewalk and had taken a big flop!

I tried to help her up. "Are you okay?"

For a girl who couldn't stop running her mouth for the last hour, she was speechless. I was stunned, and I was embarrassed for her. After all, we were in front of the Big Café and the Alpha steps. She was in full on panic mode.

"Maybe I could transfer to Howard and start over. There is no way I could spend the next four years of my life as the klutzy girl who fell in front of the Big Caf and all the fucking Alphas!" she muttered.

As I was helping her up, the prettiest girl I had ever seen came by. She looked like Naomi Campbell. She had long, healthy thick hair that was obviously all hers. I thought Simone had long legs until I saw those two poles in front of me. She was dressed to the nines. She was wearing a pair of white shorts, a white tank top, a white sweater tied around her neck in the European style, and a pair of gold wedges. But she didn't look like she was trying hard. Her look had an effortless chic to it. She stopped and helped me get Simone up... well, practically yanked her up and shuffled us around the corner.

"Holy shit!"

"I'm fine. I just need to transfer!" Simone said again. I was beginning to think she was dead serious. Although clearly, she couldn't be that shallow.

She looked down at her knee. Not only were her brand-new Seven7 Jeans ripped at the knee, but I noticed she was bleeding profusely. "Oh, my goodness, you're bleeding, Simone! You might need stitches or something. Should we go to the infirmary?"

"Okay.... you ladies need to calm down! It's time for us to do a little damage control. What dorm are you in?" the beautiful stranger asked.

"I'm in Twitchell." Simone was practically whispering.

"Oh, good! You all have air conditioning. I'm across the way at Davidson Hall and we don't have air conditioning. Those fans don't do shit! It's hot as Africa out here...And I don't need to get any darker than I already am! People already think I'm Nigerian." The supermodel started to lead us. Simone and I just stared at her. She stopped and looked back.

"Are you all coming? Follow me. Let's get back to your room and get you changed in a completely different outfit and by the time you reemerge people will have no idea you're the same person that just busted her ass in front of half the campus. But you're going to have to move fast. I know you're probably in a lot of pain, but walk through it so we can hurry up and get you to your room. By the way, my name is Jacqueline McKinley. But my friends call me Jackie." She quickly hugged me and Simone and said, "We will do introductions later."

Simone's room, at least her part, had a W Hotel vibe. She had purple, silver, and white bedding, silver vases with fresh flowers, and framed photos of Diahann Carol, Dorothy Dandridge, and Lena Horne. Her side was a huge contrast from her roommate's side, which had a basic duvet cover and just a word processor.

As soon as Jacqueline saw the photos she was in awe. "Those are my favorite actresses of all time. The original divas!" Jacqueline exclaimed.

"Thank you. I bet you none of them busted their ass in front of a bunch of people!"

"Did you ladies want some water?" she asked as she lifted a drape under her desk that hid an illegal mini fridge.

"You have a refrigerator – "

"Shhhh! I have no idea what you're talking about!" Simone winked as she handed Jackie and me a bottled water.

"Your room is insane!" Jackie was still checking out the digs.

"Thanks. My mom is an interior designer so she made it her personal mission to pimp out my room." She said it as if all mothers did that. I wondered what it must have been like to have a mother like that.

"My mother was too busy on her Blackberry to help me set up my room," Jackie said, rolling her eyes. "Okay, let's get you changed up!"

She had Simone change her entire outfit and put her hair in a ponytail. She even had her switch into big hoop earrings. When we were done, she said, "Voilà! A little damage control..."

"No one will ever know you were the same girl!"

Simone jumped up and hugged her. "Thank you so much, Jacqueline!"

"Please, call me Jackie! All my friends do."

"By the way, this is Taylor Ross, and I'm Simone Monroe."

"Well, nice to meet you, ladies!" Jackie said as she looked at herself in the mirror and ran her fingers through her hair. "Your room inspires me! Are you a theater major too?" she asked Simone.

"You're a theater major?! Wow! I didn't even know you could go to college for that."

"Yeah... Go figure, you sound like my mother," Jacqueline said with a loud laugh.

"Okay, girls! We're wasting valuable time standing here. Let's get out of here and do a take two on our campus tour,"

"Miss Monroe... I know you're in pain, but everyone will know it was you who flopped if you're limping around campus. You're going to have to walk through the pain, my friend!" Simone looked at Jackie.

"I'm just saying. It's not about how you fall, it's about how you get back up!" Jackie waved her hands in the air like she was praising Jesus.

"I like that quote!" I said. She definitely had a point.

"There's more where that came from." Jackie put up a hand for a high five. I smiled, gave her a high five, and the rest is history. The Three Amigas have been inseparable since that day.

•   •   •

At Katana, when I spotted Simone sitting at our table, the first thing I noticed was she looked tired. Of course, I wouldn't tell her this. She was probably so busy having newlywed sex that she wasn't getting much sleep at night. But I suspected there was more to it. Ever since Simone became engaged, I noticed that the light she used to have was slowly dimming. I knew better than to ask her; image was everything to her. Now, don't get me wrong. She still turned heads when she entered a room. But I could tell something was eating at my best friend. When she noticed us approaching her, her face lit up and she flashed her mega-million smile.

"Hello, Mrs. Lee!" I said as I embraced her.

"Hello there, soon-to-be member of the 40 Club! I already ordered a drink. And by the way, ladies, this round is on me!" Simone had the best expense account a girl could ask for. If we met during the week she would happily offer to pay for our drinks. She always said that since the company insisted on her keeping long hours and traveling all the time they owed it to her. We would call it Uncle Goldstein. This stood for the advertising agency she worked for, Goldstein Advertising.

"Why thank you, Simone!" I heard the relief in Jacqueline's voice. She had been super-tense as we were getting on the elevator to come up to Katana. She had insisted on trying to find street parking until I told her I would pay for the parking. The girl was always up to something. I could not understand how she had a brand-new pair of Louboutins but didn't manage to pay her car registration. But that was Jackie.

"Simone, you look tired as hell!" Jackie was never one who thought before she let the words come out of her mouth. When she saw Simone's expression she tried to soften the blow, saying quickly, "I guess it's all of the consummation sex you and your hubby are doing.

So... how is married life?"

"It is amazing. Ladies, I must tell you, having sex under the eyes of God is a great thing. I no longer have a guilty conscience after sex because I know it's my biblical duty."

Jackie and I exchanged glances and burst out laughing. I mean, who was Simone trying to fool here? We were her closest friends.

Since finding Travis, Simone seemed to forget that she was once a party girl. Simone used to get it in! She knew all the club promoters and was always on the VIP list for the hottest parties in L.A. On top of that, she worked for one of the biggest ad agencies in the country, so she was always invited to the hottest premieres as well. We never had to wait in line. We just walked up and the red velvet rope opened for us without any questions asked. Simone would usually give the doorman a big hug and kiss.

In L.A. everyone knew the doormen held the keys to the city. If you were in good, your social status rose. I can't count the numerous times I had witnessed girls being turned down at the door for either being too fat, too Black, too homely, or too country/midwestern. Doormen had no shame. They would simply point the girl out and say, "It's not happening... try again."

It was the L.A. form of hazing. Those same girls would return to the club weeks later completely made over with a head full of weave, the shortest tightest dress they could find, boobs popping out, and a face full of makeup, and then the red velvet rope would magically open for them. As for us, we were never classified as Hollywood starlets. Instead, we were looked at as regulars who brought a spot of status because of who we were. You had the top advertising exec, the well-known artist, and of course Jackie, who looked like a supermodel and never had any issues. Once we got into the club, it would be VIP bottle service all night. Simone was getting so used to putting on her new holy-roller act, she forgot from whence she came.

"Bitch, puleeze! Don't try to front with us. You were certainly doing a whole lot fucking in the eyes of God before you got those five carats on that finger!" I couldn't help busting out laughing. Simone tried to look pissed, but then she started laughing, too. There the three of us were, just like old times.

Jackie was struggling trying to read the menu, holding it at a distance to see what she wanted.

"Why won't you just break down and get some damn reading glasses!"

"Because I don't need them. There's a glare from the sun."

"Okay... that's what we are calling it... a glare?" Simone and I both laughed. Jackie was fighting 40 like she was Bruce Lee in a martial arts movie.

"Whatever, assholes!" The waiter came by and Jackie ordered a glass of champagne and I ordered a vodka martini straight up. Simone had already finished her first drink and ordered a second pinot noir.

"I sent you the final menu for your food selection, Taylor. You still haven't gotten back to me," Simone said.

"I know, I've been so busy getting the exhibit together I haven't had a chance. You pick." I wasn't in the mood to go over every single detail of this party.

"This is becoming my party. You two have to make *some* decisions," Simone whined.

"I got bamboozled into having this party, Simone. I told you I wanted a small intimate dinner with my closest friends but you have turned this into a total pain in the ass!" Simone had practically twisted my arm to go in on this party. The only saving grace was I was also doing an art show. At least I could make some money while celebrating my milestone birthday.

"Well, excuse me for wanting to plan something special for my best friends! Shoot me!" Simone dramatically fell back in her chair like she had been shot.

"I know, but you're like the party-planner Nazi! Just pick the shit out. You know what I like. I need to concentrate on finishing my pieces. Just stay in the budget." When I said that, Simone took a long gulp of her wine and looked away. I immediately knew what that meant. "Don't tell me we're over budget."

"Not by much. This is your 40th birthday, for Christ's sake! I want to make sure everything is perfect. And I refuse to use paper plates and plastic champagne glasses. It's not over by much – just a few hundred dollars."

"No, no, no. A few hundred dollars will turn into a few thousand and I am not going broke throwing a birthday party." I sipped my martini to calm my nerves.

"Taylor, please, you have so much money sitting in the bank, stop being cheap," Jackie jumped in.

"This, coming from the woman I just had to pick up because she hadn't paid her registration. I don't think I'll be taking financial planning advice from you, thank you." I snapped my fingers in front of her face for extra effect.

Simone laughed. "They finally caught you for driving around with the expired registration! I was wondering how long it was going to take!"

"That's exactly what I said!" I am busy saving my coins instead of spending them.

Jackie crossed her arms and pouted, "You are so damn frugal, Taylor. You can't take it with you. You don't ever do shit for yourself. Live a little! And by the way, I chose not to pay the registration because I don't agree with where my tax dollars are going. Why should I pay taxes as long as that orange clown is in office?"

Sometimes I couldn't believe the crazy shit that came out of that girl's mouth. She was serious as hell. "Don't call me next time your car gets towed. Pay on time."

"Are you finished with the lecture?" Jackie flipped her hair behind her shoulders, looking bored with the conversation.

Before I could get my next thought out, Simone said, "Yes, she is!"

"Thank you, Simone! For a second, I thought my mother had joined us at Katana! Anyhow, how did this get on me? We were talking about your party."

"Okay, then," Simone said, turning to me. "What's your final number on the guest list?"

"I'm still at 75 and my brother will be coming!"

"That's wonderful, T! I am so happy for you. I haven't seen Michael in years." Simone was genuinely excited for me.

"And if he's looking as good as he was last time I saw him, I'm doubly excited." Jacqueline snapped her fingers and licked her lips. "Just call me your sister-in law-to-be."

"No fucking my brother, Jackie!" I said, giggling.

"I will not make any promises I can't keep. Heh...But seriously speaking, how is he doing?" Jackie and Simone both knew how much I had been through with him and were my support system through all the roller coasters rides.

"He seems okay. They are still adjusting the levels on his meds so he's a little... off."

"But he's still taking them, right?" Simone asked.

"He promised me he was." I didn't believe it as I said it, but I didn't want to bring down the energy of the conversation any more than I already had. "But enough about me, how's Travis? Is married life all you thought it would be? And we still need to see the St. Tropez honeymoon pics!"

"It's better than ever. He's such an amazing man. He really gets me. I fall in love with him more and more every day," Simone took the last sip of her second glass of wine and motioned for the waiter to bring her another. But then her mouth dropped open.

"What is it?" I asked, turning to look in the same direction. And there was Antonio,

Simone's ex. I forgot how fine he was! He was 6'5" and chocolate, with a beautiful football build, as if his body was sculpted by Michelangelo himself. His curly hair had gone salt and pepper. He looked great in a black shirt, black blazer, dark jeans, and black Gucci loafers.

Antonio was a total man whore. He knew how to lavish Simone the way she deserved. His NFL paycheck certainly didn't put a dent in his bank account when he would lace her with a brand-new diamond necklace or ruby earrings. He treated her like a prize. I have to admit, I was disappointed when they broke up. I always thought once he retired, he would settle his whoring ways and those two could have a good life. Antonio's heart was good, but when you are in your 20s and 30s and pussy is being thrown at you left and right, it was no surprise that he failed at the faithful part of the relationship. But I always felt that Antonio genuinely loved Simone – as opposed to Travis, who seemed like he thought SHE was lucky to be with HIM, instead of the other way around. I tried to give him the hint at the wedding during my maid-of-honor speech.

I looked him dead in the eye and said, "When you think you've loved her enough, held her enough, lavished her enough, do it even more, because she deserves it." I think it went over his head.

"Oh, shit!" Jackie exclaimed. And before we could say anything, she yelled "Hey, Antonio!" and motioned him to come over.

"Are you out of your goddamn mind?" Simone said through gritted teeth.

"What the hell are you doing?" I was appalled for Simone.

Jackie leaned over and whispered, "Ladies, please. This is perfect. He gets to see Simone with a fat-ass diamond on her finger and looking fabulous. He can see what he missed out on."

There was always a method to Jackie's madness. I glanced at Simone's engagement ring and saw that her hands were shaking. This was a surprise because she wasn't easily swayed.

When Antonio saw her, his face lit up and he was smiling ear to ear as he walked over. Jackie whispered to me, "This is about to get interesting." It was like they were the only two people in the room. The chemistry between the two of them certainly hadn't been lost.

Simone got up and gave him a hug. He hugged her a little tighter. And then he noticed that Jackie and I were also sitting there. "Hey, ladies." He was still as charming as ever.

"Well, hello, Mr. Antonio. And congrats on the new gig," I said. Antonio had recently started as a sports commentator on the NFL network.

"Yes, congrats. My husband is a fan," Simone said quickly. I'm not sure if she was saying it to get to Antonio, or to remind herself.

"Yes, Simone is a happily married woman now," Jackie said, smiling and stirring the pot. "She's married to a real estate developer. He's pretty big-time."

"Well, Simone deserves the best. You are still just as beautiful as I remember." He couldn't take his eyes off of her.

"Thanks." Simone looked down to break the stare then sat back down at the table to give him the hint the conversation was over. He bent down to hug her and whispered in her ear. I could read his lips, saying, "I miss you."

We watched Antonio walk away and be greeted by a white woman who gave him a hug. She had that wannabe, broke-down Kim Kardashian look. Dark hair, overinflated lips, a fake ass, and an ultra-tight sweater dress. Antonio must have been uncomfortable knowing we were looking.

"Antonio is into white girls now?" Jackie said it before I could. "What the fuck?"

"I know. Another Black-ass fool!" I said. "We can't keep anything for ourselves. I thought he was one of the few real brothas we had left. If he's dating white women, then there really isn't any hope for us." I was sick and tired of L.A.'s Black men forsaking their Black sistahs and hopping over to white women. It was an epidemic! At this rate, I would never meet an eligible Black man!

"And why do they always pick the ones that even the white men don't want," Simone added. "At least when Black women go that route, the guy is rich and good looking!" I could hear a little twinge of envy in Simone's voice. I knew her long enough to know she was hoping he would be with some frumpy, tired bitch.

"That's why I'm keeping my options open." Jackie said, flipping her hair in her trademark style.

"They aren't loyal to us... so why should we be loyal to them? And trust and believe, if I went that route... my man will be rich and James

Bond-fine. Hell, it would be wonderful if he had a British accent. I'll pull a Meghan Markle! That bitch schemed her way right into the Royal Family. And I ain't mad at her at all!"

"And ironically, it was her white sister and father who showed their asses!" Simone and Jackie high-fived each other and laughed.

"I'm sorry," I said. "I want a Black family with a Black man and I want to have Black children. I don't give a shit if he's a prince or not. There ain't nothing better than a Black man. That's why every single race is chasing them."

"I'm with Taylor on that one!" Simone agreed. "The Black family unit is dying. It's my personal mission to ensure we don't become extinct,"

Jackie was looking me dead in my eyes. "Well, you'll be waiting forever, Taylor. You need to keep your options open,"

"Don't judge me and chastise me for wanting to be with a Black man! I'm not giving up on them!"

"I'm not judging you. I just don't want you to limit yourself. Besides, most people assume you're mixed anyway so you won't get the same side eye I would get."

I hated when people said that shit. Just because I was light-skinned, they assumed I was mixed. It drove me nuts. I used to hate being seen with my dad and his second wife because people would assume that white woman was my mother. Dating outside my race was never an option. I vowed I would have a Black husband. I just loved Black men too much. And Jackie knew this, and she was also well aware that comments like that infuriated me.

As a matter of fact, I truly believed Jackie wanted to marry a white man so if she had kids, they would come out looking like me. I would never tell her that, though. Little did she know, as much of a struggle she had being dark-skinned, I had the same issue being light-skinned. Dark-skinned girls swore that I had it so much easier being light, and that wasn't the case. I was always having to explain my blackness, and state that I was a B.L.A.C.K. woman, not biracial.

"Well, you can have your white-ass husband, Jackie, and once you have your mixed babies, you can deal with people assuming you're the nanny when your Black ass is pushing their asses around in strollers!" I lifted my glass in a pretend toast.

"Ha… ha… ha…very funny," Jackie said as she flicked me off with both middle fingers. "For the record, I have no desire to have any trifling-ass kids. I picture myself being a jet-setting auntie who appears with gifts for your rug rats from Paris, Milan, and London, and then your kids will tell me all their secrets because they will know both of you heifers are uptight and Auntie Jackie is the cool, fabulous auntie!"

Jackie took another sip of her wine. "Besides, how did we get off of Antonio? I blame Simone for him being a traitor to Black women everywhere!"

That shook Simone out of her ex-boyfriend run-in coma. "You blame me? Why?"

I answered for Jackie. "You dumped him. No matter how many flowers he sent you begging for forgiveness. You wouldn't give him another chance." Antonio had sent so many flowers to her condo at one point it looked like a funeral home.

"Have you bitches forgotten that Mr. White-Girl Loving Antonio couldn't keep his dick in his pants in our entire relationship?"

"I always thought he would grow up and things would be better," I admitted.

"Besides, people make mistakes, Simone," Jackie said. "What happened to forgiveness? Surely, you couldn't have expected a young NFL star to be faithful at that age. I'm just keeping it real. Nobody is perfect. I mean, what the fuck?" Jackie always said what was on her mind and quite frankly, that was the same thing that was on my mind too. I admired how she had the balls to say it.

"The bigger 'what the fuck' is why you called him over here in the first place, Jackie."

"Why not? He needed to see you're happily married and still looking good. And it's not my fault you acted like a babbling schoolgirl. What the hell is wrong with you?" Jackie snapped back.

Then, Jackie, in perfect theater fashion, imitated Simone. "Ummmm…. Ummmmm…. Hello…. My husband is a big fan!" She imitated Simone's shaking hands.

"Really? That's all you could come up with?" Jackie laughed in disbelief. "I was trying to help your ass out. What's going on with you?"

"It doesn't matter anymore. I'm married." Simone once again flashed the big-ass rock. "Remember?"

I rolled my eyes. "You never let us forget! But seriously, is everything okay? You don't seem like yourself, that's all."

"I'm fine. I'm fine. I just have so much going on at work. And I'm going out of town this week so I need to make sure I give my man a night he won't forget and fuck him out!"

I poked Jackie under the table with my knee to make sure she didn't say anything else, to drop it. She wasn't going to say anything else. During my last breakup, I was the opposite, I couldn't stop talking about Randy. He couldn't handle it when I started making more money than him. It didn't bother me that he was a struggling actor, but the more successful I got, the more distant he got. And it ultimately ended, after over a year.

There were times I got lonely and truly missed him. But I wasn't about to apologize for my success or shrink in order to make him feel bigger. If that meant I stayed single forever, so be it. My art was a non-negotiable and we were a package deal. When Simone was ready to talk about it she would. And we both would be there for her when she was ready.

Simone finished her third drink and motioned for the check.

The waiter came over with the espresso I had ordered for Simone. I wanted to make sure my friend had a caffeine jolt before she headed home. Although Simone could drink with the best of the best, I didn't want to chance it.

"Your bill for the evening is being handled," he said.

Jackie exhaled. "He might have been a cheating asshole, but he sure knew how to wine and dine our asses!"

"And every other woman in L.A.!" Simone downed the espresso and gave me a subtle wink. "I gotta skedaddle, ladies. Love y'all!" She gave us each a hug. And then said to me, "And start getting excited about this party! You're turning 40. That's a big deal. Let us celebrate you!"

"Thanks so much, girl. Have fun tonight!"

"And don't do anything I wouldn't do... Or would, for that matter!" As Simone went on her way, Jackie turned to me.

"We should stay and have a few more. I don't have shit else to do. And since it's on Antonio, let's order the good shit!"

"That works for me." When the waiter appeared with two glasses of Moët, we clicked our glasses and laughed.

Chapter Three
Simone

Antonio had looked so fucking good. He smelled like heaven, too! Had I jumped the gun breaking up with him? "It doesn't matter, you're married now," I reminded myself out loud. Why the hell did Jackie have to call his Black ass over? And now he was dating a trashy white bitch. Good lawd!

I took a deep breath and took in the beautiful day as the sun began to set. I was sitting in bumper-to-bumper traffic. The one thing I hated about sunny California was the traffic. In most states, people can gauge the traffic and know Monday to Friday from 7-9 a.m. and 5-7 p.m. were rush hours. But no, not in California! I had the best California girl car (Audi Cabriolet convertible), but it couldn't fly me out of traffic.

Meeting the girls for drinks had made me miss those carefree, single-girl days. It's funny; as single women we spend so much time trying to meet Mr. Right and get married and settle down. No one tells you about mourning of the loss of your singledom.

By the time I met Travis, I thought I was over dating. But now I missed the first kiss and the butterflies of getting ready to go out on a date with a guy you really liked. I even missed the feeling of uncertainty in the beginning of a relationship when I wasn't sure if a guy was really into me and not knowing what he was going to do next. And I missed hanging out with my single friends, getting numbers while hanging at Katana. My new role was the all-knowing Simone who put her mind to getting married and accomplished it.

Or, as Jacqueline put it, "One thing I know about Simone Monroe ... when you put your mind to something you get it DONE, bitch!"

That I did. I managed to get married to a man that had everything on my long laundry list of requirements. I managed to have the wedding of the century that was featured in *InStyle Weddings*. And I did truly love my husband. The good outweighed the bad... most of the time. And like I keep telling myself, and others say to me all the time, marriage is hard work.

Never once in our 20-year friendship had I lied to my girls. But I wasn't ready to admit that I was miserable and lonely as hell in the marriage. Maybe it was because I wasn't sure if it was just that I was having a bad week. Although I hated lying to them, I didn't have the heart to tell them how things really were in the Lee household.

How in the world could I tell them that after only six months of marriage, my husband spent most of his nights falling asleep on the living room couch, watching "Sports Center?" I didn't want them to think that after years and years of battle in the dating world, the married world was actually worse.

This night, before I left on my business trip, would certainly be making strides to marital bliss. I am a firm believer in making sure your man is happy and satisfied before a separation, to keep the temptation away. Travis has never given me any reason to think he would stray, but why in hell would he want to stray? I'm not one of these timid sistahs who are afraid to get down and dirty in the bedroom. I aimed to please and I accomplished that goal on the regular basis. My goodness, just the idea of having my husband make love to me tonight was beginning to get me excited. Those three glasses of wine I had certainly didn't do any harm to my libido.

Travis was a different personality in the bedroom. He knew how to lay the dick down – and WELL, might I add. With that thought I darted out of the slow lane and went to the carpool lane reserved for vehicles with two or more passengers. To hell with this bullshit traffic. I accelerated so I could get home faster and begin my passionate evening with my hubby. I prayed I wouldn't be pulled over by the cops for my traffic infraction. A minor traffic violation for Black folks could easily turn into a homicide with these shady ass cops.

• • •

In our gated community, the houses were to die for. Ours was a five-bedroom, four-and-a-half bathroom, white, Spanish-style home. The landscaping was done to perfection. Now that I'd put my touches and my furniture on what had been Travis's house, it was beginning to feel like it was my home too. I moved from my condo in West Hollywood, which was in the center of all the A-list action, to this beautiful, suburban neighborhood of Rancho Palos Verdes.

West Hollywood to Rancho Palos Verdes was a good 45-minute drive without traffic and with traffic it could take up to an hour-and-a-half. But the panoramic few of the ocean from every window and balcony of our home certainly made the long-ass commute worth it! And nights like this, when it was just the two of us enjoying being newlyweds, was what I lived for being married to Travis Lee.

But this evening, there were two cars parked in the driveway. I knew by sight that one belonged to Karen, my husband's evil-ass momma, and the other to my husband's scheming brother Jacob. I knew goddamn well Travis told these fools we had plans. We just saw them yesterday. And he knew good and goddamn well I was heading out of town and this was our night to hang out – just the two of us.

As I walked to the door I felt my heart beating really fast. I was a little tipsy from the three glasses of wine I had at Katana. Normally that wouldn't do anything to me, but since we were going to Beauty and Essex for dinner, I didn't have lunch so I could save room for their fabulous food. Shit! I pulled out a stick of gum and popped it in my mouth. The last thing I needed was to smell of alcohol. Karen would have a field day with that one. I opened the door and walked through the vestibule, which had on the round table a fresh bouquet of flowers I'd gotten from the farmer's market and arranged. I walked into the family room and was greeted by my brother-in-law Jacob, whose wife was on the floor with their son, changing his diaper that clearly had a fresh pile of shit. And she was doing it on the expensive rug I had just had shipped in from Italy. BITCH!

Jacob greeted me. His wife looked up with her usual silent smile and quiet "hello." The bitch didn't speak much. I guess she feared if she opened her mouth too much, a skeleton would come out of it. Lindsey was a stunningly beautiful woman, mixed Black and Mexican, with all the best features from each race. Her skin was flawless and the coloring of the inside of a pear. She had an innocence to her, although I knew she was fucking around.

The day my husband found out she was unfaithful to his brother, we were in Mississippi for the church convocation. He broke down crying... actually, he was sobbing. You would think the bitch had cheated on him. He kept repeating, "How could she do this? Why would she do this?" He was inconsolable. His reaction didn't make sense.

When we first started dating, I thought she and I could be friends...maybe form an alliance and be each other's confidante. But when I found out she had once fucked a friend of mine's now-husband back in the day, and used to do threesomes and all kinds of wild shit, I couldn't take her seriously. And on top of that, once Travis discovered she cheated on his brother, a friendship with her was out of the question.

And I didn't have anything in common with her. I was essentially in no-man's land...a loner. I took a deep sigh. This was the life I signed up for. This was my life, my "perfect" fucking life. Urgh!!!!!

"Hi. Where's your brother?" I put my computer bag on the end table.

"He's in the kitchen with Mom. She's making gumbo. You came just in time. It's almost – "

I turned on my heel and stormed into the kitchen to find my husband at the stove with his mother, tasting a spoonful of her gumbo. Karen was a very simple woman in appearance – rather tall, with a short matronly hairdo that had the appearance of being set with old school pink-sponge rollers at night. She came from the Pentecostal background that didn't believe in women wearing pants and lots of makeup. So she always wore a skirt that came below her knees and some sort of sweater set. And there I was in my tight-fitting pencil skirt, high heels, low-cut white blouse and a face full of makeup. I was the complete antithesis of what she believed was good enough for her "good Pentecostal son."

"Hi, Simone. Don't you look nice and professional today," she said in her typical, snide delivery. But as much I couldn't stand her, I had to admit she did have a pretty smile. It was just that when she smiled in my direction it was completely fake.

"Thank you, Karen," I said, instead of "What the fuck is your evil Black ass doing here." "I'm surprised to see you here."

"Well, of course, I'm here. I had to make sure my baby was eating since you're going out of town...again." Dig number two.

"Your son is well taken care of. We actually have dinner reservations tonight," I said as I looked at Travis expectantly, waiting for him to say something.

"Oh, I canceled the reservations once my mom told me she was going to come over and make gumbo," he said nonchalantly.

I almost grabbed one of the gourmet pots hanging over the island to throw it at him but instead I gritted my teeth "Travis, may I speak to you privately? NOW!" I didn't even wait for him to respond, and stomped down the hallway, hearing Karen yell, "Simone, you should take your shoes off so you don't mark up the floor."

I turned and looked at Travis who was looking at me as if he had no clue I was pissed. "Are you serious, Travis? We made plans!"

"What do you expect me to say? You expect me to tell my momma not to come over? She wanted to do something nice for us."

"Uh...yeah. That's exactly what I expected you to do. We were just at her house for dinner yesterday. I wanted the TWO of us to spend time together before I left."

"WE can still spend time together once they leave."

"You're missing the point. Why didn't you tell her we had plans when she called?!"

"Simone, it doesn't make sense for us to spend money going out to dinner when we can eat here."

"Since when does it matter how much money we spend on dinner? So fucking what, it's not going to break the damn bank."

"Oh... so now you're cussing at me? This conversation is over."

"No, it's not over. This is ridiculous. We never spend any time alone."

"You're tripping over nothing. They're going to leave after dinner. It's only six o'clock and then we'll have the whole night to ourselves."

Travis and I were standing not even an inch apart from each other. I was frustrated, I didn't know what to say to make him see my point.

"Look, I just want us to – " Then his little nephew ran up with my brand-new La Perla teddy on his head, laughing, with Lindsey running after him, saying, "Jordan, stop." She took the teddy off his head and handed it to me.

"I'm sorry. You know how little kids are." I gave her a fake smile. Perhaps I needed to follow in her footsteps and just go with the flow, following the master plan of the Lees. The last thing I wanted was to be arguing with my husband right before I left town. That's exactly what Karen wanted. I wasn't about to let that bitch win. So I sucked it up and picked up little Jordan. "Hey, little man. Do you want some gumbo?" Jordan began to try to imitate the word. "Guuumbooo!" I had to admit, he was a little cutie pie.

Back in the kitchen, Travis's father had joined the group. His father made the family tolerable for me. He and I connected from the first moment Travis introduced us. I didn't really care for his preaching style or some of his old-fashioned beliefs, but he was genuinely a good guy, and my husband looked up to him.

"How's my favorite daughter-in-law?" he said, giving me a hug. Luckily, Lindsey wasn't around. It was our secret that I was Mr. Lee's favorite. I think he was impressed with my drive and my background. And unlike his wife, he appreciated what I brought to the table and what I exposed his son to. He was a handsome older man.

"Hey, Daddy Lee. I'm good. I'm heading out to Toronto tomorrow for work."

"That's what I'm talking about! I have an international daughter-in-law"

"That's what you call it?" Karen chimed in.

"Well, what would you call it, Momma Lee?" I challenged. I was waiting on her to say something ignorant. She typically waited until no one was around to make obvious digs.

"Well... you know how you professional women are. Always on the go. But I guess you need to get it out of your system now before you have our grandkids."

"Actually, my mother traveled all the time for work when we were growing up. That's how I was exposed to the world and not just confined to the U.S., doing the same things over and over again." That was a dig.

One for Karen, one for me. I purposefully brought up my mother because I dared that bitch to say anything stupid. She knew which line not to cross when it came to my mother.

"And she raised my wonderful daughter-in-law," Papa Lee said, in an effort to change the subject.

"So how many days will you be gone for this trip?" Karen was not trying to let it go. Travis didn't chime in. He was so busy filling glasses with tea, he didn't even notice, or pretended not to notice his mother was back to her shit again. At that point, I knew I was long overdue for another glass of wine to calm my nerves. I grabbed my bottle of Kim Crawford sauvignon blanc and began to pour a glass but before the glass was even a quarter-full, Karen said, "Oh, Lawd Jesus. How much more are you going to pour!" She had her hand to her heart like she was going to faint.

"I'm not sure, Karen. Would you like a glass?" I knew that this "woman of the Lord" didn't drink, although I liked to picture her and Daddy Lee getting completely hammered when no one was around. I would pay money to see her buzzed. I poured my glass to the brim and lifted it in a cheers motion to Karen. Lindsey had come into the kitchen and was watching the entire interaction. And just to really be a bitch, I said, "Lindsey, would you like a glass?"

"No, thank you," she said quietly.

"Lindsey doesn't drink. She handles her stress the right way. Through fasting and praying," Karen said.

"She sure does," I said sarcastically. If only she knew that Lindsey handled her stress by fucking another man. She would probably welcome me glugging the entire bottle of wine.

"All right, y'all, the gumbo's ready," Travis interrupted, giving me a look. He decided to interrupt me now, when for the last 20 minutes, his mother couldn't stop her digs at me and he didn't say shit.

Everyone sat down at the table. I braced myself for the usual talk about their congregants. It still fascinated me how Karen talked about the people who went to their church and essentially paid their bills through their tithing. She would call folks ugly, cheap, and even talk about who was sleeping with who. I would have never expected this kind of behavior from the First Lady of a church. But this was my new reality.

I sighed and picked up my spoon to devour my gumbo, because truth be told I was STARVING. I hadn't eaten anything but a Power Bar all day because I was looking forward to Beauty and Essex with my husband. I was about to put the spoon to my mouth when I realized everyone had their heads down to say grace. *Oops.* I carefully laid my spoon down and caught a glimpse of Karen shaking her head in disgust at me.

Chapter Four
Jacqueline

My manager rarely asked me to come by her office and meet with her. I still didn't understand why in hell she got 15 percent of my earnings when most of the time, the work I booked was because of my connections. But as an actor, in order to be relevant and even book deals, you have to have an agent or a manager. There was once a period of time when I had both and was getting 25 percent taken out of my bookings.

Luckily, I caught onto that bull and dropped my agent and got a manager. I figured when I decided to get another agent, it would be with Paradigm, Creative Artists Agency (CAA), or William Morris Endeavor (WME). No more of these bootleg boutique agents!

Of course, I had to "rent" another outfit for my meeting with my manager. And this time, I was going to make sure I didn't sweat so I could return it and get all my money back. I always liked to look on point when I went to see her ass, just in case she forgot what I was bringing to the table. I settled with a pair of leather leggings and an off-the-shoulder orange Michael Stars t-shirt and a pair of thigh-high Chanel boots. I bought them with my last big royalty check. I figured they would pay for themselves.

The t-shirt gave the look a casual appearance. I didn't want to look like I had spent two hours getting ready. I wanted effortless but fabulous style. Afgter all, my motto was "fake it until you make it." As I walked through the sliding glass doors and took the elevator up to the fifth floor in the office building in Century City, I suddenly got nervous. I watched "E! True Hollywood Stories" on a regular basis and I recalled celebrities describing what it felt like the moment they got the part that changed their lives. This was actually my moment. I took a deep breath. After all this time in Hollywood, after all the years of countless auditions, countless rejections...

The rejections that had nothing to do with my acting ability. Either I was too tall, too dark, or too universal. It never had shit to do with my talent! But things were finally taking a turn for the better. I was finally about to hear a yes. Who would I pick to be my publicist? I needed to find out who Sofia Vergara was using. That bitch was everywhere and she even had a clothing line. Granted, I wasn't about to sell shit in K-mart, but I am sure Neiman's could use a new celebrity line to hit their floors.

Or better yet, Zoe Kravitz was everywhere these days and she even landed the YSL campaign. I could see me gracing the covers of *Vanity Fair* and *Vogue*. And with my new-found fame, I could definitely meet some rich baller and make shit official.

"Hello, Ms. McKinley. Can I get you some water?" Linda's assistants were always young and fresh. This particular girl reminded me of myself, back in my twenties. She had on a cute outfit, probably from Zara and a pair of Steve Madden knock-offs. I laughed to myself thinking of what I was like back in the day. So young... so hopeful. And now all of those hopes and dreams were coming true.

"Sure. But I'd like some sparkling water with a slice of lime please."

"We don't have limes, Ms. McKinley."

Did that young bitch just roll her eyes at me? Clearly, she doesn't know who she is fucking with!

"Well, do you have lemon?" I asked, failing at my attempt to not sound annoyed.

"Yes. We do." Giving me even more attitude.

"Then I'll take that. And by the way, in the future if you're not in the mood to get someone something to drink, then don't ask!"

"Well, I had asked you if you wanted water. With all due respect, this isn't a restaurant." No, this bitch didn't show respect! I was once her. I paid my dues and I certainly wouldn't speak to the future star of a hit show in that manner.

"I would suggest you kindly get me the damn sparkling water before I tell Linda about your attitude and you will find yourself working at the closest California Pizza Kitchen, dear."

"Hello, Jackie. I see you've met my new assistant?" Linda came out of her office with her glasses in her hand and a pen in the other. She was tall and when she entered a room she had a presence. She had the coloring of the outside of an almond. She wore her hair in a big funky natural look. She was in great shape. I figured Linda was in her early to mid-fifties but she looked like she was in her late forties. She had gotten a little hippy in the last few years. Hell, as a woman you struggle with your weight for so long until you realize certain areas of your body ain't going nowhere. For Linda, it was her hips. She had the flattest stomach a woman could ask for but she also had those big childbearing hips, although she'd never used them to have children.

Linda was part of the who's who of Hollywood. She started her career like most managers, in the mail room of William Morris. She then worked her way up to assistant, and eventually junior agent. After years of building her credibility and discovering great talent throughout Hollywood, she branched out on her own and opened her management firm. Of course, like most powerful women in the country, she knew my mother. I met her on my 18th-birthday trip to L.A. She had a cell phone before it was the norm, and carried it in a big bag. She also graced the cover of *Ebony* magazine and they called her the dream maker. When I first met with her, she barely gave me the time of the day. But my confidence won her over. She took me on a 90-day trial run and when I booked three national commercials in that time period, it established that I was worth her time. But lately, the auditions were drying up and my phone calls were taking longer to be returned. When she called me with the possibility of a series regular on an NBC show, I was shocked. Quite frankly, I thought she had forgotten about me. When I got the call back, she was more excited than I was. Then I went to the producers, and once again proved myself as a talent to be reckoned with. My goodness, I get tired of always having to prove my worth to folks in this town!

"I did, and she clearly doesn't know who I am," I said.

"Still a diva! Come in and have a seat, girl." She motioned for me to have a seat in one of her ultra-modern red leather chairs.

Linda's office was beautiful. Bright red, silver, and glass. Framed photos of her with Black Hollywood elites – her and Denzel Washington, her and Oprah, her and Jada Pinkett – and even pictures with her and Steven Spielberg and George Lucas. She really knew everyone.

"Well, well, well, Jacqueline McKinley! You went into that audition and killed it. The producers LOVED you!"

"Thank you. I told you I would make you proud!" I took a long sip of my sparkling water. My heart was practically pounding out of my chest. How much would I get? Series regular for a J.J. Abrams show? We could ask for at least $50,000 per episode to start off with...

"You really did! They were so impressed. But – "

I sat up as soon as she said that "but." I looked her dead in her eyes and I saw it coming. The head tilt, the softening of the eyes.

"But, *what*?" I tried not to sound like I was attacking Linda.

"You were just too damn tall for the actor they picked to play opposite. What can I say? You're just too damn tall!"

"What? I wore flats."

"I know, but they are going with a guy who is 5'7" and you are 5'10" flat footed. They just thought it was way off balance from a cinema graphic perspective."

"This is awful. That was supposed to be MY ROLE. MY BIG BREAKOUT!"

The tears started welling up. Linda had never seen this side of me. I wanted to pull it together, but I couldn't. I was so tired of all the rejection. So tired of trying to prove to people I was pretty enough, I was good enough. Not even 50 pairs of Chanel boots could fill this void. I should have made it by now. Reject me because I have no talent, but don't reject me over my height. I don't have control over that. I took three deep breaths. I'd be damned if Linda Lowry saw me fall apart. The thing she liked most about me was my diva behavior. And why in the hell would she call me to her office to tell me I didn't get a role. Then it hit me. She's about to drop me. I am about to be a 40-year-old unrepresented actress. Oh, hell no! I leaned over, put my elbow on her desk and rested my chin on my hand.

"So, why did you call me into your office, Linda? You could have told me this over the phone. So let's cut the shit. Just say it... I'm a big girl. You could have dropped me over the phone. You didn't have to call me into your office. I've been with you for 15 years and this is how you do me? Well, fuck it! I can book work on my own. This audition was the first real thing you got me in years and you have the audacity to DROP me?"

I got up, grabbed my brand-new YSL clutch and turned toward the door. And then Linda busted out laughing. I turned around. I was ready to jump over the desk and smack the shit out of her.

"What in the hell is so damn funny, Linda?"

"Jackie, sit your butt down. I wasn't done talking to you."

"That's okay. I'll stand." I crossed my arms like a defiant child.

"Why in the world would you think I was going to drop you? I called you here because although the producers thought you were too tall for that part, they wanted to offer you a starring role in another series," Linda put her glasses back on and lifted her eyes at me over the rims. "Now will you sit down, so I can finish telling you the good news."

I sashayed over to Linda's desk, put my clutch down and slowly sat.

"I'm listening... continue." I played it cool as a cucumber, but on the inside, I was doing cartwheels and leaps.

"As you know, NBC and Bravo network are one big happy family. Andy Cohen saw your audition video and called me to ask me questions about you, your background, your plight as an actress. He's looking to do a reality show about an actress who is about to get her big break. He wants it to be about you and your life!"

"A reality show? On Bravo?! And you're happy about this, Linda? I'm an actress. I have a degree in theater. I studied in London. I am a REAL actress, and you're offering me a reality show? Have you lost your ever-loving mind, Linda?"

Linda whipped her glasses off and slammed her pen on her desk in one swift motion and leaned in. "I have managed you for the last 15 years. Don't think for one moment I don't recognize your talent, Jackie. If that were the case, I wouldn't have taken you on. I only deal with A-list talent. Your mom is what got you in my door, but your personality, your dedication, your drive is what made me take someone who barely had any credits to her name. This business is changing, and if we don't do something drastic and soon, it's the end of the road for you. You're getting old and if we don't do something soon, you're going to have to think of a Plan B."

A term I hated – Plan B. But hearing it come out of someone else's mouth beside my mother's was even more scary. Linda got up from her desk, walked around it and sat in the chair next to me. "You have been offered your own reality show on Bravo. On Bravo! Do you realize what a big fucking deal this is? Look at Nene Leakes! Do you think she would have a series regular role on a hit show if she hadn't done 'Real Housewives?'"

"You're comparing me to Nene Leakes?" My voice was just above a whisper. My ego had deflated like a tire that rolled over a nail.

"Yes, I am. Because she is now rich, very rich! Look at Bethany Frankel. Do you think she would have her own talk show and a multimillion-dollar empire had she not done the 'Real Housewives of New York' and then gotten a spin-off? No! She would still be living paycheck to paycheck in that tired Upper West Side apartment, *struggling*! Look at Erika Jayne from 'Real Housewives of Beverly Hills.' Do you think her music would be heard outside of the gay club scene had she not gone on that show?"

Linda cupped my face in her hands, and like a mother looking at her newborn child, said, "Aren't you tired of struggling? Aren't you tired of trying to prove yourself? I am about to give you the knock of opportunity. The question is, are you willing to open the door?"

Linda gave me a hug. And snap, she went from loving and concerned mother type to the mega-manager she was. "Take some time to think about it. I'll need your answer by the end of the day. They want to start production right away. We'll need to negotiate your contract, and believe you me, I will be sure you are well taken care of and get the money you deserve."

I slowly got up to leave, too stunned to talk. And she added, "Sometimes the opportunity doesn't come the way we thought it would. But it doesn't mean you ignore the knock at the door."

I nodded. "I'll call you later."

•   •   •

The elevator ride back down to the garage seemed like it took hours. I could still hear my heart banging in my chest. I got in my car. When I tried to start it, the "check engine" light came on. "Come on, come on!" I yelled as I tried to restart my stalled car. That's when the floodgates opened. The tears came down my face like a hurricane. I pounded the steering wheel. "WHY? Why?"

Is this what my life had come to? I was a fraud. I had no money in my bank account. I had at least six payday loans out. My car note was late. My rent was late. "Please start, come on, come on..." I begged my car.

And now my only option was a reality show? Me? On a reality show? I would never be taken seriously. But Linda did make some good points. I was beginning to sweat. The tears wouldn't stop falling down my face.

I looked in my rearview mirror. I was beginning to look like those older actresses I looked down upon when I first moved here. I was them.

Finally, my piece of shit car started. I exited the garage and began driving west on Wilshire, and my phone rang. It was my mother. She was the last person I wanted to talk to, especially since I had just lied to her and told her I got the part. I couldn't hear another, "I told you so... time to look for a plan B... maybe you should move back to the East Coast where people have more culture..." I knew that would send me over the edge. I let the call go to voicemail.

I stopped at Whole Foods on my way home to pick up some emerald sesame kale and a bottle of wine. I already knew that bottle would be finished before I laid my head on my pillow. In line at the checkout were numerous magazines with Meghan Markle on the cover. *Lucky bitch.* I could tell by the way she sashayed, holding Prince Harry's hand that she had conned her way into that damn palace! She fucked that white boy's brains out so good, he put a ring on it. And now, her and her dreadlocked momma were sitting pretty in the palace.

Why did I never have that kind of luck? And why was I hating on her? She didn't do shit to me. If nothing else, I was proud of her. She pulled off the scam of the century and once she pushed out a mixed royal baby, she would be set for life. I switched to *People* so I could see the lives of more celebrities who were living how I wanted to live. Oh, how I wished the paparazzi chased after me. I came across a spread with Erika Jayne. Reality TV stars were taking over Hollywood. That's why my ass couldn't get a gig. All of these bitches were taking them!

"Excuse me, ma'am," an older hippie lady said with a smile. "He can take you down there."

"Thanks, I'm sorry," I said, pushing my cart ahead. The fact was, I couldn't even afford to get groceries, let alone a magazine. I flipped through it and there was another article about Erika Jayne from "The Real Housewives of Beverly Hills." I moved over to the side so I could read the article. Well, I'll be damned. It said exactly what Linda had just barked at me. Maybe I needed to get with the times. The industry was changing. Maybe I could parlay this reality show thing into a huge opportunity.

"Hey, there. Have we met before?"

I was in such deep thought I completely forgot I was standing in the checkout line at Whole Foods. I turned around and saw the girl from the audition. She still had the tired-ass weave in her head and jacked-up shoes.

"Yes, we were at the audition together a few days ago. How are you doing?" I hated making small talk with these wannabes.

"I'm great. I actually got the role!" She couldn't hide her excitement.

"You've got to be kidding me... uh, I mean... that's great. Congratulations." I looked at this bitch and saw a light-skinned version of me. We were eye level with each other so clearly, I didn't lose the role because of my height. I lost the role because the casting director was a black-ass bitch who had a color complex and probably thought, "White is right." It was the Black casting directors who usually were responsible for making it so damn hard to work in this town. Their own self-fucking hate! I was livid. I wanted to jump on the checkout counter and yell, "This isn't fair!"

But I refused to give this bitch a leg up on me. "They actually offered me the role but I turned it down. I got offered a series with Bravo. But good luck, hon." I gave her a condescending pat on the shoulder, turned on my heel, and walked out like Whole Foods was my personal runway.

As soon as I got in my car I dialed Linda. "Hey Linda, I've thought about it... I heard the knock at the door and I'm ready to open it."

Chapter Five
Taylor

When I woke up, the bright blue LED on my clock read 4:12 a.m. I'd had a bad night of tossing and turning.

But insomnia was nothing new to me. As a matter of fact, I would say not sleeping was the norm for me. That's usually when I created my best work. I flipped off the covers, went to the bathroom, splashed my face with cold water, and brushed my teeth. I made a pit stop in my kitchen and made myself a celery, mint, cucumber, coconut water, pineapple, and ginger smoothie, then headed downstairs to my studio.

If I can't sleep, I might as well finish the piece I started earlier in the week. I turned on my surround sound to some Christian Scott and I took a deep breath to escape into my private world, the world of my creation.

I took long broad strokes, then short controlled strokes. I was in the zone. I was shaken out of it by my ringing phone. It was a 626-number that ID'd as Huntington Hospital. My heart began racing. I knew this had to do with my brother.

"Hello," I answered, my voice a whisper.

"Hello, may I speak with Ms. Taylor Ross," a stuffy nasal voice on the other end said.

"I am Taylor Ross," I said, quickly walking out of my studio. It was my sanctuary, a place where I didn't allow any type of negativity or bad energy. I sat down at my kitchen table, and braced myself for the news.

"Hello Ms. Ross. I'm calling from Huntington Hospital. We found your number in recent calls on a Mr. Michael Ross's phone... Do you know Michael Ross?"

"I do. He is my brother. Is he okay?"

"Your brother was brought into our facility earlier this evening. He was found on the 134 trying to cross the highway."

"Oh my God." My hands shook as I braced myself for her next sentence.

"He was not harmed, but we have to keep him here for the next 72 hours on observation. Has your brother had a history of mental illness?"

"Yes. He is bipolar. They have been trying to adjust his meds to the right level and I think he stopped taking them due to the side effects. I need to see him."

"Visiting hours begin at 9:30." I looked at my clock and it was 8:43. I hadn't realized so much time has passed since I got in my studio.

"Okay, I'll be there. I was supposed to see him later today...it's my birthday. He was coming in town to celebrate with me..."

"Well, we have him and luckily he's okay."

"I'll bring a list of his meds. I want to make sure you guys don't over-medicate him. I'll also make sure you are in touch with his current psychiatrist." I could feel myself going into business mode. One of the benefits of episodes like these was the 72 hours of peace that came with knowing he was under watchful observation in a hospital.

"That will be helpful, to know what his meds are. The doctor in charge is Dr. Timothy Sanders. You can ask for him when you arrive."

I ended the call and immediately ran to take a quick shower. Before I got in, I sent Simone and Jackie a text:

72-hour hold. I'm heading to Huntington Hospital. I'll call you later.

•   •   •

At Huntington Hospital, an older Black lady was sitting behind the information desk.

"Excuse me. I need to get to the... to the..." She peered at me over the top of her glasses. I have no idea why I suddenly felt embarrassed. Was this lady one of those Bible-thumping Christian folks who thought mental illness could be prayed away? Was she going to look at me funny when I said, "Where is the mental ward?"

But no. Instead, her eyes softened. She pointed behind her. "Go straight back through the double doors and go outside to the right, and it is the building half a block away." I began to walk off and she touched my hand, looked me straight-on. "It's going to be okay, baby."

"Thank you so much." She was the gem I needed. I believed that your loved ones who pass have a way of speaking to you through other people. I believed she was channeling the spirit of my mother, reaching out and hugging me from heaven.

Me and this woman held each other's eyes for a quick second. I took a deep breath and began walking to the furthest end of the hospital.

There's a thing about mental wards in hospitals. They are always located somewhere at the very back of the building or on a hidden floor. Did hospitals think that mental illness was contagious? When I finally got to the separate building, I told the attendant in the reception area who I was. He asked me to have a seat and called Dr. Sanders. I sat down and waited. I tried to calm the beating of my heart, which hadn't slowed down since I got the phone call.

Thank God I hadn't had any coffee, or else my heart would surely have beaten out of my chest. It seemed like it was taking forever for the doctor to make his way to the front. Sitting wasn't working so I began to pace back and forth. At least if I kept moving, my mind could be occupied. Then, a tall African American man came out from behind the secured doors. He was just about 6 feet tall, with an almond complexion. He had a low fade that exposed his wavy hair. He was wearing Malcolm X-type glasses, and as he got closer I noticed he had a few freckles. He couldn't be any older than 45. He was in great shape and his hazel green eyes had a sincerity to them I wasn't used to seeing in these situations.

Lots of times, the doctors in the mental ward are older white men who had checked out and were very impersonal. Or they were the opposite: save-the-world, former hippies who thought they could cure everything by overmedicating the patients. But this man's energy was different. He immediately put me at ease.

"Hello, Mrs. Ross, I am Dr. Sanders." He extended his hand. I noticed it was warm and the handshake lingered for a second before he motioned for me to sit down. His hazel green eyes held a sincerity I wasn't used to seeing in these situations.

"Hi. It's *Miss* Ross, but you can just call me Taylor."

"Okay. Miss – I mean, Taylor. Before I bring you back to see your brother I have to warn you, he is quite agitated. When he was brought here, he was manic."

"I was worried about that. When I spoke with him earlier this week, I could tell he wasn't on his meds. His treatment facility in New York was in the process of adjusting them. And I know the side effects are strong, so he may have stopped taking them altogether."

"It appears he hasn't been on his meds for months now. We were able to somewhat stabilize him." Dr. Sanders spoke slowly and deliberately as he paged through his notes. "How long has it been since he was diagnosed with bipolar disorder?

"He was fifteen. But this is the longest he has gone off his meds."

•　　•　　•

Las Vegas, September 1989

My mother had been drinking most of the day. When she got drunk she was either super happy, in the best of spirits, or she was batshit crazy. On this particular day, she was the latter. I had come downstairs to watch TV and passed the kitchen table where my mom was sitting paying the bills.

"Hey..." she said, and jumped up from the table and charged toward me. "What the fuck is that?" she yelled.

"What is what?" I had no idea what had set her off.

"What's that on your lips?! What is that?"

I realized she was referring to my new lip gloss. I had bought my very first tube of Wet N' Wild, bright pink, with my babysitting money.

"It's lip gloss, Mommy."

"So you think you're grown now... I didn't give you permission to wear lip gloss! You fast now?" she shrieked. "You fast?" At this point she was nose to nose with me. I could smell the liquor on her breath.

"No, Mommy... no I'm not." I didn't understand what "fast" meant, but it was obviously something bad.

"Take it off! Take it off!" She started smacking me in my face and smearing the lipstick off of my lips. Then the smacks turned to punches. "I will not have any whores in this house! Take it off!" She was screaming at the top of her lungs.

"I'm sorry, Mommy! I'm sorry. Please.... Stop!" I tried to block my face, and she mistook that for me trying to hit her back.

"Oh, so now you want to hit me? You bitch! "You fucking fast bitch!" She kicked me. Then she ran to the kitchen and came back with a pair of scissors. I didn't know what to do. Was she going to stab me? Was she going to kill me? I couldn't slow down my breath. Tears streamed down my face. "I'm sorry, Mommy, I'm sorry..." My voice was barely a whisper,

Through gritted teeth she said in a deep voice, "I will not have any whores in this house." She grabbed a fistful of my hair. She brought the scissors up. She could cut all my hair off and it would be over in a matter of minutes. She would pass out and forget what happened. I closed my eyes...

"Mom! What are you doing? STOP! STOP!" It was Michael. He ran into the house, dropping his football gear on the floor. He pulled her off me, just in time. The moment I was free, I ran upstairs and closed my bedroom door.

"What are you doing?" I heard him yell.

"You're a fuck-up just like your dad!" she yelled back.

I heard plates crashing... glasses breaking.

"FUCK YOU!" Michael shouted. "I hate you, you bitch! I fucking hate you!"

Although I was terrified to leave my room, I had to help him. Her fury had transferred to Michael. Running downstairs, I missed a step and fell the rest of the way. But at this point my adrenaline took over and I didn't feel the pain. I didn't feel the blood from my busted lip from my mom's earlier punches.

Michael was screaming. "You touch her again and I will kill you myself! DO you hear me? If you touch my sister again, I will fucking kill you!" He started to charge toward her. But the last thing I wanted was for Michael to go to jail defending me.

"Please, Michael... don't!" I pulled him back by the arm. He calmed and put his arms around me.

"Are you okay?" he asked. He rubbed my head and kissed my forehead. My mother started to go upstairs. He looked at her and said it again, this time enunciating every single syllable. "DON'T-YOU-EVER-TOUCH-HER-AGAIN."

My mother continued to stumble up the steps. I had never seen my brother in a rage like that. If I hadn't come downstairs when I did... my mind didn't even want to process what could have happened.

"Thank you, Michael." I started sobbing in his arms.

"I got you, Sis... I got you. She's fucking crazy."

·   ·   ·

That night I went to Michael's room and knocked on his door... no answer... I knocked on it again and waited... no answer. I gently opened the door and walked in. The room was pitch-black. He had all the blinds closed. I went to the blinds and opened them. I walked over to his bed and shook him. He didn't move. Then I saw on his nightstand an empty bottle of aspirin and a half-full glass of water I immediately knew that he had swallowed the full bottle of aspirin.

"Oh, my God! Oh, my God!" I ran downstairs to use the cordless phone to call 911.

"Is this an emergency?" The 911 lady said.

"Yes... Yes... My brother has taken a bottle of pills!" I was out of breath and my heart was racing. My adrenaline had taken over, and a greater power was moving through me.

"Okay, Miss. I am sending the paramedics out there."

"When will they get here? We need them to get here right away." I didn't realize I was shouting until my mother wobbled into the kitchen. "What the fuck is all this motherfucking noise? I'm trying to sleep, goddamn it. Shut up!"

She went to slap me but before she made contact I yelled, "Michael has taken a bottle of pills! The paramedics are on their way!"

"What?" My mother ran out of the kitchen and upstairs to Michael's room.

"Miss, are you with me?" the 911 lady said in her calm voice.

"Yes... Yes... How much longer before they get here?"

"They will be there soon. I want you to listen to me. Sit your brother up so that he isn't lying down flat." I ran upstairs, carrying the phone, hoping the signal would hold. My mother was trying to shake him awake. I pushed her away, she was so drunk she fell to the floor and just sat there sobbing.

"Okay, I did that, now what?" I asked the 911 lady.

"Can you take his pulse?" I attempted to take his pulse. Luckily, at that point, the paramedics were banging on the door.

"Let them in!" I yelled at my mother. She stumbled downstairs and opened the door.

It all happened very fast. The paramedics came up and put my brother on a gurney. I followed them to the ambulance. As soon as they got him inside, they immediately gave him this thick black fluid (I later found out it was charcoal). Michael started throwing up. I got in the ambulance with him. They continued to pump his stomach when we got to the hospital.

I was 12; he was 15. That was the day he was officially diagnosed with bipolar disorder. That was his first attempt at suicide and it wouldn't be his last. It was my fault. Had that fight with my mother never happened, he wouldn't have tried to kill himself. That day was the first time I heard the words "72-hour hold…"

•   •   •

And here I was again. Two days before my 40th birthday in another hospital, talking to another doctor.

"As you know, Taylor, that's the tricky part with this disease – keeping them on their meds, and regulating them. I'd like to test him for schizophrenia as well."

"What? You think he's schizophrenic too?"

"I think he might have been the entire time, but he was just never treated properly. Lots of times, they don't test Black men for everything because there is a disconnection." He gave me that look Black people give each other. We both knew exactly what he was saying about racism.

"Doctor, may I see him now?"

"Sure, follow me this way." We went through the automatic double doors that automatically locked behind us. I flinched. Dr. Sanders put his hand on my shoulder. "Are you okay, Taylor?"

"Yes." I took a deep breath and exhaled.

We walked down the hall to a community/recreation room. There were about eight patients in there.

I spotted Michael in the corner facing a window. He'd lost a lot of weight....

This wasn't my first trip to a mental ward to see my brother. I had learned coping mechanisms, such as talking to him like everything was normal. For me, it was my reality in the midst of the chaos. I closed my eyes for a second, then walked over to him.

"Well, if you weren't in the mood to go to my party, all you had to do was tell me!" I laughed weakly at my joke. I leaned over and I hugged him. Although he seemed to be in a catatonic state the moment his eyes connected with mine I felt our sibling bond. I knew he was aware that I was there for him. My brother and I had a way of communicating without words. I reached over to hold his hands and I could feel them shaking. I held them tight and placed them on my chest close to my heart.

"I need you, Michael. I can't live without you. I'm not mad at you. We gotta get you back on track. I understand, and I love you. We are going to get through this together."

I kissed his forehead. And I just held his hands. His hands calmed me. Even in the middle of a mental ward and in his state, I could look down at his hands and see the little mole on the corner of his pointer finger and the shape of it, and we exchanged an energy. I believe that when you come into this world having shared the same womb and birth canal, there is an unbreakable bond. My brother and I had that. I couldn't lose him. I wouldn't allow it! It was my responsibility, my and mission, to get him back on track.

I felt a tap on my shoulder.

"I'm sorry to interrupt you, but we need to send Michael back for his afternoon meds." Dr. Sanders' hazel green eyes had a genuine look of concern.

"Okay. I'm just concerned about overmedicating him. He gets the shakes and he becomes very stiff. Sometimes it makes it difficult for him to eat. It really does a job on his system. Could you please just make sure... just make sure... he's – " At that point an orderly came by to take Michael away. I hadn't realized he was in a wheelchair. My strong, handsome brother had been reduced to being in a wheelchair. I didn't take my eyes off him until he was out of my view. Tears streamed down my face. You would think I would get used to this.

"Taylor, I can assure you we will take good care of your brother. My training is in medications and the long-term effects on African Americans."

"Thank you, Dr. Sanders. Michael is all I have. Please take good care of him."

He patted my shoulder. "Taylor, I promise you, I will do my due diligence."

And for some reason, I believed him. It was the first time I'd ever felt I could trust a psychiatrist. He walked me back out to the reception area. I shook his hand, and when I turned around there were Jackie and Simone, waiting for me. They gave me the biggest, tightest hug. That's the thing about true friends. They appear when you least expect it and when you most need them.

Chapter Six
Simone

I never knew much about mental illness before I met Taylor. On TV they made it seem like the mentally ill were non-functioning homeless folks. But seeing Taylor deal with Michael's ups and downs over the last two decades forced me to look at mental illness differently. It made me realize there are so many people around us who suffer in silence. The first time she told us about the severity of her brother's illness, she was so nonchalant about it, as if she was giving directions on how to bake a pie. It wasn't until Jackie and I started to cry that she realized how sad the stories were.

"Taylor, you will get through this. Michael is going to pull through. They are going to get his meds leveled out and he's going to get treatment. It's just a bump in the road," Jackie said. That's one thing about Jackie – she might be one of the shallowest people you could ever meet at times, but then she had this whole other side to her. She could be so strong and say all the things you needed to hear at your lowest point.

She pulled me together over a decade ago, and here she was doing the same thing for
Taylor right now.

"Let's get you home so you can rest up," Jackie said.

We walked out the double doors of the hospital. I have never been a fan of hospitals. They smelled of sick people. It felt good to inhale the fresh air. California sunshine and blue skies were just what the doctor ordered. We walked Taylor to her car.

I gave her a hug. "I'll give you a call later. Please get some rest. You have a big day tomorrow."

"Simone, we are *not* still having my birthday party. My brother is in the hospital for Christ's sake!" Taylor snapped at me. Usually it was Jackie who got that tone of voice, like when Taylor had to bail her out over the towed car.

"Oh no you don't, Taylor," Jackie said, annoyed as I was. "You are going to go home, get in the bed, sleep, and wake your ass up tomorrow, go to the hair salon for the appointment we booked you, get your makeup done and have your ass at that gallery for your party! Simone has worked her ass off to pull this shit together."

"Besides, what is sitting at home going to do?" I said. "You can visit Michael tomorrow morning and then start getting ready for your party. You have sacrificed too much of your time for him. You have to learn how to take care of yourself. The doctors know what they're doing. And listen, we're doing shit different in our 40s!"

"And that Dr. Sanders is FIIIIINE as hell. So I know Michael is in good hands!" Jackie chimed in. She has a way of reminding you that she is still a crazy nut, lightening the mood in the most serious times. We all started laughing.

"You got a point there, Jackie! Where were men like that when I was single?" I said it jokingly but was dead-ass serious.

"Okay, ladies. I will pull it together." It was easy to see that Taylor's energy was drained. But at least she was willing to do something for herself for a change.

"Call me when you get home." I kissed her on the cheek and closed the door to her car. Jackie and I watched her drive off.

"Never a dull moment, huh?" Jackie said, and put her arm through mine as we walked to our cars.

"Never a dull moment. Listen, can you please go by her house tomorrow at six and make sure she's getting ready?" I knew Taylor might change her mind when she woke up.

"I got you covered. I will have her there come hell or high water... Damn, Michael. I wish he could get it together. This party is just what she needs. I'll make sure she gets to the salon."

Jackie got in her car and I heard her try to start the engine. I waited to make sure the Land Rover was good to go. She rolled down her window, "Girl, don't worry about me. I'm fine."

I wasn't about to leave my girlfriend there not knowing if her car started. It stalled for a second time, and then it started. She gave me thumbs up and a smile.

•　　•　　•

When I pulled into my driveway, I was spent. It had been a long week. When I got the "72-hour-hold" text from Taylor it was only 9 a.m., and I had just landed from my business trip in Toronto. I drove to the hospital straight from the airport. Now, I was finally home. As I was getting out of the car Travis came out. He embraced me and gave me a passionate kiss.

"Hey, baby." He stroked my hair, kissed me on my forehead, then gave me another passionate kiss. "I missed you."

"I missed you, too." I allowed myself to melt in his arms for a minute. This was the Travis I fell in love with.

"How's Taylor's brother?" He kissed me again and went to the trunk to get my luggage.

"Not good. I'm really worried about him and about Taylor." Just thinking about the look on her face when she came through the double doors made my heart hurt.

"I'm glad you're doing this birthday party for her. It sounds like she needs it."

We walked into the house and there were tea-light candles everywhere. Rose petals were sprinkled on the floor leading to the staircase and going all the way up the staircase.

I looked at my husband in amazement. "Oh my goodness..."

"I know you've had a long day and I really want you to chill. Now let your husband take care of you." He led me upstairs. Candles were everywhere. For a split second I was worried our fire alarm would go off. But I was allowing myself to enjoy this. Freddie Jackson was playing on our surround sound stereo system. He brought me into the bathroom, where he had filled our Jacuzzi with bubble bath. Wine was chilling in a silver bucket. This was the man I fell in love with. Just when I thought he was lost forever, he reappeared.

"Get in and relax for a bit," Travis said, as he began to unbutton my blouse. His eyes didn't leave mine. He kissed my right shoulder, and then he kissed my left shoulder and hugged me close as he unhooked my bra. He leaned back and looked at me as he slowly peeled my bra off. I could see him getting hard. Although I wanted to have him inside of me right then and there, I was enjoying this slow dance of anticipation. He got on his knees to take off each Jimmy Choo and then straightened to unzip my pants. He gently brought his hands to my thighs and kissed me through my lace panties. I was getting wet and I wanted him so bad. He slid off my panties and let them drop to the floor. I reached down to draw him to my lips and kissed him passionately... then he slowly pulled back and helped me into our large Jacuzzi. He poured me a glass of wine.

"I'll be back..." he whispered. I took a deep breath. My goodness I wanted him so bad! My insides were wetter and hotter than the water in the Jacuzzi. I couldn't wait to feel his manhood inside of me. I wanted to kiss it and stroke it. I leaned back in the bathtub and imagined what would go down next. Travis and I – our chemistry was off the charts. With our intense passion, we were like undercover freaks. No one would ever know the freak side to this "church boy." Just as I felt myself about to drift off to sleep in the Jacuzzi, Travis came back and helped me out of the Jacuzzi. He wrapped me a towel then dried me off inch by inch. He kneeled down and brought the towel slowly up each leg. When he got to my jewel he kissed one lip and then he kissed the other. He inserted his finger in me as he lifted me on the bathroom counter. I was so wet. My insides were screaming for him.

He lifted me up and brought me to our bedroom where he had set up a foot spa for me. He slowly sat me on the rose silk boudoir chair I had just bought to add a little more femininity to our bedroom. He had placed by it, and lifted each of my feet in the swirling water. As I leaned back, enjoying the massaging bubbles on my feet, he moved behind me and massaged my shoulders and kissed my neck. Then he slowly moved in front of me and brought his hands down my body to my breasts. He skillfully took my nipple in his mouth. He sucked on it and licked the outside areola. He flicked his tongue as my nipple got harder. I wanted this man so bad I couldn't take it. But each time I attempted to grab his hard manhood he wouldn't let me.

"It's all about you tonight, Simone. Sit back and let me take care of you, baby," he whispered, his voice husky. And that's just what I did. I sat back to surrender to my husband's tongue between my legs. I was about to come, but just before I was about to release, Travis, with the skill of a pro, lifted me up and placed me on the bed. He mounted me and slowly let me have all of him. He started with long slow strokes, then moved his hips so he was so deep, deep inside of me. I was screaming from anticipation. He took my head between his hands and looked deep into my eyes with each stroke. As he sped up he whispered in my ear, "Come for me, baby. Let's come together."

I promised to obey in my wedding vows and that just what I did. I let go and came and so did he. It sounded like a chorus of passion between my screams and his moans. He jolted and collapsed on top of me. Oh, my... this was what I dreamt marriage would be...

Chapter Seven
Jacqueline

"I'll need your most recent paycheck stub and a bank statement," the young Mexican girl said behind the bullet-proof window of the payday loan place. This was the fifth loan I'd taken out and I was hoping it would be the last one. At this point, I owed them over $1,500. I reached into my Louis Vuitton purse to pull out the documents, then readjusted my dark sunglasses. I would be mortified if anyone recognized me in a place like this. As if any of my friends would be in the depths of Van Nuys at a strip mall. How ironic – I was carrying a $2,500-dollar purse and barely had $25 in my bank account. Had this really become my life? The young lady had me sign a bunch of paperwork that I didn't bother reading. I skimmed over the big bold highlighted paragraph that said the interest rate of this payday loan was 375%.

That was exactly how I skimmed over the contract Linda had handed me for the reality show. I knew I should have had an attorney to look the shit over, but I didn't have enough money to hire one. I knew it was crazy, that it was a temporary fix and not a solution... both the payday loan AND the reality show. The Mexican girl counted out the $255 that I would have to pay $300 back on in two weeks when I got a paycheck. Once I got my first check from the show, I could at least pay off all these payday loans. I'd be getting $10,000 per episode and with a 10-episode commitment, that was $100,000. I thought I would be getting more. Granted, $100,000 was a huge help to me at the moment, but I knew other reality show stars were getting paid three times that much and then some.

Of course, I pitched a shitfit, but Linda assured me that once the show was a proven success I would make the same amount as those other Bravo network celebrities. At this point, it was a lot more than I was making at that trifling-ass publishing company. I figured I could pay everything off at one time and start fresh.

That's exactly what I needed, a fresh start... a new beginning – a sense of hope. I took the cash and began my crazy-ass day. I had to buy something new for my interview with the producer of the show, after all.

•   •   •

I had told the girls about the reality show the day before. Simone was hell-bent on going to Avra, the new hot spot in Beverly Hills. The moment you walked into the restaurant you felt like you were in a magical Mediterranean island. It had an all-white décor and open-air seating. It was certainly a place to see and be seen. Of course, I was running late as usual. They were already seated and waiting for me. Ignoring Simone's annoyed glance I said, with extra pep, "Hello, beautiful ladies!"

"You're 30 minutes late!"

"Well, hello to you, too, Simone... And don't get started. I told you I was coming from Santa Monica. I'm not in the mood for your shit today!" I was annoyed she was about to ruin my moment. I loved her like a sister, but she could work my last good nerve!

"Alright, ladies... both of you need to woosah. We aren't saving lives. It's not that deep," Taylor, the peacemaker, pronounced. "So what's the news, Ms. McKinley?"

The waitress had perfect timing as she came by with a bottle of sparkling rosé. This bill had to be within my $255 payday loan budget.

"Ladies, I have an announcement." I looked at Simone, then Taylor, and they looked at each other.

Taylor jumped up and shouted, "You got the part!" She started hugging me. "I knew you would get it. I told you not to worry about the audition and it was yours!"

People around us were looking now, and I was slightly embarrassed, but still soaking up all the attention. Damn, this would have been a great scene for the show. Maybe I'll convince them to shoot a redo of this moment.

Simone took a sip of rosé. "This is the best news ever! Oh, my God! I have been praying for this moment for years. I am so happy for you!" She was damn near teary eyed. I wasn't expecting that level of a reaction. Why did I suddenly feel like I had deceived them? Before they could go any further down the NBC series-regular path, I had to take them on the detour of what I actually booked. Which I was still very proud of... That is, I was getting more and more used to the idea.

"Hold on, ladies... I didn't exactly get that part. They gave it to some broke-down, damn near white bitch. Though they told me I was too tall." The girls looked confused. As usual, neither of them fully understood what it was like to be a dark-skinned sistah. Taylor looked mixed race and Simone had the luxury of being able to maneuver in both worlds because of her caramel complexion. "But I got offered another part by the Goldstein Company. I'm going to have my own reality show!" I gave the news my all, like I was a car dealer trying to meet his quota for the month. I lifted my glass, expecting the same level of excitement from my two best friends, if not more, but they looked confused as hell. They looked at me, then they looked at each other, and then back at me again.

"A reality show? What the fuck about? You're a trained actress! You studied abroad in London, for Christ's sake!" Simone sounded like a mother lecturing her daughter. "And what in the hell did Angelique say when you told her this?"

"I haven't told her yet, Simone."

"I think what Simone is trying to say is. You always said you would never do a reality show – that it was beneath you and you hated all the reality stars who were on TV. What made you change your mind?"

"You're right, Taylor. But the definition of insanity is doing the same thing over and over again and expecting different results. Times have changed since I first moved here. There aren't enough roles and these reality bitches are getting all the work. I'm exhausted and tired of going to audition after audition and getting nowhere. I'm 40 years old. I'm sick and tired of being broke. This is my opportunity and I had to take it. So, I am hoping you all will support me in the same way I have supported each of you through these years in all of your dreams, even if I didn't always agree with them. I was there to cheer both of you bitches on."

I wasn't used to being this vulnerable in front of my friends. I always tried to put up a front like everything was okay. I didn't want them to think of me as a failure. My mother did that enough already. This was the first time I'd admitted that I was financially struggling.

"What's the basis of the show?" Simone said, softening.

"Well... it's about four actresses, each trying to make it in Hollywood. They picked four who are on the brink of something big, but it's going to center around me. Look... it's not how I thought I would get my big break, but it's a big deal. And will be airing on Bravo!"

"Well, all right, bitch... You should have mentioned Bravo in the first place. We need to hire a great publicist for you and get this cracking!" That's what I love about Simone. The second I was about to write her off as a hater, she'd turn it around and be your biggest cheerleader.

Taylor lifted her glass. "I am excited for you. Sometimes the journey is different than what we expected. Good for you for going with the flow!"

Simone joined with one of her famous toasts. "To our talented friend who is going to show Americans what a true Black American Princess looks like!" We looked at each other and clicked our glasses together. With all the uncertainties and disappointments I had experienced, these girls in the end had my back.

•　　•　　•

The damned production company wanted all my personal information. I had to fill out a bunch of fucking paperwork and questionnaires. I also had to meet with a psychologist. Apparently, this was standard practice for all reality TV shows. They had to make sure I wasn't a lunatic. I mean, really? Get the fuck out of here! Half the bitches on reality TV are basket cases! Who did their psychological evaluations?

They asked me everything from what my favorite color was to what was my most traumatic childhood memory. They asked me about all of my various relationships. When it got to my mother they spent a good hour drilling me about every single aspect of our relationship. I tried to make sure I painted a great picture of her. This was something I was used to. Growing up with a mother who was so successful and in the public eye and a member of various elite Black circles, it was part of my childhood rearing: always present the family in a good light.

I wasn't about to tell the psychologist that my mother was controlling and deep down inside I felt like I was a disappointment to her. They didn't need to know that shit. Things moved at lightning speed after I completed the preliminaries. An added benefit of my contract (which I still hadn't read) was that I would receive a living stipend.

The production company reached out to my landlord and negotiated to pay a fee to put up lighting and camera equipment in my house. At first, I was concerned my landlord would not agree, given how often I was late with my rent, and that he would kick my Black ass out. And with my kind of credit, I would have to move to a Section Eight apartment in Compton or Watts. But a $10,000 deposit was apparently all they had to pay in order for my landlord to get on board. Unfortunately, it would not apply to my back rent.

Then I had a meeting with *the* Jay Goldstein. I got to the gate and gave the security guard my ID. He looked at me like he was trying to figure out who I was. I loved every single second of this. I played it up and adjusted my sunglasses like I was a star who didn't want to be noticed and fussed over. He let the gate rail up and I took off to the offices of Jay Goldstein.

There had been so many times I was on this lot for auditions, but this was the first time I was on the lot and actually employed! And I must admit, I was looking extra good. I used my payday loan to buy a beautiful bright yellow Alice and Olivia dress, on sale for $200. It was a steal, and I felt like a million bucks! I would get Taylor a sentimental birthday card instead of the jewelry I was originally going to get her.

The receptionist had me sign in and take a seat to wait for Jay Goldstein's assistant. Jay Goldstein was the mastermind behind some of the top reality TV shows. Unlike other reality show creators who produced ratchet ghetto shows, his shows had the feel of "Keeping Up with the Kardashians" and "The Real Housewives of Beverly Hills." They were fun, upbeat, and very NOW.

"Ms. McKinley! I'm Melanie, Mr. Goldstein's assistant. Wow! You look beautiful! Yellow is your color!"

"Why thank you." My nerves were by now on edge but her compliment put me at ease

I followed her down the hall to Jay Goldstein's office. He was finishing up a phone call and motioned for me to have a seat. In his mid-50's, he was balding but insisted on keeping the hair he still had outlining the parameters of his head. He wore his glasses perched at the tip of his nose. What I could see of his suit made me guess Hugo Boss.

His office was of course massive, and his mid-Wilshire view of the city was spectacular. There were a lot of framed photos. Jay with a bunch of different reality stars like the Kardashians, Nene Leakes, Sharon Osbourne, Lisa Vanderpump, Erika Jayne... He also had a picture of him with his family on his desk, two little Asian twin girls, and another man – his husband. That immediately put me at ease. Gay men loved me! And it was always a relief to know I wouldn't have to worry about the executive producer trying to fuck me, which was always a likelihood in this town.

"Can I get you something to drink, Ms. McKinley?" Melanie came in to ask.

"Yes, please can I have water?"

"Would you like lemon or lime with that?" What a far cry from that bitch who worked for Linda!

"I'll have a lime."

"You got it!" Melanie hurried off, just as Jay Goldstein got off the phone.

"Jacqueline McKinley! My god, aren't you a sight for sore eyes!" He came around from behind his desk to shake my hand. I had no idea he was so tiny. He couldn't be more than 5'4". I felt like a giant compared to him. "You are stunning!" he said as he looked up at me with a huge smile.

"Thank you!" Talk about my head getting gassed up!

He motioned for me to have a seat on his couch and sat next to me.

"I am thrilled you have decided to sign on for the show, Jackie. I think we have a potential hit on our hands. I want the public to see the real picture of what it's like to be an actress on the rise in L.A."

Did Jay fucking Goldstein just call me "an actress on the rise?" I always thought of myself as an actress on the rise, but to hear someone like him say it was confirmation!

"That means a lot coming from you." I was trying to maintain my cool. I didn't want to come off as an overeager starlet, but I had to say something. It's not every day a powerful producer recognized my potential.

"As you probably know, the show is going to feature four upcoming actresses and show what your day-to-day life is like. The auditions, your interactions with various people in your life. Friends, family, managers, agents – "

"Friends and family?" I knew Angelique McKinley would never agree to be on reality TV. She had a reputation to uphold. There was no way she would "lower" herself to appear on a reality TV show, even if it was for me.

"We want to get the real picture of your life in Hollywood. I know this is your first time doing reality TV."

"It is... to be completely honest, I never thought I would do reality TV. You see, I studied theater and I always felt like reality shows were ... how shall I say this – "

"By all means speak your mind!" he encouraged.

"Well, I always thought it was beneath me..." I blurted out, then scrambled to make sure my Black ass didn't talk itself out of being on the show.

"Don't get me wrong. I am a *huge fan* of all of your shows. I mean I am a *loyal* viewer. I just always thought I would be doing scripted TV."

"This is exactly the kind of real and authentic moment I want to capture on the show, Jackie. I love your honesty, and I know it will translate well on camera!" He was ecstatic. "Linda said you would be great, but meeting you in person is confirmation. You are going to be reality TV gold!" He clapped his hands and then hugged me.

"Oh, I was afraid I may have offended you!"

"Offended me? How? By being honest? That is what we long for when we meet potential cast members. I want you to promise me you will be authentic and real and honest once those cameras start rolling.

According to Linda, reality TV hasn't seen an African American woman of your pedigree."

I was pleased to hear that Linda was actually doing her fucking job and pitching who I was and where I came from. So I made sure to reiterate that just in case Linda left something out. "I have to agree with you. I get so tired of reality shows portraying Black women as lower-class, angry, and uneducated. I am a fourth-generation college graduate, I grew up wanting for nothing, summers on the Vineyard, cotillions, I went to a prestigious HBCU – "

"What's HBCU?" He leaned in with a look of curiosity.

I couldn't help but laugh. "It stands for Historically Black Colleges and Universities, which are a collection of majority-Black colleges across the country. Blacks of a certain upbringing attend these schools and graduate to be major influences across the country."

There was a lot more to it, but I really wasn't in the mood to give him a history lesson on segregation and racism. So I put it in entertainment speak so he could understand: "Think 'A Different World' and 'Stomp The Yard.'"

"Aha... I see!" He was probably already thinking of an unscripted show to produce around an HBCU. If so, I needed to executive produce and get credit for it since it was my freaking idea! Whoa. Slow down Jackie... One step at a time, I reminded myself.

Jay straightened up, ready to talk biz. "The shooting schedule is intense. The first few days you are going to be in your head, Jackie. That's natural. But after a while you'll forget you're even on camera. What's important is that people see life from your point of view. Uninhibited and real. But I know you're a pro and that this is going to be the next big THING. I am so happy you have signed on to spearhead it!" Jay stood up, went to his desk and buzzed Melanie. "Bring the champs!" he said.

A few moments later, Melanie appeared with a bottle of Veuve Clicquot and two Waterford crystal flutes. Jay took the bottle and popped the top off effortlessly.

"Oh... How I love that sound!" I said as he handed me a glass. But as Jay raised his to toast, I said, "WAIT!"

Jay was startled. "What?"

"You didn't look me in the eyes. Don't you know if you don't look someone in the eyes when you do a toast that it's bad luck and seven years of bad sex?! Now, you know I love you, Jay.... But I can't have you messing up my libido!"

Jay burst out laughing. "You are going to be a star! This is what I wanted for the show all along," he said as we clicked glasses. "Welcome to the Bravo family, Jacqueline."

I took a sip of champagne and flashed him my million-dollar smile. It was finally happening. The world was finally going to know my name.

Chapter Eight
Simone

"Damn it! I asked for the oval white wine glasses, not the square. Take this shit back and get what I asked for!" I was so annoyed. Why can't people follow directions? The caterer was late setting up, the wrong wine goblets had been sent, and on top of everything I wasn't sure if the birthday girl was even going to show up! No, fuck that, she was going to show up. She wouldn't do that to me. I was well into panic mode when I got a text from Jackie:

Hey, planner extraordinaire! Let me know if you need anything. And don't worry. I will make sure the birthday girl is there by no later than 9 p.m. even if I have to drag her by her curly-ass hair. Smooches!

At least I knew Taylor was going to show up. I knew I could trust Jackie to do just that, drag her by the hair if she had to.

My assistant came up to me with a look of concern on her face. She had helped me manage my side-event gigs for the last two years. She was about to graduate from USC and I cringed at the idea I would lose her. Parker was young, hip, and kept my ass relevant. She handled my social media and knew of all the little conveniences that millennials discovered and invented. She was the one who told me about Venmo. It changed my life! I thought I was doing big things with PayPal. She wore her hair in a big curly 'fro, wore glasses that always tended to fall to the tip of her nose, she dressed sexy hip. She rocked fitted, high-waisted jeans with some Chuck Taylor All Stars, and a fitted tank top topped it off with a cute little sequin blazer.

She had style for days. And on top of that she was super-duper smart, efficient, and ambitious.

She reminded me of myself when I was her age. There were so many times I wanted to shake her and say, enjoy this time of your life. It goes by way too fast. To think I took my 20's for granted, rushing to get to the future. And now the future... well...it wasn't turning out like I'd imagined. Although Travis was really on his shit since last night. Just thinking about it sent shivers down my spine.

Tonight, I would wear the La Perla lingerie I'd bought a week ago for the night his family showed up and ruined. I wish marriage were just about fucking. If that were the case, we would be on top of the world. There was so much more to it though. I just felt... I didn't know what I felt.

But enough of my pity party. The focus was Taylor. I was determined to throw my friend the party of the century. She deserved a few hours to get her mind off of Michael.

Parker sashayed over to me, shaking her head "What's wrong?"

"We are $1,200 over budget! $1,200!" She had her iPad with the leopard leather cover in hand and on the screen was a spreadsheet.

"Damn! I figured we were over budget. But $1,200 was more than I expected." I tapped a newly manicured finger on my teeth.

"Um, Mrs. Lee, I called you when we were one cent over budget and continued to call you for each cent we went over from there!"

"I know. I know. Calm down!" I was more annoyed with myself than Parker.

"And your friends are crazy! Especially Taylor. She called me to make sure we stayed within the budget. She asked if we really needed oval goblets? The square ones are $2.27 cheaper. No one will know the difference."

"They absolutely will, Parker! I am going with a look here. Just charge it to my card. I'll cover the difference. And don't tell her. I don't want to hear her mouth either!" I handed Parker my Platinum Amex and went back to overseeing the floral arrangements, making sure they were perfectly centered.

I had to hand it to Taylor. Her two-level gallery space was phenomenal, prime real estate in the center of the downtown art district, open and full of light with exposed brick. Her art work was displayed with strategic precision. Not only was this going to be a fabulous party, she would more than have a sold-out art show. Getting her to agree to let me organize her party was damn near impossible, but once she gave me the green light I vowed to make the evening spectacular. She'd never done anything like this for her birthday before. Typically, she just met us for dinner and insisted on paying.

The caterer finally showed up. Taylor had been adamant that I use a Black caterer. I wanted us to do an Asian fusion menu, but she wanted Caribbean food. Now don't get me wrong. I'm all about "Power to the People," but the problem with a lot of these Black-owned businesses is they don't have their shit together. This motherfucker was 45 minutes late and he had the audacity to stroll in without a sense of urgency! Had I hired a Jewish-owned catering company, they would have not only been here on time, but early! I took a deep breath so I didn't cuss him out.

"Well, thank you so much for joining us. You do know you're 45 minutes late, right?" So much for not sounding like a bitch.

"I'm sorry, Mrs. Lee. The traffic was much worse than we anticipated," he said in his slight Caribbean accent. I hated when people used the traffic excuse. This is L.A. Everyone knows to give yourself an hour and change to get anywhere in this town. But the last thing I needed was to piss him off and have our food taste like shit. Besides, to be honest, knowing I was dealing with a Black-owned business, I told him to be there 45 minutes early as a buffer.

"Follow me. I'll lead you to the area where you'll be preparing the food." I happened to look down and saw he was wearing Timberlands. "Do you need anything to get started?" I asked when we got to the tiny kitchen area off the gallery.

"No, Mrs. Lee, I can take it from here."

"Okay, great. And let me know if you need anything."

"Sure thing. That's a bad haircut, by the way! I like women who wear their hair short. It takes a lot of confidence." He smiled, revealing a Michael Strahan-gap in his teeth. Unlike Michael Strahan's, it wasn't cute or sexy.

"Thank you." At least it was confirmation I still had "it." A little ego boost never hurt anyone. I decided to be a little nicer to this Black entrepreneur. Power to the people! "Do you have all the menu options we discussed?"

"Yes, Mrs. Lee. And I have six waiters who will be passing around drinks and trays of hors d'oeuvres.

"Great! Let me know if you need anything." I turned around and saw Parker urgently waving for my attention. She scurried over.

"It's about the new wineglasses, Simone. Your card was declined." She handed me my AmEx.

There was no way that card could be declined. I had just paid the bill. "There must be some type of mistake."

"They ran it twice."

"Okay, try this one." I handed her a Platinum Amex that was for mine and Travis's joint account. I would explain to him later.

Parker ran back to the rental company that was supplying all of the linens, tables, chairs, and glasses. I watched the man swipe the card and then shake his head and hand it back to her. What the fuck was going on with American Express? Maybe they saw my charges were out of my normal spending pattern? If they were trying to protect me from possible fraudulent activity this was not the time.

I took out my personal Chase Sapphire Preferred credit card. Before I got married my mother took me to the side and gave me some game. "I know you are marrying a man with lots of money. And you are joining your bank accounts together. But always make sure you have fuck-you money."

I had never heard my mother cuss. She was always so prim and proper. I was taken aback. "I love your father. He is my everything, and I know I will leave this earth as his wife. But I still have a separate account that he knows nothing about, just in case of emergency. I have set you up with an account with Chase, too. The bill comes to my office. If you ever need to use it just pay me back directly." My mother gave me a kiss and handed it to me. The same card I was now handing over to Parker. She went back to the vendor, and the vendor swiped it. A few seconds later Parker turned around with a smile and thumbs up. What a relief! I'll give American Express a call tomorrow and see what the hell is going on. Now I needed to finish setting up, head back to my hotel and change, and get my makeup done. I was so happy Travis and I decided to get a hotel room so we were close to the venue. The thought of having to drive all the way back to PV would have sent me over the edge. I was close to everything in case there was an emergency. Thank God for contingency plans!

Chapter Nine
Taylor

This time, I parked closer to the back entrance of Huntington Hospital, near the mental facilities. In reception, I told the lady at the desk I was there to see Michael Ross. Five minutes later, Dr. Sanders was buzzed through the secured double doors.

"Hello, Ms. Ross." All of the anxiety I felt slipped away hearing his calming voice. I was confident my brother was in good hands. Usually his physicians were foreigners and treated my brother as a drug-test guinea pig.

"Hi, Dr. Sanders. And it's Taylor," I reminded him.

"Sorry, that's right. Taylor. I'm not used to calling people by their first name."

"I'm not used to seeing Black psychiatrists. So I guess there's a first time for everything." We sat down and I took a deep breath, preparing myself for the worse. "So how is he doing?"

"He's doing better. We are regulating his meds. He's not in the same catatonic state he was in yesterday. But he does have severe shakes. We have him on Lithium, Klonopin, Equetro, and Lamictal. The shakes should subside soon." This was nothing new to me. This was one of the many reasons why Michael hated taking his meds.

"I want to make sure you aren't overmedicating him, doctor. He's creative and he feels like the meds stunt his creativity. And it's hard for him to write when he has the shakes. He can barely hold a pen."

"I understand..." Dr. Sanders stood. "Are you ready now to head back to see him?"

"As ready as I'll ever be." I took a deep breath and followed Dr. Sanders to Michael's room, where he left me. My brother was sitting in a straight-back chair looking out the window. When he saw me his eyes lit up. He got up to hug me. He was very stiff but at least he wasn't in a wheelchair. "Hey, T-Squito," he said, his speech slurred from the medication.

"Hey, bro! I brought you a few things." The front desk had gone through the bag from Banana Republic. I forgot he wasn't allowed to have belts. In the mental ward, belts could be used for suicide. So, his pants would be slightly saggy.

He pulled out each item one by one. He couldn't raise his arms because of the stiffness so I helped him. "I hope I got the right size. I can't have my brother in here not being fashionably acceptable."

"No, this is perfect. Thanks, T-Squito... How are you doing?"

"I'm good. How are you?"

"Never better." Even in the midst of his body trying to regulate the medication, he still had a sense of humor. Then he got really serious: "I'm sorry I'm going to miss your party."

"Don't worry about that. You'll be at my party next year – " A nurse walked in with a tray of hospital food. She placed it in front of him and took off the covers. Some chicken noodle soup, Jell-O, and mashed potatoes. He couldn't eat any solid foods yet.

I laughed. "When you get out of here, I promise our first stop will be to get you a nice steak."

He smirked, then picked up his spoon but the shaking was so severe he couldn't hold it. I gently took the spoon out of his hand and began to feed him. I started with the soup, then the mashed potatoes, and finally the Jell-O.

"Why does it have to be so damn hard, T?" I took one of his shaking hands and held it tightly. I could feel his tremors vibrate through me.

"You just have to loosen up, Michael. Shake your shoulders. You're just a little stiff." It was the same thing I told him when we were teenagers and he was home for a weekend visit after his second manic episode. He was so stiff he could barely walk. But he insisted on going to the mall to check out some cuties.

Sometimes I felt guilty that he had the bigger cross to bear. I didn't understand how he was the one who got afflicted by this disease and I wasn't.

I would not let him be another statistic. We were going to beat this thing together. I owed it to him. I put my head on his shoulder and held his hand through the shakes and the pain. I could sense the tears he was trying to hold back. And I sat there in his room with him and let him shake.

•   •   •

On the drive home I decided to call Simone and let her know I was not in the mood for a party. I parked the car and took my phone out as I was walking to my loft. Then, I heard a familiar voice.

"Hey, there, birthday girl! Time to turn Cinderella into a princess! And you won't need this."

Jackie swiftly took the phone out of my hand and dropped it in her purse. She had a hairstylist and makeup artist with her.

"Jackie, I'm really not in the mood for a party." All I wanted to do was close my blinds, crawl into bed, and sleep for the next 48 hours.

"I'm sure. That's why I brought the glam squad here because I knew your ass would flake!" She took the keys from me and opened the door to my loft. She directed the hairstylist and makeup artist where to set up. She was so damn bossy! She then went into my kitchen and opened the grocery bag she was carrying and took out a bottle of Veuve Clicquot. She went into my cabinet and took out two champagne flutes and poured them to the brim. "Here you go." She handed me a glass and we clinked them. "Umm... wait a minute, bitch. You didn't look me in the eyes. And the last thing I need is seven years of bad sex, let alone seven seconds. Let's try that again. Cheers to the most amazing person I know. Cheers for you finally allowing us to do something for your birthday."

The rest of the afternoon was spent drinking champagne and getting my hair and makeup done. The final touch was putting on the champagne-colored Hervé Léger crepe-back satin dress that Simone had bought for me. When Jackie turned me around to look at myself in the mirror, you would never have known the morning I'd had. Instead all I saw was me looking at myself in the mirror and Jackie's big smile in the background. At that moment, I made the conscious choice to enjoy my night and stay in the moment. For the first time ever, I was going to put myself first, even if it was just for a few hours. I knew that not only did I need that, but my friends also needed it. They went through so much, over months of coaxing to get me to agree to celebrate. I owed it to them to have a good time. Jackie hugged me from behind and said, "You look beautiful, my friend. Our chariot waits." And we walked outside to the waiting Escalade.

Chapter 10
Taylor

"Surprise!!!" the crowd erupted when I walked into the gallery, which had been completely transformed into South Beach, Miami. There were white leather lounge chairs, a white dance floor, and high round and square cocktail tables bedecked with white flowers and gold accents. The DJ was playing good old school jams: Luther Vandross's "Never Too Much," Frankie Beverly and Maze's "Before I Let Go," and of course some 90's New Jack Swing that brought us back to our days at Hampton, partying at the Student Union. Caribbean food was all set up, including roti, curry chicken, curry shrimp, veggie patties, and peas and rice. Waitresses in short white cocktail dresses were passing out champagne and white wine.

I grabbed a glass of champagne, then walked round the room getting hugs from so, so many friends and colleagues. Various black and white pictures of me were set up on gold easels around the room. There was even a blown-up photo of me and Michael from back in the day on our bikes.

My heart began to ache seeing it. The party was beautiful, but I had looked forward to celebrating my birthday with my brother. I took a deep breath and a long swig of champagne staring at it.

"What do you think? Are you happy?" Simone had her arm around me, looking like a little kid, begging for her mother's approval.

"Oh, Simone! You did an amazing job! This is better than I could have ever imagined!"

"Thank God! I was so worried." Simone hugged me again. She was definitely tipsy. Hell, I think I was too. I'd lost count of the glasses of champagne we'd had at my loft as I got ready. "Follow me this way!"

Simone took my hand and guided me through the crowd to the center of the dance floor where the DJ handed her a microphone. Simone motioned for Jackie to join us. Jackie, always the consummate performer, made her way to the middle of the dance floor with twirls and a curtsey, as the guests cheered her on.

Simone began her toast. "First of all, I would like to thank everyone for coming out to celebrate our girl, Taylor. But most importantly I want to thank *Taylor* for coming out!" The crowd started clapping. "Most of you already know this, but for the few of you who are new friends, and haven't heard the whole story, Taylor and I have known each other for two decades. We met at the best university on the planet... which we all know as HU – Hampton University!"

Several folks there had attended our rival school, Howard University, and started yelling, "The Real HU is HOWARD!" Of course, it was all in fun.

"But seriously," Simone laughed, "from our very first encounter I knew I had met a lifelong friend. Taylor has been there for me through all of my ups and downs. And most recently, she made sure my walk down the aisle to my amazing HUSBAND was memorable."

Jackie discreetly winked at me. We both knew Simone would find a way to make the toast about her. I saw Travis toward the back of the crowd. He seemed distracted, oblivious to the compliment she'd given him. His phone started to ring, and he actually answered it! In the middle of his wife's toast! I looked over at Jackie who didn't do such a great job hiding her annoyance.

And Simone noticed it. I could tell, even though she hardly skipped a beat.

"But this night is about celebrating you, Taylor. You are always taking care of everyone else, and now is our time to take care of you and celebrate YOU! May your best days be your worst moving forward. May you have the absolute peace you so deserve! Cheers!"

The guests lifted their glasses in my direction. Simone handed the microphone to Jackie and I took another swig of champagne. If there was one thing you knew about Jackie, she was unfiltered. She spoke first and thought about the words later. It was one of the qualities we both loved and hated about her. But that was who she was, and she made no apologies for it.

"Happy birthday to the most talented, driven, frugal bitch I know!" Jacqueline and Simone did a high-five. Only Jackie could make the word "bitch" really sound like a term of endearment and not make people feel uncomfortable. "And make sure you motherfuckers buy a painting tonight!" I laughed, appreciating the plug. I would need to sell several paintings to pay for this party. I knew Simone had gone above and beyond the budget we discussed.

"Okay, now... let's get serious," Jackie said. "Happy birthday to our sister friend. To the woman who puts everyone first, ahead of herself. To a woman who deserves all the happiness and love her heart can take. When life knocks you down, you get up and say, 'You hit like a bitch!' Your strength, courage, and tenacity are inspiring, your talent is raw, and having you as a friend is a blessing. We all love you and thank God for you. Cheers, beeyotch!"

The three of us clicked our glasses together and posed for a photo. The three amigas, tighter than ever.

As the crowd pulled back, we could talk. "This is all beyond my expectations, Simone. You were able to pull this off and keep within my budget?"

"Well... uh... Of course!" Simone said as she drained her champagne glass and motioned to a waitress to bring her another.

"Well then, how much was everything?"

"I told you, we're good to go!" she said dismissively.

"This is a banging-ass party, Simone! This is what I call grown and sexy. How do you feel, birthday girl?"

"I feel great. I just want to make sure I'm not homeless when all's said and done."

"Bitch, puhleeeze, calm the fuck down and enjoy your birthday." Jacqueline handed me another glass of champagne.

"Ha... ha... ha... very funny, heifers! Very funny!" I couldn't help but laugh.

"Enough with this mushy shit. Let's hit up that dance floor!" Jackie said, leading the way.

I was beginning to loosen up. I downed my glass of champagne and grabbed another. I had no idea what number I was on, nor did I care. The dance floor was full and the old school music was just what the doctor ordered.

"I need to find my husband! I'll be right back," Simone shouted over the music.

"And I need to retouch my lipstick," Jackie said.

I decided to stay and dance with the sexy man that appeared with dreadlocks hanging down the middle of his back. I was feeling extra flirty and dropped down and tapped the floor and came back up with my booty first. The crowd went wild! Who said a 40-year-old didn't still have the moves?!

Chapter 11
Jacqueline

The DJ was off the chain, but I needed a few minutes to myself. I had been going and going today and needed some fresh air. I headed upstairs towards and stepped out onto the balcony. Then I heard Travis and Simone's voices in the office in the next room, arguing. I leaned in so I could hear what was going on. Simone seemed on the verge of tears, pleading with her husband.

"You're being so anti-social. This is my best friend's birthday party. All I asked is that you could at least pretend to give a shit." Simone was practically begging. It was a side of her I'd never heard before. "Why can't you be supportive?"

"You're acting crazy. I was only on the phone to watch the last few minutes of the game."

"I come to your mother's house every single Sunday. I sit at the table with your family and I make myself accessible. And all I asked was that you come out and have fun with my friends. And you can't give me that?"

I never liked Travis. I thought he was a self-righteous asshole. And I didn't like the person Simone had become since she'd been with him. She was a Stepford wife. I felt like she gave and gave to him and never got anything in return. And that fucking hypocritical family of his was a trip! I tried to convince her not to marry this asshole. Although she put on the blissfully happy act, I saw another side right before her wedding.

•   •   •

Six Months Ago
It was only a week before Simone's wedding when I got a disturbing text from her: *I can't do this. I'm calling it off. I can't go on like this. I'm done.*

I tried calling her but it went to voicemail. So I sent her a text back: *Where are you?*

Two hours later Simone responded: *Shade Hotel - Room 417.*

I called Taylor. "Girl, we have a situation!" I said before she could even say hello. I caught her up on the strange texts.

"She checked into a hotel! It must be bad."

"Do you think she's going to finally call this thing off?" Taylor said, equally concerned.

"I would rather her call it off than go through with it. But let's see what's going on first. Maybe Simone is having a meltdown over the linens being a different shade of blush." We both chuckled, but we both knew it was more than that. We agreed to meet at the hotel.

•   •   •

The Shade was a chic boutique hotel in Manhattan Beach that not a lot of people knew about. "I have to give our girl props. Even in the midst of chaos, that bitch only does fabulous!"

"Okay, Jackie, focus, it's not about that right now," Taylor said sternly, as she pressed the elevator button for the fourth floor. We knocked on the door of Room 417. No answer. I knocked again, harder, and a few seconds later, Simone opened the door. Her pixie cut was uncombed. She was wearing what for her were all the wrong clothes, ripped jeans, a tank top, and Tory Birch black patent leather flip-flops. But Simone being Simone, she smiled the second she saw us. Even when she was down in the dumps she still had the megawatt smile.

"Heeeeeeeyyyyy, girls! Come on in..." We followed her into the room. "Can I gewt yous somding to drink?" she slurred.

I immediately went to the mini-bar and found a bottle of Fiji water and handed it to her.

Taylor called room service and asked for a large pot of coffee. We needed to sober her ass up before we could get the full story.

"Don't get married. It's bullshit!" She started crying. "He doesn't love me. He doesn't give a shit about me. It's all about his family." She got up off the couch and started walking around the room. "Where did I put my wine?"

"Simone, I think you've had enough wine. Sit down and drink your water." Luckily, Simone wasn't a belligerent drunk. She listened. She drank some water and sat down on the bed and began sobbing. Taylor sat on one side of her and I on the other.

When room service came with the coffee I poured her a cup, straight black. She was slowly sobering up.

"So what's going on, Simone?"

"Travis's trifling-ass brother wants to bring his infant son to the wedding." I, for the record, could have sworn Jacob was on the DL. "Travis was going to oblige, although we had already made the decision we weren't going to have any kids at the wedding! It would be rude to have a baby at our King's table while all of our guests had to get child care! He wouldn't budge..." She gulped some more coffee.

Seriously, was this bitch having an emotional meltdown over a baby at the wedding and seating arrangements? "So unbeknownst to him, I called our wedding planner and had him rearrange our seating so now instead of having a King's table in the center of the room, we now have a Sweetheart table." She took a long gulp of her water.

"Okay, so that's solved. What's the problem now?" I didn't want to tell her it really wasn't a big deal in the grand scheme of things. If I ever got married, my ass was running off to the Justice of the Peace. I didn't have the time or the patience for these types of shenanigans.

"That's not all," she went on. "We had to submit all of our final deposits today. I had already paid my portion with cash from my bonus. So as he was filling out the rest of the payment forms, I tried to help him. And he was just being so damn mean to me. He was acting like he didn't even like me, let alone love me. I don't even remember how the argument started. I was trying to talk to him and he stormed out of the dining room and went up to his office and started doing some shit on his computer. I followed him up there to make him listen to me. I snatched the keyboard away from him and then he pushed me. The housekeeper was downstairs and he pushed me so hard I fell to the ground. And then he yelled at the top of his lungs, 'Get off me,' so the housekeeper would think I had pushed him!"

"What?" Taylor had been intently listening and reserving her comments for later. But this hit her the same way it hit me. This was way beyond anything either of us could have imagined.

"He pushed you? I will kick his ass." I wanted to drive to the house that second and do it.

"But you see, I had snatched his keyboard...."

She was actually defending this motherfucker! "I don't give a fuck what you snatched. Not only did he put his hands on you, he tried to manipulate the situation and make it sound like you had pushed him! Oh, Simone, this is not good."

"What happened after that?" Taylor calmly asked. She was trying to neutralize the discussion, seeing me about to go off.

"I stormed out of the house, got in my car and waited a good five minutes. I thought he would run after me. I thought he would try to stop me from leaving. And he didn't. So I just started driving. I called my planner and asked him how much it would cost is if I called off the wedding."

"How much would it be?" Taylor was quick with numbers and figuring out totals and all that shit.

"We've already put in $125,000 in deposits that we won't be able to get back."

"You can make that money back in no time, Simone," Taylor said. "Have you heard from Travis since?"

"No. He hasn't tried to call me, text me, nothing..." She started crying again.

Taylor rubbed her back. "My goodness... I'm so sorry."

But I couldn't maintain my calm as well as Taylor. "Let me get this straight, you have been gone for hours and he hasn't tried to call you? You could be dead on the side of the street somewhere! You are his future wife!" I was beyond pissed!

"I know! I don't think he cares." And she just started bawling in Taylor's arms. I had never seen her cry like this.

I took my best friend's face between my hands and looked her in the eyes. "You don't have to do this, Simone. We will support whatever decision you make. But you don't have to do this."

"I can't call it off. People are on their way, they've bought plane tickets, they are expecting me to get married..." Her expression reminded me of that freaked-out girl back at Hampton who had fallen and didn't know how to get back up.

"Fuck them! We can just have a big party at The Montage."

"Jackie's right. You really do not have to do this. You have to trust your intuition. No one will be mad at you."

Simone took a deep breath and stood up. She walked to the mirror and looked at herself. "Wow, I look like shit." She smoothed down her hair and tried to laugh. "No, no. I'm going to do this. I can't let everyone down. I'm almost 40 years old. I'm tired of being in the game. I don't want to be one of these successful women who have everything but a husband and kids. I don't want to date again. It's hard enough dating in L.A. These brothas ain't checking for us. It's not getting easier the older we get."

"First of all, you're not going to end up alone, Simone. You've got us! Anyway, it's better to be alone than with someone who doesn't treat you right."

"Things will get better once we are married. He's just stressed out... We both are. I'll make this right.... I'll make this right," she said, almost to herself

"All anyone expects of you is happiness." Taylor walked up behind her and leaned into her shoulders.

"It's going to be fine! Just fine. I think some of your theatrics have rubbed off on me, Jackie! I overreacted," Simone said, turning to look at me.

"Well, Travis would have been picking his teeth up off the floor if I were you!" I laughed, but realized I had hurt her feelings. "And that's why you have the huge rock on your finger and not me." That worked to smooth things over. Whenever you mentioned her ring it always did the trick to change the subject.

A week later, I was holding a beautiful bouquet as I watched my friend float down the aisle. She was a stunning bride, wearing Vera Wang and a crystal tiara and a cathedral-length veil. She looked like a princess. She was beaming. Travis and Simone were the picture-perfect bride and groom.

●　　　●　　　●

Now, hearing him ignoring her pleas made me mad at myself. I should have protested more and never allowed my friend to marry this dickwad.

"I told you, I just wanted to check the score."

"Fuck the fucking game, Travis!" she yelled.

"Oh, so now you're gonna cuss at me? This conversation is over." I heard him walk off. I went back inside towards the office, and pretended like I had just turned the corner of the hallway. It took everything in me not to trip his Black ass with my Jimmy Choo stiletto.

"Hey, Travis! How's it going?" I said full of cheer, thankful again for my theater training.

"What's up, Jackie?" He didn't even try to match my level of enthusiasm. I decided to fuck with him and bring my girl's point home.

"Your wife gave a great toast a few minutes ago. You missed all the action! That girl adores you."

"Yeah...she's a good woman."

"That's an understatement. If I were a man, I would have married her, too!"

"Have a good night, Jackie," he said dismissively me as he walked past me.

"Are you leaving?" I asked incredulously.

"Yeah, I have an early day tomorrow. Gotta to make sure I'm there for 8 a.m. service. Can you make sure Simone gets back to the hotel safely? I know y'all are going to get crazy." He started walking off before I had a chance to respond. And a part of me felt slightly judged with his suggesting we were going to get crazy. That's the thing that killed me about those religious types. Here his wife was, terribly hurt, and all he could think about was getting up early for that bootleg church. I went to Taylor's office and found Simone, who was standing at the desk window gazing out on the city lights.

"Hey, girl!" I put my arm around her and gave her a hug. "Say, are you okay, Simone?" I looked straight into her eyes, sending the unspoken friendship signal that let her know I was there if she wanted to talk.

"Yeah, I'm fine. Everything's fine! It's just a little cold out here and I got the sniffles... I'm going to head back into the party." That was sure enough a signal to shut the fuck up and leave it alone. So I did...for now at least.

Chapter 12
Simone

I'd had so much champagne and wine at the party, I'd lost count. I swear, Lyft is a blessing and a curse. Prior to Lyft, I had to be responsible because I knew I had to drive home. I was not one who took those funky-ass L.A. taxicabs. I hated the smell of them, and it just wasn't a good look to be getting into one of them. So I would limit my drinks or start early in the night so by the end I had sobered up and could drive home. The last thing I wanted was to get a DUI. I drank like a fish and didn't give a shit because I knew I could Lyft back to my fabulous suite.

The first thing I did when I walked through the door of our suite at The Ritz was take off my heels and my bra. That's always the first thing I did when I got home. My feet were killing me and having my double-D breasts confined in a bra all damn day – I needed to let those suckers hang! No matter how much pain my feet were in, I couldn't bring myself to walk around in public barefoot. How gauche!

The views of downtown L.A. from the suite were spectacular. I was glad I decided to take a suite at The Ritz Carlton downtown rather than drive back to Rancho Palos Verdes after the party. Floor-to-ceiling windows gave me a front-row seat on the city lights, sparkling like the stars in the sky.

I knew my husband was going to be in the bed watching ESPN. Although he had ticked me off at the party, I still wanted to celebrate the success of the night with him. I really needed to learn how to do a better job picking my battles. After all, it wasn't that serious. Don't all men like to watch the games live? I clearly overreacted. I must have been PMS-ing. Lately, the littlest things sent me into an emotional tizzy. I didn't want to become a nagging wife so soon into the marriage. Besides, I was horny as hell and ready to fuck his brains out. As I was walking through the suite I realized I was stumbling a little... Well, maybe more than a little.

I went to the bedroom and the bed was untouched. He wasn't in the bathroom either. What the fuck? I checked the closet where he had hung his clothes for church tomorrow. The clothes were gone. I was still calling him, "Travis...!" My feet were killing me and my head was spinning.

I went back to the living room and plopped down on the couch. Travis was so unpredictable. Last night we were having hot passionate slow sex with candles and rose pedals and today he completely flipped on me. I didn't know what I was doing wrong or how to fix it. I was exhausted and confused by the emotional roller coaster. I was waiting for the man I fell in love with to come back and stay. And not just for a day. I didn't know how much longer I could put up this façade. Being single was far better than this bullshit. I reached over for my phone to see if my husband had even tried to call me. There wasn't one single solitary text from him. There were three from Jackie checking in on me and two from Taylor making sure I got back safely. I replied to both of my girls:

I made it back safely to my suite. I'm not going to make brunch tomorrow. My husband and I are in for a long night... if you get my drift. Wink. Happy Birthday, Taylor. Love you!!!

I hated to lie to them. But I wasn't prepared to tell them that Travis had not only left the suite, but he couldn't care less if I was dead or alive. I went to the mini-bar all it had was Chardonnay. I needed to numb the emotion that a part of me was somewhat relieved and happy that I had the suite to myself. It reminded of the days when I could come home and relax and not worry about anyone else but myself. I decided not to call Travis and make sure he was okay. I wasn't going to chase after him. Instead, I was going to enjoy the peaceful energy of the suite, the sparkling lights of the city, enjoy my glass of wine without being judged for how many glasses I had. Tonight, I'd sleep in the middle of the California King bed and watch what I wanted on the 60-inch TV, and not have to be concerned about waking someone else up.

Perhaps switching shit up would bring Travis to his senses. Perhaps he would actually worry about me and whether he had upset me, instead of the other way around.

I was going to enjoy a few hours as Simone Monroe. Although I almost lost her somewhere along the way, this hotel suite reminded me that she was still very much alive.

•　　　•　　　•

I woke up Sunday morning with a major hangover. Although I was completely hammered the night before, I had arranged for coffee to arrive precisely at 8:30 a.m. so I would wake up to it. Then I got in the shower and let the hot water and steam detox me.

I got out of the shower, lotioned up and pulled it together. I packed up my stuff; so much of it you would have thought I was staying for a full week. I took a look at cell phone – not one call or text from Travis, not one! How dare he? He's never wrong, it's always me...

I checked out and got my car and headed to Beverly Hills to meet my girls for brunch.

On the patio at the Four Seasons, Taylor and Jackie were drinking mimosas, laughing. Their eyes lit up when they saw me. Some time with my girls was just what my spirit needed. I decided to stay Simone Monroe for a few more hours, before I headed home to be Simone Lee.

Chapter 13
Jacqueline

"Simone! I'm so glad you made it." I got up to give her a big hug. "So, you got a 'get-out-of- purgatory-for-free' pass this morning? You sure Cornelius isn't going to trip?" I never tired of calling Simone's mother-in-law Cornelius, like the character from "Planet of the Apes." Not only did she look like an ape, she acted like one too. Taylor chuckled. We both knew the expectation that the Lee family put on Simone to be in church every Sunday smiling and acting "holy."

"Well, surprise. I don't give a fuck anymore. Fuck that bitch!" I had never heard Simone refer to her mother-in-law with such venom.

Taylor and I gave each other a WTF look. I took a few sips of my mimosa during the uncomfortable pause that followed.

"Simone, you know you don't have to put up a façade with us. We are your amigas for life, remember?"

"I'm fine. I'm just adjusting to being a married woman."

I couldn't stay on the bullshit train with Simone today. "Travis walked out in the middle of your toast last night. That was blasphemous!"

"I know. Work has him stressed out these days. I'm just trying to give him his space."

"Are you sure that's all?"

"Yes, Inspector Gadget... All I'm saying is, my Taylor only turns 40 once and this weekend is about celebrating her. So my mother-in-law will just have to deal with it. As well as Travis!" Simone ordered a sauvignon blanc.

"Well, alrighty then," Taylor said brightly. "I'm glad my turning old has this effect on you! And thanks again for the party, Simone. It was off the charts. Did you ever consider opening your own event planning business?"

"You totally should, Simone!" I said. "Party planning is your passion and I know your boss has been working your nerves. I say you cash out that 401k and start making money for yourself, instead of other people." Listen to me, sounding all financially secure now that I had a few dollars in the bank.

"I like the security of the corporate golden handcuffs. I like having insurance, expense accounts, and not having to chase down checks," Simone said as she took a long swig of her wine.

"I hear you on that! I love those perks, too!" I really loved these girls, and I could have stayed there all day cackling with them. But looking at my phone, I realized I had to get out of there. "Uh-oh, I misjudged the time for this brunch. They're coming to install the cameras and lighting today."

"So you're really going through with this?" Simone said slowly. Why did part of me feel like she was being condescending? Maybe I was just being paranoid.

"Nothing has changed, Simone. Why do you ask?"

"No reason, I just wanted to make sure you are absolutely sure about this."

"I am." I couldn't keep the edge from my voice.

"And we support whatever decision you make, Jackie," Taylor interrupted. "We know you know what is best for your career and we are happy for you." She gave Simone a look to quit it and shut the fuck up.

"Ladies, things are starting to fall into place," I said, in a grand save. "Simone, you're a married woman now. Taylor, I know you are going through it with Michael, but last night was a wonderful way to kick off 40. Not only did you have a kick-ass party, but your pieces sold out again. And now I am finally getting my big break. This is what we all dreamed of all these years!"

My training in theater came in handy. Although I put on a good show, this doing a reality show made me feel dirty. It made me feel like all those years I spent studying my craft were going down the drain. Although I made it sound exciting, you can't polish a turd. And reality TV was a big piece of shit. What the hell had I gotten myself into?

•　　　•　　　•

I had picked up a few modern silver vases, long stem wine glasses, champagne flutes with some silver bling, and some gold and silver silk throw pillows from Z Gallerie to spruce up my apartment. Although it wasn't a huge place, I had decorated it with bright colors and beautiful art on the walls – mostly paintings by Taylor. The lighting crew would be here any minute and I wanted to make sure everything was perfect. Shooting was beginning tomorrow at Penthouse at the Huntley Hotel, but then they'd be shooting here. I was arranging fresh flowers in my new silver vase when the front gate app buzzed on my phone. I buzzed the guys in, checked myself in the mirror, and applied another coat of lipstick. I looked casually cute. My hair was pulled into a bun, and I was wearing cut-off shorts and a white T-shirt tied in the back to show off my tiny waist line. We might not be shooting here today, but I wanted the crew to see the beauty they were working with. I took a deep breath and opened the door.

Instead of a lighting crew and their equipment, there stood Angelique McKinley in head to toe St. John and David Yurman jewelry.

"Well... aren't you going to invite me in? I know I raised you with better manners than this." I had been standing there with my mouth open.

"Uhh... Mom! Of course, come in." I gave her a hug, getting a full blast of Chanel No. 5. My mother was still a strikingly beautiful woman. At 67, she resembled Diahann Carroll, her beautiful salt and pepper hair swooped to the side. I called her "The Devil Wears St. John" because her cut was also similar to Meryl Streep's in "The Devil Wears Prada." I got my height from my dad. My mother was only 5'4", but her personality made her seem like she was 6'4". "I'm sorry, Mother. I wasn't expecting you ... what are you doing in L.A.? Why didn't you call me?"

She sat down on the couch and looked at me over her glasses. "I have been trying to call you and you're not answering my calls. I wanted to give my beautiful daughter the opportunity to let me know that she was about to make the biggest mistake of her life!" She took her glasses off.

"A reality show, Jacqueline? Really? And please, for the love of God, stop slouching, darling."

I immediately stood up straight. I don't know what it was about her that made me revert back to the insecure dark-skinned girl from childhood. My mother, fairer than me, was so beautiful. My mother passed the paper bag test; her skin was slightly lighter than a brown paper bag so she had more "privileges." My Hershey chocolate coloring didn't come close. I always felt inadequate.

"After all the money I shelled out making sure you were in the best private schools, the best colleges... you even studied abroad, for Christ's sake."

"I was planning on telling you, Mom, but I've just been so busy. Besides, I'm a grown-ass woman, I can make my own decisions and I don't have to tell you my every move." I went to the kitchen and grabbed two champagne flutes and poured us both a glass. I needed to fortify myself because I knew this was going to be one of those lectures, like the one she gave me when I told her I wanted to be a theater major at Hampton University. It didn't matter that I was 40 years old. I could be 60, and as long as she was aliv,e she would feel the need to control my every move. I took a long swig of my champagne.

"When were you going to tell me? Once it started airing on TV?"

"Actually... That's exactly what I planned. And how did you find out?"

"These people from the production company called me because they wanted me to shoot a scene with you!" she said indignantly.

I was shocked. Jay mentioned having family and friends on this show, but how in the hell did they get my mother's number? I was suddenly feeling embarrassed. "I had no idea they were going to reach out to you."

"Well, they did. And when I called Linda she was just basking about how you landed this huge gig! I thought you had told me you booked an NBC series, a regular role." She took a sip of champagne.

"Technically, it *is* an NBC series regular role. Bravo and NBC are all under the same corporate umbrella." I stretched the truth a little. "And Linda is excited about it, so that should put your mind at ease. She's excited about it!" I was desperate to lighten the mood.

"All Linda is excited about is being able to put 15 percent of your money into her bank account. You're better than this, Jacqueline. I didn't raise you to be ordinary – "

I finished her sentence. "I raised you to be extraordinary and if being extraordinary was easy, everybody would be doing it." I laughed.

"I know you think it's funny, Jacqueline, but it's not." She was fuming. She enunciated every syllable. Growing up my friends used to call my mother "Claire Huxtable" because she carried herself the exact same way. I swear, that character had been modeled on her.

"I don't need a lecture, Mom. I'm 40 years old. I know what's best for me." I tried not to sound like a 12-year-old kid.

"Oh, really. So much that you have five different payday loans out? So much that you were almost evicted from this place?"

How the hell did she know about the loans? Not only was I floored, but I was humiliated. I was like a junkie who attempted to keep her drug use a secret about the payday loans. It was my secret life.

"Jacqueline, I keep my eye on you. And I am extremely worried about you. When you told me you wanted to be an actress, I was on the fence, but I went along with the program. Now you are 40 years old and I know you're tired of struggling. But this isn't the way to go." She leaned in closer to me. "I know you and I do not always see eye to eye. But you have to know I love you and I only want what is best for you. This isn't not the route you want to go. You're better than this."

"Mom, the business has changed. Everybody is doing reality. I can parlay this opportunity into something else." Why was I putting on an act? This was one of the few times I actually agreed with my mother. But what was my alternative?

"I know this about you. You are the ultimate salesperson. You can and will parlay it into something else because you are that brilliant, but you will always be viewed as a reality personality. You will never be taken seriously in the business. For example, when you signed the contract, did you ask for final edit approval?"

How the hell did she suddenly know so much about the entertainment business?

"You already know producers have a field day editing Black women to look like 'coons' on these shows. You're not thinking this through.

This why I told you years ago to go back to school and study law so you had a better idea how to negotiate your contracts. You just never listen. You could have been a powerhouse agent. But that's neither here nor there. You're looking for a temporary solution to your problem."

"Mother, I have absolutely no interest in going back to school and becoming a lawyer. I have my bachelor's degree, and that's all I need. Unlike my sister, I am not a professional student. And why are you so damn controlling?" Yes, I had five payday loans out, but I hadn't asked for her help with my rent in months. I had to take control of this situation, even though she was saying everything I was thinking about reality TV.

"I am not controlling, and I resent you saying that!" She pointed her perfectly manicured red-polished finger at me. "And you should be proud of your sister for continuing her education while she is still young and can reap the rewards later in life, so when she's your age she won't be... well... that's neither here nor there. My point is, you're better than a bootleg minstrel reality show!"

"So what do you suggest I do, Mother? Swing on a pole and twerk onstage for ten-dollar tips? I'm not asking you for any more money. It is what it is." I felt defeated. I also felt exposed and embarrassed. Deep down inside, I would give anything to make my mother proud of me. I would love to be a daughter she bragged about to her friends.

But I knew she was up to something. My mother didn't do pop-up visits to L.A. from New Jersey. There was always a hidden agenda.

"Wait a minute, Mom. What brings you all the way to Cali unexpectedly? I know you didn't reserve your lecture on how to run my life for an in-person appearance. You are more than effective over the phone."

"Please save your sarcasm for your girlfriends. You are so disrespectful these days! But yes, we are both full of surprises today. I have decided to open a West Coast office."

"A West Coast office of what?" I looked at her like she suddenly grew two heads.

She stood up and went into my kitchen and poured herself another glass of champagne. "I have decided to open an L.A. office and I want you to run it!" She held up her glass for a toast like she was telling me the best news ever. I was dumbfounded, insulted, and ticked off. There was always some type of manipulation with Angelique McKinley. That's what made her so damn successful. She knew how to come in at folks' lowest points and be their savior. She couldn't give two fucks about my career. She wanted to manipulate me into running her office! This is what she wanted all along.

"Are you kidding me, Mother? You flew all the way across the country, spied on me, stuck your nose into my finances, just to make me run your business? How many times do I have to tell you that I do *not* want to be in your non-profit business?" You know those times when you are so angry you want to punch someone but you can't so you shake out of utter frustration? That's where I was at this very moment.

"You need to lower your voice, Jacqueline. When I started my company I always envisioned that one day you would take over, once you got this acting foolishness out of your system and finally decided to get a real job. I am giving you the opportunity of a lifetime. You could finally be in a place in your life where you aren't struggling."

"You like for me to struggle, don't you? You like for me to need you. To need your money, to need your help, because then you can remind me what a fuck-up I am." She winced at my language, but at this point I didn't give a shit.

"You need me to be a fuck-up so you can sweep in and save the day. You have been waiting for me to fail so I could become a slave to your company and you can run every aspect of my life. No more, Mother! I am going to make it without your help! I don't want to work in your office. How many times do I have to tell you that I am not you? I am an actress, not some boring, stuck-up, stuffy corporate woman!"

"I am going to give you a pass on your little temper tantrum. Have you ever heard the three magic words 'In addition to...?' It means you can do more than one thing at once. What is so wrong with running my West Coast office as you pursue your dreams?"

"Oh, Mother, puhleeez! Do acting and run your office? What if I got a big gig and had to quit? Would you be okay with that?"

"Well, we can cross that bridge when we get there. Before you say a fast no... I would rather you take your time and say a slow yes. And darling...cussing is so unlady-like. You know better than that!" She got up to get her purse then pulled out her checkbook.

"Mother, what are you doing?" I walked over to watch her write my name on a check. When she got to the amount part she wrote out $25,000. She ripped the check from the leather folder and reached out to give it to me. "Mother, I don't – "

"Uh-uh." She waved her red-polished finger at me. "Please don't say you don't need this because you do. Let's just say this is a part of your signing bonus... a fresh start. You can always pay me back."

I knew this tactic. I knew my mother. If I accepted this money I was basically allowing myself to become her bitch. And as much as my mother worked my last nerve, she knew me well. She knew good and damn well I didn't want to do that show. But I just didn't have it in me to tell her.

"Don't bite off your nose to spite your face. Take the check, Jacqueline." I couldn't bring myself to take the check in my hand. So she put it on the table.

"So... are you going to shoot with me?" I asked in a voice just above a whisper. Now I remembered what she'd said earlier about the production company wanting to interview her.

She laughed. "Oh, darling, I'm no actress."

"It's not acting; it's reality TV. And you could even promote The McKinley Group." I said, trying to appeal to her business side. "Mom, can you please do this for me?" I didn't want her lack of participation to hinder the possibility of me being on the show. If they called her, then they must think it would be helpful to me and my storyline.

I wanted to say that this show was my last hope, but I couldn't bring myself to say that out loud, let alone to Angelique McKinley. So instead I said, "This is my big break and I want you to be a part of it, Mom."

The front gate buzzed my phone, and this time it actually was the production team. The timing couldn't be better because I didn't like how I was begging her to be on the show.

"I'll let you get to what you were doing," Angelique said as she grabbed her purse and headed for to the door.

"Mommy, please..." I whispered to her, begging again. I needed her answer before she left.

"I'll think about it. And please think about what we discussed as well." We hugged and she left. The check was still on the dining room table. I picked it up and stared at it. I needed the money. I had so many loans out and massive credit card debt. Even with the money from the reality show, I was barely keeping my head above water. But I also needed my freedom. I wasn't ready for my Plan B. This was one of the few times in my life when I really didn't know what to do. I wasn't ready to face my reality.

Chapter 14
Taylor

I'd gone to bed early the day after the party and woke up before the sun came up. In a few hours, the 72-hour hold was going to be over for Michael. In my mind, the next steps were very clear and concise. Michael would move in with me while Dr. Sanders adjusted his meds. This way, Michael could get outpatient treatment and I could make sure he was taking his meds. The problem was, Michael loved New York. He couldn't stand the superficial people of La-La Land. So, getting him to stay for the next few weeks was going to be a challenge.

I went downstairs, made a cup of coffee, drank it, then sat on my couch and meditated. I closed my eyes and sat in silence, my legs crossed and my hands resting on my lap with the palms up. I took deep breaths and concentrated on being in the present moment. I had to get centered.

His coming to my birthday party meant the world to me because he had missed so many of them while we were growing up being in treatment facilities. I really wanted to start this next decade with Michael celebrating with me. Yet, I was back to when I turned thirteen years old and he missed my big party as I entered my teens because he had an episode. I felt like he once again cheated us out of the experience. I never thought that I would turn 40 and be back in the hallways of "the ward." I needed to deal with these feelings of anger before I went to the hospital because I didn't want to go off on him. People don't get mad at folks who are battling cancer because the remission ends. They don't blame the patient for the cancer coming back. That was something that was out of their control. I had to remind myself the same was the case for this disease. I continued to meditate for another 30 minutes. I allowed myself to not judge my anger. I allowed myself to acknowledge the feeling and breathe through it. By the time I returned to the room and opened my eyes, I felt better. My girls made fun of me meditating... but the shit worked. I felt much lighter after that time to myself. And I was clear on what I had to do.

After a long shower, I threw on some distressed jeans (no pun intended), a T-shirt, and my gold All-Stars, some gold bracelets and hoop earrings, fluffed up my hair and jumped into my new Cayenne.

First stop, groceries. I picked up all of my brother's favorite food items. I'd make his favorite for when he came to my house, red beans and rice.

Then I went to Nordstrom and picked up a few pairs of jeans along with shirts, socks, and boxers. From there I went to Target and picked up soap, razors, shaving cream, lotion, and other toiletries Michael would need.

Back at the house, I hung up the clothes in the guest bedroom, and set up the bathroom with all the essentials. The very last thing I put in his room was a large framed picture of him, me, and my mother the day she got her one-year sobriety chip.

•   •   •

My mother stood up in the small room and walked to the lectern. She took a deep breath. Over the last year she had been through a lot. She had checked herself into a 28-day rehab facility. When she came out, her skin was clearer, her hair had a shine to it, and she'd even lost weight. Now it was a year later and she was glowing. She was that stunningly beautiful mother I remembered. Her green eyes sparkled as she stood in front of the room.

"Hello, my name is Teresa and I am an alcoholic," she started. My mother wasn't a public speaker. You could tell she was nervous.

Everyone in the room responded, "Hi, Teresa."

The moment the group said hello back to her, I could see the tension in her shoulders release. "I almost lost it all because of alcohol. My children – " Michael took my hand and held it gently as she spoke. "– my home, and even my life." By the middle of her talk, she was in tears. "Every day is a struggle. Because, being completely honest, I miss alcohol. I miss drinking. But it is not worth missing another minute of the life I have left to live. I have so much to experience and look forward to."

She looked directly at Michael and me. "My handsome son..." This was the first time I'd heard her call him handsome. I knew my brother was drop-dead gorgeous. He would walk into a room and every woman and gay man would stare. He was the spitting image of my dad – even more so, now that he was getting older. He had my dad's height, build – he even walked like him and talked like him. The pain my mother used to have in her eyes when she looked at him was now replaced with love.

"My daughter is a talented artist. And I'm not just saying that because she is my daughter. She is beyond talented! And maybe one day I'll be able to spoil my grandchildren. Not anytime soon..." The room erupted in laughter at her joke. "I am so blessed to finally be able to live for the first time in my life. I plan on taking this second chance seriously. And I thank God every day for giving me the chance to live again."

When she was done, tears over, everyone said, "Thanks, Teresa." Then the chairperson came up and gave her the One Year Chip. It was a beautiful, gold and blue, small chip with a big meaning. We came up front and took a picture with her as she held her coin with such pride and joy. She took Michael's face between her hands and said, "I love you, and I am so sorry. Please forgive me for not being the mother I should have been to you."

He quietly whispered back to her, "I love you, Mom, and you are the mother I need now." She then held me in her arms and said, "I love you and I am so proud of you. I am so sorry. Please forgive me for all the times I lashed out and I hurt you emotionally, physically, spiritually, and mentally."

I whispered back to her, "I forgive you and I love you."

At the end of the meeting, we stood next to our mother and held her hand as the Serenity Prayer was recited: "God grant me the serenity to accept the things I cannot change, the courage to change the things I can, and the wisdom to know the difference."

•　　•　　•

My mother was diagnosed with cirrhosis of the liver two years later and died a year after that. But that lovely Vegas fall day had been the happiest day of our lives. I stared at the photo of us. I put my finger to my lips and kissed it and then put that same finger on my mother's image in the photo.

Downstairs, I took a seat on the barstool at my kitchen counter and wrote out a list of "house rules" for us while Michael was living with me. For me, the main thing was making sure he was taking his meds and going to his doctor appointments. As for him, he was already a neat freak. He would probably come here and start cleaning his damn self. I was determined to make this new arrangement work. Perhaps this was what needed to be done years ago. I always hated that he lived on the opposite coast from me. Maybe if I presented this plan in a desirable manner, he would consider moving to L.A.!

On the drive to Huntington Memorial, I turned on some Pat Metheny to calm my nerves. I focused on the road and my breathing.

By the time I pulled into the back parking lot of the hospital, I was calmer. I turned off the engine and just sat there for a few minutes. All of the times I had to do this when we were teenagers were so different. It was like me and Michael in our own world. I think what scared me deep down inside was this could have been me. To be honest, I lived with the constant fear that I was next. Perhaps his illness lived deep within me and it hadn't been triggered yet. Whenever I was feeling depressed or having a down moment, I would work relentlessly to make sure I "pulled it together." The fear of it not subsiding lived with me and I didn't want to go into the deep hole of depression and not know how to get out of it. Even when my mother passed away, I made it a point to go to my art. I lost myself in my private world of creativity in order to avoid my feared world of depression. And so far, it had worked. I don't know if it was luck. I wished my brother could have the same luxury.

But after dealing with this disease for decades, I knew he couldn't help it. It would be the equivalent to asking someone with cancer *why can't you kick this? Why can't you make the disease go away?* Those times when I felt myself slipping into a dark place, I was often terrified I wouldn't be able to bring myself out of it. I didn't understand how I was able to dodge the mental illness bullet. Growing up in our household could have driven anyone to insanity. My survival method was my art. That was the only world I had control of. But I always lived with this dark suspicion that at any moment, I could slip into darkness. And I also lived with guilt that I managed to escape the chokehold of this disease, and Michael didn't. It just didn't seem fair.

I took another deep breath and shook my head. I shook my shoulders and pulled it together. Now wasn't the time for me to attempt to psychoanalyze myself. Before I got out of my car, I checked myself in the mirror and put on some lip gloss.

The receptionist remembered me this time.

"Good morning, Ms. Ross, how can I help you?"

"Hi. I'm here to discharge Michael Ross," I said as I reached in my purse to get the paperwork.

"Dr. Sanders would like to meet with you prior to his release. Please have a seat and I'll page him."

I went and sat down. Although there were 15 old issues of magazines I could read, my mind was racing too much to concentrate. Although I'd spent a lot of time in these facilities, the feeling of emptiness and darkness, and most of all a coldness, never went away. This was the very reason I was getting Michael the fuck out of there today! He needed to be somewhere comfortable. Not in a stuffy-ass mental ward.

"Hello, Taylor." Dr. Sanders' voice startled me. "I'm sorry... I didn't mean to startle you."

"No problem, just a lot on my mind." I looked up at him and those hazel eyes were doing their calming thing. I guess that was what separated him from all of the cold psychiatrists I had come across over the years.

"That's to be expected. Before we discharge Michael, I wanted to talk to you one on one about his treatment plan. It will only take a few minutes."

I followed him through the secure double doors when they buzzed open. I always hated this part of the process. It felt like a prison. And it was fucking intense. The doctor's office faced the afternoon sun. The sun on my face had a calming effect. Timothy Sanders's degree from Morehouse was prominently placed on the wall, and right next to it his Harvard University Medical School degree. That was a great combination. There was a picture of a little girl and a little boy on his desk. They must have been about 7 and 9 years old. They were adorable.

And it was obvious the mother had to be a Black woman because they were clearly Black.

This was something you don't see often in L.A. The brothers move here and suddenly seek out Kardashian look-alikes. So it was nice to be able to look at a picture of his kids and not have to scrutinize to tell if their mother was Black. There were no pictures of a wife. As Dr. Sanders sat down at his desk I looked for a wedding ring and did not see one.

"Are those little munchkins your kids?" I looked at the picture of them again and they reminded me of me and Michael. The little boy had his arm around his little sister the same way Michael did with me in pictures as kids.

Dr. Tim picked up the photo and smiled with so much joy. "Yep. These are my babies."

"They are adorable. You and your wife make some beautiful kids." What I really wanted to say was, thank you for being a real brother and having a Black wife and Black babies.

"Ex-wife," he responded, almost cutting me off. There was an awkward silence. "Taylor – and by the way, please call me Tim – let's talk about your plan for Michael."

"Well, uh, Tim, I hope to bring him to live with me for the next few weeks while you adjust meds. I want to make sure he is seeing you daily. I am also going to make sure he is getting acupuncture, taking his meds, and exercising. For the first time, I feel like he is in good hands with you. He's never had the opportunity to have a Black psychiatrist. And let's be real, Michael isn't going to consent to being in inpatient treatment longer than the obligatory 72-hour hold. He's 43, for God's sake."

"Yes, I understand. There is an outpatient program affiliated with UCLA that I would like him to participate in. This program provides a full spectrum of evaluation, treatment, case management, and rehabilitative services for individuals with schizophrenia and related disorders. The program has special expertise in the care of patients with treatment-resistant illness." Dr. Sanders pulled a brochure from a folder desk and handed it to me. I saw that the program included acupuncture, nutrition plans, consistent counseling, and experimental drugs.

"This seems promising. My two concerns are the experimental drugs and how these will affect his system. And I'll feel much more comfortable knowing that you are his assigned psychiatrist. Would that change if he is a part of this program?"

"Not at all. I would remain Michael's designated doctor. This program is a more intense outpatient program designed specifically for African American male patients with the disease. I would not recommend something I do not totally believe in."

I took a deep breath of relief, hearing the African American part. "If it's a program you believe in and trust, then I am willing to try it with him. How long is the treatment program?"

"It's depends on his progress. As you know, his disease isn't cookie cutter, and it's important we have treatment that is specific to Michael's issues."

"Oh, boy, I hope I can get him to agree to stay in L.A. He hates it here."

"Good news... I talked to Michael about the program and he has agreed to it as well. He is very fortunate to have a job where he can work remotely from anywhere."

"Wait a minute, you convinced Michael to stay in L.A.?" I asked not truly believing my ears.

"It didn't take much convincing."

"Wow, you really are a gift from God." Tim actually blushed as a slight smile came to his face.

"Thank you. Michael is lucky to have a sister like you. You are clearly a gift too." Our eyes locked for a second. I found myself biting my lip. Why was I suddenly nervous?

"So... Is he all set for discharge?" I asked, changing the subject.

"Umm... yes. Yes, he is," Tim said, going back into "doctor" mode. "We are still trying to stabilize the levels. So, he is having some strong reactions."

I knew exactly what Tim was referring to. He still had the shakes. This always happened when his medications were readjusted. Tim went over his medication schedule with me and we scheduled his appointments for the next week. Then we went to Michael's room.

"Hey, Michael! Time for you to bust out of here," Tim said in an enthusiastic voice.

"Cool. Thanks, man," Michael said, standing up stiffly. Although his hands were shaky he still managed to give his doctor the "brotha" handshake. That's one thing about us – no matter the circumstance, we have an unbreakable bond as Black people.

"Your sister has your schedule set. The shaking will subside in the next 24 to 48 hours. Call me if you need anything, man." It was one brotha talking to another brotha. Tim actually gave a shit about Michael's well-being. He felt like... family. Michael and I signed some more of the discharge paperwork, then as we were leaving, a woman's voice called out from behind us.

"Michael..." We all turned around and saw a young white woman hurrying down the hall. A blonde, blue eyes, thin and tall with big fake-looking breasts. "I just wanted to make sure we had a chance to say goodbye!" she said as she spread her arms to hug my brother. I looked at Tim like "What the fuck?"

"Okay, Amber," he said, "You know our policy on patient-to-patient physical contact. Taylor, this is Amber, she's being released from treatment tomorrow."

"Amber has been a godsend while I was here," Michael said, smiling.

Amber looked at me all starry eyed. "You're Taylor, OMG! You're beautiful. Michael talks about you all the time," she said, clearly high from her meds. I had no interest in entertaining this bitch with a response.

"Yes," I said dismissively. "Okay, Michael, let's head on out before rush hour."

"That's a wise choice." Tim said as he walked us out. I felt his hand on the small of my back and I didn't bother to move it. It felt reassuring.

"Bye, Michael... bye..." This Amber person was still waving goodbye. Michael was waving back. Now I knew why Michael had suddenly become a fan of La-La Land. He still could make a woman swoon, even in a mental ward.

In the parking lot, when Michael realized the brand-new Porsche Cayenne was mine, he said, "Damn, sis! This is the shit!" The car was a man's dream car.

"Hop in. You'll love how it drives. So let's get the fuck out of here!" I said.

"You got that right!" he shouted.

•   •   •

I was giving Michael a tour of my loft. I was proud of my three-level oasis. I showed him around the main level where the kitchen and living room were, and the balcony that was off the living room. I walked him upstairs to the third floor and showed him his room. "This is where you'll be staying." I then walked him to the closet, "I also picked up some clothes for you."

"You work fast, T-Squito. Thanks for this. But you know this is temporary. I don't need my little sister taking care of me. As a matter of fact, how much was all of this, I'll send the money to your Venmo." He said as he took out his phone.

"You don't have to pay me back, Michael," I insisted. "It's fine."

"T, I'm not letting you pay for all of this." He was insistent. Before I could tell him to not bother, he said, "I just sent $1500 to your account. Done! And not up for discussion." He put his phone back in his pocket. Michael walked over to the window and looked out. "You have a great view of downtown L.A. I'm proud of you, sis. You are doing exactly what you said you would do."

"Mom would be proud of you, too." He said as he came over and put his arm around my shoulder. "You showed me every place in here except for where you make the magic happen." He was referring to where I did my artwork.

That area of my house was sacred. I never let anyone in there. But this wasn't just anybody.

"Follow me this way..." Michael followed me back downstairs. And we took a turn to the right and we walked down a few steps.

Before I opened the door, I motioned for him to take his shoes off. I slowly opened the door. My painting sanctuary was beautiful. I took a lot of time decorating it to make sure it reflected the serenity that painting gave me. There were floor to ceiling windows that faced downtown L.A. I had sheer white curtains that blew in the wind when the windows were open. There were white candles everywhere. The room was simple and subtle.

"Voilà!" My latest masterpiece was in the center of the room. There was still a ladder in front of it, since it was so massive compared to my petite frame. It still wasn't finished. It was missing something. Wasn't quite sure what it was, but I never brought a piece of work out of this area until it was entirely complete. Michael walked up closer to the painting.

"Damn, T. This is off the charts. You created this?" he was in amazement. Michael had missed most of my art showings. Actually, he had never been to any of them. He missed out on so much. I was hoping this new arrangement would change things. Maybe this was the beginning of a new relationship. I had sent him pictures of my artwork. But that never did them justice. You had to be in the same room and feel the presence of my pieces. My artwork spoke to people. I painted with my heart and soul and I left a piece of me on every single painting I created.

Michael was just looking at it in awe. He finally turned around and looked at me and came up to me and gave me a hug. "I am so damn proud of you. I am so sorry I missed out on your party and the showing. I know I have missed out on a lot of your moments. And I am so sorry. But I want you to know that I am so very proud of you. That I brag about you all the time to anyone within hearing distance. My little bratty ass sister is living life and that makes me so happy."

Michael was dead serious and he was looking me in the eye. It felt comforting. It had been so long since I had this type of time with him. Thinking back on it, we hadn't spent this much time together since we were teenagers.

"Thanks, Soul Brotha. I love you, too. And we aren't going to dwell on the past. We are going to move forward." I started directing him towards the door. As wonderful as this moment felt, this was still my sacred space and I had to be very aware of the energy I allowed in there. Michael followed me out and we went to the kitchen. My pot of red beans and rice was smelling sensational. It was his favorite dish and I was sure he wanted some homecooked food after being in the hospital for three days. I took a spoon and dipped it into the pot and took a taste of my own creation and it was perfect.

I placed the bowl of red beans and rice in front of Michael and he smelled it. "Smells good. Much better than that crap food they were feeding me I the hospital... although I am going to be blowing your bathroom up after I eat this!"

He laughed as he picked up the spoon and attempted to eat it. His medications were still stabilizing and his hands were still shaking. It was difficult for him to take a taste of the food due to the shakes. He tried a few times but was only able to get a few bites in. "This is why I don't fuck with these meds. You see this shit?! I can't even enjoy my damn food. This is why I stop taking my meds. You see this." He held up his hands that were shaking. He was genuinely and understandably frustrated. And I was mad at myself. Why didn't I make something easier to eat? That was so damn stupid on my end!

I came around the counter and sat next to Michael. I turned my chair so we were face to face. "I know this shit is hard. I have been there right with you for the struggle. For all these damn decades. I'm just as tired as you are. But you know you HAVE to take your meds! I would rather you have these damn shakes and take ten hours to eat some damn red beans and rice than not have you sitting here next to me. Michael, we have been down this road before. These pills are your lifeline."

I picked up the bottle that happened to be in front of me on the counter. I shook them in Michael's face. "Without these... you die. You fucking die. Why don't you get that?!" At this point I was yelling.

"You die and I am left here alone. I can't have that. I can't lose you. We are the only two left. You're all I got. Don't you get that?! What do I have to do to make you understand? It's not just about you Michael!" I started crying. All the frustration I was holding in for the last few days just came out. I couldn't hold it in any longer and not just a few tears, I was sobbing.

"I hear you, sis. I'll take them." He took the pills from my hands.

"You promise?" It was so silent you could hear a pin drop.

"I promise." He acquiesced.

Maybe this time things would be different. Maybe this was all Michael needed at this time in his life; he needed to be closer to family. If I was completely honest with myself, I needed this even more than Michael. I felt complete with him being here. I felt whole. I felt like that black cloud that constantly hung over my head was beginning to dissipate. I had my big brother home with me. I was hopeful for the future... for his future for the first time in a long time.

Chapter 15
Jacqueline

My call time was for 5 p.m. at the Huntley Hotel, a perfect time to shoot with the sun setting in the background. With the awful Cali traffic, I had given myself an extra hour and a half in case there was some high-speed chase, accident, or disaster that hit the freeway. But now I was an hour early, which showed desperation, so I pulled over on a side street where there was a nice ocean view in front of me. The call sheet had the location and time, but under Other Cast Members, it was left blank. I hated all the vagueness of this shit. At least with scripted, I went on set knowing all my lines and when the director yelled "Shoot," I was on. But this was a different scenario. Producers were purposely not telling me shit in an effort to get a genuine reaction. They wanted to see the "real me."

I began to get nervous. This was a foreign feeling – what did I have to be nervous about? Unlike auditions and other acting gigs, I didn't have to memorize lines or do extensive character work. After all, I was playing myself. And then the thought occurred to me – actually, a scary fucking thought. I spent most of my life studying other characters and memorizing their lives and actions, and did deep dives into why they did what they did. This was something I never did for myself.

Who the fuck am I?! And more important, how can I do a reality show when I don't know who the fuck I am. What am I going to portray to the audience? Who is this character I am going to bring to this project? My heart started racing and I could feel beads of sweat starting to trickle down my back. I rolled up the windows and closed the sun roof of my newly fixed car and turned on the AC. Thanks to the first check from the production company, I was able to get my car fixed.

Thank God they hadn't installed the cameras in my car yet, so I had a moment to myself. While we were shooting today, they would be installing the car cams so they could get footage of me driving around L.A.

I knew Taylor was picking her brother up from the hospital today and I didn't want to disturb her, so I called the person who I could always count on when I was having one of these down-in-the-dumps moments."

"Good morning, Sunshine!" Simone always sounded chipper when she answered the phone. It immediately put a smile on my face.

I cut right to the chase. "Simone... what in the hell am I doing?!"

"What do you mean? You said this is what you wanted to do." I could hear honest concern in her voice.

"I know that's what I said, but it is hitting me hard. What was I thinking?! I am about to shoot the very first scene for this show. They keep telling me to 'just be yourself,' but Simone, who the hell am I?"

"You're motherfucking Jacqueline McKinley! The one and only...infamous... classy... beautiful. And a damn star. You're the bitch who walks into a room and counts how many people are looking at her. Don't you forget!"

Simone was in full-on PR mode. I chuckled because it was true. Even when I go to Rite-Aid to pick up toilet paper, I count who's looking. "I hear you, but I am beginning to feel like a failure. This wasn't the life I imagined back in Hampton. I was supposed to be a success. I should have won an Oscar or an Emmy by now. I should have been the lead in a hit show. But I'm not. Instead, I'm doing a reality show. This was not my plan!"

"Oh, Jackie... fuck plans. I think we are always so damn focused on our plans that we don't take into account the reality of what a situation is. Sometimes in life we have to take the road less traveled to get to the destination of 'happy.' I know this isn't how you thought you would make your breakthrough in Hollywood. But who gives a shit? You have bitches out there who suck dicks to get parts! And you're tripping over a show produced by Jay Goldstein, who sounds like a decent guy?! You better walk on that goddamn set and own it! But most important, you have to stop worrying so much about what people think and start living your life for Jackie and making Jackie happy. Your happiness in life is the only thing that will sustain you. You gotta stop living for other folks."

It had begun to feel like she was giving herself this pep talk. I debated whether to ask what was going on with her. Well, fuck it, I'm just going to ask.

"Simone, you're right. And that's enough about me. Now I have to ask, are you okay?"

"Girl, I'm fine. Not to worry. Today is about you and your first day. I want the world to see the Jackie that I love. Don't waste this opportunity worrying about random motherfuckers."

As much as I wanted to dig into what was going on with her, I didn't have time. The clock on the dashboard said 4:42 p.m.

"I love you, girl. I'll call you later and let you know how it goes."

"Break a leg, Jackie!" Simone shouted as she hung up.

•   •   •

The production team was in place at the hotel, ready to mic me up. I was wearing a fitted purple Ted Baker dress. The PA stared at me, trying to figure out where to put the mic. "Do you mind if I put this on your bra strap?" he asked.

"Wow... shouldn't you take me out to dinner first?" We were both laughing when the executive producer walked up.

"Are you ready?" she asked.

"I was born ready." My talk with Simone helped motivate me.

"Great! OK, now get back in your car and drive up to the hotel again. You're going to get in the elevator and go up to the penthouse restaurant. Your reality TV life begins now!"

I did as instructed: went back to my car, which now had camera-cams in place, exited the parking lot, and drove back to the entrance. When the valet ran up to the car I smiled and handed him the keys and slowly walked to the elevator. It was strange having a camera guy in my face when I wasn't saying shit. I was also hoping this fool was catching me on my good side. I discreetly angled my face to the right to ensure he did just that. I was used to being in front of multiple cameras. That part was easy. The part that was making me totally self-conscious was being in front of the camera as "myself." I took a deep breath and hit Penthouse in the elevator. When the elevator doors opened, I was greeted by the all-white art deco feel of the Penthouse at the Huntley Hotel. And it was an absolutely beautiful late afternoon. The sun was beginning to set, the sky was different shades of lavender, gray, and pink. You could see the waves of the ocean crashing onto the sand. It looked like a scene Taylor would paint. For a moment, I forgot that there were two cameramen following me.

The young hostess greeted me. "Hello, ma'am. Follow me this way, the other person in your party has already arrived." I hated when these young millennials called me "ma'am." What the fuck? I wasn't a damn senior citizen! Young bitch. To be 27 again! I still had no clue who the hell I was meeting. I was not liking this unscripted, yet staged, reality one bit! We turned the corner and there, sitting at a table looking regal and ever so classy, was my... mother.

She was wearing a crisp white button-down shirt with the collar up, black cigarette pants, a pair of Chanel loafers, her famous black pearl earrings, and her red reading glasses. She looked up on cue and her face lit up seeing me. She got up from the table to give me an elegant hug.

"Hello, darling. You look beautiful. But of course you do... You're my daughter." I couldn't remember the last time my mother was this happy to see me. Her greeting threw me for a loop. Turns out she's an actress too!

"Mother, I'm surprised to see you here," I said as we sat down. You look beautiful yourself."

I was grateful she had agreed to do the shoot, but I also knew there had to be an angle to this. Angelique McKinley was no fool, and there was no way on God's green earth she would agree to appear on this show if it didn't have some sort of benefit to her.

"I'd like a bottle of your Veuve Cliquot Rosé," she said to the waiter who had suddenly arrived at our table. She looked at me and smiled, then placed her forearms on the table and leaned in. "So... have you thought further about our conversation yesterday?"

There it was... she was actually going to ask me about this on national television! I was floored. She had no fucking limits! And the fucking production company knew this was what she was up to. "You would do an amazing job running the McKinley Group's brand-new West Coast office, Jacqueline."

I rolled my eyes and this time I didn't even try to hide it. "I did, Mother. I thought long and hard about it."

"And...?" She was beaming and enjoying every single aspect of this. But if she was going to go there, then I would, too!

"Mommy, I am NOT you. You always told me that I was not destined for an ordinary life and I completely agree with you. But that doesn't mean I am supposed to live the life you want me to live. When I am onstage or on set, I am happy. It is my happy place. I feel free and alive. I really want you to understand that acting isn't just a passion for me it, is a place of freedom. A place where I feel like I have control, in the same way you feel you have control when you are at your office and in board rooms." I was being extra careful with this so if any studio executives or casting folks were watching, I could make them see my passion. But I was also being honest with her.

"Okay, but why can't you do both? You're 40 years old, Jacqueline. I think it's time you are more realistic with your life."

I glared at her. How dare she mention my age on television!! Was she trying to destroy me?! For a millisecond I considered cussing her out. But as the waiter came up to the table with our bottle of champagne I saw one of the cameramen off in the corner shooting us. How quickly I forgot the cameras were there. So, although I was pissed off, I would be damned if I cussed my mother out on national TV. The waiter popped open the champagne and poured some into my mother's glass for her to taste. She nodded her head, tapped her glass and he poured each of us a full glass. I took a long gulp. Liquid courage was always a great thing. And then I went on with the conversation.

"You're absolutely right, I am not where I thought I would be at this point in my life. I thought I would be a series regular, be married, and have my 1.5 kids by now. I have no idea what's in store for me. And Mommy, I am scared. But I am not ready to give up on this dream because a part of me feels like I am about to have a breakthrough."

"What exactly are you saying, dear? And Jaqueline, for the love of God, please stop slouching!" She sounded irritated. And I wasn't even slouching!

"I am not going to run your West Coast office! I am not ready to give up on the dream that keeps me living and feeling alive. I don't want to disappoint you, but I can't disappoint myself. Why can't you respect that and support my dreams!" I felt like a teenager at this point.

"I've been supporting your dreams for the last four damn decades, Jacqueline! I have been supporting you financially when you couldn't pay your rent, I helped you get the publishing job... which I just found out you quit. I helped you get your agent. I have been there for you in more ways than you give me credit for. I have gone along with your program. And quite frankly I am tired of watching you struggle all the damn time!" She enunciated each word, never raising her voice. Hers was the ultimate read. It was stunning.

"I'm not strug – "

"And please don't try to tell me you're not struggling. You are! This acting thing was cute in your 20's, and in your 30's, I was still going along with it. But now you're 40! 40! It's time to grow up and be realistic about things."

I couldn't believe she was calling me out on my age again. If she thought she could embarrass me into submission and make me agree to take over her company she had another thing coming.

"Do you think I don't wake up every morning and mourn the life I thought I would have by now, Mother? Do you realize how many times I have been turned down for roles because I'm too tall, too Black, not urban enough, not pretty enough? You don't think that hurts?"

I forgot the cameras were there. I had my mother's undivided attention and I needed her to hear me out. "I'm not working for you. I will not give up on my dreams. I know you think I'm a failure and I know I have always disappointed you. And yes... I am 40. But I would be a fool to give up on this now. I won't quit whether I have your blessing or not. I love you, Mommy. You are such an amazing woman. You have built a great life for me and the family. You are a force to be reckoned with. But, Mommy...I AM NOT YOU." I looked her dead in her eyes.

We sat there in silence for what seemed like an eternity. This was the ultimate mother-daughter face-off. And the sad thing was there wasn't going to be a winner.

I was not about to cry my first day shooting. I would not let my mother or the world see that. I grabbed my clutch and got up from the table. "Goodnight, Mommy." I bent down, gave her a kiss on the cheek and went to the elevator as a camera followed me. I needed to get out of there and fast. What the hell was taking so long for the elevator to come? I started banging on the down button and the doors finally opened. I got inside and attempted to press the door close button before the cameraman could get in with me. But of course, I wasn't fast enough. I managed to bottle up the tears as the motherfucker was zooming in close on me. The valet had already pulled my car around. I got in and turned the corner out of the hotel and found a place to stop.

I leaned my head on the steering wheel and just cried my heart out. I cried for all the parts I didn't book. I cried for every single bad decision I made. I cried for not being the daughter my mother wanted me to be. I cried until I was cried out.

Finally, I stopped. I had no idea how much time had passed. It was completely dark out at this point. I took one final deep breath and started the car. Then I saw the small red light blinking from the dashboard. In my emotional state, I had completely forgotten that the production company had installed the car cam and this entire moment was being filmed.

What the fuck had I gotten myself into?

Chapter 16
Simone

Jackie's call was a great distraction from my own problems. It was day 7 of Travis ignoring me. Last night I woke up and found him in his office staring at the computer screen, all hunched over. Normally, I would come behind him and give him a shoulder massage, but I was tired of acquiescing to him. I went back to our room and slammed the door loud enough so he knew I went back to bed. When I got up this morning he was already gone. And today had been such a crazy day at work. My boss was on his period and moody as fuck. I thought once I got promoted to V.P., all of my problems would disappear. However, it was just mo' money, mo' problems, and I was stuck smack dab in the middle of all the corporate politics. I didn't know who was going to make the next move to try to stab me in the back and take my accounts.

How ironic... it was just like my marriage. I thought once I got married, all of my problems would disappear. Travis wasn't the man I fell in love with. The man I fell for was affectionate, supportive, and passionate. He loved cooking me dinner and cracking jokes. He was fun and we enjoyed being around each other. What the hell was happening?

I pulled into our long driveway. I was relieved Travis's car wasn't there. I went into the house, immediately took off my heels and bra, and went to the wine rack and opened up a bottle of pinot noir.

Lately, my usual favorite sauvignon blanc would get me nauseous, so I'd switched it up to red. I swirled the wine in the glass and took a sip. Then I heard the garage open and a few moments later Travis walked in. I tensed up. Maybe he would realize this silence shit was ridiculous and actually have a conversation with me. But he walked right past me and went upstairs and I was left there standing with my glass of wine and my thoughts. Asshole!

I went upstairs to take a shower. Travis was in the walk-in closet changing out of his suit and putting on his sweats. I purposefully left the bathroom door open so he could see me. I started to run the shower and took off my clothes. If he was going to ignore me, at least I could attempt to remind him what he was missing. But he stormed out of the bedroom like I had the plague. I took the shower, put on lotion and a splash of Victoria Secret Heavenly Body mist. I put on a fitted pair of sweatpants and a fitted white tank top and went back downstairs. I could smell food. And it actually smelled really good. Travis was sitting on the couch watching ESPN highlights. In the kitchen there were various Tupperware containers of food, which made it abundantly clear he had been to his mother's house and brought home some of her cooking. And it looked like...just enough food for himself.

Wow! This was a new level of low. I started to pull out some lettuce, tomatoes, cucumbers, and onions to make myself a salad. I started humming just to annoy him. He grunted. Got up off the couch. Came into the kitchen. And for a second, I thought he was finally going to say something to me. Instead, he grabbed his car keys and left. I heard his car ignition and then heard him speed out of the driveway.

I wasn't sad – I was infuriated. I had never had a man treat me like this, *ever*. If we were dating, I would have broken up with him and gone back to my condo in West Hollywood and call my girls for a cocktail. But this was marriage. I was stuck, and I didn't know how to get this train back on track. I could take the high road and ask him to talk. But I was so tired of always having to do that.

Our house was feeling more cold and distant each day. I had more peace in a suite at the Ritz than my own home. I was missing my condo in the heart of West Hollywood. I loved it there. I was missing my gay neighbors who always looked out for me. Most important, I was missing the calming energy and positive vibes I used to feel when I walked in the door of my own place.

My phone buzzed for a text message. Well, it's about damn time... the Negro finally decided to talk to me! But it was just a text message from my assistant letting me know she had emailed the receipts for the charges I'd put on my secret "fuck-you" credit card.

That reminded me – I needed to call American Express and find out what was going on with our other accounts. "Never a dull moment," I said out loud and called American Express. A soft voice with a heavy East Indian accent answered the call. After giving her all of my information to verify my identity I got down to business.

"Two of my cards were declined a few days ago and I know I am nowhere close to the limit on either one of the cards." I quickly checked the edge of annoyance in my voice. After all, it wasn't this outsourced Indian girl's fault that my cards had been declined.

"I am so sorry for the inconvenience, Mrs. Lee Let me see what's going on..." After a few seconds of her tapping on her keyboard, she said, "Umm... Could you please hold on while I connect you with my supervisor?"

"Supervisor? Why does this need a supervisor?"

"Yes, ma'am, I understand. Please hold on for a moment."

I began tapping my perfectly manicured nails on the kitchen counter. This was absolutely ridiculous. As I was holding I looked around the family room at our perfectly framed weddings picture of our first kiss, in black and white, the perfectly placed fresh flowers... The house was spotless. Finally, a new rep came on the line who was clearly American. Talk about around the world in 30 seconds! "Hello, Mrs. Lee. Thanks for your patience. It's my understanding you were calling regarding declined transactions on your card?" She sounded very about business.

"Yes, that's correct. What's the problem? My husband and I are nowhere near our credit limit." I had now been on the phone with American Express for 10 minutes. These were 10 minutes of my life I would never get back.

"Well, Mrs. Lee, I'm afraid your cards have been suspended."

"WHAT? That's impossible! Why?"

"They have been suspended for well over a month. We have been trying to call you for quite some time now and have not gotten any response. We talked to your husband on Tuesday and explained what was going on."

"Well, what is going on?"

"We have suspended the cards ending in 0023 and 3052 for fraudulent activity."

"What? Fraudulent activity? What are you talking about?" My head was starting to spin. On top of everything wine was no longer giving me the comfort I needed.

"Mrs. Lee, have you spoken to your husband?" the woman asked in a calm voice. No, this bitch didn't! Now I was going to have to check her ass too. But quickly decided to take a different direction. I needed this woman's help to get the information I needed. I took a breath and said, "What is your name, Miss?"

"Claudia..."

"Claudia, I am an authorized user on this account and unfortunately my husband has not shared anything with me. I need your help. Men! Are you single?" I asked.

"Um... yes, Mrs. Lee." She sounded taken aback.

"Here's some advice... stay that way! Being single is the best thing ever. Marriage is overrated."

The Claudia woman laughed on the other end, "Thanks, Mrs. Lee... I'll take that advice!" Our mutual laughter loosened her up.

"So, let's start again... what fraudulent activity are you referring too?"

"It's not good, Mrs. Lee. It appears that your husband was taking out cash advances from several company American Express cards to pay the balances on other Amex cards. He was doing business with a Lee Bros. company, and we discovered he has part ownership in that company. That is against our policy. We warned him once in the beginning of July and informed him if the activity continued, we would need to terminate his card privileges and suspend the accounts. Unfortunately, the activity began again two months ago, and happened more frequently. All of the AmEx cards in his name as the primary card holder have been suspended, and American Express will no longer be doing business with him in the future."

Lee Bros. was his brother's business. I was stunned. What kind of ghetto bullshit was this? We got married in July – was he doing this to pay for wedding expenses? But two months ago was when he found out about his brother's wife' affair. Somehow his broke-ass, trifling brother was behind this.

"Mrs. Lee, are you still there?" Claudia asked on the other line.

"Yes... yes I'm still here."

"Do you have any other questions, Mrs. Lee?"

"Actually, yes, I do. How is this going to affect my credit and relationship with American Express?"

"You have nothing to worry about, Mrs. Lee. The cards for which you are a primary cardholder are not affected by this and since the other cards are in his name and you are not a co-signer, this will not affect your credit."

"Could you do me a favor, Claudia? Could you please email me all the statements for the last year for both of the cards Mr. Lee and I have jointly?"

"Sure."

I gave Claudia my personal email address. The moment I hung with American Express, I ran upstairs and stormed down the long hallway to Travis's office. I went to open up the drawers of the desk, but they were locked. Suddenly, I felt really nauseous. I ran to the bathroom and violently threw up. My stomach had been fucked up since that damn Jamaican food Taylor insisted on us eating at the party. I didn't have time to diagnose myself, however. I didn't have much time to figure out what the fuck was going on with my husband and his finances. I came back to the office and grabbed his silver envelope knife and tried to jimmy open the desk drawer. I began banging the envelope knife until the desk drawer burst open and I cut my finger. It started to bleed and I sucked the blood. At this point I didn't even care. I pulled out the files out the desk and prepared myself to discover the truth.

I felt like my eyes were deceiving me. I couldn't believe the shit Travis had been hiding from me. He had been living another life. But I couldn't understand why. He was a successful businessman... college-educated, and a good "Christian" who was active in his father's church. But he was participating in what seemed like bank fraud. What the hell had I gotten myself into?! He had purchased two properties in Vegas. When he went to Vegas for what I thought was his bachelor weekend he and his other trifling cousin were actually purchasing properties under another company name. For wedding expenses, he had opened up fake American Express accounts so that he could charge those companies for business expenses.

I logged onto my email account on his computer and looked over all of the statements that American Express sent over. There were a lot of charges for dinners as well as hotel charges. Was he cheating on me?! How would that be possible? But then I thought back to a text message I saw on his phone a few days ago: *Hotel is booked! ~J*

I assumed this was regarding Valentine's Day, and he had used a connection to surprise me with an amazing weekend getaway, but who the fuck was J? Shit wasn't adding up. I couldn't make sense of this. I began to print out the next credit card statement.

"What the hell are you doing?!" I hadn't heard Travis walk into the house. The office looked like a war zone. There were papers everywhere. I immediately snapped back into the present moment. If anyone was going to be angry today it would be me. He leaves my best friend's party early, leaves me in a hotel suite by myself, hasn't spoken to me in days, and now I am discovering I could be married to a fraud. Oh, hell no, I wasn't going to let him be angry with me

"The bigger question is what the hell are YOU doing, Travis?!" I flashed the stack of American Express statements in my hand. "I went to use the credit card and it was declined, and then I called American Express and they told me they've suspended our accounts. Why don't you tell me what going on?!" I was trying not to scream too loud, I was trying not to cuss.

"This place is a mess... And you broke the desk, an antique – "

"I don't care about the damn desk. I need you to answer my question. What is going on?" I was beginning to feel nauseous again. "What are all of these companies and these cards, and you have properties in Vegas you didn't tell me about? What else are you hiding from me?"

"You had no right to go through my personal documents, Simone. It's none of your business." He was so nasty. I couldn't believe this was my husband speaking to me like that.

"What do you mean it's none of my business? Didn't your dad say in our marriage counseling session that once you get married there's no such thing as personal? I'm not some little housewife who doesn't contribute to this household. I'm your wife and an equal partner here. It *is* my business when I can't use my damn credit cards at my own party and you are keeping things from me in my own house!"

"First of all, this isn't YOUR house, it's MY house and you moved in."

"Your house? YOUR house? What the fuck do you mean YOUR house?! I am paying bills here and I am sick and tired of your brother bringing you down. He's going to wind up getting your ass arrested. You need to tell him and cheating whore wife that the money train has come to a stop. How dare you – "

Travis snatched the papers out of my hand, grabbed me by the neck and slammed me against the wall. Through gritted teeth, he growled, "Don't you ever fucking talk that way about my family again." When I started to respond, he shook me and said, "*I mean it.*"

I couldn't breathe. He finally let me go and pushed me to the floor. He stormed out of the office. I should have been scared. But I wasn't. I was more pissed off that he'd threatened me. I ran after him. When I got outside he was getting into his car. "Don't you walk away from me! We aren't done here. Are you fucking crazy?"

Travis waved his hand in dismissive fashion as if he were shooing off a fly and got in his car. I grabbed the door. As I tried to open it, he accelerated and I was jerked forward and fell. Blood started running down my leg. Ahead I saw him stop the car. For a quick second, I thought he was going to come back and make sure I was okay. When he saw me wobble my way to a standing position, he sped off. My jeans were ripped. My knees and palms of my hands were scraped and bleeding. I came back to my senses. I didn't want anyone to see me like this out front of the house. I didn't want to embarrass myself and Travis and have our dirty laundry aired in public.

I limped back into "his" house. And I felt the vomit coming up. I didn't even make it to the bathroom. I threw up in the front vestibule and all over my clothes. I felt so damn sick. Here I was sitting in my mansion with vomit all over me and a tear-stained face. Why did Travis marry me? How could we get back to where we were?

I got up and limped to the laundry room and threw my shirt and jeans into the washing machine. I went back to the hallway and mopped up my vomit. My knee was in pain. I went upstairs and took a long hot shower, washed my hair and put on some leggings and a sweater. I went into the guest room. The furniture in it came from my West Hollywood condo. It was the one place in the house that felt like my own. It was my own personal oasis in this big, cold house. I got under my old comforter. Maybe I would wake up and find out today was just a bad dream.

Chapter 17
Taylor

I made a pit stop at Gelson's on the way home from the gallery to pick up some sea bass for dinner. Things were going so well the first few days of our cohabitation. It had been years since we spent this kind of quality time together. It was nice to come home and see Michael sitting on the couch, relaxing, watching TV, or cleaning up, or cooking. He loved cooking and we'd been having some great gourmet meals. He was typically up before me in the morning, sitting at the table writing. And I painted at night. So we tended to be out of each other's way. His new meds were helping – he no longer had the shakes and the stiffness was gone. He used my old Ford Explorer to go back and forth to his appointments.

Walking into the loft delicious smells were coming from the grill on the balcony. Another one of those gourmet meals.

"Oh, shit! You done brought out the big guns! If I keep eating like this I'm going to be two tons of fun!" I shouted as I chucked the sea bass in the fridge and went out to join him.

There was Michael barbequing some swordfish on the grill, and to my surprise, there was that blonde, Amber, from Huntington Hospital on my balcony, in *my* chair, drinking *my* wine from *my* wineglass. I stopped dead in my tracks. She looked very comfortable. Most people are slightly uptight about being in someone else's house, but she'd made herself right at home. She even had her shoes off.

"OMG! Hi, Taylor!" Did she start every sentence with OMG?

"Hey, T-Squito, top-quality grade swordfish from your favorite bourgeois-ass Gelson's."

"I see...uh, nice to see you, Amber... Can you excuse me for a minute...I'll be back." I didn't wait for them to answer me. I went straight to the kitchen and poured myself a scotch and club soda with a twist of lime. I looked in the fridge and saw that the bottle of Kim Crawford Sauvignon Blanc I had bought only yesterday was opened and almost empty. What was the fucking point of putting the damn bottle back in the fridge when there was only less than a half glass left?

Michael came into the kitchen. "You good, T?"

"No, I'm not good. Why didn't you tell me we were having company?"

"Come on, T. I know you're not tripping over Amber. She's cool. And she's harmless," he said nonchalantly.

"I'm not questioning her coolness... but what is she doing *here*... in my house. You've only known her for two goddamn minutes!"

"She and I had a connection. She got me – in a way no one has. Yes, I've only known her for a few days but it feels like a lifetime." He was dead-ass serious. That's the beauty and the curse of my brother. He was so damn handsome, and so damn charming that no matter where he went he attracted women. It was effortless. And he was a genuinely a good guy and knew how to make a woman feel like she was on top of the world. My brother had never brought a white girl home. Yes, he fucked a bunch of them in high school, but he was *always* into Black women... usually sistahs that were chocolate, classy, stylish, and sophisticated. My brother had been in L.A. for a little over week and he had already become victim to the BAF (Black-ass fools) club? BAFs were men who moved to L.A. and in record time, started dating anyone and anything, as long as they weren't Black.

"A connection? Really? Come on, Michael, you were high on your meds at the hospital...She's not even a fly white girl!" I didn't mean to say that out loud. Maybe the scotch was going to my head too quickly. He was giving Amber all this credit for understanding him when I dropped everything to get shit together for his arrival to my house and almost missed my own birthday party to deal with his treatment? "And speaking of your meds, did you take them today?"

"Goddamn Taylor. You are trippin'! And yes, I took my meds. Damn."

"I'm just making sure. That was one of the conditions of you staying here."

"Yeah, one of your conditions. You didn't say I couldn't have company. Right now, I'm starting to feel like I'm back in the mental ward, with all your rules and shit. I'm a grown-ass man. I appreciate you letting me stay here for a while. But damn, stop riding me."

Michael had a point. Fact was, I was loving this one-on-one time with my brother. Call me selfish, but we hadn't had this type of time together in years and I was enjoying every second of it. And I was frustrated. I never thought my brother would be seeing a white girl, and a rather trashy-looking one at that. Who would have ever thought a white bitch would pick up my brother in a mental hospital? Was I in the twilight zone or what? But at the same time, I recognized I was being a nag. I took a deep breath to calm my nerves. "My bad, Michael. I'm not trying to ride you. I want you here. I like having you here. I just thought you and I were going to have some time together, just the two of us."

Michael came around the counter and put his arm around me. "You got me, sis. I'm here. But a brotha does have needs that even his superwoman sister can't fulfill," he said, winking. We both laughed. "But for real, T. Is the real issue that she's white?" It was the typical defensive reaction Black men use when they decide to step out and date outside their race. "You can't hate every single white woman because of Dad."

"What are you talking about?"

"Come on, T! You never got over the fact that dad married Fiona and adopted her child when he was never there for us," Michael said. I couldn't allow myself to go there. Dad was a topic I usually shot down. My dad abandoned us and went on to become the picture-perfect father to Fiona and her mixed child, and even adopted her. It made me sick thinking about it. These are feelings I pushed down – and I wasn't ready to unbury them. I needed to keep them where they were... buried.

"No, fool! The issue is that you met her in a mental ward. How do you even know she's stable?!" I asked as I squeezed more lime into my scotch.

"I was in the same ward she was in. And she didn't judge me. I'm no different than her, T. She didn't question my stability. I'm not better than she is. We were both two people in a bad place who are trying to do better."

I felt like a judgmental piece of shit for saying what I said. Although, the fact remained that there was something about her I didn't like or trust. I couldn't put my finger on it. I knew this bitch was bad news. But I would be damned if I'd let this chick win. My brother was finally with me in L.A. and I was going to enjoy every moment of having him here. Besides, it wouldn't last. She would run her course and he would be on to the next woman or back in New York.

"Okay, agree, you're a grown ass man. I apologize." I patted him on the shoulder. "Just curious, have you reached out to Tammy?" Tammy was his ex-girlfriend. They had met in high school. She had called him here and I had relayed the message.

"No, I'll give her a call tomorrow." He sounded dismissive. "You really should give Amber a chance."

I took a deep breath and a sip of my scotch. "Okay, I'll try…and say, tell her she owes me a bottle of wine," I said, laughing, trying to lighten the mood. Then the thought dawned on me: should she be drinking? I knew Michael wasn't supposed to be drinking while on his meds. I decided to pick that battle another time. Michael was a Taurus, a stubborn man's man, and he would put me in my place if I went too far. He was still my big brother and there was always a certain amount of respect I would always give him.

"Come on out eat on the balcony with us. It's a gorgeous evening."

"You two should get started. I'll come out later," I lied.

"You sure? We can wait for you." I hated how easily he used the words "us" and "we" when it came to that bitch. Although I was starving, the last thing I wanted was to sit outside and make small talk with that Amber.

"No, go ahead and get started," I said.

I watched Michael go out on the balcony as Amber stood up and kissed him, at the same time handing him a glass of wine. The red flag was up when I saw Michael take a long sip. He was drinking, too!

Chapter 18
Jacqueline

Today was a big day on the show. I was heading to an "actor's retreat" for the next few days. This was how the entire cast would finally meet. I was looking forward to that, and I was also looking forward to spending three days at the location, a fabulous mansion in the Pacific Palisades. My car was packed with my Louis Vuitton luggage, filled with the best of my clothing, shoes, and handbags. You would have thought I was staying for a few months. A sistah had to make sure she had options. I also needed to make sure I slayed in every single scene I was in. The higher I drove up the street, the more spectacular the ocean view got.

I pulled up to gate of the address that was on the call sheet. I entered the code and the gates slowly opened revealing a show-stopper of an estate. The mansion was all white with a glass facade. You could see directly into the house. The cameramen were waiting for me, their large equipment on their shoulders ready to get me on video. I took a deep breath and got into my "Jacqueline" mode. After all, I was about to meet my competition.

Although this show purportedly had an ensemble cast, I knew that when it came to reality TV there was a pecking order, and I wanted to make sure I was the queen bee on this set. Bow down, bitches! I laughed out loud at my own foolery. I parked the car at the entrance and began to unload my luggage. I took out the Louis Vuitton wheelie and the shoulder bag. I'd gone with a casual look: white jeans, a white wrap shirt, Jimmy Choo wedges, and a Gucci belt with a silver buckle. Of course, I wore my Chanel earrings and my oversized Tom Ford sunglasses. I was very careful not to get any dirt on my all-white ensemble. I knew the white against my chocolate skin would resonate well on camera.

As I was entering the house, a camera almost hit me in the face. I wanted to cuss the cameraman out but I knew the importance of not breaking the fourth wall. The estate was even more breath-taking from the inside.

The furniture was all white and cream with hints of silver and gold and blue that accentuated the blue ocean, which could be seen from every floor-to-ceiling window. It was the perfect California day. There wasn't a cloud in the sky and there wasn't a hint of smog. Waitstaff greeted me holding a tray with glasses of champagne. Ocean views... champagne.... waitstaff – when I dreamed of heaven, I swear it looked like this! I wanted to run through the and spin around in a reenactment from "The Sound of Music." But I was reminded this was a working gig when I glanced over my shoulder and saw the camera zooming in on my face. It really was amazing how quickly one forgot that there was an entire crew shooting your every move. And I would be damned if I was caught on camera acting like this was my first time in a fabulous ocean-front estate.

After all, I am Jacqueline Motherfucking McKinley! I immediately snapped back into "character" and walked over to the waitress holding the tray of champagne, and before I picked up a glass I asked in my most upscale voice, "This is champagne, not sparkling wine, correct?"

As most common white folks have never met an upscale black bitch, the waitress was taken aback, turning slightly pink, "Yes, ma'am, it's Perrier Jouet."

"Oh, in that case, I'll take two." I walked to window carrying one in each hand. I said, over my shoulder, "I'm assuming there is someone here to take the luggage to my room?" I still hadn't taken off my sunglasses. It was nice to have a layer of protection so I could hide my excitement. The waitress said, "Yes, ma'am, once the rooms are selected the staff will bring it upstairs."

"Rooms selected...?" I took a long swig of champagne and realized if I was indeed sharing this estate I had to make sure my Black ass was the first to pick out a room. My initial reaction was to sprint up the steps, but then since I was on camera I decided to saunter casually up the stairs like I was checking everything out. Clearly, I was the first to arrive. Thank God! I looked for a room with large double doors. Anyone who had stayed in an estate would know the master bedroom was always the farthest down the hall with the largest double doors. I walked down the hallway, and there it was, the master bedroom. It was fit for a queen... me. I put my Celine handbag in the middle of the bed. I took out my cellphone charger and plugged it in. I took out my makeup bag and put it in the bathroom so that it was clear the room was taken. I walked over the glass doors that led to a balcony and went outside. I could smell the ocean and feel the breeze on my cheek. This was really the life. I was beginning to understand why these reality stars became addicted to showing their asses on TV. I was being treated like royalty! I took another sip of champagne and allowed myself to take a moment, making sure my good-side profile was positioned for the camera. I also arched my back a little so the camera behind me could get a full view of the body I worked so hard to maintain. I was going to give these 20-year-old bitches a run for their money. This wasn't so bad after all. Why the hell did I wait so long to do a reality show?

Just as I was beginning to do a mental hallelujah dance, I heard a strong New York accent yelling from downstairs, "Helloooo.... Helllllloooooo.... Who else is here?" A cast mate had arrived. The voice sounded very familiar to me. Before I headed downstairs I pulled down the comforter. I didn't want there to be any misunderstanding that this room was taken. Too bad my luggage wasn't up here yet so I could have hung a few clothes in the closet. But I think my point was made.

I went downstairs and my mouth dropped open when I saw LeTisha from "Love and Hip Hop L.A." She was ghetto fabulous, loud as shit, had a weave down to her butt, and was wearing ripped-up denim booty shorts with a half-top to show her well defined abs and oversized tits. She was overly made up, dark magenta lipstick and all. What the fuck was she doing here? I knew she wasn't a damn actress.

"Who are you?" she said in her thick New York accent. She had the audacity to ask ME who I was? I was about to check this bitch, but I also wasn't stupid. I might be able to fight with my words, but I knew this heifer could kick my ass. I had to slow my role. I decided to act like I didn't know who the fuck she was. Let her know "Love and Hip Hop L.A." was ghetto as hell and beneath me. Although I watched it religiously, she didn't need to know that.

"I'm Jacqueline. Nice to meet you. And you are...?" The look on her face was priceless.

"LeTisha, but my friends call me Tisha." She was looking me up and down and sizing me up.

The waitress came over and offered her a glass of champagne. "I don't drink this bougie shit. Y'all got some tequila in this mothafucka?" The waitress left and came back with a glass of tequila. Tisha downed it and motioned for another one. "What do you do?" she asked as she motioned for another one. This was why those bitches acted like fools on those shows. They were taking shots of tequila. It explained a whole lot!

I needed to be completely coherent so I asked for some Pellegrino. Two glasses of champagne were more than enough.

"I'm an actress..."

"Fo' sho. I knew you looked familiar. What have I seen you in?" I absolutely hated this question. When people asked me that it was a constant reminder I hadn't done shit.

"I've done a bunch of commercials and guest starred on a bunch of shows." I didn't feel like going through the laundry list. And before she could ask, I flipped the script. "How about you?" I still had to pretend like I had no idea who she was.

"I was on 'Love and Hip Hop' and my man cheated on me. The usual. Now I'm ready for a fresh start." We just sat there in silence. This girl couldn't be more than 23 years old. We had absolutely nothing in common.

Thank God the door opened and the next cast mate walked in. And Felecia Skye needed absolutely no introduction. She was popular back in the late 90s/early 2000's, but fell off after her marriage to a corrupt mayor who was now serving time for embezzlement. Her signature color was yellow. She never left the house in anything that wasn't yellow or in the yellow family. She had to be pushing 50, but the bitch looked great. She was proof that Black don't crack. She was no stranger to reality TV. Her wedding was a reality show in its own right. I had met her a few times at various parties and she was always cordial. But I had no idea she was back in the reality show arena. I thought I was the star of this show. There is only one *I* in the word DIVA, so there wasn't room for two of us.

"Well, hello, beautiful ladies." Felecia Skye grabbed a glass of champagne. And yes, you had to say *Felecia Skye*, not just Felecia.

"Oh, my God, I know you!" Tisha ran up to her and gave her the biggest hug. Felecia Skye almost spilled her champagne. I could tell she was annoyed but she was still gracious. "Felecia, I am one of your biggest fans. I can't believe I'm going to be living with Felecia!"

"It's Felecia Skye," she said gently to correct her.

"I know... that's what I said."

"No, you said, Felecia. It's Felecia Skye." Tisha looked at her, then looked at me. She was genuinely confused.

"What the fuck ever. Felecia... Felecia Skye whatever the fuck your name is. Welcome." She shrugged and plopped back down on the couch with an attitude.

"And you are...?" she asked as she came over to shake my hand.

"Jacqueline McKinley, welcome." We shook hands and then Felecia Skye went to the windows to take in the views of the ocean. "This place is beautiful." She turned back to me and asked, "Where do I know you from? You look so familiar."

"We met at a few parties. And auditions." I kept it nonchalant, even though I was feeling extremely inadequate.

"Yes, bitches! Let the party begin!" shouted the literally larger-than-life former comedian Bianca who had just joined the group. Both Tisha and Felicia Skye ran over to give her a hug. Bianca spotted me hanging back and looked me up and down, "Who the fuck are you?"

I looked to my left and looked to my right and didn't respond. When I didn't, she let out a loud-ass laugh. "Psych! I'm just fucking with you... I've seen your commercials and shit." She looked around the room. "This place is off the hook."

So, this was the cast? This is what I signed up for? A show with a young ghetto bitch, an old has-been, and a fat, loud comedian who never made it big. What kind of foolishness was this? This was feeling more like it was being filmed for public access, not Bravo! This was some bullshit.

At this point some random older white woman who resembled Vanna White from "Wheel of Fortune" walked in. "Hello ladies, and welcome!" she said, full of cheer. "The next three days are going to be an intensive acting workshop. We are going to dive into your past and help you shape it to create characters and bring them to life on film. We are going to get those acting chops going!"

I was highly irritated. And before I could think, my mouth took over, "I don't understand. You sound as though we are newbies. I studied acting in college and abroad in London, and she has been in numerous movies." I pointed to Felicia Skye. "I don't understand the purpose of this."

The Vanna White wannabe didn't lose her fake plastic smile, "I understand. But we want to start from the ground up and rebuild those acting muscles." She kept her cheerleader act going. What the fuck was this corny shit? Not only was I sharing the TV screen with bum basic bitches, but was also being treated like some starlet who had just gotten off the bus. This was beginning to be too damn much! All I could say was, "Whatever!"

Then she said, "Why don't you ladies make yourselves at home. Pick out your rooms, and then we can start with our first exercise." She smiled as she exited the room.

"Has anyone seen the bedrooms?" Felecia Skye said.

"I already have my room." I piped up, happy I got here first.

"Oh really, how did you already get a room?" Bianca looked at me like she smelled dog shit.

I wasn't about be steamrolled by these ghetto bitches and I certainly wasn't about to have them check me on national TV. The cameras were still rolling.

"It is what it is... There are more than enough rooms for everyone. I just so happen to have chosen my room."

"All right, ladies, let's just take a look at the rooms before we start to trip." Felecia Skye reasoned. She and the Ghetto Evil Sisters. They went upstairs and I leaned back on the couch and relaxed. I took a deep breath and tried to find the silver lining in this situation, outside of the fact that the house was beautiful.

"Oh, hell nah... Who does that bitch think she is?!" I heard Tisha shriek in her annoying New York accent. And let me be clear. When I say New York accent I'm not talking Upper East Side. I'm talking boogie-down Bronx accent.

Bianca stomped down the stairs, yelling, "Why the fuck does the bitch that nobody knows who the fuck she is get the biggest goddamn room in this motherfucking house?!"

I continued to sit calmly on the couch, my legs crossed, unbothered.

Then Tisha chimed in and got in my face, "You ain't got nothing to say?" I could smell the tequila mixed with a blunt on her breath.

"I am not giving any of you bitches my energy. There are five other rooms in the house. Pick the one you want. Mine is already taken..."

"Now, Jackie – " Felecia Skye tried to chime in in her yellow outfit.

"It's Jacqueline... Only my friends call me Jackie." With that I stood up and walked over to the waitress who looked terrified and took another glass of champagne. "You snooze, you lose! Cheers to new beginnings, ladies!" I lifted my glass for a toast.

"Oh, hell no!" Bianca came up to my face, grabbed the champagne glass and threw it against the wall. I was shocked, mortified, and my first instinct was to grab that fat bitch by her bad weave and throw her out the window. I remembered the cameras in the nick of time. Plus, security guards had come rushing out to hold her back as she screamed in my face. I looked at her and started laughing. Because one, it was funny as hell, and two I didn't want this bitch to think she had one up on me. I was officially done!

"You know what, you bitches can have the room, this house, and this tired-ass show. I don't leave trash in my house long enough for it to stink and I certainly won't live in a playpen with you animals. Toodles, ladies." I calmly went upstairs, grabbed my stuff and came back down the stairs. I looked each of those tired desperate bitches in the eye and made my exit out the front door.

As I walked out the cameras were still on me. I wanted to cuss Linda out for putting me in this position. I wanted to torch Jay's office for getting me associated with the likes of these trashy bitches. I knew this wasn't the right move for me. Not all money was good money. I allowed myself to be pimped and now I was documented as being part of a piece of trash show with bitches that were beneath me.

I never got along with the Black kids at my high school. I was always being taunted for talking "proper" and thinking I was a white girl. They called me names like "Oreo," "Wannabe," and "Tar Baby." This incident had brought back all of those memories.

I ripped off my mic, no longer giving a fuck about breaking the fourth wall. "Can someone bring my car around... Now!" No one was responding so I yelled for the supervising producer, "Diana! I'm done. Take this mic, get my shit out of this rat hole, I'm done!" A few moments later Diana, came running out of the production room in her headset.

"I'm out, Diana. I didn't sign up for this. I don't hang out with ghetto trash. This isn't the show you pitched me. Get my bags from my room and I am out." It was hitting to close to home and I would be damned if the cameras would catch me crying...again!

Tisha, Felicia Skye, and Bianca were now out front watching my mental breakdown. Although I was calm in my delivery I couldn't keep the utter frustration out of my voice. "If this is what show business is I don't want any part of it. I have sold my soul to the devil long enough living for other people and what the fuck they want. And if you bitches had any damn sense you would get the fuck out, too."

I walked up to them and addressed them one by one. "Tisha, people watch you to see you fail. They think you're a big fucking ghetto joke. You're too young to sell out like this. You're better than this. You have your whole life ahead of you. Don't end up a washed-up has-been by the time you're 30. Stop letting these reality shows use and abuse you like men did when you were stripping on the pole. Bianca, you're fat. People like to see the big fat girl make a fool out of herself and be loud ghetto and obnoxious. It makes for great TV, but now what? How far has it gotten you? And Felicia Skye. Felecia, Felecia, Felicia... you have been in this business for three damn decades. Aren't you tired? Don't you just want to finally be you and wear red or black? I'm exhausted for you. Isn't it time to figure out the next move and stop doing the same thing over and over again? It's fucking pathetic."

All three of them stood there gaping at me. My hair was in my face. I combed my hands through it and wrapped it on the top of my head into a topknot. "Diana, where the hell is my car?"

"Ms. McKinley. You are contractually obligated to shoot with us – " she was trying to say it discreetly.

"I don't give a fuuuuuuccccckkkkkk about a goddamn contract. Sue me. I will not stay in this prison and subject myself to these animals. You want a show. Now you have one. I'm OUT! If you do not bring my car around and my luggage I will call LAPD and tell them I am being held here against my will. You fucked with the wrong bitch. I'm done!"

A production assistant come out of the house with my luggage, and a few moments later, my car was pulled around by another production assistant who handed me my keys. I clicked the button for the trunk to open and motioned with a single nod to the production assistant to put my luggage in the truck. At least these motherfuckers didn't think I was about to load my own luggage. Fuck that!

Diana attempted to reason with me again. "Ms. McKinley, I'm begging you to rethink this. This show is nothing without you."

"I agree it sure isn't. But Diana, you have to understand. I went to Hampton University, I have an education, and unlike those bitches I have options. I will NOT make a fool out of myself and subject myself to some bullshit all at the price of fame. I studied abroad in London for Christ's sake. You have a good few days and hours of footage to use. And that's all you're getting from me."

I got in my car and sped the fuck off.

• • •

I stormed into Linda's office and walked right past her little bitch of an assistant. She jumped up from her desk and started running in my direction. "Excuse me, Ms. McKinley, Linda is on a call – "

I put my hand up and said, "Save it!" and barged into Linda's office.

"Linda! We need to talk." Linda motioned that she was on the phone and signaled me to wait. I went to her desk and clicked the button to hang up. "Now!"

"Have you lost your damn mind? I get you the gig of a lifetime and you walk off the damn set?! I was on the phone with the production company trying to fix the mess you've made."

"The bigger question is, have you lost *your* damn mind. How could you put me on a show with a bunch of ratchet, wannabe has-beens!"

"You need to get back to the set."

"I walked off the damn set. I would have never signed up for some shit like that!" I was face-to-face with her when she suddenly started laughing hysterically. She was laughing like Dave Chappelle was doing a standup routine in her office. And then I realized she was laughing at me!

"I don't see anything funny about this situation!"

"It's funny that you think you're better than the other girls on that set. They work more than you, Jackie. I had to beg Jay to even consider using you on the show and now you come barging into my office like you're fucking Dorothy Dandridge? Child... please."

"You have a lot of fucking nerve, Linda. I might not be working but I'm certainly NOT desperate."

"I only took you on as a favor to your mother. If you're not happy with my services you and I can cut ties right now."

"It's too damn late. The ties have been cut. The moment I left that set I knew you didn't have my best interest in mind. You had no problem cashing in the 15 percent when I was booking commercials left and right. Instead of finding me real work, you booked me on some bullshit. You are motherfucking fired, Linda. One day you'll be groveling to have me back as a client but it will be too fucking late!"

I slammed the door so hard leaving the office that the glass almost shattered. What had I just done? I cussed out a production company, I cussed out and fired my manager, I cashed the check for the show I just walked out on, and I had no idea how the hell I was going to pay them back. My reality started hitting me hard. This was my life. This is what it had become.

Chapter 19
Simone

"Can we take a break? I need to catch my breath before we hit the stairs." I needed a moment to sit down. My knee was still throbbing from my fight with Travis. Each step was painful. I was still nauseated too. But this hike with Taylor and Jackie was a great distraction, and the views from this part of Runyon Canyon were spectacular.

"Damn, Simone, usually we are trying to keep up with your ass," Jackie said as she kept jogging in place. She looked at her Apple watch. "Cool... got my 10,000 steps in." She stopped jogging and sat down next to me.

"I can't believe you cussed out the whole crew and that bitch Linda, Jackie. Now, this is some shit you need to write about!" Taylor stood in front of us stretching her legs and arms.

"It had to feel so damn liberating. I am so proud of you. I hate to ask this next question... but now what? What's your next step?" I planned out every single area of my damn life. But Jackie lived life by her own rules and marched to the beat of her own drum, even if it was not in sync with the rest of the band. A part of me admired that about Jackie.

"Well..."

"Well, what? Don't tell me you're doing another reality show," I said, attempting a joke. Taylor shot me a look. "Too soon?" I slouched down and mouthed *sorry*.

"No, smart ass. I was thinking I could take Angelique up on her offer."

"What? You know you can't work for your mother. That would drive you to insanity for sure!"

Although I was one of Angelique McKinley's biggest fans, there was no way she could be seriously considering her mother's offer.

Now me, on the other hand, I would have jumped at the opportunity to run a McKinley West Coast office. Jackie's mom and I were cut from the same cloth. We often joked that we had been switched at birth and my mother was actually her mother and vice versa.

"I have to agree with Simone," Taylor said. "You know how your mother is. Are you sure she didn't orchestrate this entire reality TV stunt just to make you quit acting?"

"If it wasn't so utterly crazy, I might believe that, but even Angelique couldn't have created that type of foolery. I have to be honest, girlfriends, I'm considering it. I'm sure I will owe legal fees for quitting the show."

"Oh shit, Jackie. How are you going to pay them back?" Taylor and I were well aware of Jackie's overspending and her financial situation. She had been financially irresponsible since college. I remember the day there was a campus fair and the various credit card companies were taking applications for credit cards. Jackie filled out seven different applications, was approved, and then went on lavish shopping sprees until all her new cards were maxed out. And now, though she was struggling she would show up for drinks with us wearing, say, brand-new Gianvito Rossi heels and carrying a new YSL clutch. Knowing her, she'd probably already spent the $25,000 check from the Goldstein company.

"I have no idea. The production company started calling me early this morning. And I have been ignoring them." At that moment her phone vibrated. The held it up to show us it was the production company calling her again. "See...? I have no idea what I'm going to do..."

"You can't ignore them forever. You're going to eventually have to figure out a plan."

"No shit, Sherlock! Obviously!" She rolled her eyes in annoyance.

"I'm sorry, I don't mean to kick you while you're down," I said.

"I know. I didn't mean to take it out on you, Simone. To be honest, I'm terrified. I have no money, I have no savings, I have taken out payday loans to pay my rent. I haven't been the most mature about my financial decisions and it's all coming down on me. That's the honest to God truth ladies. I've fucked up my life." I had never seen Jackie look so deflated. This was the first time in almost two decades of friendship she was completely honest about her money woes. As she rested her head on my shoulder, I looked over at Taylor and she shrugged as if to say *What should we do?*

Taylor got up and squatted in front of Jackie. "No, you haven't, you have pursued your dreams and you were trying to survive. Don't be so hard on yourself"

"We won't allow you to play that tape, Jackie. You're not a fuck-up. As a matter of fact – I am so proud of you for standing up for yourself and not staying on some toxic reality show set. You didn't sell your soul to the devil for 15 minutes of fame. That's something you should be proud of."

"Thanks, girls. But I think I'm going to take my mom up on her offer. It's time for me to give up acting. It's just not working. If she could sacrifice and make an appearance on this show for me, then I can do the same for her. It's time for me to figure out a Plan B."

We all sat there in contemplative silence, gazing at the view. Sometimes it's nice to sit with your girlfriends and just ponder life and feed off each other's energy.

"Michael is dating this white bitch he met at the psych ward – " Taylor suddenly blurted out after a while.

"What? Michael is dating a white girl? He's never dated white girls!"

"He's barely been here two weeks and he's already become a BAF – " Jackie stopped herself. "I'm sorry, Taylor. I don't mean to insult your brother and be disrespectful... And you say they met at the hospital? How did that happen?"

"I know! I just don't get it. I came home the other day and this bitch was chillin' in my house like she owned the place."

"Is dating another patient even allowed?" I was utterly confused how her brother could have met someone while getting treatment.

"I have no idea. I am thinking about calling his doctor. I'm concerned about this."

"I would be too. Is he at least taking his meds?" I knew the routine. I would have never known about mental illness had it not been for my friendship with Taylor.

"I think so. But on the other hand, he's also drinking," she admitted. "I actually stopped bringing alcohol in the house. So now he is rarely home and when he gets home it's late."

"Hanging out with his new 'girlfriend?'" Jackie said, using air quotes.

"Exactly!" Taylor shook her head. "I have no idea what to do. I find myself acting like a nagging pain in the ass."

"I'm so sorry, Taylor. It's all going to work out. At least he's here in L.A. so you can try to keep an eye on it."

"That's true. Who knows what was going on in New York... the city that never sleeps. Thank goodness he can work remotely and is still writing for the magazine. Between the book he's writing and the magazine, he has a few hours of the day where he is forced to be coherent." Taylor shook her head and took a deep breath and continued, turning to Jackie. "Well, enough about that, Jackie. I don't think it's time for you to give up on your dreams. And I certainly know the last thing you need to do is work for your mother.... I'll give you the money to tide you over."

"Are you crazy? I can't accept that. I didn't tell you all this to get money from you. I'm just venting," Jackie said.

"I know that, Jackie. But you are my sister. I have more than enough to help you. That's what friends do. We help each other."

"But Michael is living with you. I know you have extra expenses." Were those tears beginning to form in Jackie's eyes? I had never seen Jackie cry.

"Trust me. All those years of me being frugal and cheap has given me a good nest egg!" Taylor laughed.

"Are you sure?" Jackie asked. "What happens when it's time for your eggs to be in the nest?"

"We'll cross that bridge when we get there. I'm positive," Taylor said.

"And I can give you $5,000," I said. "I have an emergency 'fuck-you' secret account."

"I can't accept your money, ladies," Jackie said, her voice breaking. "To be honest, part of me is embarrassed. I'm embarrassed I have lived my life so irresponsibly... embarrassed that I haven't made it... embarrassed that I have even had this conversation. I'm exposed and so tired of living a lie."

"You have to allow us to help you. Jackie. You would do the same thing. Allow us to help you. You can pay us back when you have it. Your story isn't over, it's just the beginning," Taylor said, taking Jackie's hand.

I grabbed her other hand. "The fact that you are being so open and honest with us right now shows you're ready for a change. I'm proud of you, girl! Don't give up on you, because we haven't."

We all hugged and stood arm and arm at the top of Runyon Canyon, overlooking the city. From this view, the City of Angels looked so peaceful. Yet, there was so much chaos happening out there. I took off my jacket and tied it around my waist. "Are y'all ready to hit the steps? I think I've caught my breath!" I began to jog in place.

"Simone, what happened to your arms?!" Jackie yelled. I had totally forgotten about the bruises I got in my argument with Travis. For the whole hike I'd been trying to hide them.

"It's nothing. I banged my arm on the car door." I jogged over to the steps of Runyon to begin the hardest part of the hike.

"No, Simone... Stop! You're not brushing this off." Jackie was dead-ass serious. I turned around and her hands were on her hips.

"Simone, what's going on?" Taylor begged.

"It's nothing. We just had a disagreement. I pushed too hard. I should have just left it alone. And I said something about his family and he got upset. I shouldn't have even said anything. I know how much he loves his family." Saying the words out loud I realized how pathetic I sounded. I started up the steps.

"Stop, Simone! He's putting his hands on you? This is some bullshit. I will kick his ass!" Jackie was in full on warrior mode.

"You're talking about my husband, Jackie. Not some random I'm dating!" I yelled back.

"Ladies! Stop! We will not do this," Taylor said. "Simone, honey, you have to tell us what's going on. Please! We won't judge you. We are your sisters. Please... what's happening?"

Looking at how upset both of them were, I turned around and slowly walked back to the bench.

"He hates me...I don't even know why he married me. We haven't talked in almost two weeks. When he looks at me, it's with disgust. I'm trying to make things better, but nothing I do works."

"Have you told him how you feel?" Taylor asked.

"Better yet, have you cussed his ass out?!" Jackie said aggressively. "This isn't the Simone we know. Where is the confident you? Don't let this man steal your soul. Tell him how you feel. He knew you weren't a wimp when you married him. Maybe he just needs to be cussed out one good time."

"When I cuss, he stops talking to me."

"Who the fuck cares? He's not the only one in this marriage!" Jackie was making a lot of sense. "And where did he get this violent streak? Is the Bishop at home kicking the first lady's ass?"

"I have no idea. His brother has a streak in him, too." That was a good question, though. Where did Travis and Jacob get this rage from?

"This shit is ridiculous. The fucked-up first family! I told you those religious folks are the biggest hypocrites! They preach one thing and do another." Jackie shook her head. "So now what? You can't just keep taking this shit!"

"Look, Simone, all Jackie is trying to say is, you cannot be a prisoner in your marriage. You need to tell him how you feel. And this – " she said as she held up my bruised arm, " – this is NOT acceptable. I don't care what you say."

"My marriage is falling apart. It's only been six months. I don't know what to do." By now tears were streaming down my face. They both sat next to me on the bench with their arms around me.

"Have you talked to your mother?" Jackie suggested. "You know she would get on the first plane and be here for you."

"I can't. We just spent a shitload of money on this wedding. I don't want to tell her because even she would insist that I leave him."

"Well, yeah..." Jackie clearly agreed with that concept.

"It's only been six months, I know the man that I fell in love with is still there. He is stressed from work. A couple of deals didn't go through and he's just stressed. I'm going to play this out and see what happens." I was trying to convince myself. I looked at Jackie and Taylor. They were really worried. I started crying. "This isn't what I thought marriage was going to be."

"How about counseling?" Taylor suggested.

"He wouldn't to see anyone except his dad. When we got married, his dad was our counselor. When I begged to try outside counseling he went for two sessions and made it seem like I was the problem."

"That's some bullshit. You don't need his family in your business. Do they even know that your sister-in-law fucked another man? I bet you they ain't telling the father that." Jackie was trying hard to contain her anger. "This man and his family are controlling you, Simone."

"This is what I signed up for," I conceded.

"No, it's not. You didn't sign up to get mistreated."

"You love this man. And if he loves you he will listen to what you have to say. I'm worried Simone, I'm really worried about you."

"We both are," Taylor said. "You need to take your power back. Where is the Simone we know and love? Tell him how you feel. We aren't judging you. We are just worried."

I took a deep breath and looked at both of them. "I don't know how much longer I can do this. I think I've made a mistake. I think I need to get a divorce." It was the first time I'd said it out loud. Or even thought it.

"Simone, we won't judge you if you decide to walk away." Taylor's voice was so calming.

"I know... I know, you're right. But it's only been six months!"

"Who gives a shit?! Better to get out at six months than wake up in your sixties and realize you have been stuck in a loveless marriage to an asshole." Jackie was adamant.

"I don't want to be single and 40. Who wants to date a woman in her 40s in L.A.?" That was the truth of the situation. I was terrified of being alone, super successful but with no man.

Taylor cocked her head to the side and looked at me like I was crazy. "You really gotta stop with that shit. You're beautiful, have a banging body, you're successful, and fun. You will be fine."

"We got your back, Simone," Jackie said, standing up to embrace me.

"You got this," Taylor reassured me. "Now let's ditch this hike and go home."

We walked back to our cars. Before I got in my car, I felt the nausea hitting me again. I threw up on the ground and leaned against a tree for a few minutes. I hadn't even told them the American Express part of my troubles.

Chapter 20
Jacqueline

When I got home I checked my email, and both Taylor and Simone had already wired the funds to my checking account. I went straight to my closet and began pulling out my designer clothes. I had so many of them, some of them still had tags. I pulled out Seven7 Jeans and Joe Jeans that I hadn't worn for 20 years. I pulled out five pairs of Louboutins that I only wore once before I gave in to the fact that they hurt my damn feet and gave me corns on my pinky toe. I took out evening dresses by Ralph Lauren and Tahari that I bought for my corporate gigs. By the time I finished I had five big bags of clothes filled. I dragged them into my car and drove up the street to Crossroads Trading Company. I had gone there many times when I needed cash to tide me over until my next paycheck. The manager went through my items and I left there with a check for $3,000. Some of the items were on consignment and I would get paid once she sold them.

It didn't make sense for me to be wearing designer clothes when my friends had to loan me money. This was the new and improved Jacqueline McKinley. I drove back home and the sight of my almost empty closet sent me into a panic attack. My addiction to designer labels was all about impressing other people and making people envy me. I bought those clothes to play the part of the fabulous Jacqueline McKinley, the movie star, the Hollywood actress. All I was at this very moment was Jackie... no savings, no husband, no kids, no property, bad credit, and living paycheck to paycheck.

Linda did have one thing right. I wasn't any better than those other girls on the set. I might have been able to fake it better because I was a trained actress. But they actually had more going for themselves than I do. I looked at my reflection in the full-length mirror. It was not who I was. I had no idea who this woman was sitting on my bed staring back at me in the mirror. I got up and walked closer and stared at my face. My complexion was perfect, though I could see a few hints of 40. My eyes had lost their innocence, replaced by the "experience" and "life lived" of a woman in her 40s. This person I was looking at felt like a stranger. Most of my life was spent studying and becoming other people. When I got a script, I picked apart the character's life. I made up their backstory, their insecurities, their fears, their wants and desires. I had never done that for myself. And clearly, reality TV wasn't the best place to figure that shit out. I needed to figure out who Jacqueline McKinley really and truly was. She deserved the same care I put into all those characters I played over the years.

I sat back down on my bed and took a deep breath. *What's next for me? Who am I? Where do I go from here?*

The ringing phone snapped me back to the here and now. More than likely it was someone from the production team trying to track me down. Those folks didn't take no for an answer. I let it go to voicemail. I wasn't quite ready to return to reality.

I stretched out for a few more minutes and then grabbed my phone, prepared to listen to another message about how I was reneging on the contract and blah... blah... blah. I gritted my teeth and pressed play to listen to the new voicemail:

This message is for Jacqueline McKinley. This is Dr. Connors. I'm calling from Cedars-Sinai Hospital. You were listed as Angelique McKinley's emergency contact. Your mother has been admitted to the hospital...

I dropped the phone. "Oh, my God!" I shouted. I didn't even bother listening to the rest of the message. Without hesitation, I grabbed my bag and ran to my car.

•   •   •

Reception gave me my mother's room number. I ran through the hallways of the hospital, sweating. When I finally found Room B-1032, there was my mother, the great, strong Angelique McKinley, lying in a hospital bed, connected to tubes.

She was bald! Her head was shiny and smooth. A wig lay on the night stand beside the bed. How could this be? This didn't make sense. I was just with her a few days ago and she looked wonderful, as always. She had no makeup on and her skin had a slightly gray tinge that she could have covered with makeup. She was sleeping. I took her hand. She slowly opened her eyes. When she saw me, she managed to force a smile in her delirious state.

"Mommy, what happened?"

An older man, slightly balding, walked in. He wore a doctor's white jacket, glasses, and sneakers. He had to be in his late seventies, but he had a hipness to him.

"You must be Jacqueline. Your mother speaks so highly of you. I'm Dr. Connors."

I shook his hand and then I looked back at my mom who was sleeping again. "What is going on?" He walked me outside of the room.

"Your mother has stage 4 brain cancer. She came here for a special treatment this hospital gives. We managed for a while to keep it contained but it has spread to the lungs, liver, stomach, and kidneys. Her body hasn't handled the treatment well. She didn't want me to call you until it was necessary. I felt like now was the time for you to know," he said gently. He went into some other medical talk but I couldn't hear a thing. His lips were moving but I couldn't hear a word. I was paralyzed with shock. My mother...cancer... chemo.

This just couldn't be happening. Everything was going in slow motion. The world was silent except for the sound of my heart beating. Boom...boom... boom-boom. Boom-boom. The room was spinning. I regained focus when it started to register what the doctor was saying.

"How long?" I asked. "How long does she have?" I said slowly.

Dr. Connors gave me the look that everyone fears. It was that look doctors give when you know they are about to deliver more bad news on top of bad news. I leaned against the wall and prepared for the worse. "Give or take, three months. She has decided not to do any more chemo, and now it's just up to us to give her the best quality of life during the time she has left."

"How about alternative treatments... acupuncture... herbs... surely there is something that can be done." I wasn't about to take this bad news for gospel. "I'd rather you say a slow yes than a fast no." I had fallen into using my mother's lingo.

"Angelique had already done alternative treatments prior to deciding to move forward with chemo. And they worked at keeping her comfortable for a while. But the cancer has been too aggressive. At this point the chemo will give her another month, maybe two months, but her quality of life will not be enjoyable, for lack of a better word."

This couldn't be happening. This explained why she appeared in L.A. unexpectedly. This also explained why she wanted me to take over the business. Not my mommy! Dr. Conner patted my shoulder. He had a nice bedside manner for a doctor. He wasn't cold and distant like so many doctors are. I started to pull it together. My mother didn't need to see me break down. "Thank you, Dr. Connors," I said and shook his hand.

"I'll give you a few minutes with her, and then we'll discuss treatment options." I watched him walk down the hallway. And it became quite clear, this wasn't a dream.

I began that counting exercise I did with Taylor over the phone. "1-2-3-4." I did it 3 times and took 3 deep breaths. It was working until I went back into my mother's room and I pulled a chair next to her bed and took her hand. She immediately woke up.

"Mom, why didn't you tell me sooner?" I asked.

"I didn't want to bother you. I didn't want you worrying about me. And I didn't want my clients to know and lose business," she said weakly.

"Oh Mommy, to hell with the clients!"

"Work and clients have kept me busy. It's nice to keep busy and not have to think about this."

"If you wanted me to take over the business you didn't have to go and get cancer!" My feeble attempt at a joke got a chuckle out of her. I laid my head on her shoulder. "Oh, Mommy, you can't leave me. I need you." Then I thought about my sister, Julia. "*We* need you!"

"I know, baby, I know," she said as she stroked my hair. "You know I love you, Jacqueline. We may not see eye to eye, but know I love you and I want the best for you."

"Does Julia know?" I asked.

"Not yet. I hadn't told anyone, I thought I could... I have been successful at so much in my life. I thought I could beat cancer. And I tried, but, well...."

I didn't want her to finish that thought. "I understand. I'll talk to Julia." This was my time to become the big sister. I had no idea how she was going to react. I looked at my mother lying helpless. I felt guilty for every bad thing I'd ever said about her. I felt guilty for the times I mocked her ambition. I felt guilty for not being the boss bitch she wanted me to be. I should have taken over her damn company. I felt selfish. I felt like the most self-interested bitch on the planet.

"I'm so sorry, Mommy. I am so sorry I haven't been the daughter you want me to be."

"That is not true! I admire you for following your dreams. You don't think I support you, but I do. If you want to do that show, then do it."

"Mommy, we don't need to talk about the show anymore. I quit it and now I absolutely know it was the right decision. These next few months are important."

"What do you mean, 'quit?'"

"It wasn't what I thought it was going to be, Mom. You were right – I was making a big mistake."

"Jacqueline... we are not quitters! I don't know what happened but I won't allow you to quit," she said, attempting to sit up in bed.

"Mom, you are my priority. To hell with that show!"

"I appreciate that, but you must finish what you started. And I will be here to support you in whatever way I can."

"What are you saying?" I was so confused.

"What I am saying is if we can inspire people and touch people with our story, then I think this show won't be the disaster you make it out to be."

"But Mommy –"

"Please let me finish." She had a coughing spell. I picked up the cup of crushed ice that was next to her bed and rubbed a few pieces on her dry lips, and then put a few bits of the ice in her mouth. "I want to be there for you, Jacqueline. I want to show you that I care."

"Are you sure about this, Mommy? Are you sure you want all this to be documented?" I asked, indicating the hospital room with my hand.

"I love you, Jacqueline. And for you, yes. I am willing to do that," she said. "I'm not gone yet. We have some time."

Dr. Conners came into the room, accompanied by a young blonde a woman in black slacks and a black sweater set. He pulled up a chair on the other side of my mom's bed. "This is not the easiest part of my job. But we need to discuss hospice options. This is Sara, and she handles hospice care for the hospital. I'll leave you all to discuss."

Sara sat down and opened one of the folders she was carrying. "There are quite a few options..." She started to hand us a brochure.

I stood up. "Absolutely not! I'm not putting her in hospice. She can stay with me."

"Ms. McKinley, your mother needs 24-hour care and treatment. This is something you can't take on by yourself," Sara calmly said.

"Jackie, please listen to her. Go on." My mother motioned for her to continue and took the brochure.

"I think you will like this location, Mrs. McKinley. It is in Malibu and has beautiful views of the ocean. The staff is top-notch. Their goal will be to make you as comfortable as possible."

I looked at the brochure with my mother. The brochure did all it could to make death "happy." It's a damn hospice and the models were smiling like it was happy time. Like people at a resort for vacation.

"Okay... when can I check in?" Even in her sick state she was still about business.

"They will have your room ready in a week," Sara said.

Mom took a deep breath and closed her eyes. "Okay... Okay..."

It seemed to me that being in this hospital was making her worse. Maybe all she needed was some fresh air and some time in the Neiman Marcus shoe department and she would be back to her normal self. I wasn't accepting this shit! I refused to accept that my mother was going to die. No!

"In the meantime, can we check her out of here?" The hospital room was so depressing. "I can arrange for a full-time nurse to attend to her at my apartment while we wait for her room to become available in hospice. I don't want her sitting in a hospital." I was surprised by how I was suddenly so about business myself.

"We can arrange for that," Dr. Connors said. "I'll have the hospital draw up the discharge paperwork for tomorrow and work with admin to get home care set up for the next week."

"Thank you, doctor."

"Mommy, we are going to make these the best months of your life. I promise you that." I took her hand in mine and kissed it and held it to my cheek.

I sat there with my mother for what seemed like hours, until she fell into a deep sleep. My mother was dying, but I was going to do everything I could to make her last days golden.

Chapter 21
Taylor

The tea kettle started to whistle. I made a cup of chamomile tea, with extra honey, ginger, and lemon in it. I took it over to the couch where Jackie was sitting staring into space.

"You're going to get through this," I said.

"I just can't imagine how it feels to know you're dying. I just can't imagine…" She started crying again.

"I know… I know. Get it all out. It's okay to cry, Jackie. I'd rather you have your moment now with us." It hurt me to see my friend hurting like this. I couldn't help but think about when my mom passed away.

"So, let's think of a plan." Simone was in business mode. I could see Jackie tense up.

"Don't start, Simone. My mother is dying and you're about to take out your day planner and make a plan?"

"Simone, this clearly isn't the time for that," I agreed.

"I'm not trying to be disrespectful. I just feel that if we're going to make these next few months the best months of her life then we do just that. I think we should plan a trip somewhere for the two of you… we throw her a birthday party… we take her to some of her favorite spots until she can't do it any longer." She knelt down in front of Jackie. "Allow me to be your strength while you are weak, like you have been for me." Her sincerity was real. This was the old Simone, not the weak, submissive, insecure Simone we had been forced to be around lately. Instead, this was the confident Simone that kept things going at the hardest of times. I hoped she would stay for a while.

"You would do that for me?" Jackie asked just above a whisper.

"Of course, I would. I am doing it for us. You are my sister, you are my friend. We got you. You're going to get through this," she said as she took her hand and my hand.

I repeated, "We got you, Jackie."

•   •   •

After the girls left I went to the gallery do business. After that all I wanted to do was go home, pour myself a glass of scotch and go to bed. As I approached my loft the sounds of "Black Coffee" played at top volume boomed to welcome me. I turned the key to the loft and was greeted by wonderful smells of cooking. I turned the music down.

"What's up, T-Squito!" Michael bounded from the kitchen and put his arms around me. I was surprised that he was at home, considering that he spent most of his time hanging out with that Amber bitch, or she was here, acting like she was paying my mortgage.

"I have created an entire menu tasting for you!" Indeed, he had created a feast, a gourmet feast. Branzino, sea bass, chicken, shrimp skewers, a turkey – a full-on fucking thanksgiving turkey! – kale salad, Caesar salad, grilled octopus, seafood pasta, fettucine alfredo. Everything that was in my fridge and cabinets had been cooked. I was stunned. But most of all, I was concerned. He was more hyper than I had ever seen him. He described each dish in detail. "Here, try this…" he took a forkful of branzino and fed me a piece.

"Are you expecting guests?"

"No, no, I was just trying out some different recipes. I have renewed passion for cooking." He started mixing the various pots and pans he had going on the stove.

I looked at his eyes, which were bloodshot. "You good?" He couldn't keep still.

"Yeah! Why do you ask?" He started slicing the turkey. "I'm great!" He grabbed a plate from the cabinet and handed it to me. "Here, fix yourself a plate."

I slowly took the plate from him. "Michael, what are we going to do with all this food?"

"The good thing about a lot of this is you can freeze it. And I know you're always hanging out with your girls so you can bring some to them. And I'll take some to Amber. You know she loves my cooking...in addition to other shit!" he laughed slyly. He was all over the place. He was opening the lids to the pots, putting more seasoning on the fish, sampling the turkey, stirring the pasta. It was exhausting watching him.

"So, what do you think?"

"Everything is delicious, Michael, I'm just trying to understand why you felt the need to cook everything in the house."

"You know when you have those moments when you're craving more than just one thing? Well... I was craving all of this so I decided to test it out. Amber and I are going to open a restaurant together," he said. He leaned on the counter and crossed his arms, a big goofy smile on his face.

"What?! Why would you open a restaurant, and more important, why would you open a restaurant with a bitch you barely know?"

"I'm going to need you to stop calling the woman I love that name, T!" He was agitated.

"You barely know her. What about Tammy? She's been there for you for years and then you come to L.A. and forget about her because of this this trashy white bitch? What about loyalty?"

"I don't see color. All I see is love." He sounded pathetic. He sounded like my father.

I lifted my hands in protest. "Really... really... well, good for you. When a cop shoots your Black ass just for being Black I bet you'll see color then!"

"You don't like Amber because she is white!" This was the typical bullshit Black men who dated white women used to justify themselves. He was acting just like my father.

"That's one of the reasons why I'm pissed. The affection you should have shown to Tammy, you're showing to this podunk trash! It's not right. You're damn right, I'm pissed!"

"I can't help who I fall in love with."

"Yes, you can!" I threw my plate in the sink and headed to my studio. This day had been just too emotional and I needed a few hours to escape the world.

"Where are you going? You haven't even tried half the shit I made!" he yelled.

"I need a fucking break!" I yelled back and stomped out like a big kid.

I went into my sanctuary, my oasis. I dimmed the lights, turned on some Atjazz, lit a few candles, and sat on the floor in front of a blank canvas in the lotus position. I closed my eyes and took long, deep slow breaths. In the background I could still hear the clanging of pots and pans. I tried to focus on my breathing and tune it all out. But it was impossible. My vibe was off between thinking about Jackie and her mother, hearing the banging in the background, and knowing that my brother was in a state of mania. Opening a restaurant, writing a book, pursuing Amber...I couldn't focus and knew I wouldn't be able to paint. Urgh! I got up, blew out the candles, turned off the lights and went upstairs to my room.

•　　•　　•

In the morning I threw on a pair of jeans, a Prince off-the-shoulder T-shirt, and my All Stars. In the kitchen, Michael was at the computer typing away. It was clear he hadn't slept.

"Good morning," he said sheepishly.

"Morning..." There was nothing good about this morning.

"Look T, I'm sorry about last night."

"Water under the bridge, Michael," I said, as I turned on my Keurig. "Did you want some breakfast? We have plenty of leftovers." I rolled my eyes in exaggerated fashion.

"I see in addition to being one of the great American artists of our time, you haven't lost your talent for sarcasm," Michael said, still typing away.

I saw his meds on the counter and discreetly opened the morning bottle and dropped a pill into a glass of orange juice. If this was the only way I could get him to take his meds... well, then so be it!

"Here, at least have some orange juice." I handed him the glass. "Did you get some rest?" His bloodshot eyes told all.

"You know once you get hit with your creative wave, you have to ride it before it's too late," he said. "Besides, I'm at the most intense part of the book."

"Even Shakespeare took a nap or two." I finished my coffee. "Next time you decide to do a tasting menu, could you at least give me advance notice so I can invite some folks over? The food was delicious, but I hate to see it go to waste."

"Yes... sir... Mr. Taylor, sir!" He saluted me.

"I really hate when you do that. I just don't like wasting food. Damn!"

"I heard you the first time, T! You done, drill sergeant?" He went back to his computer and continued typing.

"Whatever, asshole!" I flicked my two middle fingers at him and he flicked his right back at me. This was just like when we were kids and he had pissed me off. I went to my studio to paint, and get away from two kids pretending to play grown-up.

• • •

When I emerged a few hours later, Michael was gone. I checked his room and was shocked to find it a mess. This was not normal at all for him. His room had been immaculate in the first few weeks staying with me, now there were clothes all over the floor, including a pair of panties and a bra – obviously Amber's. My house was being disrespected not just by him, but by that whorish interloper. I picked up Michael's clothes to put them in the hamper and as I picked up his jeans a small plastic bag with white substance fell out of the pocket. I bent down to pick it up from the floor, and there it was, cocaine. Motherfucking cocaine! I knew it, I knew this bitch was no good for him! I would have been more understanding if it was weed, but cocaine? This was next-level shit. So Michael had been smoking and drinking – AND now he was using drugs!

I sank down on the bed, paralyzed with anger, disappointment, and fear of what this meant. I took the packet and flushed it down the toilet. I had decisions to make.

• • •

At Huntington Memorial Hospital I went straight to the receptionist and demanded to see Dr. Sanders.

I couldn't sit. I paced back and forth, waiting for him. He looked perplexed when he emerged from behind the double doors.

"Tim," I said, not even giving him a chance to say hello. "I know I should have called ahead of time. I know you have a very full schedule, but please, may I have a few minutes of your time?"

"No need for apologies, Taylor. Let's take a walk," he said as he ushered me through the sliding glass doors outside. I was relieved we went this way rather than going back to his office in the mental ward.

We walked through the garden of the hospital, which had lovely grounds I'd never noticed.

"Thanks so much for seeing me. I just had to go with my gut – " I started.

"It's okay! I'm glad I was here and available. As a matter of fact, I was planning on reaching out to you this week." He motioned for me to sit with him on a bench.

"You were?"

"Michael hasn't shown up for his last four appointments."

"Oh no, that's just what I was worried about. It's obvious he's not taking his meds and he is in a manic state right now. And I think he is self-medicating with other substances."

"Like what?"

"He's using cocaine," I said, cutting to the chase. I told Tim about the scene last night. He listened intently. "And I am concerned about his relationship with Amber, the woman he met here."

"Amber Wescott?"

"Is that her name?" Tim looked flustered. He'd violated patient confidentiality policy by saying her last name. "Were you aware they've been seeing each other since they were released?"

"No, I wasn't."

"She's bad news. I feel it in every fiber within me. What is her deal?" I leaned in closer so Tim could let me in on it.

"Taylor, I cannot give you patient information."

"I understand that, but I need to get her away from Michael. She's a bad influence."

"I'm sure you realize Michael is an adult. He's responsible for his own actions. There is only so much you can do."

"But Tim, I need your help. I don't know what to do. Can you help me get him to start coming to his appointments? Is there any way I can force him to be readmitted for a longer period of time?"

"I understand your concern, but involuntary hospitalization is only considered if the courts find the patient to be a grave danger to himself and others and is not functioning."

"This is grave danger! You know what happens once he's out of the manic state. That depression state is next. This is clearly dangerous." I didn't try to mask my frustration.

"Well, patients have rights and judges typically rule in favor of the patients."

"This just doesn't seem fair!"

"I'm sorry, Taylor. I know this is difficult. The most we might do is put him on another 72-hour hold, but that would have to be based on whether he presents a clear threat and that isn't the case right now."

I took a deep breath and leaned back in the bench. "I feel so hopeless. I thought having him here in L.A. would make things easier. I don't know what to do. I even put his meds in his orange juice this morning." I admitted.

"You have to careful with that, especially if he is using other substances. Coke mixed with the meds could trigger severe reactions..."

"Please, Tim. You're my last hope!" I begged. He looked at me as if he were evaluating me. "Please?" I put my hand on his shoulder.

"All right. This isn't something I normally practice but I want you to feel supported. Let's clarify the problem. What is it you want to accomplish with this meeting?" he said in stern doctor mode.

"I want him to agree to take his meds, stop using drugs and go to his appointments." I was very clear on that.

"Are you prepared for him to say no? I can come help you with this intervention, but you have to be very clear with him on the consequences if your boundaries are not respected. What would the consequences be if he refuses?"

"If he doesn't agree to it..." I took a beat. I wasn't prepared to say it out loud, but I had to. "If he doesn't agree to it, then I will have to ask him to leave." I couldn't bear the thought. At least having him in my house, I knew where he was. "On the other hand, I think it will work out. I think an intervention with you there will make him realize that he needs to take his treatment plan seriously."

"Okay, Taylor. Let's do it."

Chapter 22
Simone

I didn't realize how long I'd been sitting in my car in the driveway, thinking after I left Taylor's. My heart ached for Jackie. To find out the great Angelique McKinley had brain cancer really shook me to the core. It made it even more evident that life was way too short to be unhappy. That led to me thinking I couldn't live my life like this anymore, and I was ready for the conversation I needed to have with Travis. He was home, his car was in the garage. Maybe when I went into the house he would greet me with a hug, kiss, and an apology. Maybe he'd been having a bad couple of weeks with all the financial shit he was dealing with, which I was still in the dark about. Maybe this time things would be different. Maybe...

He was in the family room, watching "SportsCenter." His tie was loosened, he was wearing his glasses and his feet were up. He looked super-duper comfortable. Maybe the timing was right, maybe he would acknowledge me and admit that this no-speaking passive-aggressive shit was immature. He looked at ease...

Then he realized I was in the room. I could see his shoulders tense up and the expression change to one that reeked of annoyance. I changed course, and went to the kitchen and put my keys and purse down, and took off my shoes. I poured myself a glass of water, closed my eyes, and practiced what I was going to say. I went back to the living room and stood in front of the TV.

"Travis, we need to talk," I said, forcing my old confidence into my voice.

"You're blocking the TV," he said flatly.

I wanted to say "Fuck the TV!" but I knew if I went there the conversation was over. So I went with the speech I practiced. "Travis, I can't live like this. I've tried to give you your space. But I am in the dark. I need to know what's going on with Amex."

"That's none of your business!"

"It *is* my business. I am paying half the bills here; I am your wife, for God's sake!" My voice was getting louder.

"Then act like one," he said.

I was floored. "What does that mean, Travis? Am I not a good wife to you? Am I not making you happy? What am I not doing? Tell me! What do you mean?!" I could feel myself shaking. "Please. Tell me what I'm not doing so we can fix this."

He leaned to the side so he could see the TV and used the remote to turn up the volume.

"No! You're going to talk to me." I went to the couch and grabbed for the remote to turn down the TV. He pushed me away. "Oh, so you're going to push me away?! You are going to talk to me! We are going to have this conversation whether you like it or not!"

I ran to the rack of electronic equipment and began to pull the cable box off the shelf. Travis then came from behind and shoved me aside. I fell to the floor and watched him sit back down and turn up the volume to the loudest decimal. And that's when it happened, I snapped.

"Fuck you, you bastard! You're going to listen to me, damn it! You're going to listen! I'm tired of this shit. Why did you marry me? You're a fucking asshole. I hate you, you're a piece of shit." I grabbed the glass of water I poured for myself and threw it at him. That got his ass up off the couch. I followed him into the kitchen, where he was going to dry off the remote, and his pants. I took the plates that were in the kitchen sink and started throwing them on the floor. I was having an out-of-body experience. I saw myself screaming at the top of my lungs as I was crashing plates, spoons, glasses on the floor. "You fucking asshole! I'm going to fucking kill you! Fuck you, fuck your brother and his whore-ass wife. You probably fucked her too. Fuck you, fuck you! I HATE YOU! YOU LISTEN TO ME GODDAMN IT! LISTEN TO ME!!!!"

Everything I ever thought and held in was spewing out of my mouth. "You want a divorce I'll give you one and I'll take you for everything you've got! You piece of shit!" Before I knew it, Travis had grabbed me and was dragging me to the door. I was kicking and screaming and hitting him. I even bit him. I was an animal. I knew why the caged lion roared... I was roaring and I couldn't stop myself. He opened the door, threw me out, then slammed it shut and locked it. I started pounding on the door, screaming, "Let me in, goddamn it!" I kept banging on the door, kicking it, screaming.

I don't know how much time passed in that state but at a certain point I lost all my energy and stopped banging. My own spirit reentered my body. I realized I was outside, barefoot. I have no idea how long this episode lasted. I looked up at our security cameras, looking dead at me. So Travis could see that I had calmed down. I waited a few minutes to see if he would come to the door and let me in. I gently knocked on the door and waited for Travis to come open it. Surely, he was going to let me back inside...

I gave it a few moments and knocked again. "Travis, open the door," I said in a low voice. He didn't. I didn't know what to do. I just sat on the bench on our porch waiting for him to let me in, and the longer I sat the longer it felt. It had to have been a good hour. It was dark and I didn't know where to go or what to do. I had no shoes, no purse, no car keys no cellphone. I tried knocking again... useless.

At this point I had no other choice. I walked barefoot two blocks over to his brother Jacob's house. I didn't know where else to go. I knocked on his door and Jacob answered. obviously on the phone with Travis. He beckoned me in. Even though I was desperate I still felt animosity toward him. I felt like 70 percent of our issues had to do with him and his wife. And I refused to allow him to feel like he was helping me.

"No, I don't need to come in. Could you please tell your brother to at least give me my purse and my car keys?"

Jacob said into the phone, "Travis, come on, man, let her have her keys and purse." I could tell by the interaction over the phone his brother was able to get through to him. Before he could say anything else to me, I walked the two blocks back to my house in my bare feet. I reached our doorway and there was my purse in front of it. I picked it up and my car key dropped to the ground.

Travis had taken my housekeys off the key ring and just given me my car key. I tried the door again and it was still locked. I knocked and waited. I still didn't have any shoes! I couldn't believe this was happening. I remembered that my gym bag was in the trunk of my car and my shower slippers were in it. I grabbed the slippers and got in the car. I didn't know where to go. I didn't want to bother Taylor because I knew she was dealing with her brother. I didn't want to go to Jackie because she was dealing with her mother and preparing her apartment for her mom to get discharged.

I started the car and just began driving.

When I got to a stop sign, I went to take my cellphone from my purse so I could call my mother. I wanted to tell her what happened. She would help me; she would know what to do. I kept digging until it dawned on me that Travis had taken my phone out of my purse. I looked in the mirror and my hair was uncombed. My mascara was smeared. I looked like a lunatic. I figured I would check into a hotel. At least I could get a good night's rest and pull myself together. I would call in sick to work tomorrow, even though I had a major presentation. I went back to my purse and then realized Travis had taken out my wallet too. I had no ID, no money, no credit cards, no phone. I had nothing. I pulled over to the side of the freeway

This couldn't be happening. This is just a bad dream. I'm going to wake up and realize I was only having a nightmare. I sat there for a good hour. Then I made an executive decision to go to the only place that made sense.

• • •

The moment my mother-in-law opened the door and forced out a "Hello," I knew I had made a mistake. I didn't think this decision through. I wanted to talk to Daddy Lee. He was always supportive, an advocate for me. And since Travis had forced us to do our pre-marital counseling with him, I figured I could talk to him about everything that was going on and he would help us. In addition to being my father-in-law he was my pastor. But somehow, I forgot about the fact that Karen would be there and want to know what happened to her baby boy. I should have just gone to Jackie or Taylor. I wanted to turn and run. But it was too late.

"It's cold out there. Come on inside," she said. I could feel her looking me up and down. I was always so put together and now I looked a mess, but I didn't have a choice. The humiliation was starting to make its way into my spirit. Just as I contemplated running, I heard the happy-go-lucky sound of Daddy Lee's booming voice "There's my favorite daughter-in-law!" Once he got close to me and took in my disheveled hair, smeared makeup, and red and tearstained eyes his smile went to a look of distress. "Oh my, what's going on?" he said.

I whispered, "Can I talk to you?" Instead of leading me to his office in the house, he motioned for me to sit on the couch in the living room. And Karen sat right next to him, her mean and judgmental eyes looking me over head to toe. At this point I had nothing to lose, so I told him about the last few weeks. How Travis was ignoring me, how he was treating me. I told them how he drove off with me trying to grab the door handle and I even showed him the scrape and bruises on my knee strangely enough, they didn't have the level of shock I expected. Even amid all of this, I still tried to protect him. I didn't tell them about the alleged fraud with American Express.

The first thing Daddy Lee said after I went through the story was, "What did you do to make him react like this? This isn't like him. What did you say?" And I went through the entire story again, and he said, "You must have said something or done something to make him attack you like this."

I was so confused. This wasn't the Daddy Lee I knew. Karen didn't say anything, she looked down at the floor. And then it clicked... Travis learned this behavior from his father. That would explain why she couldn't stand me. The Bishop was abusive to her. On top of her feeling like I was taking her favorite son away, she resented my independence. And now, here I was, just as helpless.

Daddy Lee came over to the couch and hugged me and I cried in his arms. "Now, now, it's all going to be okay." He got up went to the kitchen and grabbed his keys. "Come on, you need to go home and we are all going to talk."

•　　•　　•

The drive back to my house felt like the longest drive of my life. Daddy Lee' jovial self was replaced with sadness and concern – for his son. When we got there, Daddy Lee used his key and let us in. This was the one time I was glad I lost the fight about his parents having the key to our house and never knocking when they stopped by.

We walked into the house and the evidence of my outburst was all over. I didn't realize how many dishes I had slammed on the floor, or how many glasses I had crashed against the wall until now. And suddenly, his father started sobbing. Loud sobs. Travis came downstairs in his gym shorts and wife beater (that irony wasn't lost on me).

"Why did you go to my dad?" he said angrily, through gritted teeth. He then consoled his dad. And there I stood, alone, embarrassed, ashamed, in pain, bruised, humiliated with no one to comfort me. After a while, they remembered the monster, me, was still in the room. His dad pulled it together and directed us to sit at our kitchen table. We sat down on opposite ends. Travis wouldn't look at me.

"What's going on, son?" he asked.

"She's crazy," Travis said.

I was so embarrassed by my actions, and I didn't want to say the wrong thing. I didn't have anyone there who would take my side. I finally was able to get a few words out. "You won't talk to me. You treat me like you don't even like me."

"Son, you have to talk to your wife. That's not right." It was a weak attempt to defend me but at least it was something. "Son, you two have to work this out. This is your wife. You can't kick her out."

"I'm not comfortable with her staying here. I don't know what she's capable of. I value my life! Do you see this place?" He said as he pointed at the broken glasses and plates on the floor.

His father shook his head in agreement. "You can't react like this, Simone. These things are expensive. You all spent a lot of money to get these things. You can't destroy your home."

"I'm sorry." Was all I could say to his lecture. I sat there with my head down.

"Well, you two are going to stay under the same roof tonight. And alone here may not be safe. So pack up some things and you are both coming with me." Daddy Lee was in full-on "Bishop" mode, taking over the whole situation. I didn't want to go back to his house and have to feel the disapproving looks of Karen. But I found myself dutifully going upstairs to the bedroom and grabbing my items for the night. Daddy Lee followed us like he was a police officer protecting his son in case I had another outburst.

After I packed up my things for the night in my Vuitton overnight bag. I remembered that Travis still had my wallet, cell phone and house keys. "I need the rest of my things, Travis." He reluctantly took my things out of a drawer and gave them to me. Only because his father was standing there.

I got back in the car with his dad and Travis got in his car and followed us back to his parents' house.

His mother was waiting in the kitchen. She had a fresh pot of coffee brewed. Her son fell into her arms. "My baby," she said, over and over. We sat at the table. His father spent the next two hours walking us through the Bible and talking to us about marriage. "Just because you tithe, that doesn't mean anything. You can tithe the most in the church but that doesn't mean anything if you aren't one with the Lord. A demonic spirit came over you, Simone. You allowed the devil into your home. You must ask God for forgiveness and fast and pray to cast out that demonic spirit and honor your husband."

Karen had her eyes closed and her hands in front of her face with her palms facing up. She was slowly rocking back and forth. "Yes Jesus. Fix it Jesus..."

By the time the Bishop finished I was exhausted. What about what Travis had done? What about how he'd treated me? Travis went upstairs to his childhood room, and his parents went upstairs to their room. I was downstairs in the guest room. I was the interloper... the wild beast that attacked their son... the demonic spirit. I was surprised they hadn't locked me in the room. But I was so damn tired I cried myself to sleep instantly.

When I woke up the next morning the sun was shining directly in my face and burning my eyes. Then I remembered I was in the guest bedroom at the Lees' house. I sat on the edge of the bed and the by now familiar feeling of nausea hit me again. I managed to make it to the trash can in the corner of the room. Since I hadn't been eating much, nothing came up.

I got my cell phone out of my purse. My mother answered on the first ring. As soon as I heard her voice I started bawling. "What's wrong baby?" she said as I tried to calm down. "I knew something was up when I got the bill from the emergency credit card I gave you. Is he cheating? What have those yahoos done to my baby?"

"Mommy, my marriage is over..." I told her everything that had happened and she was enraged. She wanted to call Karen.

"Don't, Mommy, you're only going to make things worse," I pleaded.

"What can I do, baby? I'm getting on a flight and will be there tonight."

One thing about my mother, she didn't play. I didn't fight her on this because I knew that she was going to come regardless of what I said and, to be honest, I needed her.

"Okay," I sighed.

"Now listen to me, Simone. You have told those people enough... I want you to pull yourself together and get out of that house. They are not there to help you. They are there to protect their son. As a matter of fact, I bet they are sitting having a conversation right now while you're not in the room. You will NOT let them see you like this. I will be there as soon as I can. I also want you to take pictures of your knee and the bruises on your arms."

"But Mommy – "

"Promise me you will do this. You might not even need to use them. But promise me you will do as I say as soon as we hang up, and then send them to me so they are time stamped."

I couldn't believe we'd just had that conversation. I started taking pictures. The bruises were darker than they'd been last night and there were more than I thought. My knees were scratched up and swollen. When I walked, I had to limp. I sent my mother the pictures.

I took a hot shower, combed my hair, brushed my teeth and managed to put on some lip gloss. Downstairs, Travis was in the living room with his mother, who was applying more ointment on his bite marks. The marks I had caused. His dad was sitting at the table. It was obvious they had been up for a while, just like my mother predicted. Karen asked me if I wanted coffee.

"No, thank you," I said. Travis didn't look as angry as he did last night. He looked indifferent. I limped over to the couch and sat down next to him and asked, "Can I go back to the house and can we talk later?"

He nodded. And I whispered in his ear. "I love you and I am so sorry."

"I'm trying to forgive you," he responded coldly, I put my head down and then I heard my mother in my head. *You will not let them see you like this.*

I stood up and walked to the kitchen where both Daddy Lee and Karen were sitting. "I am so sorry for last night. I am so sorry I put you and your family through that."

Karen kind of shook her head and Daddy Lee responded, "We still love you."

I went up to the bedroom, grabbed my stuff, and to my surprise Travis walked me to my car. And he hugged me. He couldn't look me in the eye but this was the most attention he had given me in over two weeks. "I am so sorry, Travis. Please forgive me. Let's me make this right."

"I'm trying, Simone... I'm really trying," he said as he pulled away.

"I'll see you tonight?" I asked.

"Okay," he said and then he went back inside his parents' house.

•   •   •

Back at the house I called in sick to work and then spent hours sweeping up the broken glass and plates and cleaning the kitchen. Finally, I sat down on the couch with a glass of wine. Although I no longer liked the taste, I needed something to calm my nerves.

I heard the door open. Travis walked in and to my surprise his brother Jacob was behind him. My heart was palpitating and my hands were trembling. This must be how O.J. Simpson felt when the verdict was about to be read. I was confused as to why Jacob was here. But before I could even ask the question Travis spoke up and said bluntly,

"This isn't going to work, Simone. I want a divorce. You can stay here until you find a place. I'll stay at my parents' house. Just continue to pay half the mortgage and the bills while you look for a place." It was like he was reading from a teleprompter. He didn't wait for me to respond. He went upstairs to the bedroom.

I looked at Jacob and said, "This can't be happening. I don't want a divorce. I thought we were going to work things out."

"Y'all need to talk, man." Jacob shook his head and looked down.

I ran upstairs. Travis had taken out the luggage we used only six months ago on our honeymoon in St. Tropez.

"Please, Travis, can we talk about it? Please don't do this. I love you!" He moved faster, suits out the closet and putting them into the suit carrier.

"There's nothing to talk about! Except that I value my life! You said you were going to kill me. Every time I close my eyes I picture you hanging over me with gun or a knife trying to kill me. No, no, no. I value my life!"

"You know I didn't mean that. I said it out of anger. I would never kill you!" I pleaded.

"No, you were dead-ass serious. You meant it! You meant it! I value my life!" He couldn't stop repeating it.

I attempted to touch his arm so we could talk. "Get off me!" he shouted and pushed my hand away.

At that point, Jacob appeared. "You good, man?"

"I'm good!" Travis said. Jacob had run upstairs like I was going to do something to his brother, which explained why he was with him. He was there to protect his brother from the wild beast... Me!

"I'll be downstairs if you need me." Jacob quickly went back downstairs.

"Travis, I made a mistake, I don't know what came over me. I'm sorry. But we can work through this! Please!" I fell to my knees and grabbed him around his ankles. "Please don't leave me! Please don't leave me!"

He ignored me. He was in a zone. He was moving with determination and precision. He was leaving me and there was nothing I could do to stop it. I followed him downstairs.

"Let me know when you make your arrangements to move out." Those were his last words before he left. Jacob looked back at me, and for a split second I glimpsed empathy in his eyes.

I stood in the middle of the vestibule of this big house. Alone... the same way I'd felt since I moved in. After only six months, it was over.

•　　•　　•

I sat on the couch staring at the blank TV screen for hours. Then the doorbell rang. It was my mother.

She immediately dropped her luggage and enfolded me in her arms. "It's okay, baby, Mommy is here." Yes, I had my girls, they were always there for me. But there is nothing like having your mom to hold you when you are at your lowest point.

"Why didn't you tell me sooner?" she asked after we settled on the couch.

"I thought you and daddy would be disappointed in me. You two have been married for over 40 years and I can't make it past the six-month mark. I didn't want to embarrass the family." There was one person I couldn't lie to, and that was my mother.

"Oh, my baby, you could never disappoint me or your father. We have been married for so long because we have mutual love and respect for each other. And please know we have had many valleys and trials. Your father can work my last nerve. But one thing we have always maintained no matter what is RESPECT. This – " she gestured toward the room, " – this is not love. This is not respect. This is all material things."

"Mommy, you didn't see how I behaved. I was an animal. I don't know what came over me."

"Why aren't you holding him accountable for his part? You didn't just come home and start trashing the house out of nowhere. You were pushed to that point. I will not allow you to take the blame." She cradled my face in her hands. "Where is my confident daughter? I didn't raise you to lose yourself to a family like that! Don't you realize it was only going to get worse?"

Although I hated to admit it, she was right. I always thought abused women were weak. How did I become that woman? "Mommy, I just don't know who I am anymore. I always wanted to be married. I know the first year of marriage is hard work, but this is just too much."

"You're right. The first year of marriage is hard work, but this isn't a marriage. This is bondage. Hear me when I say this, I am still proud of you. You're not a failure." My mother was managing to address every fear of disappointment I'd had. "I also want you to know that I had to do some major convincing to make sure your father didn't hop on a flight to kick Travis's ass himself. He backs you 1000 percent; we just need to keep him in New Jersey to avoid him going to jail for murder."

I had to laugh, though it took an effort. "So now what? Travis said I can stay here until I find a place."

"Absolutely not! You're not staying here. For what? So you can pay his mortgage? You are getting out of here!" Mom jumped up and started heading up the stairs. When I didn't follow immediately, she stopped and said, "What are you waiting for?"

In the bedroom she grabbed a Tumi suitcase out the closet. "Pack up enough clothes for the week. And don't take your toiletries. We want him to think that you're still here as you're looking for a place. You will not give him any information. The only information you will give him is when you find your place and move out. That's when we will pack up the rest of your things. Understood? *Capiche?*"

I did as I was told and began packing clothes for the week. "Do you think I need more clothes than just for a week?"

"No, you'll find a spot very quickly. Now get the remote for your outdoor security cameras. Let's turn them off – he doesn't need to see you leaving with a suitcase." I turned them off as instructed.

We then got in my car and drove to the Casa Del Mar Hotel in Santa Monica. With its ocean view, it provided exactly the right amount of tranquility I needed. She checked us into a suite for a week. It was beautiful. I immediately took a long shower. By the time I came out my mother had ordered room service. We sat the small dining table in the room and ate and started strategizing my next moves.

This would be my temporary home while I looked for a place to live. I would go to the house once a day to appear like I was still living there.

I was not to give him any indication that I was leaving in case that would set him off. I needed to make him feel like he was still in control. Once I found a spot, I would only ask him for money toward my new place and nothing else. He was also not to know where I was moving to.

Thank God my mother took the reins. She made me realize I needed to accept the fact that my marriage was over and I had to start over with my life. This was my reality. I couldn't fight it any longer.

Chapter 23
Jacqueline

I was dreading this meeting with Jay Goldstein. I frowned as the production assistant put on the mic as we stood the lobby of his building. This conversation was already going to be hard. But then to have to do it on camera didn't make the shit any easier.

I had dressed to look understated and classy, contrary to what I was feeling inside. I wore a pair of high-waisted, bright green, Alice and Olivia flowy pants, nude-colored Prada suede pumps (a pair that actually fit me that I didn't sell to Crossroads), a denim button-down shirt tied in the front, and a pair of gold hoop earrings and matching chunky bracelet. I had my hair slicked back in a low bun to accentuate my face. I wore very subtle makeup and a nude lip. There was no need to walk in like I owned the place when just a few days ago I had exited the set of the reality show like a tornado.

As the elevator rose to the top floor, with each passing floor making an annoying ding, I decided to treat this like I was in a movie playing the character of a confident woman who knew what she wanted. *Fuck this nervous shit, I am Jacqueline Fucking McKinley!* I straightened my shoulders, smoothed my hair down and walked in to Goldstein's offices like the star I always believed myself to be.

Jay's assistant came up to me, smiled. and gushed, "Ms. McKinley! We're so happy to see you. Jay is waiting."

I was taken aback. I expected her to give me a look of disdain. And Jay was waiting? Was I in the fucking twilight zone?

I tried to ignore the camera in my face as I followed her into his office.

"Well, here she is! My favorite AWOL actress," Jay said. I couldn't tell if that was a dig or a joke. But hey, at least he hadn't cussed me out upon arrival.

I figured I would just cut to the chase, rip the band aid off to take the pain in one swift motion instead of a slow and steady burn.

"Jay, this project wasn't what I was expecting at all – "

"Well, that is the understatement of the year, Jacqueline. You walked off the set," he reminded me.

"Yes, I am aware of that. But I was already on the fence about doing the show. And Linda wasn't exactly upfront with the premise. And with all due respect, you weren't either." When your mother is dying of cancer, it's easy to have a sudden boost of confidence and not give two fucks. "You see Jay... I am a real actress. I studied abroad in London. I live, breathe, eat, sleep my craft. This is why I am where I am, not where I want to be in this business, because I never compromised the foundation of who I was. Unfortunately, in this case I allowed myself to think about the money instead of my art and agreed to your project. I know you have made a successful career making hit reality shows, but that's not me and it will never be me." I reached into my purse and took out the check. "Here's the repayment of the bonus in full. I am so sorry this didn't work out, but I can't compromise my dignity and not honor who I am just for 15 minutes of fame."

I laid the check on his desk in front of him. I began to walk toward the door, forgetting the cameraman and boom operator were right in my path. I rolled my eyes directly at the camera.

"Hold on, Jacqueline, listen to what I have to say," Jay said. I turned around. "What do you plan on doing next?" he asked.

I didn't have the time or patience to beat around the bush. And since my mother was now making her condition public and letting her clients know, I didn't feel the need to put on a façade.

"Jay, my mother has stage 4 brain cancer and they are only giving her three months to live." I suddenly felt dizzy. I reached for the closest chair to steady myself. Jay quickly rushed around from behind his desk to help me sit down. I needed to pull myself together. I had already given this show too much of me. And now, here I was in Jay Goldstein's office, not getting paid for a real "reality TV" performance. This was my real life.

"I am so sorry, Jacqueline." Jay sounded sincere.

"Thank you." I blew my nose really loud and tried to dab my eyes so my mascara didn't smear, although I think it was too late. "Right now, I have to focus on making the best of the time I have left with my mother."

"I understand. I lost my mother to breast cancer 15 years ago." I could see the pain in his eyes as though he were reliving those final moments. Then, he abruptly switched to business mode. "You know, I watched the dailies and the scene with you and your mom at the Huntley Hotel was very powerful. It was real and raw, and I think you and your mother will resonate with the audience." I wasn't sure how to respond to this. Although my mother had agreed to continue on with this show, I was not going to pimp her out for national TV.

"When I first met you, I knew you were a star. I still believe in you. And I saw the footage of your...well, let's just call it a 'moment,' and to be quite frank, it was brilliant. It was honest, it was refreshing, and it was real. I want to work with you, Jacqueline."

"You do?" This might have been one of the few times I was at a loss for words.

"Yes. I haven't come this far in this business without having an eye for talent and knowing who has star potential. And you do. I'm really sorry to hear about your mother, but I think there is something there. No reality show has gone deep into the mother-daughter relationship and especially when there is, well, limited time. "

"But Jay, I am not interested in doing a reality show. That's not who I am. And I certainly am not interested in shooting my mother dying for national TV."

"Let me be very clear, we would shoot with the utmost dignity. I can assure you of that."

"After what happened the other day, I can't trust that, Jay."

"Jacqueline, if it were anyone else, I would be meeting with my legal team to set up action for breach of contract. But I see something in you. I see the potential of a spinoff – about you and your mother. It could move millions of people."

Suddenly, Jay's fancy mid-Wilshire office felt like a pig's den. I got up and started taking off my mic.

"What are you doing?" he said, startled.

"I come here and I tell you my mother is dying. She's fucking dying and all you can think about is a reality show?!" I was seething. "Fuck you, Jay Goldstein!" I ripped the mic from under my shirt and threw it on his desk. "If I am in breach of contract then sue me! But what I won't do is sell my mother's soul to you devils! How dare you? How dare you?!"

"Jackie – " Jay was following me to the door.

"It's Jacqueline!" I said through gritted teeth.

"Jacqueline, you're making a big mistake."

"That's the first thing you said that I actually agree with. Yes... I MADE a big mistake by agreeing to do this chitlin' circuit show! But at least I have enough sense to move the fuck on. My mother is dying! She's fucking DYING and all you can think of is ratings for this trifling-ass production company!"

I slammed the behind me, and strode by his bewildered assistant. The camera crew followed me. "Leave me alone!" I yelled. But they followed me down to the lobby where I pushed the camera off his shoulder and it slammed it to the ground. I have no idea where all that strength came from, the camera had to be at least a good 200 pounds. "Fuck off!" I took off my heels before I ran to my car and sped off.

I was done with Hollywood for good.

●　　●　　●

When I got home there were flowers all over the apartment. "Did you go and buy all these flowers at the farmer's market, Mom?" She must have called an Uber, even though I'd told her to wait for me and we'd go together.

"Jacqueline, I want to enjoy my flowers while I'm still living. I won't be able to appreciate them at my funeral." There she went, with another joke. I'd never realized my mother had such a great sense of humor. Why hadn't I ever taken the time to see this side of her?

She saw the look on my face. "Honey, we can't spend these last few months being down. We have to make light of this situation and find the humor in it." She kept cutting the stems of the flowers and arranging them in vases. After about 10 minutes I could see she was losing her energy.

"Mommy, why don't you let me give this a try and sit down and relax. I'll make you some tea." And for the first time I could remember, Angelique sat down on the couch and propped her feet up. I filled the tea kettle then began to try to duplicate my mother's perfect flower arrangements.

"Well, Jacqueline, are you going to tell me how it went with Jay Goldstein?"

"Of course I was," I kind of lied. "Um, things went rather differently than what I expected. I quit."

"Oh, Jackie, why? I told you that McKinleys don't quit! And I told you I was willing to be on the show with you." Was this real? I was finding it hard to believe that my mother, the great Angelique McKinley, was still showing interest in my reality TV career. And it seemed to be genuine interest.

"I so appreciate you were willing to do that for me, but no, I would not feel comfortable with that. And it's not fair to you. I want us to spend these last moments to the fullest and enjoy each other." The teakettle started whistling. I added a little bit of fresh turmeric to the brewed tea. According to my research, turmeric helps with cancer prevention. I brought it over to my mom and sat next to her on the couch and crossed my legs. I knew how much my mother hated when I crossed my legs on the couch. She started to say something but stopped herself. Wow! Who was this woman?

She took a sip of her tea. "I don't want you to let my situation stop you from living your life. This sounds like an interesting opportunity." I noticed she had a folder on her lap.

"Now there is something I want to talk to *you* about," she said, turning serious.

"Okaayyy..." I said slowly. Another bomb to drop?

"It's about my will, Jackie I never want you to take on projects because of money. That is something you will never have to worry about again. I took out a life insurance policy years ago, I have savings, and assets – you will be taken care of for life if you are responsible with how you spend and invest the money. You have power of attorney. I am leaving the house to your sister because I know you have no intentions of ever moving back to the East Coast and she needs that stability."

Normally I would have interjected and regurgitated all the reasons why my sister didn't need to have access to a 4,500-square foot house. But just like my mother had just bitten her tongue in front of me, I was going to do the same thing. Besides, she was right; I was never leaving Cali and if I did, I wouldn't be moving to the burbs.

My mother continued in Angelique McKinley business mode. "I have specific instructions in my will on how I would like you divide the money between you and your sister. But both of you will be taken care of."

"Mommy, do we have to have this conversation now? I have hope. Miracles do happen. Why are we just accepting this diagnosis? I've seen people on their deathbeds and miraculously, they bounce back."

"Oh, dear. Now isn't the time for you to write a Hollywood script and be stuck in a fantasy bubble. That's not going to help me or you. We need to be realistic. Trust me, this isn't easy. This wasn't part of my plan. But I have accepted that I do not have control over this. So, I have to focus on what I do have control over."

"But I don't want you to focus on the end."

"Jackie, unfortunately we have to. I want to make sure you are clear about my wishes and that you ask me any questions you have while I am still here to answer them." She paused. It was so quiet you could hear the sound of silence. "Now I'll be honest and contradict what I said before. I was _proud_ of you for walking off that set and standing up for what you believe in. I never want you to a make a decision out of desperation again, do you hear me?" She was firm but kind as she said that.

"And I'll be honest, Mommy. I thought I would be married with kids by now. My life isn't exactly where I thought it would be. I thought I would have an Oscar or the series regular part on a hit TV show. I guess Shonda Rhimes doesn't have my number on file."

"At your age, Jackie, I had two kids to take care of and was divorcing my fourth husband. So don't beat yourself up for not being married. Husbands can be a pain in the ass. I know it's hard for you to believe, but I push you so hard because I believe in you. Look at you, you're tall, beautiful, you take chances, you live life on your own terms and you are unapologetically you. I can't keep trying to impose my life on you."

She finished the last of her tea. "I'm feeling like having a little nap." She gave me a kiss and went to her bedroom.

I turned on the TV. A "Real Housewives of New York" repeat was on. I could always count on those crazy bitches to give me a chuckle and make me realize life isn't that bad, after all. And before I knew it I fell into a deep sleep on the couch. I woke up hours later to the sound of choking noises coming from my mother's room. I found her in the bathroom, throwing up violently. Her vomit was all over the bathroom floor. She had tried to make it to the toilet. "Mommy!" I cried.

She waved me away. "I'm... I'm okay. I'm okay."

"No, you're not." I grabbed a wash cloth and put cold water on it and held it to her face. I then turned on the shower. I got my mother out of her clothes and helped her into the shower. I was so thankful that it was a stall shower and not a bathtub. It made it so much easier. I stepped in with her, fully clothed, and let the cool water run over her body and clean her. I dried her off and lotioned her from head to toe. I helped her into her pajamas. At this point, she was weak but she was able to walk on her own from the shower. I helped her get in bed and pulled up the covers. She looked at me with loving eyes. "I'm not ready to go.... I thought I had more time. I thought I had more time..." she said softly.

I took her face between my hands and rubbed my nose against hers and smiled. She mouthed the words, *I love you*. And I said, "I love you to the moon and back... Get some rest, Mommy."

I held her tight until she fell asleep. Then I went into the bathroom and washed it down and put the bath mats to the washing machine.

This was cancer. It wasn't pretty. She wasn't ready. I wasn't ready. Cancer didn't give a fuck about time, or all someone accomplished in her life. Cancer was unforgiving and relentless. This was not a game, this was not a reality show. This was motherfucking cancer.

Chapter 24
Simone

"I'm sorry, Mrs. Lee, but I cannot rent this apartment to you," the landlord of the beautiful West Hollywood building said in his thick Armenian accent.

"Sir, I don't think you understand. I have *never* lived in Rancho Cucamonga, San Diego, or Corona. And I've never been evicted in my life! I told you, someone stole my identity." The owner looked at me like I am sure he looked at others who tried to rent with bad credit. But my credit had been immaculate all my life. I was raised to be financially responsible. I didn't even think to check my credit before I started apartment hunting.

"All I can suggest, Mrs. Lee, is that you check with the three credit bureaus and have the evictions removed."

"How long will that take?"

"About thirty days. And then you can come back when it's all – " he held up his fingers for air quotes " – cleared."

"You don't have to be nasty!" I grabbed my purse and stormed out.

On day two of apartment hunting, this was the second place that had rejected me due to that bad credit report. I had finally convinced my mother to go home. As much as I love my mother and as helpful as she was, I knew I needed to handle this on my own. Not to mention, each day she was in L.A., the angrier she became. I didn't need to hear again that she thought Travis's family was a bunch of "country-bumpkin yahoos." I didn't need to hear again how I was too high-society for him and his family. Although most of the shit she was saying was true, I just wasn't ready to receive it at this moment. I had to find a place to live. My mother's main concern was that "he thinks you're going to stay there and pay half his bills for another month. I don't think so."

I got back in my car to go to the third and final spot on the list. On the way, I passed a CVS and decided to stop. This morning it had occurred to me that I hadn't had a period for a while. Any other time, the possibility of being pregnant would have made me do cartwheels. But the timing of this couldn't have been worse. I was praying that I was just stressed out and that was the reason my period was almost three weeks late. I was on the pill from the time I was 18 until the day of my wedding. Now, the happiest possibility of my life was scarred with the bullshit of my reality. In the drugstore I grabbed four pregnancy tests – two First Response, and two Clear Blue Easy. The checkout cashier smiled, and said "Good luck!" In her mind, she saw the huge diamond ring on my finger and thought that this was a joyous occasion.

I felt like a fraud. From the outside looking in, I was living the best life ever, but the reality was I was looking for an apartment to rent since I didn't have time to look for a place to buy.

I stared out into the sunny blue skies of Los Angeles. The tall palm trees were standing still and looked regal against the blue skies. Who would ever think in the midst of this beautiful day, I was having the hardest time of my life! I leaned my head back and closed my eyes, hoping that when I opened them, I would realize this was just a bad dream. After a few minutes, I slowly opened my eyes only to the reality that I was still in front of the CVS and I looked over at the passenger seat and saw the bag with the pregnancy tests. "URGH!!!! My life!" I yelled and slammed my fist on the steering wheel. I thought letting out a good yell would make me feel better. It didn't. I felt empty, I felt lost, and most of all, I felt like a failure and I was scared. I was 40 and scared as hell.

I got back in the car. I didn't have time to fall apart. I had one last spot to look at, in West Hollywood, on Kings Road.

The property manager was waiting outside for me. She was an older white woman, mid-70s, with perfectly coifed and teased hair, red nails, red lipstick, and she was wearing a caftan. "You must be Simone." She put her hand out. "Nice to meet you."

"Nice to meet you too," I said, looking at the building. The picture on Westside Rental didn't do it justice. Almost hidden behind trees, there was a beautiful swimming pool in the middle of the 14 units. One of the tenants was walking in behind us with groceries. "Hi, Mrs. Patton," he said as he passed by.

"Hey, Justin, make sure to tell David happy birthday for me!" she said.

"Sure thing." Justin smiled. He made eye contact with me and said "hello" in a friendly way.

It felt like a family atmosphere. "I just love him and his husband. They got married a few months ago. The wedding was beautiful." I followed her to Unit 7 in the back corner. Inside we were greeted by bright sunlight. The place was beautiful. There were dark hardwood floors. The kitchen was huge, with stainless steel appliances and light granite countertops with hints of teal. There was a fireplace in the living room and high ceilings, and it had two bedrooms. But most of all, the energy was calm, unlike the environment I was leaving.

Mrs. Patton was going over all the amenities. "You're just two blocks from Santa Monica Blvd. But this place is very quiet. There aren't any kids, and everyone knows each other and looks out for each other."

This place was perfect. It had to be my new home. I didn't want to move from a 5,000- square foot house in a gated community to a dump. I still wanted a fabulous lifestyle. I turned around with excitement I didn't have to muster. "I'll take it!" I said as I clapped like a kid being handed the largest Christmas present under the tree.

"Wonderful. I think you'll love it here. I can already tell your energy fits right in." Mrs. Patton said. "I'll just need the first and last month's rent and you can fill out the application here."

My balloon of excitement popped. I had one of two choices. I could fill out the application and hope the false eviction reports didn't come up this time OR I could tell her the truth upfront and see what happens.

As Mrs. Patton handed me the pen and application, I went with the latter approach. "Mrs. Patton, I must tell you that I discovered today that I am a victim of identity theft. There are false evictions listed on my credit report. I am filing to get those fraudulent marks off my credit. I can give you the first six months' rent, I can give you my previous landlords' info as a reference, I can also give you my job number to verify

I have been with the same company for the last eight years. But I really want this apartment."

"Why don't you fill out the application and let's see what comes up. Maybe the other places were using a different system. I'm sure you'll be fine." She was so reassuring. She left me alone in the apartment while she went to run my report.

I walked around the apartment, enjoying how light and airy it was. Standing in it gave me a sense of hope. I ran my hands across the beautiful granite countertops. I went back into the master bedroom with its fireplace and looked at myself in the bathroom mirror. I looked tired. I pulled up my what I perceived was sagging eyes. Didn't help. How had I allowed myself to become a person I couldn't recognize? I walked back to the living room. Mrs. Patton was taking a long time to return. Was she calling the police on me? She probably ran my credit report and thought I needed to go to jail! Lord have mercy.

"Okay! So, I ran your report," Mrs. Patton said, appearing with my application in hand. "And yes, there are three evictions listed. But I did some digging and the evictions are listed for the same months you were living at your apartment on Fountain Avenue. Which made no sense. Why would you rent three different apartments at the same time? Anyone who took the time to look up the dates would see that's ridiculous. Luckily, I know your former landlord Hasson and gave him a call. He assured me that you were one of his favorite tenants who paid on time each month and sometimes early. He also said you kept an eye on things around the building too. So that's all good. I have to be honest, you have to fix your credit reports. There are a lot of derogatory remarks on them."

"I know, I know. But I have to wait 30 to 45 days to get them cleared off. You see, I'm going through a... through a..." I took a deep breath. "I'm getting divorced, Mrs. Patton." It was my first time saying it out loud. My lips started to tremble, a giveaway that I was about to cry, but Mrs. Patton caught it and put her arm around me.

"Now, now dear. Everything will be fine. I was married four times!"

I was shocked. This sweet old lady had lived! "You were?"

"Oh, yes. My first husband was the love of my life. I think we just got married in the wrong decade, but he gave me two beautiful children.

Then my second husband was my best friend. And that marriage ended when I walked in on him wearing my favorite evening gown and a wig. My third husband was a cheating bastard. And my beloved Henry passed away five years ago."

"I'm so sorry," I said with sincere sympathy, though reeling from her perhaps too-colorful history.

"Oh, dear, life has a way of taking you down unexpected roads, and sometimes you have to take detours to get to that destination called happiness. Listen, I'm going to take a chance on you. The apartment is yours. Just give me the first three months' rent and this month's rent."

I hugged her. I took out my checkbook and immediately wrote out the check. She handed me the rental agreement. I read through it page by page, then signed it.

"Perfect! I'll give you the keys on Friday and you can move in then. Let's not even bother prorating for the extra days you'll be here. This is a small building, and what's important to me is that we have good people living here. Welcome to the neighborhood, Mrs. Lee... Wait, is Lee your married name?"

"Yes, it is," I answered.

Mrs. Patton looked at my application and then said. "Let me correct myself. Welcome to the neighborhood, *Ms. Monroe*!"

"Thank you so much, Mrs. Patton!" And I hugged her again.

Chapter 25
Taylor

When I got home from the hospital, I called out for Michael. When he didn't respond, I figured he was out with that Amber. Fine, I needed some downtime. I poured a generous amount of scotch in a glass, squeezed lime into it, and added a splash of club soda. I would need to hide the bottle before Michael came home. I took a long sip and it was so damn refreshing and relaxing. I finished it and made my way down the steps to my studio, hoping to have some sort of creative renaissance in the peace and quiet of my sanctuary.

Instead I found Michael sitting on the floor in a corner, rocking back and forth. My concern allowed me to overlook the fact that he was in my sanctuary, which I'd told him was off-limits. I sat down next to him on the floor. I put my arm around his shoulder and leaned in so I could see his face.

"Michael, what's wrong?"

He was quiet for a while, just rocking back and forth. He finally spoke. "Why does it have to be so damn hard, T?" He started sobbing.

"I don't know, Michael, but I do know God doesn't give you more than you can bear." I felt like if I said that I would believe it too.

"God is dead. He doesn't care out me. Why would He bring me into this world fucked up?" The sobs continued.

"You're not fucked up, Michael. You're not! I want you to hear me when I say this: there is nothing wrong with you. You are not fucked up. You just have to deal with your situation differently. You're ill."

Tim was coming in the morning, but in this moment I knew I couldn't wait until the morning.

"Michael, I know about the drugs."

He started to deny and before he could, I cut him off. "I found them in your laundry. They aren't helping you." I said. "I'm not judging you, but you can't keep doing this and thinking you're going to be okay."

"I know, I know... I sometimes just want to escape. I want to escape this madness that constantly goes on in my head. I can't turn it off. It won't stop. I want to escape myself. I don't know how much longer I can do this. I can't live like this much longer. I am so tired. I am so fucking tired."

I didn't know what to say. I decided to sit there with him for a while in the dark and in the silence. I understood this is what it felt like to be him. Constantly in the dark and silence with only the bad thoughts playing in your mind. We sat in silence for a while. He finally broke the silence. "I've been thinking a lot about Mom lately."

"What have you been thinking about?"

"That day... that day everything changed."

There was so much chaos in our childhood, I couldn't even guess which incident it was, but then he reminded me.

•   •   •

Michael was in sixth grade. My mother had to go pick him up from school. He had gotten suspended for drawing a penis on the wall in the boys' bathroom.

"Go to your room and don't come out until I tell you to!" my mother was screaming as they walked into the house.

As Michael passed my room I mouthed, "What happened?" He just shook his head and went to his room. In the kitchen my mother was, of course, pouring herself a glass of vodka. When she realized I was standing there she snapped, "What are you doing here? Go to your room, too. I don't want to see either of you!"

It was quiet for a while. After an hour so I heard her stumble into Michael's room where he was lying down. "So you want to draw pictures of dicks in bathrooms?" she screamed. He didn't answer. She said it again, "You can't hear me? Answer my question!"

He didn't speak. Then she ordered, "Take off your clothes! You heard me! Take off your clothes, now!" I tiptoed to my door and watched

Michael strip. She had a belt in her hand and began to beat him with it. I lay down on my bed and buried my head under the pillow to shut out my brother's screams of pain. "Mom, please stop! I'm sorry. Please!" he begged.

At one point I ran into the room and tried to make her stop. "Mommy, please!" She looked at me with venom and then smacked me. "Get out of here!" I ran back to my room. When the beating finally stopped she said, "Keep your door open and stay just like that.' She made him sleep with his door wide open, naked, his back covered with bloody welts. He was never the same after that.

• • •

I didn't speak until my spirit gave me the right words to say. "Michael, I wish I could take away this pain. I wish that you didn't have to go through this. I wish we'd grown up normal, I wish we had parents who gave a fuck more about us than themselves and their own bullshit."

"I know you do, T. I know you do...."

"Michael... you have to take your meds and you have to stop self-medicating."

"I've only taken heroin one time," he admitted.

"Heroin? I was talking about the cocaine!" How things went from bad to worse in only a matter of seconds I would never understand.

"That stuff is only going to make matters worse. I'm not judging you. But you have to pull it together. I'm saying this because I love you."

"I know you do. I love you, too."

"And you know Mom loved us. The alcohol fucked her up. Remember how much better it was when she got sober?"

"I do. She was a different person. I wish she had gotten sober sooner."

"Me, too. Just like she got better when she stopped drinking, the same can happen if you stop using." There was a long pause in which he did not respond. "Can you promise me you'll get back in treatment? If the meds they have you on aren't working, then we can work with Dr. Sanders to get you on a different regimen. As much as I love you, I can't be in your corner if you're not willing to fight. You have to be on your meds and you have to stop using. Can you promise me that?"

He stood up and went to look out the window. I leaned my head on his shoulder. "You got this, Michael. I know you can beat this once and for all." We looked at the lights of the city for a long time in silence. I finally felt my eyelids getting heavy.

"Why don't you stay in here for a while. I find my studio gives me such peace. I think it will do the same for you."

He nodded and continued to look out window. This was the scary part; after the mania, the depression entered.

I gave Michael a hug and left him there and went to bed.

•   •   •

I hadn't intended to sleep this late. But I was so agitated when I went to bed that I'd popped a ZzzQuil to sleep. Dr. Tim was coming in the next hour so I wanted to make sure everything was all set. I threw on some jeans and a t-shirt and knocked on Michael's door to see if he was up. When there was no answer, I went to my studio to see if he had fallen asleep in there. When he wasn't there so I assumed he was dead asleep in his room. I decided to leave him alone until the doctor got here. It was imperative to get him back on his treatment plan because the depression had set in.

I buzzed Dr. Tim upstairs a few hours later. Michael still hadn't appeared.

"Well, are we ready?" he asked.

I caught him up on everything that happened last night.

He agreed we needed to level out his meds and get him into detox. I offered him coffee or water, and he chose water.

I poured him a glass and settled him in the living room where we would have the talk with Michael.

"I'll go get him." I took a deep breath. I felt nervous. I felt like I was betraying him. I felt like I was doing something wrong by having his doctor there and not telling him. Dr. Tim immediately sensed my apprehension.

"It's going to be fine. This is a good thing," Tim assured me.

"You're right." I went down the hall and knocked on Michael's door. He didn't answer. I knocked again. Still no answer. "Michael... Michael!" I was loud enough where he could hear me. When he didn't answer I opened the door. Fuck privacy at this point! By now Tim was standing behind me. I was stunned... the bed was stripped. I went into the bathroom and all of his toiletries were gone. And then I went to the closet and all his clothes were gone. The only thing that was left behind were his meds, my house keys, and my car keys for the Explorer. Next to them was a note. I sat down on the bed and read it out loud. "I love you and I appreciate you. But I need to figure me out on my own. I have to quiet these demons..." When in the world had Michael left? And how did I sleep through it all? This was crazy! I thought we were on the same page!

"I'm so sorry, Taylor," Tim had taken his glasses off and was massaging the bridge of his nose.

"If I hadn't taken that damn ZzzQuil, I would have heard him leave. How could I have been so stupid? I should have stayed up until I knew he was sleeping."

"Are you beating yourself up for getting sleep?" Dr. Tim asked incredulously.

I ignored Tim's question. It was obvious where he went. I needed to get to Michael. I grabbed my car keys.

"Wait. Where are you going?"

"C'mon, Tim. We're heading to Amber's house. You and I both know that's where he is. Just give me the address or I can follow you over there." I headed toward the door with my keys and purse and stopped when I realized Tim wasn't rushing to follow me.

"Taylor, I can't do that. I can't give out patients' confidential information, I could lose my license."

"But, Tim, Michael is a danger to himself and others. There is no way that being around that piece of trash is going to help him. As a matter of fact, it's her damn fault that he's going down this path in the first place." I didn't have the time or the patience to be PC when it came to that whore anymore. When Dr. Tim didn't move I really started to be impatient. "Why are you just standing there? We don't have the luxury of wasting time."

"Taylor, please sit down." He was, as always, his calm professional self. When I didn't move he insisted. "Taylor, please have a seat."

I slowly walked to the couch and sat down and he sat next to me. "Taylor, I have watched you be Michael's biggest advocate. You have provided for him, made sure he made his appointments, given him a place to stay, a car to drive... you even convinced me to help you do an intervention. You've snuck his meds in his food and drinks. At what point are you going to say enough is enough?"

Tim took off his glasses and laid them on the coffee table. "Michael is 44 years old. He is responsible for his own decisions and his own actions. You can't keep following him around like he's a child. That's not helping. You're being an enabler, Taylor."

"So, what am I supposed to do? Give up? What if I don't go looking for him and something happens and I could have saved him?" Waves of fear started to hit me.

"This isn't a way to live. You are so busy trying to save him, but what about you and your feelings?" Dr. Tim looked at me with intensity. "You have to let him go, Taylor. I know it's not going to be easy. But you have to. Michael has made it clear that he is unable to meet you where you are and he needs his space. You have to respect his decision. If not, you are enabling him and that's not going to help him either."

"I don't – I don't even know what 'letting go' means. How do I do that? Why does it feel like I'm just giving up on him? What if something happens to him? How would I be able to live with myself knowing that I didn't do everything I could... knowing that I left stones unturned?"

"Taylor, you have done everything you possibly can at this point, except letting go."

I closed my eyes. I didn't know what my life was like without worrying about Michael. That had been my default for so long. If I lost Michael, I had nothing left.

"Thank you for everything, Tim," I said as I got up from the couch and walked him to the door.

"I know this isn't easy, but if you need anything I am here. Please don't hesitate to call me."

"I really appreciate your help." I gave him a warm hug.

He hugged me back and whispered, "You're going to be fine. You'll get through this."

I leaned against the door after he left, listening to him get the elevator. Maybe Dr. Tim was right. What would my life be like if I let go?

I guess now I would be forced to examine that, whether I was ready or not.

Chapter 26
Simone

I peed on the fourth and final stick. This one said **PREGNANT** before I even had a chance to put the damn thing on the counter. I placed that one next to the other three that were sitting on the bathroom counter and each one blared the same word: **PREGNANT.** That explained the nausea, my moodiness, and the fact that the smell and taste of wine made me sick. As if on cue, I turned around and threw up into the toilet for the second time since I started peeing on the sticks. I rinsed my mouth out and took the pregnancy tests with me to the living room and placed them on the coffee table. I didn't even give a second thought to the fact that it was unsanitary. I plopped down on the couch. I was at Travis's house, as my mother instructed to give the appearance that I was still living there.

Holy shit, I'm fucking pregnant. I got off the pills right after we got married. I figured it would take a few months for the birth control hormones to get out of my system. I thought I would probably have to do IVF in order to get pregnant. Most women my age had such trouble getting pregnant. Go figure – I was Fertile Myrtle.

This isn't good. This isn't what I planned. And at my age, I couldn't even think about having an abortion because this might be my last chance. So now what? I was going to be a single fucking mother? All these years I spent trying to do things the "right" way, and I was going to be exactly what I feared most, a single, divorced mother. On the other hand, it wasn't like I was having a baby out of wedlock. I was still married. I'm really pregnant! This is crazy as hell. I had a human being inside of me.

A sudden calm came over me. I was going to be a mother. I was fucking pregnant. *Wow! I'm pregnant.*

I placed my hands on my stomach and rubbed it, imagining my unborn child growing inside of me. "We are going to be okay, little guy. Mommy is going to take care of you." I picked up the pregnancy tests and went upstairs to our bedroom. I rinsed my face with cold water. As I wiped it dry I saw the reflection of my engagement ring in the bathroom mirror. I looked at the ring. It had no meaning anymore. The shine, the size, the clarity was all bullshit. I found the ring box in my bedside table – the same box that Travis held when he proposed. I sat on the edge of the bed, looked at the ring one last time, slowly slid it off, and returned it to the box. I looked back at my finger without the ring on. It was an adjustment, but I was no longer going to live in this fantasy I had created.

I no longer had myself to think about. I had to think about my child. I put the pregnancy tests in a small Ziploc bag and put it in the front zipper part of my suitcase. I started packing clothes from the closet and out of the dresser. I left all my lingerie. No need to reuse them. Not to mention, the idea of sex made me sick to my stomach. I also left the tank tops I wore before we got married that said "Future Mrs. Lee" and "Bride." I put the ring box right next to the pregnancy tests in the zippered compartment. The engagement picture of the two of us happy stared at me as I packed. It wasn't my plan to be a single mother. It wasn't my plan to get married and separate after only six months. Plans were what got me in this position in the first place. Life isn't about plans.

• • •

In the morning I called the moving company and arranged for them to come Friday morning. They brought over packing boxes immediately. I went to the bank and opened up new accounts. I took my name off the joint accounts. I sent a text to Taylor and Jackie:

Sorry I have been missing in action. I am fine. So much to catch you ladies up on. Can we meet in Manhattan Beach Sunday at 4 p.m.? I'll bring some sandwiches and food and you ladies can bring the wine. Let's meet at our usual location.

They both immediately responded:

Jackie: *I'm glad you're alive. Taylor and I were about to do a drive-by. See you then.*

Taylor: *Let us know if you need anything before then. The beach sounds like a good break.*

I sent Travis a text, short and simple:

I am moving out tomorrow.

I didn't want him to know where I was moving to. All he needed to know was that I was leaving. He responded within seconds: *Leave the keys and the garage opener on the counter upon your exit.*

Asshole! I started taking my knickknacks off the shelves and paintings off the wall. I was the person who brought life to this place. I counted out the wedding plates, making sure I took half of everything and left him half. I took six of the twelve plates and four of the eight long stemmed Waterford crystal white wine glasses. I knew Travis would be taking inventory of everything I took. After all, this was a business deal.

I was packing up my throw pillows from the couch when I heard keys unlock the door. I looked up and saw Travis walking in with his cousin Daniel behind him. He'd brought someone with him so I couldn't attack him, I guess. He had no idea I wasn't the same desperate woman of recent weeks. Once my mother gave me her blessing, once I found a place I loved to move to, and once my pregnancy was confirmed, Travis had become an afterthought.

"Hello, Travis," I said, as if he was a work colleague I barely tolerated.

"Hello, Daniel." Like Jacob, Daniel looked extremely uncomfortable being stuck in this position.

"Hi, Simone." Travis could barely look me in the face. It was pathetic. A family full of grown-ass male PUNKS!!!

I walked past him and started putting bubble wrap around the plates. He opened the kitchen drawer where we kept gift cards people had given us as wedding gifts, started taking inventory of what was there. He was so damn predictable. All he cared about was monetary shit. Now I realized why my mother wanted me to wait until the very last minute to let him know I had found another place to live. She must have anticipated him showing up like this the moment he felt like he was losing control.

"Where's the $250 Bloomingdale's gift card?" he demanded.

I took a deep breath. "I put it toward our new bedspread. I left the bedspread on the bed. You can have it."

He then went to the kitchen cabinets and counted the plates that were in the cabinets and then the plates that were in the box I was packing. He was so fucking pathetic and petty.

"I am only taking half of them." I said calmly, and continued to bubble wrap.

"Where are you moving to, Simone?"

"That's none of your business," I said and walked around him to the drawer with our cooking utensils.

"So... what is it that you want?" he said impatiently. I could tell he was beginning to freak out, which was making me nervous. At least having Daniel here, he wouldn't try to put his hands on me. Or maybe he would. I could no longer assume I knew this man and what he was capable of.

"All I want is the moving expenses and money toward my first and last month's rent for my new place."

"That's contingent upon you giving me back the rings," he said.

I stopped dead in my tracks. "Have you lost your mind? I'm not giving you back the rings. Those are mine."

He then lunged at me and grabbed my hand thinking I was still wearing it. I pushed him off as Daniel said, "Yo, cuz, chill!"

"Where are the rings? Where are they?" he demanded. I ignored him. He ran upstairs and I knew he was going to look in the bedside table where I kept the ring box. Relief washed over me that I had placed the ring and pregnancy tests in the suitcases that were lined up by the door. He charged back downstairs. "Did you pawn my rings? You had no right to do that!" I chuckled because he looked so asinine and continued packing my shit. I also laughed to fuck with him.

"Where are the rings and where are you moving to?" he demanded.

"That's none of your fucking business. You wanted me out, and now I'm out! You can send anything you don't need to Taylor's gallery. You know, the one where you couldn't stay for the party because you needed to watch a basketball game."

He looked at me in disbelief. I no longer cared that Daniel was standing there. I was no longer interested in perpetrating this fraud any further. "Grow up, Travis! You pushed me and pushed me until I broke so you could blame me for everything. Now if you have nothing else to say let me get back to my packing. And don't worry, I'm not taking any of your shit. And you can keep the gift cards and go buy a pair. I'll leave the keys on the counter upon my exit as you requested. Now you can go back to your mommy."

I turned my back on him and continued to pack my boxes. I heard Daniel mutter, "Come on, cuz, let's go. She ain't taking your shit." I didn't turn around to look at them. I wanted to give the impression I no longer cared. When I heard the front door close I exhaled. I felt a sharp pain on the side of my stomach. I rubbed it "It's okay, little guy. It's okay." And the sharp shooting pain stopped.

•   •   •

The next morning, movers took out the last two boxes. I did a final walk through. Our wedding pictures were still hanging on the walls. We looked like the perfect *Essence* magazine couple. We looked so happy, like the couples I would see in magazines and say, *I want to be just like them.* I shook my head at how misguided I was. I went upstairs and did a walk-through of the master bedroom. I went into our walk-in closet. All of his clothes were hung up neatly on his side. The evil part of me wanted to cut all of his ties in half. But I knew I wanted to leave in the same way I came in, with class. I didn't want him to be able to say I was crazy and have it be justified. I had to take the high road. I had to regain the dignity I lost in this relationship. It was going to take a while for that to happen, but this was the beginning. I looked on my side of the closet and everything was cleared with the exception of my wedding bouquet that was hanging upside down with the dried flowers. It was the perfect analogy of our marriage. I was trying to hang on to something that was dead. I thought that the beauty of when it was fresh would return. But just like dead flowers, once the relationship is dead, it's dead, and there's no turning back from that. The dead flowers will never be bright and shiny, and smooth to the touch. I took a deep-breath and rubbed my stomach. I walked downstairs and grabbed my purse. I took out the garage clicker and the keys and lined each key on the counter individually next to the clicker.

I took one last look at this house, and I walked to the door and never looked back.

Chapter 27
Jacqueline

Although I wasn't in the mood to fight the traffic to Manhattan Beach, once I got there, I knew it would be worth the drive. I hadn't been to the beach this entire year. It was a welcome distraction from dealing with all the paperwork, medications, and my own thoughts about my mother's illness. My mom was at the condo with the nurse we hired, so I knew she was in good hands while I was gone.

I passed Sepulveda and the view of the ocean was closer. I found a parking spot and grabbed my grocery bags, beach chair, towel and a sweater – because my white t-shirt, and cutoff jeans wouldn't keep me warm once the sun set. Los Angeles beach weather could be three seasons in one day. As I walked across the sand, I spotted Simone and Taylor. I could see Simone's diamond studs blinging in the sun. As I got closer, I could tell she wasn't wearing her wedding ring. This was serious.

"Hey, girls!" I said, as I got closer.

"Hey, I thought you bitches could use some real food." I started pulling out small sushi trays, kale salad, chicken salad, and lastly, a bottle of Moet Rosé. "Here, Simone, I bought your favorite – rainbow roll."

She opened the plastic container and then closed the lid back up. "I'll eat it later. I'm good for now," she said. "So, how are you doing, girl?" She tilted her head with concern and touched my shoulder.

I responded with the most honest answer I could. "I'm hanging in there. This shit is intense." I quickly changed the subject. I needed a break from thinking about cancer and death. "I feel like I haven't seen you ladies in forever. What's going on?"

"Well..." Taylor began, and told us about the shocking Michael situation.

"My goodness, T. That's awful! These white bitches come in and just fuck up our brothas."

"Michael has never been into coke, has he?" Simone asked.

"Not that I know of. I'm sure he smoked a little bit of weed here and there. But cocaine and other shit? That's some new shit."

I was curious what "other shit" meant. Clearly, she wasn't ready to divulge that information.

"What are you going to do?" Simone said, pouring herself a glass of Perrier.

"Right now, I do nothing. He knows where I live, and he knows my door will always be open to him. I've done everything I can. It's hard, but I can't control a grown-ass man. Learning to let go of control is something I'm not used to."

It was strange hearing Taylor say what I have wanted to tell her for years. She was finally facing the sobering fact that she could not have the same kind of control in the "real" world as she did in her art. I couldn't control my mother's sickness either.

"That's a hard lesson I am learning, too." Simone said, staring out at the ocean.

"What's going on with you and Travis?" I picked up Simone's hand and pointed to her ring finger, which was now bare. "What's going on? We have been worried sick about you."

Simone told us everything that happened, from beginning to end. She didn't cry. She was, in fact, unusually calm.

"Are you sure it's over? Do you think Travis will want to reconcile?" Taylor asked slowly. I knew she wanted to be tactful in case Simone decided to get back together with him. I chose to bite my tongue. I didn't want to reveal my true feelings until I knew it was over for sure.

"It doesn't matter what he wants anymore. I have been so focused on what he wants, his needs, and what I need to do to make him happy, that I forgot who the hell I am. The moment I walked out of that house I knew I would never return, ever." She was definitive in her response. "And even if I did, my mother and father would personally kick my ass for being stupid enough to go back!"

"Praise God! Hallelujah!" If she told her parents what was going on, she was finally done. The old Simone Monroe was coming back! I leaned over and hugged her.

"Simone, it has been so hard watching you lose yourself in this marriage. I'm sorry this happened to you, but sometimes God has a way of forcing you to get out of something that is toxic when you won't do it yourself." I had no idea where my sudden sense of spirituality was coming from. But lately I woke up every morning and prayed thanks that it was getting me through handling my mother's illness on the day to day.

"I'm sorry if I came off harsh. I'm just so happy you're out of that Pentecostal cult and that joke of a family. Seriously. Did you finally tell his parents about the daughter-in-law they need to be watching and that their oldest grandchild isn't biologically theirs?"

"No. I wanted to tell them so bad, but I figured her karma will come around and bite her on the ass. It's no longer my problem. Time for me to focus on me."

"My friend is back! The invasion of the Pentecostal body snatchers is over!" I yelled, and stood up and twirled on the beach.

"Thanks, girl. I needed that laugh!" Simone was laughing so hard she was almost in tears.

I flopped back down on my beach chair and took out the bottle of Moet. I popped it open. "Oh, how I love that sound! It never gets old!" I poured three plastic wineglasses. "Cheers to new beginnings! You're going to get through this Simone. I know it's hard, but I am so proud of you for seeing the light." We clinked our plastic glasses together.

"I'm pregnant," Simone blurted out as she handed her untouched champagne back to me.

I literally spit the champagne out of my mouth, "What?!"

"You're pregnant?" Taylor said in utter disbelief.

Simone went in her purse and took out a Ziploc bag with four pregnancy tests, and each of them proclaimed, in bold letters, **PREGNANT**.

"Those tests are often not accurate…" Taylor tried to go into her usual first destination, denial. She always did that after someone told her something she wasn't prepared to hear.

I decided to go easy on her since she was dealing with all her issues with Michael. "Bitch, please, these are *four* different pregnancy tests. Simone is preggers!" I shook the Ziploc bag in Taylor's face for extra emphasis.

"Not to mention, I went to my doctor today and he confirmed it. I am eight weeks pregnant," Simone said.

It hurt my heart that this was how she told us her good news, with sadness in her eyes. Simone had always wanted to be a wife and a mother. She had the names of her kids picked out by the time we were juniors at Hampton. This was certainly not how she'd imagined it.

"Soooo...?" I said slowly. I didn't want to make any assumptions. But considering she had just moved out of her marital home and was about to get a divorce, I wasn't sure if she was going to move forward with the pregnancy. Maybe she was telling us prior to arranging to terminate it.

"I'm going to keep my baby." Simone said. "I'm 40 years old. I ain't no spring chicken. This might be my last chance. I can't believe this is happening." I could see her eyes getting glossy with tears. I took her glass of champagne and drank it. I wasn't about to let it go to waste.

"I know this isn't how you planned this, but it still doesn't change that you're going to be an amazing mother," Taylor said.

"An amazing *single* mother," she corrected. And I knew Simone, she was embarrassed that in a few months she was going to be walking around with a belly and no ring. I know how much she cared about what people thought about her and wanting to give people the perception she had a perfect life.

"It's not like you're on "Teen Mom." You're a grown-ass, 40-year-old woman with a thriving career," I pointed out.

"I have a job I hate with a boss who is psychotic, I'm about to go through a divorce after six months of marriage, and now I'm going to raise a baby on my own. Life..." she said, shaking her head.

"I know...life." I had to agree.

Taylor addressed the elephant in the room: "When are you going to tell Travis?"

"I have no idea. I know he'll try to get custody of the baby before he's even born."

"He?" Taylor asked.

"I just have a feeling," she said as she rubbed her stomach and looked down at it, smiling.

"I'll kick his ass!" I said. "That bastard and his crazy cult family aren't going to come near my nephew!"

"But enough about me. I looked up some destinations for you and your mom to visit, Jackie."

"You did? With all you have going on, you still did that?"

"Of course. It was actually a lot of fun." Simone poured herself some more sparkling water.

"How is your mom doing?"

"She's trying to put up a good front, but... Angelique is dying. Every second of the day is a second I am closer to losing her."

"Oh, honey, I'm so sorry." Taylor rubbed my leg.

"Thanks, ladies. This is so much harder than I ever thought it would be. It is certainly not something you can prepare for." I wanted so desperately to get a call that a miracle had happened and the cancer had disappeared. But I knew that wasn't going to be the case. I didn't have the luxury of being in denial and acting like everything was business as usual.

Simone took a small binder out of her bag and handed it to me. "Out of all the places I looked up, I think you and your mother need to experience a Santorini sunset in Greece together. They say it's spiritual."

People say the moment a woman finds out she is pregnant, her maternal mode automatically kicks in. I believed this was the energy I was feeling from Simone.

"That's a brilliant idea," I said. Simone had divided the binder with different tabs – one for airfare, another for hotel recommendations, another one for restaurants, and she even had a tab about international travel for someone who has cancer. "Wow, Simone. I can't believe you did all of this. Thank you so much. But I don't think she'll be cleared for travel. I don't want this trip to be the trip that takes her out of here."

"At this point, what does it matter? You mother should do whatever the fuck she wants," Simone said. "It's better than just sitting in the hospice looking at the clock tick. I thought the whole purpose of her getting off chemo was to enjoy the time she has left." This was the old Simone, the Simone who was so full of life.

"I love you, ladies. You two really get it. I've been feeling guilty for all the years I was so hard on her. Wasted time. She wasn't that controlling; she was just concerned – "

Taylor stopped me. "With all due respect, Jackie, I love your mother. She is brilliant, successful, and respected. But I won't let you run that tape. She *was* controlling and she didn't exactly support your decision to go into acting. That doesn't mean she didn't do it out of love. But you had every right to bitch and complain about it. It doesn't make you a bad person. That doesn't mean you loved your mother any less. It just means you had a typical mother-daughter relationship like most folks. The beauty and the blessing of this tragedy is that it is bringing you and her closer, and you have a chance to really get to know each other and bond before she leaves this earth. I never got that chance with my mom. I had to make peace with what happened. But what I wouldn't give just to have five minutes of what you are experiencing with your mom right now. You get to know her and love on her during her final days. And the fact that she is choosing to spend her final days with you should give you reassurance of how much she loves you." She squeezed my hand. "Don't discount that."

"You're so right. I hear you."

The three of us sat there in silence for a while and listened to the sound of the ocean. Simone was the first to break the silence. "So, this is 40, huh?"

We looked at each other. I shrugged and sighed. "Well, we still look good!" I toasted with another glass of sparkling rosé.

"Ladies... I'm fucking pregnant! What the fuck?!" Simone shouted, laughing.

"I can't wait to see how you're going to look when you start showing," Taylor said as she looked down at her stomach.

"Oh, my goodness! That's going to be crazy!" she said with amazement and excitement.

I placed my hand on her stomach and said in a singsong voice, "Everybody is going to know you were fuuuuuucking!" And the three of us busted out in thunderous laughter.

•   •   •

Mom was more thrilled over the idea of us going to Santorini than I could have ever imagined. But we both knew there was a hurdle to get over before we booked our flights.

So now we sat in Dr. Connors office waiting on her latest MRI results. He came in after a few minutes. He opened his laptop and pulled up a black and white picture of my mother's brain. It had more white specs than the previous one.

"So, the cancer is spreading, and it is spreading aggressively." Dr. Connors cut to the chase.

"How can we slow down the process?" I asked.

"I suggest aggressive rounds of chemotherapy – "

"No. No. No," my mother said, shaking her finger at him. "I'm not doing chemo. What's the point of prolonging my life if it is spent being sick, losing my hair, and dwindling into nothing? I'm not doing chemo." She was adamant.

"I do not recommend you take an international flight. There are too many risks involved. During the flight, air pressure and oxygen levels change when the plane reaches high altitudes. The swelling of the brain increases pressure inside the skull. Symptoms of increased intracranial pressure include headache, decreased consciousness and vomiting. Your brain could swell and cause blindness, and there are risks for seizures. Then they would have to do an emergency landing and inconvenience all the passengers. Not to mention, who knows what hospital you would end up in and in what country?"

"Quite frankly, I could care less about other passengers right now. I have only one concern." I pointed at my mother and took her hand. "Her."

"Are you suggesting I just sit and be a prisoner to this cancer and just wait to die? Or the other choice – live a few months longer with chemo and having an awful quality of life? Those are my options? You have to do better than this." She sounded like she was negotiating a deal for the McKinley Group and not talking about her best options for cancer. Angelique was used to being in control most of her life. This was the first time being in control wasn't an option.

I placed my hand on her arm to relax her. "Dr. Connors, if we chose to move forward with this trip, how could we avoid some of the potential challenges?" I wanted to come from a place of positivity.

"I could prescribe Lorazepam, which would help in preventing seizures. You would need to walk around every hour to reduce the risk of blood clots and stay hydrated. Also, anticipate the fatigue. It will be much more significant after traveling a long distance." Dr. Connors took out his prescription pad and wrote out the prescription for Lorazepam and handed it to my mother.

"I want you to come in the day after you return for a checkup."

"We will." I got up and shook his hand.

•   •   •

Travelling with my mother meant traveling first class all the way. On the 14-hour flight, we had flat beds so we could sleep comfortably, but I couldn't allow myself to relax. I set my cell's alarm to make sure my mother got up to walk around every hour. I kept asking the flight attendants to bring her more water. She seemed calm, but I was a nervous wreck. I kept drinking champagne to try to calm my nerves.

We landed at the Santorini airport safely; no medical emergency had caused the plane to make a landing on our account. Our driver was waiting for us with a sign that said "McKinley."

The drive to our hotel was magical. The white buildings with hints of blue roof, the glimpses of the Aegean Sea – it felt like we had entered a fantasy world. Our hotel was at the top of a cliff that overlooked Santorini. When we stepped out of the limo, we were greeted by hotel staff serving us champagne. When my mother went to take a glass, I quickly took it from her, "Let's not overdo it, missy!"

"Yes, Mommy!" she laughed.

The presidential suite was spacious and airy with doors that opened onto spectacular views of the ocean. We even had our own infinity pool. It was 5 p.m., so we had to get ourselves situated for the sunset. I ordered room service as my mother rested. I could tell the flight had taken a lot out of her. She wore a silk Hermès scarf over her bald head. I prayed that this trip hadn't worn her down. When room service arrived, I had them set everything up on the terrace.

I shook her lightly to wake her. "Mommy, it's time." She slowly opened her eyes and looked around as though she had forgotten where we were. I held out my hand and walked her outside.

We sat down and watched the sky start to turn the color of burnt oranges, then lavenders, pinks, and reds. The sun was putting on a show, magical and spiritual. My mother and I sat side by side in our lounge chairs. I looked over at her silken scarf-covered bald head, her high cheekbones, and her beautiful eyes. I held my hand out for hers.

I had never seen anything like this sunset. Two birds flew by, in front of the sun. Inch by inch, the sun took its time as it made its way below the horizon for its final curtain call of the day.

Tears streamed down my mother's face. She looked at me and said, "You are the joy of my life, Jackie. I am so proud of you, and I am so blessed we can share this. This is one of the happiest moments of my life."

All was peaceful and so serene.

Chapter 28
Simone

I couldn't win. I had just separated from an emotionally manipulative, mean, nasty man, only to have to deal with the same bullshit from my boss! Today I was two seconds away from walking and not turning back. But those golden corporate handcuffs held me captive. The expense account, insurance, salary, and perks of working at one of the top PR firms in L.A. were the tradeoffs. I had a baby on the way and couldn't risk not having a job. So, I put up with the political landmines every day I walked into the building.

Although I wasn't visibly pregnant yet, my body was starting to change. My once flat tummy was beginning to get a post-Thanksgiving bloat. In the past, I would stop at the bar and have a cocktail after a hard day of dealing with my psychopath of a boss. But now, my favorite pastime was to stop at The Grove and go to Janie and Jack and look at their high-end designer baby clothes.

Today, I actually bought my first pair of blue booties. It was pretty exciting. The lady at the register asked if I needed a gift receipt and I proudly said, "No...these are for me." Her excited smile when she said congratulations made the stress of my fucked-up workday disappear.

I'd told my mom and dad the news. They were excited and concerned at the same time. Definitely not how I thought my pregnancy announcement would come. But I was learning to ride the waves as they came.

My new apartment was my safe place. All the boxes were unpacked and I'd decorated the way I liked. I didn't have to ask anyone's permission to hang shit up. I didn't have to worry about coming home to a houseful of people who really didn't like me. I hadn't spoken to

Travis since the day I left. He hadn't tried to call me and I didn't try to call him. I'm sure he told the deacons at his bootleg church to look out for me and block me from coming in. I know he made me out to be a monster so that he and his family didn't look like the bad ones. After all, these "Christians" were the "first family." They could do no wrong! It didn't shock me that Travis didn't reach out. That was who he was. What shocked me was that Daddy Lee had not. I thought that he genuinely cared about me. All that "my favorite daughter-in-law" crap was just a charade. I shouldn't have been surprised. I had seen him lay hands and pray for his congregants and then put down those same people during our Sunday dinners.

But everything else aside, he wasn't just my father-in-law, he was my pastor. I was a faithful, tithing member of his church. He was the man I was forced to do premarital counseling with. You would think just as a "Christian" and being a "Bishop" of the church, he would have reached out to see how I was doing. That would have been the right thing to do. But one of the things I was learning was that my plan and how I thought things in life should go were out the door. I was no longer trying to plan shit out to the year, month, day, hour, and second as I had done all of my life. I was learning to go with the flow.

When I got home, I just wanted to put my feet up and relax. I parked my car in the garage and was coming out to enter my building when I saw a female police officer. We made eye contact and gave each other a friendly smile.

"Simone Lee?" she asked. I was surprised she knew my name.

"Yes?" I responded.

She pulled an envelope from her back pocket. "You've been served." She handed me the envelope. She then said, "Good luck." And walked off.

I felt like I had been punched in the gut. I knew exactly what the envelope contained. For the last few weeks I had felt safe and secure. I had told Travis to send anything to Taylor's gallery, not wanting him to know where I lived. Taylor had been on the lookout for my divorce papers. I had called her every day and she would tell me every day that nothing came.

I looked around to see if someone was in the bushes looking at me through binoculars. Was he watching me? Had he been following me? I started to get light-headed. I went straight to my apartment and locked the door behind me. My safe haven suddenly felt like someone had come in and pissed all over it. I made it to the bathroom just in time. I couldn't stop puking until my body had discharged everything I ate and changed to dry heaves. I leaned back against the wall and wiped the sweat off my forehead. I thought my "morning sickness" had subsided. But clearly it had not. I washed my face and then grabbed some ginger ale from the fridge.

This was another Travis "fuck you" to me. And it wasn't as if I didn't want the divorce. I had made myself okay with the idea I was getting divorced. But I wanted to do it with class and dignity because I felt like during the marriage I had lost that. I didn't want him to add any more fuel to the fire in his efforts to make people think I was crazy. But Travis wanted me to know he was still in control. I could run as much I wanted, but he was still in charge of my life...and the divorce.

My attorney was a friend of a friend of my family. Gary Johnson had to be at least 75 years old, had a thick gray mustache, and silver hair that was slicked back. When I first met him at his office, I thought this old-ass man couldn't possibly be the bulldog I needed to fight Travis and his barracuda family. But if my mother's friend recommended this guy, I had to trust it.

Gary flipped through the paperwork, talking to himself, "Uh-huh. Okay. Hmmmm. Interesting."

With each utterance, I couldn't tell if he thought things were good or bad. Perhaps this is what made him a good lawyer.

"You sure know how to pick 'em," he said, when he finally finished looking through the documents. "Your husband has requested spousal support, the wedding expenses reimbursed, and, this is interesting... as a matter of fact, I have never seen this in the 45 years I have been in practice."

"What?" I asked leaning in toward the desk to see what he was talking about.

"Your husband kept all the receipts form every single date you went on when you were dating – every single trip, including hotels and rental cars, every gift he ever bought you, including jewelry and clothes, and he wants you to reimburse him for half of all of it. He also is requesting that you return the engagement ring and wedding band. There's even a request for reimbursement for a bottle of Dom Perignon." He shook his head.

This couldn't be happening. The bottle of champagne was a running joke I had with the friend who had introduced us. I had told him if we got married I would buy him a bottle of champagne. During our rehearsal dinner I presented him with the bottle as a joke. And now Travis was asking for half of that! My head was spinning.

"Gary, I paid for half of our wedding, as a matter of fact more than that. All of my expenses were paid in cash since I had just gotten my bonus. He paid his half with credit cards. So he is essentially asking me to pay for the entire wedding. And most of the guests were his!" I was feeling like I had to defend myself. "And I sold my wedding ring and engagement ring so I could pay for my new apartment."

"I wouldn't worry about the rings. By law the engagement ring is looked at as a conditional gift. That is, a gift given to another in expectation of marriage. If there is no marriage, many states have laws that say the ring should be returned, but in your case, there was a marriage, so you keep the ring. Is there any way you can get a list of people who attended the wedding and send that to me? I'll need you to specify which guests were his and which were yours."

Wow. Marriage really was just a business arrangement. Divorce was just the final paperwork.

"Yes, I can call my wedding planner and have him send over the paperwork." David had kept very precise records of all of our wedding expenses. And I'm sure he still had all the receipts.

"That will be helpful." Gary made a note on his legal paid.

"Since we were only married six months, can't we get it annulled?"

He went through the laundry list. "Unfortunately, in the state of California, a marriage can only be annulled under specific conditions. For instance, if the couple is related by blood; if one spouse was already married before entering into the second marriage, otherwise known as bigamy; if the person requesting the annulment was not 18 years old at the time of the marriage; or if either spouse perpetrated a fraud to obtain the other party's consent to marriage. With fraud, it has to go to the heart, or essence, of the marriage. A good example would be when one spouse persuades the other to marry because of a secret desire to remain in the United States, or one of the spouses has an 'incurable physical incapacity.' This typically refers to male impotence that prevents the couple from having sexual relations. It could also be when one or both spouses are of 'unsound mind,' meaning there is a mental condition that prevents them from understanding and appreciating the nature and duties of marriage – including severe intoxication. Another example is if one spouse forced the other to get married."

"What's next?" I asked, my head spinning.

"How much spousal support are you requesting? We should counter his. And we should also show proof that he made more money than you. I will send over a discovery request where he has to provide a list of all his assets."

"I don't need spousal support from him. I just want him to pay for my moving expenses." and my first three months of rent." I said.

"I would advise you ask for more. You two don't have children together so we don't have to worry about child support and custody. But I would advise we request that he at least pay for your first year of living expenses since you were essentially thrown out in the street without notice. And we should also ask him to cover all my fees."

The mention of kids made me reflexively rub my stomach. Now would be the time that I should tell my attorney I was pregnant. But this was already getting too complicated. And I was scared of what Travis and his family would do to get custody of my unborn child. If he was fighting like this already, it would get downright dirty if he had any idea I was carrying his child. For better or worse, I decided that I would cross that bridge once we got there. I wanted to get this divorce over and done with, and then I could start a separate custody battle once the baby was born.

Gary went through the long list of documents I needed to provide and the next steps. "Your husband seems to be very greedy and vengeful, so be prepared for this to get ugly. But don't worry, I've been practicing for a long time. This isn't my first rodeo." He smiled reassuringly.

I left the office emotionally, physically, and mentally drained, not to mention financially drained. Old-ass Gary wasn't cheap. But I had to fight not only for me, but for my unborn baby. This wasn't going to simply be a matter of me signing paperwork and going about my business. I had to take the gloves off and fight fire with fire. I was now at a point where I looked at Travis as my enemy and no longer cared about making sure he was okay. I had to worry about me and my child. This was my new reality.

Chapter 29
Taylor

3 Months Later...

This Is 40 looked perfect in the center of my gallery. It was one of those pieces that I loved so much, I wasn't sure if I wanted to ever sell it. My gallery was packed. Although this was a private showing for my inner circle of friends, I had already sold six out of the 18 pieces in the collection. At the rate I was going, I might not need to do another showing for the public. I caught a glimpse of myself in the mirror. My curls were cooperating for a change. My royal blue pants romper was just the right touch for this event. I stood out, but wasn't dressed over the top. This collection had been a great distraction for me over the last three months. *This is 40* was the first piece I created as I refocused on art. The painting explored the twists and turns of life and the milestone of turning 40. It had vibrant and intense colors. It was powerful.

With painting, I was able to get my mind off Michael. I hadn't heard from him at all and to say I was worried was an understatement. But he knew my door would always be open to him.

"This collection might be one of my favorites." Simone had come up behind me and gave me a hug. She looked the epitome of what people called "pregnancy glow." She was wearing a fitted white dress that accentuated her growing bump. At first glance it looked like she'd just ate too much and was gaining weight. But her breasts were looking like they could give Dolly Parton a run for her money. It was obvious she was pregnant, and she was embracing it.

"You like?" I asked like a little girl begging for her mother's approval.

"No, I don't like... I LOVE!" she said. and hugged me again.

"How is it going?"

"I'm hoping for the best, but expecting the worse. I hope we can come to an agreement during the mediation." Simone had shown such a huge amount of strength. She went from living in her own fantasy bubble to emerging as a confident and strong woman, ready to take on whatever was thrown her way. I really was proud of her. I was also nervous for her.

"It's going to be okay," I attempted to reassure her, or maybe I was really trying to reassure myself. The waiter came by passing glasses of champagne. I grabbed a glass and looked at the front door of the gallery.

"Do you think she's coming?" Simone asked.

It had only been two months since Angelique McKinley lost her battle with cancer, and although Jackie was taking it better than expected, it was a day-to-day thing with her. Before I could answer, she walked into the gallery looking absolutely stunning. Her hair was straightened and parted in the middle and hung in the middle of her back. She was wearing sequined black pants with a black DVF wrap shirt, a Van Cleef and Arpels necklace, and a beautiful pair of open-toed, red Jimmy Choo sandals with gold and silver studs. Her lip gloss was bright red to match her oversized red clutch and sandals. I always loved to see people's reactions when she walked into a room. But now, it was even more entertaining because the promos from the show she walked out on were starting to air. People were starting to recognize her because the promos were airing on E!, Bravo, WE, and all the other female-targeted networks non-stop. Although the show hadn't premiered yet, you knew it was going to be a hit, and her appearances were at the center of all the promos they were airing. Talk about a blessing and a curse.

I waved my hand in the air and she came over to us. Since her mother died, Jackie's arrogance when she walked across a room had been replaced with an elegant confidence. I gave her an extra-long hug and Simone did the same.

She rubbed Simone's stomach, "It must be so nice to eat whatever the fuck you want to and not have to worry about sucking in! I'm so jealous." Jackie was still Jackie. We all chuckled.

She flagged a waiter and grabbed a glass of champagne, took a sip, then looked around. "Wow, Taylor! You outdid yourself with this one!"

"Thanks!" I loved when I got the stamp of approval from my girls. "You know we've been worried about you. Have you eaten today?" I could tell she'd lost a lot of weight since her mother's funeral.

"Oh, T, food is overrated!" she laughed, attempting to make light of the situation. I flagged the waiter, who had sliders. I took two off the tray and handed them to Jackie.

"Eat!" I insisted. She took the plate and actually wolfed them down faster than any of us anticipated.

"Are you happy now?!" she asked, like a bratty little sister proving she was right.

"Now I am. You know I love you, girl. Just want to make sure you're okay."

"You don't have to put on a façade for us," Simone chimed in. Funny how the tides had turned.

"I know. But if I think about it, I might just burst into tears right here in the middle of your gallery."

"If you do, it's okay," I reassured her.

"I know, and I appreciate you two. I don't know what I would have done without you these last few weeks." She took a shrimp roll from the waiter passing by and another sip of champagne. "So, how's that asshole, Simone?"

"Still an asshole. I just want this to be over. Although to be honest, this is only the beginning. Once the baby gets here, that will open an entire new can of worms."

"Do we finally have permission to kick his ass?" Jackie was serious as serious could get.

"Or at least key his car. Something!" Even I no longer tried to be politically correct when it came to that asshole Travis!

"You can't do shit, Jackie. You're a bona fide celebrity now. The last thing you need is to have a mugshot!"

"Simone, with these promos running, a mugshot is the least of my worries." Jackie sighed.

"How does it feel to see your face always on TV? The promos are on everywhere."

"I'm mortified! I'm going to be known as the bitch who had a temper tantrum on national TV for the rest of my life! People are already coming up to me asking if that was real!" She shook her head in disgust. "Well, I wanted to be a star. Be careful what you wish for."

"It's all going to work out for the best. You have an extra guardian angel up there protecting you." I put my arm around her to reassure her. It was still hard for me to believe that Angelique McKinley was gone.

"And besides, your nephew will be proud of his auntie regardless," Simone said.

"Wait, what?!" From the beginning Simone kept referring to her growing baby bump as 'little guy.'" But she hadn't had the sex of the baby confirmed.

"Yep. I had my ultrasound today and it's definitely a boy!" She pulled out the little black and white sonogram picture and pointed to a tiny white spec. "There's his little penis! Isn't it cute?!"

"So, you are literally growing a dick as we speak!"

"Oh, my God, Jackie, you are so damn crass!" As the three of us laughed in our own world like we were the only three people in the gallery I glanced at the front door and stopped laughing. Tim Sanders had shown up. I really didn't think he'd show up. I hadn't seen him since the day he came over for Michael's unsuccessful intervention. Was he coming here to deliver bad news? I could feel my heart skip a beat. When our eyes connected I was relieved to see him smile. Okay, clearly he's not here to deliver bad news. He walked up to the three of us. "I'm so glad you could make it, Tim!" I said and gave him a hug.

"Jackie, Simone, this is Dr. Tim Sanders. He was working with Michael. Before, well...you all know the rest of the story."

"Nice to see you again, Dr. Sanders. Do you have any Xanax or any other good strong pills with you, by any chance," Jackie said as she shook his hand.

"Sorry, they're in my other coat." I appreciated his sense of humor and quick wit.

"Please excuse her, doctor, we just met her on the corner," Simone said. "But now we're going to take a look around." Simone grabbed Jackie's arm and they purposefully walked off to see the rest of the collection.

"Thanks for the invite, Taylor." His voice was warm and heartfelt.

"Here, let me show you some of the pieces." I guided him around, showing him about four paintings and explaining my inspiration for each.

"This one is... wow! You are so talented." Tim was mesmerized by the first piece I created that inspired the entire collection. Ironically, that was the piece that Michael saw and loved when he first came to stay with me. I let him take it in for a little while longer. "Michael *did* say you were an exceptional artist. But seeing your paintings in person really embodies it."

"Thanks." My heart sank at the mention of Michael's name. "So, I guess you haven't heard from him either?"

"Unfortunately, I haven't." He seemed just as disappointed.

"Can we talk for a moment?"

"Sure, Taylor."

I motioned for him to follow me upstairs to the balcony. It was a beautiful California night. There was a light breeze gently blowing.

"I appreciate everything you did to try to help me with Michael. You went above and beyond the call of duty. I felt safe with you because most of the time he was being treated by doctors who really didn't get it. You really were a saving grace to Michael as well as to me."

"You don't have to thank me, it's my job."

"You always say that. I know it's your job. But I was just desperate to do whatever it took to help Michael. And clearly, I failed at that, too."

"You didn't fail. You can't help someone who isn't ready to help himself. Michael hasn't been in treatment in over three months and I haven't seen him. But I don't want you to think that this is your fault. You have been a great support system to him."

"I understand that. I just wished we had a magic wand and we could make everything magically perfect. But life doesn't work like that does it?"

"If only it did." He chuckled to himself.

This was the only person who knew about my brother's struggles and understood. I didn't have to explain anything to him. I felt the tears start to well up. Tim took the pocket square from his jacket and handed it to me.

"Sorry... I didn't think I would still be so emotional. What you said about me having to let go and stop enabling Michael resonated. For the first time in my life, I'm actually working on looking out for me. Most of my life has been spent either caring for my mother with her alcoholism, worrying about my brother, or being mad at my dad for abandoning us and starting a new family. I have never ever taken the time to look out for me. It's certainly an adjustment. I'm not sure why I'm telling you all of this."

"Take the adjustment one day at a time. You can't just expect to switch overnight." He was so understanding.

"I just wish I could see him one more time and try to get him to come home with me. I still haven't given up."

"And you shouldn't, but I think it's important that you no longer be enmeshed in it. You should have realistic expectations of what to expect and what not to expect, and know what you are capable of doing," He looked at me. "You understand what I'm saying, right?"

I took a deep breath, "I do, I do. Well, I can't keep you out here all night. But I wanted to take the time to thank you away from all the hustle and bustle."

"I need to get back downstairs before someone else buys the piece I want!" He laughed.

"I can assure you, you get first dibs." I attempted to laugh.

"If you ever need anything, I am here, Taylor. Please don't feel like you can't call me or you're a burden."

"I appreciate that and I plan to take you up on that offer. Please send me the bill for this therapy session!"

Tim laughed. "Don't worry, this one is on the house." We started to walk downstairs. "By the way, you dropped something." Tim pointed to a small piece of white paper on the ground.

"I did?" I picked it up and saw that it had writing on it: *Amber Westcott's address.*

I looked back at Tim. He winked and continued down the stairs.

• • •

I'm sure I left skid marks on the streets driving to get to Bakersfield in the morning. I didn't realize how much horsepower my car had until I was hugging the curves of the freeway. An hour into the drive, my navigation told me to make a left and a quick right. I turned into a trailer park. I checked the address Tim had given me and confirmed it was the right address. My brother was living in a trailer park, with a trailer park bitch!

I had to get him out of here. Instead of knocking the door down and beating that bitch's ass, I decided to wait and pray he would come out soon. *Please God... Please God.* I was begging for God to have him come out. I closed my eyes and leaned my head back until I heard the sound of the trailer door opening. I saw Michael, carrying a large trash bag. He was wearing jeans and a black T-shirt. He still had his muscular shape but his hair was grown out and he was sporting an unkempt beard. A cigarette was dangling from his mouth. He threw out the trash and started walking back to the front door. I jumped out my car and ran toward him, "Michael!" he turned around and when he saw me, to my relief, he smiled.

"T-Squito, what are you doing here?" he asked. His eyes were still bloodshot red. And he wasn't fully present. His eyes were empty. The usual life that was always present, even during his depressed or manic episodes gone.

"I need to talk to you. Can we take a walk?" I asked.

"Hold on, let me let Amber know." He went back in the trailer. I hated this bitch! But I had to proceed very carefully. The fact that he was actually talking to me was a good sign, and I didn't want to fuck it up by pissing him off and discussing Amber. He came back out and lit another cigarette and we started taking a walk. I noticed he had a new tattoo on his arm, an angel with my mother's face.

At a park nearby, we sat on a bench that overlooked a small pond. In the midst of the trailer park homes, it was peaceful there. We sat in silence for a few moments.

"They did a good job," I said, admiring his tattoo. The tattoo artist not only captured my mother's beauty, but also her intense eyes. It felt like my mother was looking at me. The angel wings wrapped all the way around to the other side of his arm.

"Thanks," he said, as he looked at it himself. My brother had never been into tattoos. But I had come to accept the Michael I'd known was no longer.

"I've been thinking a lot about Mommy lately," I said. "I know she did the best she could. She did what she knew. Kids come into this world with a clean slate, and it's the adults that fuck them up." Only Michael could understand our own unspoken hidden secrets. He was holding a small object. I reached for it. It was my mother's one-year sobriety pin. I kissed it softly than placed it back in the palm of his hand.

"I think about her every day, too. I think if she was still alive she would be disappointed in me and think of me as a complete fuck-up."

"Don't be so hard on yourself. I think she would be proud of you. She would think you were handsome, strong, and she would see you are trying. And just like she was able to kick her habit, you can kick yours, too. It wasn't easy, but look how much better she was when she finally got sober."

"She got better, then she fucking died! What was the point? Where was God then, T?" I could feel his pain and hurt just by looking into his eyes.

I put my hand on his shoulder. Between his new tattoo and my mother's sobriety pin it felt like she was sitting there with us.

"All I ever wanted was to be normal, T." He leaned back on the bench. "Without meds. Without doctors. What's the difference between these drugs the doctors give me, and what I give myself, huh?" I couldn't fight him on that. They were both controlled substances. And they both made him feel unlike himself.

"I wish I had the answers. I don't, but what I do know is I just want you to be okay, whatever it takes. I never wanted you to leave my house. You can come back anytime. My door is always open to you."

I was trying to find the right words to convince him to come back. Not having him in the house with me created a major void. In the little time he spent with me, I got used to having him there. "You can even cook another Thanksgiving meal and all the shit from my fridge. I won't get mad. I know I was acting like a bossy bitch while you were there. I'll loosen up!"

"T, I'm *your big brother*. I'm supposed to take care of you. Not the other way around. As a man, I can't let my baby sister take care of me."

"Michael, you *have* taken care of me. You have looked out for me and protected me all of my life. There was so much chaos happening in our house growing up... chaos that only the two of us knew about. At the end of the day we took care of each other. That's how it's always been, and how it will always be."

Michael nodded. "I wonder if God can hear me when I call out. Why did he make me like this? Why can't he fix me? Am I being punished? It's been 44 years of this pendulum that goes back and forth. And the only fix is to take meds that make me a zombie? That's not living, T. I feel like I'm the walking dead here on earth."

"Michael, come back to my place. We can figure this out together. If you don't want to get back on your meds we can try something else. Maybe acupuncture, or some other New Age shit. Just come back."

My words seemed to be getting through. He was contemplating what I was saying. I spoke from the heart. "Michael, having you as a big brother has been the biggest blessing I could ever ask for. I know you don't see it, but you have protected me all my life, you have looked out for me. I have always admired you even when you were getting on my nerves. My life has been filled with so many ups and downs and so much pain and sorrow, but there has been only one consistent thing I could count on, and it has always been you. I wish I would have been a better sister to you growing up. I wish I understood this bipolar disease then like I know now. I want to apologize to you for all those times when we were growing up and I didn't get it. I couldn't understand your pain because I didn't understand the disease. I wish I would have protected you more, like you looked out for me. I wish I would have had your back more. I wish I would have understood more. But I do now. And I'm here. Please allow me to help you. Please, Michael, come back home and we can figure this thing out together. Please."

The tears were rolling down my face...tears that I had held in for the last few months. I cried for our lost childhood, I cried for the abuse we endured, I cried for the pain he felt, I cried for the time we would never get back, I cried for his hurt and his pain. I cried for him. I cried for us. But most of all, I cried because I was scared of what the future held. I was begging him to come back and I didn't care.

Michael, wiped the tears from my cheeks. "Don't cry for me, Sis. You're not alone. I'm here and I will always be here to protect you..." I leaned into his arms and suddenly the roles were reversed, Michael was now comforting me. It felt so safe to be in my big brother's strong arms. He kissed me on the top of my head. "You know I love you, T-Squito."

"Will you come back with me? Let's start over. Let's figure this shit and find something that works for you."

He looked down at our mother's sobriety pin again. "Yes... I'll come back... I'll be there tonight."

"I can wait for you. We can leave together now." I needed to make sure we left together. I wasn't comfortable leaving him alone with Amber.

"No, T. I got this. I have some business to handle first."

We walked back to the trailer. I gave him another big hug. I hugged him for a long time. I just wanted to hold onto this connection with him for as long as I could.

"I can wait for you outside. I'm not in a rush," I tried to reason.

"I said I got this, T."

"I'll see you later, then?"

"I'll see you soon." He turned toward the trailer. He stopped and turned around.

"Love you, T. Always have... always will..."

"Love you too, Soul Brother Number One."

•　　•　　•

I waited in front of the trailer for hours. I didn't want to leave. If I left, I didn't know when I was going to see him again.

Finally, I accepted he wasn't coming, and I drove home.

I took a long shower, one of those showers where the water was scalding hot then your skin started to burn from the temperature but it felt so good hitting my skin. I put on lotion and brushed my hair into a bun. I got in bed and fell asleep instantly. At 3:14 a.m. I was jolted out of sleep. I heard something drop or a bang. My head was pounding. I felt fine when I went to bed but I had a massive headache. I hated the idea of getting out of bed to get Advil. I went to the kitchen where I kept my meds. I noticed that the light in my studio was on... Hmm... that's odd. I hadn't been in there all day. I went downstairs to my sanctuary and found the window open. A breeze was blowing the white curtains gently. I went to the window and looked outside. I felt the breeze hit my face. It was the gentlest, softest night breeze. I closed my eyes and breathed in the air and allowed it to calm and relax me. My headache had subsided. I closed the window, turned off the light and went upstairs to bed.

I was awakened by my phone ringing later that morning. I picked up the phone and saw it was 6:38 a.m. and that it was a Pasadena number. Possibly Huntington Hospital but the prefix didn't match.

"Hello?" I already knew, my spirit told me.

"May I speak to Taylor Ross?" A man with a deep voice said.

"This is she."

"This is the Bakersfield Coroner's Office. We need you to come down and identify a body. Your number was the last number he called on his phone and we assumed you are a relation."

"I'm his sister." I was eerily calm. "I'll be right there." I wrote down the address and made a phone call for the support I needed.

•   •   •

The coroner slowly pulled the body out of the slot. He slowly unzipped the bag that held it on the cold slate of metal. All I had to see was the tattoo with my mother's face and it was confirmed – the cold dead body lying there was Michael's. I nodded my head and he pushed the body back into its slot.

I could see the coroner's mouth moving but I couldn't hear what was coming out. Suddenly I felt so cold. I had lived my entire life waiting for this call. I didn't know when it was coming but I lived with under a constant cloud anticipating this very call.

"We are so sorry for your loss. Your brother suffered from a self-inflicted gunshot wound to the left temple at 3:14 this morning."

"Wait... what time did you say?" I asked.

"The time of death was 3:14 a.m.," the coroner repeated.

"Oh, my God... Oh, my God..." I put my hand on my chest and fell back in the chair as if I had been pushed. The reality of what he was saying hit me: 3:14 a.m. was the exact time I woke up this morning with a splitting headache. The light on in my studio and the soft breeze – that was Michael. He had come to say goodbye. Michael had come to say goodbye. A calm came over me, a lightness.

"Are you okay?" Tim asked. He was the first person I called after I heard from the coroner's office. He insisted on picking me up and driving me there.

"I – I will be."

The coroner had me sign paperwork and a few minutes later brought me a bag with Michael's belongs including his wallet, his watch, and his rings. I hugged them to me.

"Can you do me a favor, Tim? If you don't mind I just need a little bit of time to myself."

"Sure, anything you need."

I asked him to take me to the park where Michael and I had our last conversation.

"Take all the time you need. I'll wait for you at the car."

I opened the plastic bag with Michael's belongings. I took out Michael's wallet. Inside was a browning jagged-edge old photo behind one of his credit cards. I pulled it out – it was a picture of me, him, my dad, and mom. How happy the family looked prior to everything falling apart, before the chaos. I went to put the picture back and something fell out – my mother's one-year sobriety pin. The last time I touched my brother's hand, we were holding it together. I held it tightly in my hand. I sat there, my eyes closed, and suddenly I felt the gentlest breeze blow on my cheek. The breeze rocked the world to stillness and peace. The breeze was Michael. I could feel his presence next to me. I knew he was there with me. "I understand..." I said.

•   •   •

Tim drove me back to my loft. And as I'd expected, there were Simone and Jackie waiting for me outside. I'd texted them to come but they didn't yet know the details.

"Thanks for everything, Tim," I said gratefully. He understood that I had to be with my sisters.

Jackie ran over and embraced me. "Oh, Taylor, I'm so sorry."

"You're going to get through this," Simone said, hugging me as well.

"I'm okay. I'm fine. Let's go upstairs." I needed to keep it together. I couldn't allow myself to fall apart.

When I opened the door to the loft it was eerily quiet and calm. It felt empty yet it felt peaceful.

Jackie was the first to speak. "I can't believe he did it. I'm still in shock."

"I have been dreading this phone call most of my life. I knew it was going to come one day." I was surprised by how calm I was. I sat on the couch and just looked out. I felt like I was dreaming. I felt like I was going to wake up at any point and realize there was a mistake. But then I looked at plastic bag the coroner's office gave me with his things and the reality hit me. I took a deep breath and started to count silently...10, 9, 8, 7, 6... breathe deep... don't fall apart... I wouldn't allow myself to fall apart. I wouldn't. By the time I got to 1, I opened my eyes. Simone was sitting next to me and Jackie was kneeled down in front of me.

"You don't have to keep it together, Taylor. You have to allow yourself to cry and to grieve. You don't have to stay strong for us," Jackie said.

"I'm fine." I could tell Jackie and Simone didn't believe me. "Really, I am. And I really appreciate you ladies coming over... but I'm so tired. It's been a long day. I need to go to bed and start planning for Michael's – " I couldn't get it out. I couldn't allow myself to let the words out. "His... funeral." I put my head in my hands.

That's when it hit me. Michael was gone. He was gone! I would never be able to talk to him again. He was gone. I let out the loudest scream. And I fell to the floor and started banging the ground. "WHY? WHY? HE'S GONE!"

Simone and Jackie stood in shock. They were paralyzed not knowing what to do. "HE'S NEVER COMING BACK! HE'S GONE!" Then I let out another scream. This scream came from my soul. It was a loud piercing scream. I was on my knees, my hands were balled in a fist and I was shaking uncontrollably. "MICHAEL!" I was shaking uncontrollably. All the years I spent holding in my anger, frustration, sadness was coming out in each scream. I had held it I for so long and now it was all coming out. At a certain point Jackie rushed to my side and I fell into her arms, "It's okay... Let it out. Let it out," she whispered in my ear. She rocked me like a baby.

I looked up at her, "Michael is gone?" this time I said it in a whisper. I looked at her eyes and searched for her to tell me that he would come back. I begged for her eyes to have a look of hope. Maybe this was all a big mistake.

"I'm so sorry, T." was all she could muster to say. Then the screams started again. She didn't try to stop it. She just rubbed my back and allowed me to scream. "I can't make it without him. I can't go on without him." I couldn't control myself. I didn't even try to.

Eventually, the screams became sobs, then the sobs turned into whimpering, and the whimpering turned to silence. My heart started to slow down. I sat up. Jackie was still kneeling next to me and Simone was standing in front of me with a glass of water. I looked up at her and let the tears fall down my face. I didn't bother to stop them. "I'm so tired. I'm just so damn tired."

"I know, I know." Simone put the glass of water down and came over to the other side of me. They helped me up. I draped one arm around Jackie and the other arm around Simone. They helped me into my room. Simone pulled the covers back. I sat on the bed, and Jackie lifted my feet up and took off my shoes. I whispered, "He's gone... My brother is gone. I don't think I can make it without him."

"You can and you will. You will have to take it one day at a time." Jackie took a strand of hair that had fallen across my eye and pushed it back.

"One day at a time." I remember my mother saying that at her one-year sobriety ceremony at the end when all the guests and the members of Alcoholics Anonymous said the Serenity Prayer out loud. It was almost as though my mother was speaking through Jackie to me. I felt reassured and I felt like she was with me. "God grant me the serenity to accept the things I cannot change, courage to change the things I can and wisdom to know the difference." I closed my eyes and fell into a deep sleep.

Chapter 30
Simone

Urgh! This was the third dress I tried on and it still wasn't working for me. I still hadn't told my attorney about the pregnancy and the last thing I wanted to happen at the mediation today was for everyone to find out I was pregnant and it would start a custody battle. I didn't want anything to delay this divorce being final. My bump was showing. It wasn't huge; all those years of working out in the gym made my body hold on to its pre-baby shape for as long as possible, but last night my bump decided to pop out and make its debut for the mediation. I decided on a black and white Tahari dress. Since it was flowy, it could hide my bump.

My hands were shaking as I put on my mascara – so much so, it made it difficult to put it on to the level of perfection I was used to. I applied a pale, subtle pink lip gloss and made sure every hair was in place. I knew it didn't make a difference, but the last time Travis saw me I was not at my best. I was not *me*. That woman had been replaced by a strong, confident, mother-to-be. I had earned my battle wounds and I was proud of the scars.

I was at peace with the idea we were getting a divorce. I actually wanted to see Travis today. I wanted him to see that he did not break me. He and his family tried, but they didn't succeed. I wanted to see if he could look me in the eye as a man and ask for alimony, half of the money back from our dates, and for me to pay for the entire wedding. How could a real man even think to ask for some shit like that? I wanted Travis to sit across from me at the table and see that I was okay. As a matter of fact, I was stronger and better.

• • •

By the time I got to Westwood, my heart was palpitating. On the elevator, I watched each floor light up, and as I got closer to the 25th, my hands started to shake. I rubbed my stomach, and said reassuringly, "Everything is going to be okay, little guy."

When the door opened on the 25th floor, I was greeted by my attorney. I didn't like the look on his face. "What's wrong?" I asked with sincere concern.

"Well, there has been a slight change of plans." He said as he directed me past a conference room where I could vaguely see the back of Travis's head and two other men I assumed were his attorneys. My attorney took me into a small office with a couch and two chairs. I sat down and Gary closed the door behind him.

"What's going on?" I asked, beginning to worry.

"Your soon to be ex-husband refuses to be in the same room with you. So, we are going to have to mediate differently than we expected." I could hear the annoyance in his voice.

"What? That's ridiculous." I was beyond insulted. Travis had three fucking months to get over his bullshit. Was he worried I was going to jump across the table and try to kill him right here in the offices? Then I realized this was just another control tactic of his. "So how are we supposed to mediate?"

"This is a stall tactic. We, meaning the attorneys, will literally be walking back and forth to settle each of your points."

"Wow! That's crazy."

"You're telling me. This is one for the books. I'm 73 years old. My knees aren't made for walking back and forth. Your soon to be ex-husband is quite a character!" He shook his head. "Okay, let's get to work."

A few minutes later an older white woman came into the room and introduced herself as the mediation facilitator. She explained that the overall goal of the mediation was reach a resolution so we could sign our papers and send them off to the judge without having to go to court.

For the next four hours I sat there while my attorney walked back and forth to Travis's attorneys going through each item we needed to cover. At one point my attorney came in with Travis's attorneys. These two boys looked like they had just come out of law school. Gary was saying to them, "You can make the request but I will be advising my client to decline." They came in and sat down and Gary said, "Simone, Travis's counsel has a proposal for you."

"Hi, Mrs. Lee," A boy attorney said to me.

"It's Ms. Monroe," I immediately corrected.

"Ms. Monroe. Mr. Lee is willing to offer you $5,000 and you can both go about your separate ways."

"$5,000?!" This was a slap in the face. All I wanted was for him to cover my attorney fees and moving expenses – a total of $25,000. I wasn't even asking for spousal support.

"Exactly! Now if you would please excuse us, I need to speak with my client," Gary said. Gary shut the door behind them. "I'm glad I didn't have to convince you not to take that B.S. offer. Listen, something is up. When I mentioned the businesses and houses you told me were under his brother's name, which were not included in discovery, they went from refusing to give you anything and asking for spousal support to wanting to settle for $5K. He's hiding something. Do you have any idea what?"

I told Gary about the American Express fraud situation, the property in Las Vegas, and the marks against me on my credit report when I was looking for an apartment.

Gary looked disgusted. "Your soon to be ex-husband is up to fraudulent activities. Be happy you're getting out of this now. Because if you were married to him when the house came tumbling down, you would be under the rubble with him." He paused. "We need to get you out of this marriage ASAP. Now that we have found a weakness, we are going to use it to our advantage."

Gary left, and I began to pace back and forth. All that glitters isn't gold. I fell for the façade Travis presented to the world. When I met him, I was so impressed with his success... so impressed by how much he had "accomplished." I loved the S-Class Mercedes, the gated community, the big beautiful house, the possibility of the life we were building together. But when it came down to his overall character and the core of who he was, I didn't take the time to look deeper. He could buy a house because he lived with his parents until he was 35, rent-free. I let it go when I discovered he replaced the S500 emblem on his Mercedes with one that said S600, so people would think he had the more expensive model. He and his family were all about façades. I never fit in. I was never meant to fit into a box. My mind was racing and my stomach was cramping. I sat down and drank some water.

Gary returned with a big smile on his face. "So, it looks like we have come to an agreement. But let me run it by you first. And let me just say that if you want to go to court I can get you more. But it's up to you.

"I have got him to agree to a $45,000 settlement to be paid to you in one lump sum, as well as all my fees. He'll have to pay you within the next 30 days in full. He will not get ANYTHING from you, no spousal support, and he does not get any of the other ridiculous payments he was asking for. Based on the information you gave me and what this man has put you through I would have no problem taking him to court and getting you more. I have him and his attorneys by the balls." Gary was so confident. The bulldog had come out! This is why my mother's friends recommended him

"Where's the pen?" I asked.

"Are you sure you want to sign this?" he said looking at me over his glasses. "I can get you more."

"This was never about the money. I just want this to be done." I meant it, because I was truly done.

"Okay, I'll go and get his signature and I'll be right back." A few minutes later he came back with the paperwork with Travis's signature on the second page.

I signed next to his signature on the same page, similar to how we signed our marriage license. The irony wasn't lost on me. The mediation facilitator came back in and gave my attorney copies in an envelope.

"We will send this paperwork over to the judge and once he signs it, you will be officially divorced. It should be within the next 14 business days."

When she left, I looked at my attorney, "So there's nothing else left to do?" I asked.

"You're essentially divorced. We are just waiting on the judge to sign it. The date of the judge's signature will be your official divorce date."

We walked to the elevator together. We got in just as Travis and his bootleg attorneys appeared. Gary put his hand on the door to hold the elevator for them. Travis shook his head no. Gary shrugged and let the elevator doors close. "Ms. Monroe, you dodged a bullet with that guy. Thank God you didn't have kids with him. That would be a nightmare!"

At the front of the building we shook hands. "Thanks for everything, Gary."

"You're welcome. And when you get married again, I will do your pre-nup, pro bono."

"I don't ever want to get married again!"

"Oh, you say that now. It's still fresh. What you want to say is you won't ever get divorced again. It's all about the lesson, young lady."

"We'll see."

"Trust me, I know these things." He patted me on my shoulder. "You'll be okay." And then he was off, dragging his rolling file briefcase behind him.

Since my stomach was still cramping up, I walked across the street to Starbucks and ordered a tea.

"Mint tea!" the barista called out. I went to take it and my hand touched another woman's who had come to grab the same tea.

"I'm sorry, I thought this was mine," I apologized. I was so much in my head I wasn't paying attention.

The barista and moved the tea back and forth between the two of us. "Jovana?"

"That's hers," I said.

"Yours is coming right up." I could feel this woman staring at me. She was Black, had long straight hair, and was slightly overweight, probably about a size 14. She seemed kind of basic until I saw the huge rock on her left ring finger. It was beautiful. It reminded me of a slightly smaller version of my ring. I was going to compliment her on the ring and tell her good luck but she was acting like I had tried to deliberately steal her tea. Was it that serious? I continued to ignore her and grabbed my drink once it came out. She finally left. I didn't have the time or patience to get into an argument with a random bitch over tea. I was hoping this tea would soothe my stomach. I could feel the cramping again.

I tried to distract myself by sitting in the window and watching the various people walking by. And then in the distance I saw Travis approaching. That man used to be my husband and now he seemed like a random stranger. How does this happen? He just gets to walk away like nothing happened. This motherfucker! I could feel the anger heating up in my face. It wasn't fair. He put me through all this and all he needed to do was write a check and he thought I would disappear. How dare he? How dare he do this to me? How dare he do this to us? His son deserved a better father than that. I no longer needed to walk on eggshells like I was his submissive wife! No, fuck that. I was finally going to give this bastard a piece of my mind.

And I was going to tell him I was pregnant. I got off my stool, threw out the rest of my tea, and pushed the door open in one swift motion. I was pissed! I was angry! I started to charge toward him. I wanted to move faster but my stomach was cramping so badly I had to stop for a second. I leaned over for a few seconds and when I stood back up I saw the woman who had been staring at me in Starbucks run up to Travis and give him a passionate kiss on the lips. He kissed her back – the same way he used to kiss me when we were dating. They held each other and I could see her consoling him.

I watched them in utter disbelief. So the "J" in the text message that Travis got months after we got married stood for *Jovana*! He had been cheating with her the whole time! And now he was engaged to her? Our divorce wasn't even final until a few minutes ago!

They walked off arm in arm in the opposite direction and never saw me. The sky started spinning. I felt light-headed. And I collapsed to the ground. A young woman came running out of Starbucks. "Oh, my God, she's bleeding! Call an ambulance!" People walking by ran over to try to help. The last thing I remember was looking down at my knees where my dress stopped and seeing blood dripping down my legs...

Chapter 31
Jackie

Two Months Ago
Alexandria, VA

My sister and I had become much closer since my mother fell ill. We spent the last three weeks of her life with her in the L.A. hospice. Taylor and Simone understood when I told asked them not to come to hospice. I didn't have to explain to them that this was our time together – the three McKinley ladies getting along, supporting each other, and most of all, loving each other.

And I didn't want them to see my mother like that. Those last few weeks were rough. Seeing her in her hospice bed, fighting to breathe, watching her chest heaving up and down and clinging to life, made me understand the expression "She fought the good fight."

There finally came a point when neither Julia nor I could stand seeing her in pain. If she were able to speak, she would have said she was ready. I was actually angry at God. It wasn't fair to put her through all of that. It seemed so unfair and so cruel. Hearing my mother cry out in pain and watching her deteriorate changed the fiber of who I was, what I thought was important, and how I treated life. Why couldn't it be like in the movies, where dying is peaceful, looking up and saying, "I see the light," then drifting off into the afterlife? This wasn't at all like that.

I gave Julia some time alone with my mother to say her final goodbye. When she left the room, I went in to say my final goodbye. I lay down on the hospital bed and I put my head right next to hers. "Mommy, I am so blessed God chose you to bring me into this world. I love you so much and I thank you for making me who I am. I thank you for allowing me to become the woman I am, I thank you for providing for me and loving me unconditionally. I thank you for understanding my temper tantrums and bratty moments. Thank you for loving me despite me. I thank you for making me extraordinary. If being extraordinary was easy, everybody would be doing it."

I was going to miss hearing her say that. "I know you will look out for me, protect me, and guide me in death, as you did in life. I love you forever." I kissed her forehead, and I went out to the hallway where my sister was waiting. The doctor arrived and administered morphine. Two hours later, Julia and I held each other's hands and watched our mother, Angelique McKinley, take her final last breath and transition.

The memorial service took place two weeks later. My mother had every single detail planned out: the location, the time of day, the colors, the flowers, the program, the picture for the program – she was just as bossy in death as she was in life. The hardest part was getting her cremated. Before she passed away I begged her to let us get her a coffin and embalm her. "Absolutely NOT!!! They never make dead people look like themselves. I do not want people looking at my corpse. That is a non-negotiable. I want to be cremated and my ashes will be split between you and Julia. This is not open for discussion!" She gave me that look that only a mother can give you, that tells you to keep your mouth shut. I did. The memorial was just as my mother instructed us, a celebration.

She wanted the repast afterward to be a big party at the McKinley and Associates offices in Alexandria. Only Angelique McKinley could pull off making her death a networking opportunity, and not seem tacky! Once family members had a few cocktails and the music was playing, people started dancing as my mother's favorite songs played. In another room, friends of my mom were laughing and telling funny stories about her in different stages of her life. Her colleagues told tales of her in business meetings, and how she could check people in two seconds. Simone and Taylor talked to my sister in the corner. They were in their own little world.

I walked around the offices by myself and took everything in. She worked her whole life to build this company. Each room had a different look and was based on every element of her life. All these years, I fought trying to be like her, but now I was able to admire all that she had accomplished. At that moment, I was numb. It felt like an out-of-body experience. I entered the corner office at the end of the hall. I sat in my mother's huge leather chair behind her mahogany desk. Her reading glasses were sitting on top of the desk. I picked them up and put them on. I wanted to see the world through my mother's eyes for a moment. I took a deep breath and let out a long exhale. After seeing her in hospice, I didn't take breathing for granted.

The room had the same silence as the hospice – eerily quiet and peaceful. I knew she was with me. I could feel her undeniable presence in this room. I leaned back in her chair, closed my eyes and allowed my mother's spirit to console me.

•   •   •

They say death either brings people closer, or tears people apart. I was relieved it was the former for Julia and me. We spent the two weeks after the memorial service going through my mother's estate. I knew Mother had left a very detailed will, but that was an understatement. She didn't just outline how much money we each got, she outlined who got which purse, which pieces of jewelry went where, which organization she wanted to donate her clothes to, where her furniture should be sent. Even the artworks that hung on the walls of her house had names of who should get each piece. Julia and I didn't have to figure out anything. She did it all for us. She didn't leave any room for us to argue and try to figure things out. It was all done.

"I think that's the last of everything," Julia said as she packed up the books from my mother's library. We gazed at the empty bookshelves. My mother's executive decision had been to only own first editions ,or books that were signed by the authors themselves.

"It looks so empty," I said, in disbelief.

"I didn't realize how many books she had up there until now."

"What do you think you're going to put here now?"

"Who knows? I might hire a contractor and have the shelves taken out and turn this area into a champagne room." Julia was still Julia, which made me chuckle. "What's so funny? Mommy liked champagne," she reasoned with a smirk.

I shook my head. "It will be interesting to see how you bring your own personality to this place."

"You know I loved Mom. But I was never a fan of her decorating. I am about to make this place so damn swanky. I'll keep the office the same. I don't ever want it to lose her touches. But as for this place, I have it to make my own home." She looked at me, awaiting my approval. She would always be my baby sister. But I could feel the shift; my approval meant more to her now than ever.

"I understand, Sis. I am so proud of you for taking over Mom's business." I had no idea how much time my mother had put in grooming Julia to take over her company. To my surprise, Julia had admitted that Angelique made her work for the company in exchange for fronting her living expenses. I had always assumed she was pimping my mother! So, McKinley and Associates would live on through Julia. It's crazy how the stars line up.

"Thanks, Jackie. I hope I don't let her down."

I hugged her tight, "You won't. You got this, Sis."

"I'm scared, Jackie." She sounded like the little girl I remembered when she came home after some other little girl beat her up on the playground. I'd gone to the school and tried to find the bully but was stopped by the principal. Regardless, Julia always knew I had her back.

"That's natural. You have big shoes to fill. But I know you will take Mommy's company to the next level."

"We have to make Mommy proud, and we will. We are her legacy. And don't forget, if being extraordinary was easy..."

"Everybody would be doing it!" We had a good laugh, finishing in unison.

Los Angeles
The Present
I woke up and peeled off my sleep mask. The sun was peeping into my room. I hadn't even bothered wrapping my hair and putting on my scarf. Since my mother's funeral, it was hard for me to get out of bed and start the day. Nighttime and the mornings were the hardest.

This morning was exceptionally hard because last night I watched the episode of "Hip and Hollywood" that I appeared in. Thank God Taylor and Jackie were with me as a support system. Although they tried their best to convince me it wasn't as bad as I thought, they didn't have the ability that I did to hide their true inner monologues. They were mortified. At certain points I could tell they were trying not to laugh. This was no laughing matter.

I looked at my cell phone and I had a dozen missed calls and text messages. Some folks who'd called me or texted I hadn't heard from in years. My phone buzzed with a new text as I was holding it.

Hey sis. Just checking in on you. It's not as bad as you thought it was going to be. That scene with you and Mom gave me chills. Love you and call me later...

I smiled as I read my sister's text and responded:

I think I am about to go into the reality witness protection program until the last episode airs! I'll call you later. Love you too.

The irony of life wasn't lost on me. My sister was running my mother's company, and she was good at it. With all of her millennial knowledge of social media, McKinley and Associates was everywhere. It was the place all the youngsters who were looking to start nonprofits went. She made the company hip and cool! Meanwhile, I was essentially unemployed and the laughingstock of Hollywood! Maybe I could become *her* assistant. I knew this was going to be a day from hell. I knew it was coming.

I got up to get a cup of coffee. As I passed the fireplace, I did my usual morning ritual. I rubbed the gold and black urn that sat on top of the mantle, and said, "Good Morning, Mommy." Behind it was the large framed picture of us in Santorini, the sunset in the background. I missed her so much. She was the only person who knew how to shake some sense into me. My new normal without my mother was too damn intense. But I had to keep it moving. That's what she would have wanted.

I turned on the Keurig and waited for my cup of coffee to brew. I contemplated putting some Bailey's in there to ease the embarrassment of last night. I was now being forced to relieve it like it had just happened yesterday, because that's when America saw it.

"Urgh!" I grabbed my coffee and turned on my TV. The channel was set for "Live with Kelly and Ryan."

Kelly: Clap if you watched that new show on Bravo, "Hip and Hollywood." (Majority of audience claps). Ryan, did you watch it?
Ryan: No, but I heard all about it.
Kelly: You have to watch this Jackie woman. She did what most of us in show business only dream of. I think we have a few seconds of the clip.

I watched myself storming through the set. "Diana, I'm done. I'm out. This isn't what I signed up for. I don't hang out with ghetto trash. (bleep) this business, (bleep) my life, and if you (bleep) had any damn sense, you would get the (bleep) out too!"

Then it flashed to the scene with Jay Goldstein and me going off on him. They cut back to Kelly and Ryan.

Ryan: That's awesome. That's great! We gotta have her come here on the show.
Kelly: We will just make sure everything is nailed to the floor in case she wants to throw something.
(Kelly, Ryan, and the audience erupt in laughter)
Kelly: Her mother passed away a few months ago.
(Audience says aww... in unison)
Ryan: That's so sad. I actually admire her for leaving the show to take care of her mother.
Kelly: Not a lot of people would give up fame and fortune and do the right thing.

Oh, my God... Oh my God! This was BEYOND embarrassing! Since I was clearly a masochist, I turned on Wendy Williams. A part of me was hoping that maybe, just maybe, she hadn't seen the show. I was hoping that maybe, just maybe, she was busy gossiping about real celebrities and watching the Real Housewives. I took a deep breath and watched my favorite Jersey girl daytime host, and hoped that she would either have some sympathy for me (or she hadn't watched the show).

Wendy: It's time for....
Audience: Hot topics!!!
Wendy: How many of my co-hosts watched that new show "Hip and Hollywood" last night?
(Thunderous applause from the audience)
Wendy: Now that Jackie is a Jersey girl after my own heart. Watch this clip and we'll talk.

The clip they played was the same clip they played on "Kelly and Ryan."

Wendy: First of all, I couldn't get past all that hair! (Audience laughs) And you could tell that's all hers. If you're going to act a fool at least make sure your hair is blowing perfectly in the wind. And then... why would you agree to do a show and not have all the details? Guuuurrrrrlllll! Some people will do anything for a paycheck!

Shit! I wanted to turn off the TV, but as much as I hated having to hear what she had to say, I kept it on. It's like watching a train wreck; you can't look away.

Wendy: I tell you, though, kudos to her for walking off that set. I wonder if she still got paid. Hmmmm... But I gotta be honest, there's something about her that's likeable. She made the show. She needs her own show. I'll be watching! How you doin'?
(Audience erupts in laughter and starts clapping)

To torture myself even more, I switched to The Real. They seemed to be slightly more sympathetic than Wendy.

Lonnie Love: I don't blame her for walking off the set.
Adrienne: I remember when I did reality TV for just a short stint. Those producers don't care about you. They are all about creating drama for ratings. I don't blame her for walking off the set. Kudos to her.

Tamera: I hear you all. But she knew what she was signing up for before the cameras started rolling. She was unprofessional. When I did the reality show with my sister, there were many times I wanted to walk off, but I had to maintain my professionalism and go with the flow because that's what I signed up for.

"Self-righteous bitch!" I yelled at the TV screen.

I was being judged in broad daylight on national TV and there was nothing I could do. This was the beginning of the end.

My phone was ringing off the hook. I eventually had to turn the damn thing off. I couldn't take it. I stayed home the rest of the day and managed to avoid phone calls. I drank two bottles of champagne and passed out on the couch. I woke up there the next morning and realized didn't have shit to eat in my fridge.

I threw on some jeans, a T-shirt, and flip-flops and headed over to Ralph's. In the store, I noticed people staring at me and whispering. What the fuck? I felt like I was walking around with a big scarlet letter L, that stood for "loser." Instead of buying everything on my list, I grabbed the essentials, six bottles of wine so I could get a 30% discount, coffee, creamer, and kale. I still had to maintain my slim figure in the midst of all this foolery. That would tide me over for the next day or so. On the checkout line I glanced at the gossip magazines. And when I looked closer, I saw I was on the cover of one of them! It was headlined, "When Reality Goes Wrong!" and the subhead read, "Behind the Breakdown of Jacqueline McKinley." And there was a freeze shot of me screaming on the set! It was the worst picture of me they could have possibly picked!

"Shit!" I said to myself. Or at least I thought I said it to myself until the person in front of me turned around and recognized me. Before he could say anything, I pulled my sunglasses down over my face and walked out and went home.

Jesus Christ! I had no idea that many people watched Bravo! The show just aired and I was already on a tabloid?! This is a fucking nightmare. I paced back and forth in my living room. I didn't want to turn on the TV because I feared there would be another segment about my meltdown. Apparently, I had become the poster child of everything that is wrong with reality TV. It was like I had started a movement on the mistreatment of reality stars. That's not what the fuck I wanted.

I finally turned my phone back on and of course I was barraged with all the texts and calls I'd missed. The only people I would be speaking to were Simone and Taylor, the only two people I could trust. My phone began to ring again. I'd had it. Whoever was calling was going to get cussed out.

"WHAT?!" I yelled into the phone.

"Ms. McKinley? This is Joan Stevens," the voice on the other end said.

"I don't know a Joan Stevens and I have no fucking comment about 'Hip and Hollywood.'"

"Well, that tone and answer certainly isn't going to help you with damage control." Something comforting in her tone told me not to hang up.

"Who is this again?" I was still irritated, but I managed not to yell.

"My name is Joan Stevens. I worked with your mother years ago on a project," she said.

I went to my couch and sat down. "You knew my mom?" I said, just above a whisper.

"She was a friend of a friend. My condolences, Jacqueline. Angelique McKinley was a brilliant businesswoman, and she will be missed."

"Thank you." I looked at the urn on the mantle. "So, what is the reason for your call?"

"Well, I saw your show the other night."

"You and the rest of America!" I interrupted. "I really don't have a comment. It is what it is and I have moved on." I was about to hang up on her. Although she was a friend of a friend of my mother, the last thing I wanted to do was talk about that train wreck of a show.

"Jacqueline, you're going to have to figure out your angle and get ahead of this. And I can help you," she said.

"How can you help me? I am the laughing stock of reality TV." I was going into self-pity mode.

"I'm a publicist. I can help you flip this and work it to your advantage," Joan said convincingly. But I was so tired of people promising me the moon and stars, while I didn't get shit in return. That's how I got into this mess in the first place – trusting that bitch Linda, and Jay Goldstein.

As though Joan was reading my mind she continued, "I am sure you have gotten a lot of broken promises. But I can help you sift through the bullshit and flip this on everyone. We can take these 15 minutes of humiliation and turn them into an empire. Let me help you."

"Why would you want to help me?" I needed to understand why this woman I had never met before wanted to come in and save me. And then it hit me, "How much are you looking for?" It was always about money in Hollywood.

The funny thing was, now that I was financially set, I was more frugal than I had ever been in my life. I knew what it felt like to be broke and living paycheck to paycheck. I wasn't about to squander my newfound wealth. I not only made that promise to my mother, I also made that promise to myself.

"Your mother gave me a shot when I young and fresh out of college, Jacqueline. She believed in me and let me handle the press for one of her biggest projects because she believed in me. She believed in me before I believed in myself, and I am forever grateful. I can help you, Jacqueline."

I thought about it for a few seconds. I looked at the picture of my mother and I in Santorini and decided to meet Joan the following day for lunch.

•　　•　　•

I was still trying to go unnoticed so for lunch with Joan I settled on wearing black jeans, a black tank top, black Gucci slide-ons, a black Gucci baseball cap, dark Gucci sunglasses, and a black Gucci fanny pack. As I walked into Gratitude Café, a popular vegan restaurant in Beverly Hills, I actually stood out more than I blended in. Gratitude Café was light and airy and had your typical cheery Southern California vibe to it. Meanwhile, I looked like I was going to a funeral. But wasn't I? Shit, I felt like my career was dead. So, the significance didn't go unnoticed by me.

When I asked for Joan Stevens at the host stand it occurred that I had no idea what Joan looked like. I didn't know if she was Black or white, tall or short, skinny or fat. I learned many years ago I couldn't go by what people sounded like on the phone. When most people talk to me on the phone they think I am a blonde-haired, blue-eyed, white girl from Laguna Beach.

The friendly girl at the host stand said, 'Follow me this way." Joan smiled and stood up when she saw me. Joan was short and wore a pair of YSL heels that must have been at least six inches, white cigarette pants, a crisp white button-down shirt with the color popped up, a statement necklace, and can't-miss, large, pear-shaped diamond earrings. She had a short haircut, and her makeup was BEAT! She looked like a younger version of Liza Minelli. It looked like she had a professional glam squad in the next room, just waiting to touch her up. And I know, I'm a shallow bitch for noticing, but seeing her immediately put my mind at ease.

"Nice to finally meet you, Jacqueline," Joan said. I almost shushed her because I didn't want anyone to know who I was. I also didn't like that she picked a table that was in the middle of the restaurant. I was hoping we would be in a back corner.

"Nice to meet you as well. Please, call me Jackie," I whispered and pulled my hat down.

"So, you got yourself in a little bit of a pickle, huh?" She smiled.

"That is the understatement of the year."

"Can I just be blunt right off the bat with you?" In the few seconds I'd known Joan, I had a feeling that my answer didn't matter – bluntness was her middle name.

"Uh... yeah." I answered.

"You gotta own this. You can't go into hiding. You have to cease this moment." She pulled two binders out of her briefcase. "So, here's our game plan."

I took one of the binders and opened it. It had a detailed strategy of how we were going to move forward. She walked me through it, page by page.

"First off, moving forward, you're Jackie, not Jacqueline. Do you realize you have started a movement? Producers are going to think twice before they fuck over more unsuspecting folks with bullshit reality shows. People relate to you. Moving forward, you go by 'Jackie.' It makes you more relatable."

"Okay," I agreed.

"I have set up some interviews and shoots with *Us Weekly, People,* and *In Touch.* We need to hit these magazines with your story, your background. They need to see you as the polished, educated African American woman who is the daughter to the late great business mogul Angelique McKinley. And with all the PR and social media hype around your mom's company, the timing couldn't be better." Joan was good. I loved how she said "business mogul."

"Then we are going to book you on some late-night shows. This is all going to happen very fast. We have to ride this wave now. We have a very small window to get in front of this and set up your next gig."

Joan went over every single page of the binder. "And last, but not least, this all-black funeral look shit isn't going to work. Own your shit. I could have had you meet me in my office, but it's important people see you out and about. I also have my own connections to make sure you are featured in the right publications. If you look over to the far left across the street, you'll see my friend with a camera. He's sending shots now to "TMZ," various gossip blogs, *US Weekly, In Touch, People,* etc. – 'Jackie McKinley, out and about after her reality debut!'" I looked across the street there was a photographer taking pictures. "I need you to trust me. Stars aren't born, they are made... by their publicist."

Joan was a gift from my mother.

•　　•　　•

Within two months, Joan delivered on everything she said she would, and more. She even helped me secure my new powerhouse Paradigm agent, Camille. I was able to create my own story and become the face of the change needed in reality TV. And now, it was time to make my next big move. Camille, Joan, and I met with the head of development for NBC.

"The ratings for 'Hip and Hollywood' were through the roof, and your scenes were the highest-rated. When you were onscreen, the ratings were up. When you were offscreen, they were down," Jeff said. "Have you thought about the format you would want for your show?"

"We have. We thought long and hard about it. We want a syndicated talk show." Camille didn't beat around the bush. "Jackie is hot right now. The people want more of her, and it's up to us to make sure they get just that." I loved how Camille was speaking like I wasn't sitting there. "AND, we want executive producer and creator credits and privileges."

"I don't know about that, Camille. You're taking my balls and putting them in the blender before dessert?" That was Jeff's idea of a joke.

"That's a non-negotiable. And I don't want a bullshit executive producer title, Jackie gets authority to make final decisions, including final edits."

Jeff nodded. "I need a few days to think about this."

"I'll give you 48 hours and after that we shop it to another network. What's there to think about? Let's not play this game. You'll lose and I'll bring her right over to CBS. We are giving you first dibs since Bravo was the network where 'Hip and Hollywood' originally aired."

"Jackie is hot right now," Joan added. "We have other networks interested, but we are doing you a favor by coming to you first."

"So, don't leave us waiting," Camille concluded for Joan.

This is what it felt like to have a team of people representing you. All I had to do was sit there and literally be pretty. A talk show?! I wanted to run around like I was in "The Sound of Music," but I remained calm.

"Well, ladies, thanks for your time," Jeff said, as he got up to leave.

"Thank you, Jeff," I said. Just then the waiter came with the bill. "He will be paying," I said, motioning to Jeff. We all started laughing as Jeff took out his wallet.

Chapter 32
Simone

One Year Later
The little guy already had a strong grip. His tiny fingers were wrapped around mine and he was looking straight at me, smiling. "Hey, little guy... How's life on this side of the world?"

"Smile!" my neighbor Justin said. I smiled cheek to cheek with the baby he and David had adopted five months ago. He was adorable. He looked like... well, he looked like he could be my son. He was my complexion with a head full of curly hair. "Thanks so much for all these clothes," Justin said.

"And they're from Janie and Jack – you spent a pretty penny on our munchkin," David said as he pulled out the overalls from the gift box. At least all the baby clothes I had bought for my little guy would not be wasted.

"Oh, no problem. He is so precious," I said, handing the baby back over to Justin. "I am so happy for you guys." I knew how long they had waited, and the struggle they went through to give this precious baby a home. "As much as I would love to stay, I gotta head to the office. I have so much going on. See you guys later."

I got in my car and headed to my office. It took me damn near a year to feel like me again... to get over the pain of losing my baby. It was not an easy road.

8 Months Ago
"Simone. You're awake," Taylor said as she rubbed my forehead.

I attempted to sit up, but my body let me know I was too weak. I tried to take the oxygen mask off my face. Jackie gently rubbed my hand as she stopped me.

"What's happened?" I managed to ask. I looked at Jackie and she couldn't look me. Then I looked over at Taylor and I saw the tears welling in her eyes.

A doctor came over. Her long brunette hair was pulled back in a ponytail and she wore glasses. "Mrs. Lee – "

"That's Ms. Monroe," Jackie said softly.

"Jackie! Not now." Taylor reprimanded. I knew something was wrong.

"Ms. Monroe. I am so sorry to tell you that we had to perform an emergency D&E." She started speaking in doctor language that I didn't understand. I was too weak to ask any more questions.

"Can you please speak to her in English, doctor?" Jackie was sensing my confusion and getting annoyed for me.

"A D&E is also known as a 'dilation and evacuation' and is done during the second trimester. Your baby was suffering from a malfunctioning heart, and when you arrived at the hospital you had lost a lot of blood. We are not sure what caused this. It could be extreme stress, or this condition could have developed on its own. We tried our best to save both you and the baby, but, unfortunately, he didn't survive. We had to use vacuum aspiration to remove the tissue – " I started to tune her out. Reality was hitting me hard.

I pulled the oxygen mask off. "My baby... where's my baby!" I started yelling. I tried to get out of the bed. Jackie and Taylor were trying their best to calm me down. The doctor rushed over and put something in my IV, and I passed out. All I remember thinking was *my son is gone. I've lost my son.*

•   •   •

I was released two days later. I'd lost so much blood, I had to have a blood transfusion. I was still weak. Jackie and Taylor took me home to my apartment.

"Let's put you to bed. You need to get some rest." Taylor said. I hadn't talked since the day I found out I lost my son.

"Close the curtains." It was the first thing I had said in days. My voice was deep and groggy. Jackie looked at me with heartache and did as I asked. I couldn't look at her or Taylor, I couldn't look at anyone. I was sore and on pain meds. I started to sob. I screamed and punched the bed. Taylor and Jackie stepped back and allowed me to get it out. I cried out of regret that I ever met Travis, I cried that my need for perfection had taken over my senses, I cried because I was mad at myself. And now, my baby was gone. I let it all out. I cried so hard that there were no more tears left.

Jackie and Taylor didn't leave my side. When I calmed down, I hugged my legs and rocked back and forth. Taylor held me, Jackie left and came back with a glass of water and a little blue box with a silver and blue bow. I looked up at Jackie and Taylor, "What's that?""The hospital gave this to you. But maybe you should open it another time," Taylor said, giving Jackie a look.

I pulled the bow and opened the box. Inside was a square of blue cardboard with the tiniest baby footprints and handprints. They were no bigger than a Monopoly game piece. I knew they were my dead son's prints. I held the paper to my lips and kissed it and held it to my heart.

Jackie pulled a tiny figurine, a silver baby angel with wings, from the box. "This is beautiful," she said as she handed it to me.

"Never again. Never again."

I didn't need to finish the sentence. They already knew what I meant. I would never again lose myself. I would never again stop loving myself. I would never again shrink in order to allow someone else to feel big. I would ever again dim my light to let someone else shine. This was the moment when I took control of my life.

•   •   •

I returned back to work just two weeks later. I wore a DVF wrap dress. My baby bump was still visible to me. It was a reminder of what I had lost, and what I needed to gain back. The receptionist was her usual cheery self, "Hi, Mrs. Lee!" I didn't bother to tell her I was now divorced and back to being Ms. Monroe. I passed my psychotic boss's office and heard him on the phone talking to one of the "boys" in the studio executives' "Boy's Club." When he saw me pass, he yelled out, "You're late!" He went back to his conversation on the phone.

I picked up my office phone and called my lazy assistant. "Deena, could you please come to my office."

Five minutes later, she came over with her usual, low-energy self, cleavage exposed, and a notepad. "Please get me some boxes, and here are all my recent receipts. Could you please make sure you submit the expense report in the next hour?" She attempted to give me some lame excuse as to why she couldn't do it that fast, but I cut her off. "Thanks. And please close my door." I then got on my computer and started deleting all my personal information. Within a few minutes, my lazy-ass assistant came back with three cartons.

I started packing up. Over the weekend I had already taken all the offices supplies that were in my drawers as well as paintings on the wall so when I came in today, I would need only one small box. I asked for additional boxes to increase the dramatic effect. One of the many things I learned from being friends with Jackie for so long was how to make a dramatic exit. An hour later, my asshole boss barged into my office without knocking. He had no concept of what privacy meant, or he did and just didn't give a fuck. He looked at the boxes. "What the fuck is going on?"

"I fucking quit! That's what's going on, Zale. You are mean, nasty, and unprofessional and I have had enough of you. I didn't leave my last company to come here and be treated like an entry-level coordinator and a second-class citizen. You have me twisted. I have paid my dues and I know what I bring to the table." I was putting the last items in my box.

"You can't just quit... We have a campaign launching this week and you just got back from being sick." He was dumbfounded.

"No, *we* don't have anything this week. *You* have a campaign to launch this week. And maybe if you weren't so concerned with what time I came and went and weren't so busy looking at Deena's tits, or gossiping with your homeboy in Chicago, you would have had more time to see all the hard work I put into this place. But you can't see past you own super-inflated ego. I'm done!" I picked up my box and started walking out.

"And by the way, I have already contacted HR with all of my documentation of your unprofessionalism and sexist behavior."

I had been building a file on him for the last year. I wasn't about to leave a major corporation without a backup plan. While I was on sick leave, I had daily conference calls with our human resources person to go over my severance package. I not only negotiated two years' salary, I also negotiated two years' health insurance, as well as receiving my full bonus for the year.

The elevator door was open and waiting for me. Talk about perfect timing!

•　　•　　•

My next stop was in Century City. Kimberly, my commercial realtor, was waiting for me in the lobby. "Shall we have one last look at the new office space?" she said.

"Absolutely! This is so exciting." We went up to the 11th floor and she opened the door to my new corner office space. It wasn't a huge space. It had an area for the receptionist, and to the left was my office. It was all white and airy.

"This is a great spot. You're in the heart of everything. You're close to Beverly Hills and the freeways. You have the corner space, so there won't be a bunch of noise. And look at that view!" Kimberly was still selling me on the office. Between my severance and my divorce settlement, I was flying high financially and I was ready to take some chances. I was no longer playing things safe. This was what my heart desired, and I was going for it. "What is the name of your business again, Ms. Monroe?"

"SEE Me, for Simone Extraordinary Events, Monroe Enterprises," I proudly answered.

"Oh, I like that! That's a great play on words." Kimberly gave me the exact reaction I wanted. "Here are your keys!" She dropped them into the palm of my hand. "I'll leave you be."

She left and I took a moment to walk around. This was my space. This was my new beginning. No one could take this away from me. I could decorate it however I pleased, and I would play by my own rules.

I would take chances. I was going to make this a success. •　　•

Seeing my logo on my office door always put a smile on my face. Taylor did a great job and the teal, gold, and white colors popped. I opened the door and was greeted by my hip millennial assistant, Reign. She kept me relevant. She ran all my social media, kept me abreast of the growing trends, and she was fun and spunky. But most of all, she was a go-getter.

"Good morning!" she said with a smile, handed me my coffee, and followed me into my office.

I had done great things with the space. The desks were white, the chairs were a white leather, and there were accents of teal and gold that brought out the colors of my logo. It was a neat and pristine office, but it also had a hip edge. In a short time, I had managed to secure quite a few clients. And the next event I was working on was one of the biggest and most important.

Being in business for myself was exciting but scary. There was a certain level of security in wearing the golden corporate handcuffs. But the freedom of having my own thing outweighed the expense account and the top PPO insurance I got from the advertising company.

"We have a lot of shit to do this week to prep for the event this weekend," I warned Reign.

"No worries. So, you saw the news?" Reign reluctantly asked.

"No, I didn't. What's going on?" Driving to work in silence was now part of my daily regimen. When I got in my car, I turned off the ringer and the radio and allowed myself time to think. I gave myself 15 minutes to have "me" time.

Reign turned on the TV that hung on my office wall and turned to the news. And there were Travis and Jacob, handcuffed, walking into the FBI offices. "That's your ex-husband, right?" Reign asked.

I was floored. I sank down on the couch. "Reign, can you get me some water?" I was too mesmerized by the TV to even look at her.

"Ummm. Sure, boss."

I turned up the volume to listen to the reporter. "Travis Lee and his brother, Jacob Lee, have been indicted on ten counts of real estate fraud. If found guilty, they face up to thirty years in prison."

The screen flashed to Jovana, walking beside Travis with her head down. The news of their marriage a few months ago was no surprise. Of course, I had to look the new bride up in all the social media pages. She fit right in with the family. I did my digging, I found out she was born and raised in Watts, didn't have a college degree, and came from a small family. She was perfect for the Lees because she didn't come from much. Karen could feel like she was in control, and Jovana probably felt lucky to be with a family like the Lees.

Based on the pictures, she and Jacob's wife looked like they were best friends. Did she know that Lindsey cheated on Jacob? Did she sit in the front row of the church next to her and Karen and play the role of the perfect first family? I wondered what his father's congregation thought. How did they explain this one? The ink on our divorce papers was barely dry, and my ex-husband was married to another bitch. But that was no longer my problem. He and his brother let their greed take them over. I was so relieved I was spared! I could have been all up in that.

I was happy. I wanted karma to hit Travis in the ass. There were times I got mad because it wasn't happening fast enough. I regretted I didn't get a chance to cuss him out and give him a piece of my mind! But now, looking at these two crooks on TV, and his sidepiece wife trying to look all dutiful, I was thrilled! This was the biggest "fuck you" he could ever get. I busted out laughing. I laughed so hard I was crying. I was clapping my hands and waving them in the air, "Thank you, Jesus! Karma is a bitch!"

I pulled it together. I heard a light tap at my office door. I smoothed my skirt and stood up straight and turned off the TV.

Reign came in. I appreciated that she was wise beyond her 24 years on the planet. She knew how to read body language, so she waited to speak. One of the things I've learned is to keep the lines of demarcation clear. She worked for me; she wasn't my friend. I learned that lesson the hard way with all my other assistants. I kept our work environment light and breezy, and made sure she respected me as her boss and mentor.

I handed her a schedule. "Here's the list of our action items for this weekend. If you have any questions, please ask. We can't afford to have any missteps or mishaps. Everything has to be perfect!"

"You got it, boss." I was glad she didn't say anything about what I just saw on the news.

"And, Reign, please close my door on the way out. Thanks, dear." She gently closed the door. I felt in control, allowing things to flow naturally. I was no longer obsessed with what things looked like to the outside world. I was light and free. I patted my now flat stomach. I had been devastated by losing my baby. But ultimately, it was for the best. I once felt guilty feeling that way, but now I had accepted it.

I went over to the large window and looked down at the cars turning onto the Avenue of the Stars. There was once a time I had my life planned down to the minute. I thought if I was prepared and went for everything with gusto, I could live in a fairy tale. Life sure had its way of knocking that theory down. Looking back on it, I understand why everything happened the way it did. I'm 40 years old. I can't live the next 40 years of my life trying to plot and plan. I finally learned how to go with the flow. The sun was shining bright, and so was my future.

Chapter 33
Jackie

"You guys have been a great audience today. Be sure to tune in tomorrow! It will be a special show – world-renowned artist and mental health advocate Taylor Ross will be on to talk about her brother's best-selling book, *The Pendulum*. It will be a very special show. Make it a great day, and always remember – " I started my slogan... the slogan that people would yell out to me when they saw me in the streets... the slogan I had trademarked, so no one could steal it as their own: " – if being extraordinary was easy..." My audience completed the sentence:

"Everybody would be doing it!"

My show's theme music started playing and the audience danced along. I went into the stands where the audience was seated and did my usual meet-and-greet and shaking of hands after the show. Taylor had created my "Jackie" logo. The set was bright and bold, just like me. The seats were a merlot leather, and there were silver and gold accents.

"You are awesome!" one of the ladies in the audience said. Another young girl asked for a selfie. I loved this part of my job. I loved connecting with my audience.

My assistant came and led me backstage so they could begin to dismiss the audience. I walked past framed press shots of me that lined the walls of the studio offices. The energy of my audience was always so magnetic. I would have stayed there speaking to people all day if it was left up to me. Some days when I woke up, I still found it so hard to believe that I was living this life. I knew Angelique was up there making magic happen.

I entered my dressing room still full of the adrenaline rush that always followed a taping. "Hello ladies!" Joan and Camille were sitting on the couch in my dressing room. I was used to them popping by. Joan was a regular fixture on the set. We usually discussed all my press for the upcoming week. I sat down at my makeup table and took out a MAC makeup remover wipe to remove the heavy stage makeup. I wasn't about to have my pores clogged up from having to wear all this shit on my face. I liked when I ran into fans on the street and they commented on how beautiful my skin was. *People* magazine had just done an entire spread about my beauty regimen.

"Well, to what do I owe this pleasure? The two of you together in the same room! What's up?"

I turned around – they both looked so serious. Ever since my mother's death, I had been waiting for the other shoe to drop. I thought I was going to wake up and realize this was all a dream and be standing in line at a payday loan spot again.

But I knew my ratings were through the roof. I was averaging 4.2 rating among women 25-54. That was unheard of for the first season of a talk show. This hadn't happened since Oprah. I'm not saying I was the next Oprah, but my ratings were following her same track record.

Camille busted out a big smile and yelled, "You've been renewed!" She started jumping up and down.

My heart resumed beating.

"You guys got me good!" I said, as we all hugged.

"We wanted to be the first to tell you," Joan said. "I'm not surprised, though. They know they have ratings through the roof with you."

"And not only have you been renewed, you've been renewed for three seasons!" Camille was beaming.

"And I also renegotiated your rate. We upped you to $3 million for the season!"

"What?! $3 million?!" Although my mother left me with plenty of money, it wasn't *that* much. I was floored. I had to take a seat. I got a little emotional, because this was a day I would have wanted her to witness. She would be so proud.

"Yes, ma'am! Three million and a 20% increase each year, as well as a bonus!" Camille was one killer agent.

Joan came over and sat next to me. She knew where my mind was going. She whispered, "Angelique would be so proud of you. She always knew you were destined for this."

"So... there is one other thing." Camille sat down in my makeup chair and Joan and I sat on the couch.

"There's more? This is too much good news for one day," I laughed.

"'Good Morning America' wants you to be a part of their morning team."

I jumped up from the couch "THE '*Good Morning America?*' They want *me*?"

Surely, I was being punked. This much good news didn't happen to someone all in one day. But this was even more than I could have ever imagined. But then, I paused.

"Wait, 'Good Morning America' shoots in New York. Do they want me to join via satellite, or are they creating a studio here in L.A.?"

"Not exactly," Camille said hesitantly.

"If you took this gig, you would have to move to New York," Joan blurted out.

"But wait, my show just got renewed for three more seasons." I was confused and I wasn't about to give up my own talk show to go to "Good Morning America." I liked having my own shit.

"We are still ironing out the details but the production for "Jackie" would move to New York. They would re-create your set in New York. You would do "Good Morning America" and then head over and do your show." Camille was in full on agent mode.

"I know it sounds like a lot," Joan said, "but it's doable, Jackie. This is your time. You are building your foundation. They are willing to work around your schedule. You know I would have shot the whole thing down if I didn't think it was beneficial to you."

As each of them tag-teamed on their pitch of why this was such a great opportunity I tuned them out. I hated New York! I thought it was dirty and the people were rude and obnoxious. They spent astronomical amounts of money on 2 x 2 apartments with roaches and lived on top of each other. The idea made my skin crawl. I hated the winters, I hated the smell of chestnuts roasting on a food truck open fire during the holidays, and I had no friends there.

I had absolutely NO interest in moving to New-fucking-York! I loved L.A. L.A. was my home. L.A. was my lover. I was finally in a position to really enjoy L.A. I finally had money, and the career I landed was even better than the acting career I thought I wanted. I was living the dream! I was already thinking of the beach house I would buy now that I was making money. I didn't want to move to New York!

"NO! I'm not going. I'm not doing it." I sounded like a child having a temper tantrum.

"You can be bi-coastal," Joan reasoned.

"Here's the bottom line," Camille said. "You're on top of the world. If you turn down this opportunity, someone else will take it and guess what, you're only as good as your last gig. This town is always waiting for the next big deal. Don't hand it over. I can negotiate your living expenses and rent into the deal with "Good Morning America" so L.A. can be your primary place of residence during hiatus." Unlike Joan, who tried to ease shit in, Camille went straight for the gusto.

I understood what was being said. My Black ass was moving to New York City. That was the price of fame. The network owned my ass. I had nothing keeping me here in L.A. I didn't have a husband or children in school. My career was my husband. My show was my child. After two decades in a city I loved, I was moving to New York.

My goodness, God had a funny way of laughing at my plans.

•　　•　　•

I watched the moving truck pull out. It was driving cross-country with all my belongings, Los Angeles to New York. I had found a fabulous apartment in the Meatpacking District. It wasn't the two-bedroom, two-bathroom I currently lived in here in L.A. It was a one-bedroom, one-bathroom, loft-style apartment that was three times the rent I paid here. But if I was going to live in New York, I wanted to live in a neighborhood I actually liked.

I waited for the truck to get far enough down the road until it turned right and was no longer in view, then went back inside my empty apartment. This place had taken me through some tough times. This spot had been my safe place. And in the end, it was my mother's safe place too.

The past year had so many ups and downs. I realized you couldn't have it all. Although I knew my mother was watching over me, it wasn't the same as having her here. In getting to know my mother, I also got to know me and discover who I was. Through her death, my life had begun. I had no idea what the future held, but I was ready for it. I was enjoying living out my dreams and open to every single possibility. I was no longer in my own way.

I was moving to New York City. My mother got her wish after all; I was moving back east! The irony of it all... Angelique McKinley always got her way, even in death. I had to believe that I could make a life for myself there in the same way I made a life for myself here. This chapter of my life had come to a close, and the next one was beginning.

Chapter 34
Taylor

I needed a few moments to just be by myself and alone with my thoughts. I took a sip of coffee and looked out on the ocean. The sun was just rising. I looked at the colors in the sky. God had painted this canvas perfectly, with lavender, deep orange, and pale blue. I could see the sun coming out above the ocean. It was like the sun was giving me a private dance.

I inhaled the scent of the ocean and wrapped my white robe around me a little tighter. Although it was going to be a warm beautiful day, at this early hour it was still a little brisk. I leaned back in the chair, closed my eyes and reflected on the past. year. Since my brother's death, I was sleeping through the night without any sleep aids. I no longer had to wait for "the call." It had already happened and I knew my brother was safe.

That epiphany allowed me to give myself permission to get to know who I was, besides an artist. I finally took care of myself. Most of all, I allowed myself to be happy. I allowed myself to be free. I was finally free from co-dependency. His death allowed me to live.

I stayed on the balcony until the sun was all the way up in position and ready to shine for the day. I took a long shower and after I finished putting on lotion, I heard three gentle knocks on the door of my suite. Then the suite doorbell started ringing over and over again. I already knew who it was. I opened the door and was greeted by Jackie and Simone, wearing their pink silk robes with "Bridesmaid" written on the back. They were identical to my robe, except mine was white and the back said "Bride."

"Happy Wedding Day, Taylor!" Simone cried.

"Simone, you and your team did such an extraordinary job planning this." Simone had finally followed her calling as an event planner. She didn't let one detail go unattended. And her event planning business was booming.

"You know, weddings *are* my specialty!" She winked at me and smiled. She was finally at a point where she could make jokes about the whole wedding thing.

"And, of course, I brought us a little bubbly-bubbly!" Jackie held up a bottle of Veuve Clicquot.

Simone laughed. "Your ass is always pulling bottles of champagne out of the sky!"

"I'm only having a sip. I don't want to be drunk when I'm saying my vows. I want to remember every moment of this," I said.

"And I still need to make sure everything is in place before I get into my dress, so I'll have a little sip too," Simone said.

"Party poopers!" Jackie gulped down her glass.

"And I don't want you stumbling down the aisle, Jackie!" I knew I sounded like a mom.

"I won't, I won't!" she insisted.

"This is our official last hurrah before you become an angry New Yorker, Jackie," I said. I was excited for her, but I was going to miss being able to have our impromptu moments like this.

"Don't even think about that. Today is *your* day!" she said, smiling at me.

"We wanted to make sure you had something old, something new, something borrowed and something blue," Simone said. After all Simone had been through, she was still sentimental when it came to weddings.

"You have your wedding gown, so that's something new," she continued. "And here's something borrowed."

Jackie handed me a little box. I opened it and it was a beautiful diamond bracelet. "This was my mom's." Jackie placed the delicate bracelet on my wrist and closed the clasp. It sparkled so brightly in the sun.

"It's beautiful. Thank you." I hugged her.

"It matches that beautiful ring Dr. Tim put on your finger." Jackie lifted up my hand and looked at the ring and the bracelet.

I looked at the ring and smiled. Tim Sanders had become the support system I needed. He helped me with the funeral plans for Michael, and he sat by my side during the service and held my hand. He was with me every single day during that time. Our love affair began naturally, and so effortlessly. I hadn't had a boyfriend in years. For the first time, I didn't feel judged. I didn't need to explain my past to Tim because he already knew it, and he didn't judge me for it. He took care of me. For the first time in my life, I was cared for and loved. I could talk to him about anything.

But what connected us most was our love for Michael. He understood my brother. And he understood and loved me unconditionally. I wasn't expecting to get married. I had made myself okay with being alone. I made myself believe I didn't need a relationship. Then I met Tim, and he showed me how to be loved. He showed me how to be taken care of mentally, emotionally, and spiritually. He got me. Our love was intense, passionate, and real. Michael left, but he made sure his little sister was well taken care of. He was still protecting me.

Simone went to the area of the suite where our bouquets were soaking in water. She took out the bridal bouquet. It was a beautiful bouquet with peonies, lilies, and roses, all in whites and cremes.

"Here's your something old," she said, handing the bouquet to me.

I smelled the roses and then I noticed that tied to the ribbon were three rings. I looked closer and recognized they were the rings my brother used to wear. That's when the waterworks started. I finally managed to get the words out amid my tears. "How did you get these?"

"Dr. Tim got them for me," Simone said. "He's a good man. You got it right! You're marrying a man who loves you unconditionally. I'm so happy for you!"

"And he loves us, too! We're a package deal." Jackie always lightened the mood. "Okay, ladies, we need to pull it together. She can't have red eyes and bags under her eyes in her wedding pictures."

"And now for your blue." Simone handed me a small box. I opened it up and there was my garter, with the Hampton University shield.

"That's where it all started – that's where our sisterhood began," I said, looking at our alma mater's logo and thinking about the first time I met them.

"Do you all remember when there was a time that 40 seemed so damn old?!" Simone said.

"It still feels old. I don't feel 40 going on 41, and I certainly don't look it!" Jackie shimmied over to the mirror.

Simone laughed. "I bet you can't drop it like it's hot like you did on Ogden Circle the night before graduation!"

I ran up to Jackie as she was about to drop into a low twerk and grabbed her arm. "Before you try it, wait until after my wedding. I don't want you walking down the aisle with crutches! Your ass is 40 now. If you break something, you'll need screws, metal plates and physical therapy to get healed again!" I stopped her.

"I remember women who were in their 40s telling me that once I hit 40, life would change drastically. They would say that your perspective on life, how you react to situations, and the energy you put out into the world changes. They said that there is a reawakening and shift that occurs. And now I get it," Simone said.

I shook my head at the thought of it. "It is so true. Think about all of the reawakening we went through. I couldn't have survived this in my 20s."

"I want to make a toast." Simone held her glass up in the air.

Jackie and I rolled our eyes. "Simone, keep in mind my wedding starts at 2 p.m., so make it short!" I looked at the clock and saw it was only 9 a.m., but we knew Simone loved a good long toast.

"Ha, ha, ha. So before I was so rudely interrupted..." We all raised our glasses. "Never in a million years did I think we would have to go through all the things we have experienced over this past year to get to where we are now. As our realities hit us – and my goodness, they hit us hard and knocked us down – and through the chaos, there was always one thing we could count on: each other. That's what sisterhood is about – being able to be each other's strength when we are weak. I thank God he brought us together. Cheers to the next 40 years, ladies!" Simone raised her glass and we were about to clink them.

"Wait!" Jackie yelled, "You all better look me in the eye."

We laughed and touched our heads together and looked into each other's eyes. In our unspoken words, we knew what each of us were feeling. We survived our emotional battle wounds because we knew that through our friendship and sisterhood, we could get through anything. Through the chaos in the storm, we would be each other's umbrella of safety, love, and comfort, always.

Acknowledgments

What a journey writing this novel has been! First and foremost, I would like to thank God for bringing these characters into my life and being able to tell their stories with truth, dignity, and compassion. I pray that all the people who read this novel leave with a little piece of Simone, Jackie, and Taylor embedded in their hearts.

To my mother Rosalyn McPherson, my rock, my biggest cheerleader, my best friend, my strength, my inspiration. Words cannot begin to express how blessed I am that God chose you as my mother. You kept me going when I wanted to give up. You believed in me before I believed in myself. Having you by my side during this process has been a blessing beyond words. Thank you for being you. I love you to the moon and back, Mommacita!

Much love to my family! Extra hugs to my Grandmama Lillie McPherson, my "Bruncle" (uncle who is more like a brother) Dr. James G. McPherson, and my cousins Danielle, Ashley and Laura – your love and support mean the world to me. You may be younger than me, but I learn so much from you. Special shout out to my cousin Clarence Nero – thank you for guiding me through this process, and for the constant pep talks. Love you, cuz! And a big thank to my talented cousin Sharika Mahdi for painting and designing my book cover! To my brother, Jackie Robert Kelley II, the "Jekyll" to my "Hekyll," your spirit continues to live on. Not a day goes by that I don't think of you. May you continue to rest in peace.

To my friends, thanks for being patient with me when I had to go into hibernation to write this book. I know I missed a lot during this process, and when it was done you all were there with open arms to congratulate and welcome me back into real life. Special shout out to my sister friends Audrey Owens, Pilar Fort, Antoinette Crawford, Vivian Ham, Monique Johnson Thomas, Sonia Lewis, and Nicole Tucker. In life you get to pick your friends – I'm so glad God crossed our paths and I was able to pick you. Blessed to have you ladies on this journey with me.

This book wouldn't be possible without the hard work of my literary agency, Carol Mann Agency. Carol Mann and Agnes Carlowicz, you are both gems! You encouraged and believed in this story and my talent. To Hampton University, my home by the sea. The day I stepped onto that beautiful campus was the day my life changed forever. I met lifelong friends, learned meaningful lessons, was prepared for what life would bring me, and most importantly, created wonderful memories. "Oh Hampton, a thought sent from heaven above. To be a great soul's inspiration.... O Hampton, we never can make thee a song, Except as our lives do the singing, In service that will thy great spirit prolong, And send it through centuries ringing!"

Note from the Author

Word-of-mouth is crucial for any author to succeed. If you enjoyed *Reality in Chaos*, please leave a review online—anywhere you are able. Even if it's just a sentence or two. It would make all the difference and would be very much appreciated.

Thanks!
Monique

About the Author

Monique Kelley is the high-powered Hollywood player and blogger behind *Confessions of A Serial Dater in LA*. This former Studio-Exec-by-day-blogger-by-night found her passion in helping women in their dating journeys. Kelley is a proud graduate of Hampton University where she completed her degree in Performing Arts. She also spent a semester studying Shakespearean Theatre in London.

Kelley is the resident dating expert on various syndicated talk shows. She has also been featured in numerous publications.

Thank you so much for reading one of our **Women's Fiction** novels.

If you enjoyed the experience, please check out our recommendation for your next great read!

City in a Forest by Ginger Pinholster

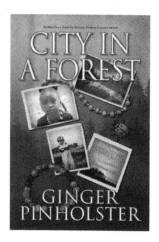

Finalist for a *Santa Fe Writers Project Literary Award*

"Ginger Pinholster, a master of significant detail, weaves her struggling characters' pasts, present, and futures into a breathtaking, beautiful novel in *City in a Forest*.
–*IndieReader Approved*

Printed in Great Britain
by Amazon